Archibald Clavering Gunter

Billy Hamilton

A Novel

Archibald Clavering Gunter

Billy Hamilton
A Novel

ISBN/EAN: 9783337041359

Printed in Europe, USA, Canada, Australia, Japan

Cover: Foto ©Andreas Hilbeck / pixelio.de

More available books at **www.hansebooks.com**

Billy Hamilton

A NOVEL

BY

Archibald Clavering Gunter

AUTHOR OF

"Mr. Barnes of New York," "Bob Covington," etc., etc.

———

NEW YORK
THE HOME PUBLISHING COMPANY
3 EAST FOURTEENTH STREET

CONTENTS.

BOOK I.

HOW STONEWALL JACKSON CAME TO FREDERICK.

BOOK II.

THE PROVOST-MARSHAL AT BALTIMORE.

BOOK III.

A BEAUTIFUL ENIGMA.

BOOK IV.

THE BATTLE FOR HER LIFE.

BOOK V.

THE BATTLE FOR HER LOVE.

BILLY HAMILTON.

BOOK I.

HOW STONEWALL JACKSON CAME TO FREDERICK.

CHAPTER I.

THE CAVALRY PICKET AT NORTON'S FERRY.

It is night on the Potomac—the night of the 4th of September of the year of our Lord eighteen hundred and sixty-two ; when one man's hand is against another man's hand ; when the shadow of a bush may conceal a Confederate sharpshooter ; when the light of a firefly may develop into the flash of an Enfield whose whistling bullet will bring death—this night when I, William Fairfax Hamilton, captain in command of a troop of the First Union Kentucky Cavalry, am guarding Norton's Ford on the Upper Potomac, and preventing the carrying of goods contraband of war, medicines for the Confederate service, despatches from Washington spies, and the crossing of innocent Maryland farmers into Virginia to give the Southern generals notice of our movements.

In addition to this, my instructions specially charge me to furnish, by courier riding for his life, the earliest news of the crossing of the advance divisions of the Confederate army under Stonewall Jackson, now expected to invade Maryland.

The bulk of my command occupies a knoll covered with second growth of pine and fir, distant fifty yards from the river, along whose banks my sentries are placed.

Immediately behind me, a few yards away, is the Chesapeake and Ohio Canal, crossed at this point by a small bridge, which of course is also guarded. Beyond this is the rolling valley of the Monocacy River, which running down from Frederick City joins the Potomac some mile and a half away. To the north, Sugar Loaf Mountain rises. To the west, something over two miles distant, is The Point of Rocks, where the Baltimore & Ohio Railway, coming through the great limestone cliffs of the Potomac gorge from Harper's Ferry—now occupied by General White and Colonel Miles and eleven thousand Union soldiers—turns sharply to the north and runs up the Monocacy Valley on its way to Washington, passing south of Frederick.

These details of scenery are not apparent to my eye, everything being shrouded in the gloom of a summer night, the sky just now made dark by some passing thunder clouds.

To prevent surprise, or loss of men by sharpshooters, I have ordered no camp-fires shall be lighted this warm September evening.

I peer into the inky blackness and my feelings are more gloomy than the night itself, as I think of the demoralization in the capital, which I had left but five days before, being hastily ordered on this service, when Washington was shaking with fear of capture, after Pope's defeat at the Second Battle of Bull Run, and the Cabinet and War Office were appealing to General McClellan to reorganize the army and save Maryland to the Union.

I have just returned from my rounds, after very carefully inspecting the sentries posted near the banks of the river, which is now in this September so low as to be easily fordable, and consequently more difficult to properly patrol and guard. My ears being very wide open to catch any sound from the direction of the Virginia shore which may proclaim the approach of Lee's victorious legions to the boundaries of Maryland—my State—the conversation from some near-by members of my troop, who do not discern me in the darkness, comes sharply to my hearing proclaiming that my subordinates appreciate my situation as clearly as I do.

"I jist about guess," floats to me in Yankee twang,

"that if the Rebs swoop over here and capture 'My Maryland,' it ll be tarnation hard on the Cap."

"Sure, if his State turns traitor, what'll become of the poor divil? Begob, they say the Cap's the only Union one in the houl family."

This last is in the tones of Sergeant Lommox, a hard-riding Irishman who somehow has found his way from the British light cavalry service into my Kentucky regiment ; although, wherever hard blows are plenty and gunpowder is burnt freely, there are sure to be some of his combative race.

"Bedad, this is a mixed up scrimmage anyway," the sergeant continues. "Some say we're fighting to free the niggers ; some say we ain't. Tare an' ages, I'm always asking myself when I'm sober what am I fighting for anyway? It isn't for grub ! Sure, army rations are too divilish bad to make a cat enlist. As for the Cap, they say his own family has cut him dead ; his father fired him out of the house in Baltimore, and his sweetheart spat in his face, because he's fighting for the Union."

These last remarks as to family and sweetheart are a libel. I have no sweetheart, therefore none spat in my face, and my family are at present blissfully ignorant that I am a Union officer, and think that I, wearing a Confederate uniform and carrying a Confederate commission in my pocket, am fighting under Lee and against my country.

As I think of the deception I have been compelled to practise on the dear ones of my home, my thoughts of war are obliterated by reflections upon my unhappy social environment. For as soon as it is known to them that I, William Fairfax Hamilton, wear a blue uniform, my hosts of friends in my native city of Baltimore will be my friends no longer, and my loving sisters and doting father will be mine no more; because I am doing what I was educated to do—fight for my flag.

My peculiar position has come about in a rather curious manner.

Before interstate trouble was imminent, in 1857, my father had obtained for me an appointment to the national military academy at West Point. After the secession of South Carolina and formation of the Confederacy most of the cadets from the Southern and Border States had tendered their resignations.

These one and all had been refused by the War Department. Thereupon, most of the Southern cadets had, without leave, returned to their own States, and were forthwith entered upon the records of the War Department as having deserted their colors in the face of the enemy. Not wishing such an implied stigma to be placed upon me, *my state not having seceded,* I, who had always taken a very strict view of a soldier's discipline and duty, had remained, and received my commission in that year of the double graduation, 1861, when, with the desire of placing officers in the field as rapidly as possible, the term of instruction at West Point had been greatly shortened ; my class being the later one, B of June, my name not appearing on the rolls as from Maryland, my appointment to the academy having been made at large by President Buchanan.

But during my cadetship, I had, perchance from northern associations, perhaps from more conservative and later reflection, but most probably on account of my views of military honor, determined it was my duty to support the flag of the United States. Without going over the pros and cons of a matter that has been argued in the halls of Congress, in all debating societies, in every cross-road tavern of the country, suffice it to say that for reasons sufficient to myself I had made up my mind to serve in the army of the Union ; though greatly fearing it would bring upon me the displeasure of both friends and kindred.

So, having graduated, instead of resigning and joining the Confederates, as my family doubtless hoped and expected, I was still true to the banner under which I had marched from Plebe to First-classman.

In order to fortify myself in this resolution, I had, without visiting my home, journeyed to Washington and secured from the War Department my commission in one of the new cavalry regiments just being formed, in an attempt to make efficient that branch of the service, which in the first year or two of the war was the jeer of the Rebels and the disgrace of the Federals, its condition being so pitiable that McClellan took as few cavalry as possible with him to the Peninsula, many so-called troopers being such incompetent horsemen that they could scarce manage their arms and steeds at the same moment.

In an effort to overcome this, several new mounted regiments were being raised in the Border States, Kentucky, Maryland, and Missouri, whose men had been cavaliers from childhood. These were now being rapidly instructed in the school of the trooper, and the nucleus of that great cavalry armament which under Custer and Sheridan did such fine work in the last years of the war, was being formed.

In the hope of doing my share towards this, I had accepted a captain's commission in the First Kentucky Cavalry, and with this document in my pocket had immediately gone to that State to drill and equip my troop—very glad that my duty took me far away from my friends and family in Baltimore.

Though thoroughly determined to fight upon the Union side, I still shrank from the ordeal of proclaiming myself one of the army of Uncle Sam, to the friends of my boyhood in Baltimore and the father and sisters who loved me—all rabid Southerners, and made bitter against all who differed from them by the potent passions of that awful time, when neighbor turned against neighbor, and brother against brother, and friend shot down friend, in the so-called Border States, which suffered more from the war than any other of their sister commonwealths.

After my regiment was organized, equipped, mustered in and drilled, at the end of the opening campaign in Tennessee where my command proved its effectiveness at Forts Henry and Donelson and also at Shiloh ; in very desperation at the inefficiency of the cavalry of the Army of the Potomac, the War Department had ordered us east.

Here, in the summer of 1862, on reporting at Washington, I succeeded in obtaining a few days' leave of absence. Desperately anxious to see my father and sisters, after telegraphing word of my coming, I, dressed in mufti, had made my appearance at the town-house of my ancestors, in Charles Street, Baltimore, to be received in a manner of which perchance I had had some suspicion, but which my imagination had painted in by no means the vivid colors that actually took form before my eyes.

Pretty little Birdie, my younger sister, a maid of sweet eighteen, meets me in the hall, looking most charming, her blonde hair done up in fashionable waterfall, and her pretty feet in their Balmoral boots peeping out from skirts enormously crinolined to the extreme of fashion, and throwing her arms around me, cries : "Billy, thank God you're back !—Where have you been these six months ?—Of course it's been something for the cause.   How soldierly you look !"   Then between kisses, she suggests : "Now papa has a surprise for you.   How well you'll look in Confederate gray !   But don't let those horrid Feds know of it, or they'll arrest you at once."   This last is whispered in my ear, as if the walls might betray us.

A moment later, Virginia, my elder sister, a stately young lady of about twenty, makes her appearance, and with equally fervid embrace exclaims : "Billy, thank Heaven you've come—at last !   We've all been anxious for you since you did not return to us after graduation. We sometimes thought you had feared arrest and gone straight to Virginia.   Where have you been ?"

"That I—I had rather not tell you," I answer between kisses.

Something in my manner impresses her.   She mutters : "Ah, I understand.   God bless you, Billy !   You do not wish to compromise us by your revelations."

"Yes ; you—you had better not know," I stammer shamefacedly.   To this I add, stroking a moustache which, cultivated assiduously during one campaign, is now quite soldierly : "Is the guv'nor in ?"

"Yes ; he's waiting for you in the library.   He didn't wish to speak to you before the servants.   You know, some of them—ungrateful creatures—have political sympathy with our invaders.   The poor foolish things think they'll be made free, and do not know they'd starve if they were."

"Very well ; I will go in and see father," I remark, my face growing so gloomy that the two darling girls put a pang in my heart by gasping sympathetically : "You must have bad news.   You—you've been captured."

"No, not yet," I mutter.

Then Birdie suddenly falters : " You've been wounded," and cries : "A—a sabre-cut just healed,

I see it upon his cheek," and the next instant the two stab me with their sweet lips as they kiss and cry over a scratch I had received at Shiloh, and whisper: "Thank Heaven! you've been in *our* army."

"Pooh, it is nothing!" I mutter, in a hang-dog way, as I put them tenderly from me and open the library door, to be cordially embraced by my father, a gentleman of old-school manners.

"My dear boy," he says, his grizzled moustache twitching a little, "you have come home at last. You did not even write to us when you left West Point. I imagine, for fear your letter might be opened by the damned Yankee postmaster, one of the spies upon us. Neither I nor your sisters could bear to go up and see you march under that infernal flag, therefore none of us could witness your graduation. I feared you thought we had slighted you. Where have you been?"

Receiving no answer to this, he asks almost severely: "Not shirking your duty, I hope?"

"No!" I answer proudly.

Then as he sees the slight sabre scratch, his old eyes light with pride, he whispers: "My own boy! your wound shows me!" and taking me in his arms, blesses me.

Good God! How can I tell my father I received it fighting against the cause he worships?

Then he inspects me anxiously, his lips trembling. His eyes have love and even anguish in them as he mutters: "You are the last who bears our name. Still, you must bear it honorably, even if to death."

Before I can reply to this, he suddenly astounds me; by whispering, extreme significance in his low voice: "Across in Virginia, Lee, Jackson and Davis know what a West Point education means. The proof of it is here!" With this he goes to the door and locks it, then draws down the blinds of the library windows, to ensure absolute privacy. As I gaze at him wonderingly, he opens a secret drawer in the old-fashioned wainscoting of the room and produces from among some papers a document of official form. Placing it in my hand, he remarks with a profound bow: "Major Hamilton of the *Confederate* Army, I greet you."

As I inspect this document blankly, in a dazed sort of way, I see, with a start of horror, that it is a commission made out to William Fairfax Hamilton, and signed by Jefferson Davis, President of the Confederate States of America, and by Randolph, his Secretary of War.

The old gentleman chuckles, "A pleasing surprise for you, eh?" then suddenly ejaculates, "Curious, they did not tell you of this in Richmond."

"I—I was in the West!" I stammer.

"Ah, that explains it!" remarks my father. "I applied for it a year ago, but only received the document recently, the difficulties of transmitting it through the blockade were so great. You see the Southern leaders appreciate your military training : the commission of Major indicates that. Your wound does not incapacitate you from active duty?" he asks nervously.

"Not at all, I am happy to say."

"Then you'll be anxious to get into the field once more—to free your native city—all the more eager when you see infamous Federal soldiers marching in the streets of this unhappy town—when you behold accursed Northern guns threatening our very homes— when you note Yankee officers flaunting their damned blue tyrants' uniforms in our streets."

These remarks give me a shudder. A blue cloth "tyrant's" uniform is packed securely in my trunk. This, the noise from the hall indicates, is even now being carried upstairs by Jonas and Jumbo, our darky footmen.

"Of course it is hard to part from you," continues the old gentleman almost brokenly, "but every man must do his duty. Your sisters and I always knew you were doing your *devoir*." For into his mind never seems to come the thought that my West Point education may have placed in me different views from his as to my duty in this crisis of the nation —that I can fight on any other side but the one he loves.

Under these circumstances, although with no thought that I will be anything but what I am, an officer of the Union, I can't bring myself to contradict him ; perchance because I wish a few more kisses from my dear sisters, a few more tender looks from my beloved father, which I know will be no longer mine after they know.

"Still, I can't carry that accursed paper about with me," I think.

So, remarking nonchalantly: "For my sisters' safety this had better be destroyed," I am about to place my commission in the Confederate Army in the flame of a wax taper, burning for convenience in sealing letters, after the old-fashioned custom which being a gentleman of the old school, my governor always adheres to.

But his hand is on my arm. He mutters hoarsely: "Don't shame your sisters, sir, by thinking they would not risk as much as you or I, for the cause they love."

"If you take it in that light," I return, a choking sensation in my throat, "the document remains with me." With this, I place it carefully in my breast pocket, buttoning my coat over it. For into my mind has flown suddenly the idea that this little paper of Jeff Davis' may in some supreme crisis enable me to do a great thing for my country. "Still, with this on my person," I mutter, "I had better not remain in Baltimore very long."

"Of course not," he answers. "Go and do your duty. Now step out and join your sisters. I—I will see you, Billy, before you go."

As I turn from him, I feel I am playing traitor to those I love so dearly; for the old gentleman has sunk into a chair, and putting his head upon his writing-table, is striving to conceal his emotion.

In the dining-room, at lunch with my two fair sisters, the prospect seems no more reassuring. Guessing what they will say to me when they discover I am one of the blue uniforms they hate, I feel it is almost a relief that my loved mother died ten years ago, for I fear I could never have resisted *her*, had her arms been put about me and her sweet voice lured me from what my Western campaign has confirmed, even more than my West Point education, as my duty.

Even now, though they do not guess I am recreant; every tone of my sisters' sweet voices is a temptation to me to fight against my flag.

As darling Virginia pours out my coffee, she murmurs, tears coming into her brown eyes: "It'll be hard to part with you again, Billy. I see what papa has told you has already saddened your countenance;

but I would to heaven I were a man," her pretty white teeth come together with a snap, "that I might go and strike with you for the South.   As it is, we women can only pray for you, and nurse you if we have the opportunity."

"Oh, don't be so gloomy, Virgie!" cries dear little Birdie from the other side of the table, attempting a whimpering lightheartedness as she plays with her oysters.   "There's a girl in Virginia who'll nurse him in a manner more to his taste.   'Deed she will!"

"Who is that?" I ask, astonished.

"The girl to whom you're engaged, sir, *of course.*" This comes indignantly from my elder sister.

"The girl to whom I am *engaged!*   What girl?"

"What *girl?*   Oh goodness, he's *forgotten* his little sweetheart!" giggles Birdie.

"Your affianced wife, William, Eva Vernon Ashley. I am surprised at you!" remarks Virginia in stately severity.

"That chit?" I laugh.   "By George! she had slipped my memory."

"*Chit?*   Wait till you see her!" ejaculates my elder sister.

"Oh, yes!   Cadets have so *many* sweethearts," sneers Birdie.   Then she cries with a shudder: "Oh, if I thought you loved some hateful Northern thing!"

"No," I reply, stabbing a soft-shell crab, which delights my palate after campaign rations.   "Behold a free heart."

"Ah. then, it's all right; true to Eve yet."

"True to her as to any woman.   By-the-by, so Eve is already a woman?   The last time I saw her she was ten—a pretty enough nursery witch.   But then I was a *man of fourteen*, and disdained her."

"She thinks you *protected* her!   I can recollect now, as a little tot, how you—you guarded her—though in a very lordly manner," laughs Virginia.   "Besides you must remember, my brother, that it has been an understanding among the families that William Fairfax Hamilton is to wed Eva Vernon Ashley."

"Yes, I believe there was some talk of that when I was in pinafores and Eve in short skirts," I reply, adding with military nonchalance: "Still, I think I have seen girls who looked better."

"Not girls more beautiful!" remarks stately Virginia. "Eve is the most lovely thing on either side of the Potomac. She came to us over a year ago—before the fighting began—accompanied by her half-brother, Charlie St. George."

"You know he's a captain in Colonel Mumford's Second Virginia Cavalry, and awfully handsome," throws in Birdie with a suggestive blush.

"But the young lady?" I question sharply.

"Oh! Eva!" cries my younger sister. "She was nineteen then and lovely enough to make Baltimore men *crazy;* and you know we've got some few beauties in this town—at least Captain St. George said so."

"To you *personally?*" I query with a smile that makes dear little Birdie's face redder. Then I go on philosophically: "I suppose the young lady has forgotten about the old-time idea of our parents?"

Virginia's answer startles me. "On the contrary," she says, "I am sure Miss Ashley thinks a great deal about it. She knows it was her dead father's wish— our Virginia properties adjoin. Her mother still keeps it before her."

"Great goodness!" I cry, "you don't mean to say Eve considers herself as my affianced!"

"I know she did when she came here, for she was always asking about you—though she, of course, was too maidenly to write to you. But I am sure when you reach Virginia all you have to do is to go up to Miss Ashley, in your Confederate uniform, and you'll find it all right!" The Confederate part of this is in a whisper.

"She didn't leave any ambrotype, daguerreotype or photograph for me, did she?" I ask in uneasy facetiousness.

"Certainly not. Your fiancée, sir, has been brought up, I am happy to say, in Virginia old-school manners," remarks my elder sister severely.

"But she stole a photograph of you—the one in the West Point uniform," giggles Birdie.

"Glad it impressed her favorably," I laugh, in the easy assurance of military youth.

"Well, I should think it would," murmurs my younger sister, who seems proud of me. "Five feet ten; dark, savage eyes ; long, drooping moustache, a Cavalry-man's figure."

"And a most unblushing assurance ! " laughs Virginia, who is proud of me also. "But seriously, William, you must think of this affair. The young lady evidently expects some communication from you. Papa said the other day that if we did not hear of you soon, he should strive to forward a letter to her mother."

"So Miss Ashley is very beautiful ? " I ask rather eagerly.

"Ah, the Stoic has given cry at last ! " murmurs Birdie archly.

"Beautiful ? " remarks Virginia scornfully. "Wait till you see her, my military philosopher. Oh, what a belle she'd be if it wasn't for this hateful war. She was in Washington not long ago at her aunt's—the wife of that horrid Border-state Union Senator—but of course Eve would look at none of the Yankee officers who fill that unfortunate town."

"Well, if she's spent much time in Washington at Mrs. Rufus J. Bream's," I remark cynically, "Miss Eva Vernon Ashley has probably very little of the old Virginia ideas in her now ! "

"Wait till you see her," laughs Birdie. "She will be a *surprise* to you—as much as the surprise we have for you in the closet upstairs."

At this both girls sigh, and edge up to me, and place their arms round my neck and whisper, wiping away stray tears : "We put it there when we got your telegram."

"What surprise ? " I ask, masculine curiosity overcoming military nonchalance.

"Run upstairs and see ! "

Taking them at their word, this I do—to my consternation.

A moment after I am in the room that has been mine since boyhood. On the table are flowers to greet my coming. The next second I have opened the closet door.

I utter an imprecation of rage ; then my eyes fill with tears. For I am staring at a full-dress, gray, Confederate major's uniform, silk sash, glittering military collar and magnificent sword. Pinned on it is a paper that shows the Rebel garb is the work of the loving hands of my two sisters—for me, their Union brother.

Filled with almost despair at the situation that confronts me—for it is worse than I even imagined it would be—I stride downstairs and, leaving the house, wander aimless and dazed about the streets of my native city. Here my peace of mind is not increased by seeing a handsome Federal lieutenant, apparently of the artillery, and stationed at Fort McHenry, step into a street car, and every lady, young or old, turn their faces from him, and, as at various times they pass by him, draw their skirts away, as if contact with his uniform were contamination.

I shiver as I think : "What if I loved any of these fair ones ?" as I remember the fate of my poor friend, George Arden Thornton, of Virginian birth, who graduated two classes before me and took his place in the Union army. After being brevetted for great gallantry at the first battle of Bull Run, lured by the eyes of a lovely Virginia girl and stabbed by her cutting invective, he had resigned his commission, and, when his resignation was refused, taken French leave and galloped across the Potomac to join the Confederate legions of Lee and Jackson.

Even now there is a curious record written against his name in the annals of the War Department.

"Dismissed. Having tendered his resignation when in the face of the Rebels."

Though from all accounts, the said George Arden Thornton was never a coward after he joined the Southern ranks, as many a slashing charge with the rough-riding troopers of Stuart and Fitz Lee bore record. Besides that, *he got the girl!*

I stroll into the Maryland Club. There it is no better ; in fact, it is worse ; for many of my old friends, thinking of course I am one of them in sentiment, talk what I consider *treason.* So, fearful of my temper and to avoid altercations which would surely arise if I expressed my feelings, I leave its charming billiard parlor, where the "Chief" is making one of his famous runs, convinced that Baltimore and I will very shortly be on exceedingly bad terms. If I did my duty, half of them would be in Fort McHenry by evening ; if

I did my *full military duty*—Good Heavens !—what would happen to my dear father ?

I cannot stay. I must end the thing, and end it quickly.

With this idea in my mind, I stride home and impress upon my father and sisters that circumstances convince me I must go to the front at once.

"Ah, I understand," whispers my governor. "You feel with that paper in your pocket, you must be in the ranks of battle." You'll run the blockade across the lower Potomac from Leonardston, I presume," he continues. "Ask for Wat Bowie ; he can get you across if any man can," adds the old gentleman, his tones easy though I note his moustache is twitching.

Then my loved ones almost shake my resolution. My sweet sisters, sobbing as if their hearts would break, whisper : "Go, dear brother, and do your duty ! "

My father takes me in his arms and mutters : "Present my compliments to Jefferson Davis in Richmond, my boy ! "

"I hope to !" I answer, scarce noting the significance of my remark.

Then as if to drive the gloom of parting from his mind, my governor suggests : " Of course you'll see your affianced. Tell her mother, with my love, we'll have a grand wedding in a year or two, when the Yanks have fled to Canada."

"Oh, you mean Miss Ashley," I try to laugh. "Yes, I'll marry her after the Yanks have fled to Canada."

With this half-jeering promise on my lips, followed by their blessings, their tears, their love, I get away from the house and fly from Baltimore, cursing myself for not having the moral courage to tell them I am the enemy of their cause.

In my trunk is the gray Confederate uniform. To leave it were to create astonishment, perhaps doubt, in my sisters' minds.

In my pocket is Jeff Davis' commission—a very dangerous document for a Union Border-State officer to carry, in Maryland in the year 1862. Found upon my person, this would be *prima facie* evidence of my treason.

This I must guard against !

Therefore, arriving at Washington, I order the hack-man to drive straight to the War Department, and send up my card.

To my astonishment, I am almost immediately shown into the private office of that man of blood and iron who held Washington—ay, even this whole country—so firmly in his hand during the last three years of that frightful struggle—Edwin McMasters Stanton.

As Madison, the darkey factotum of the secretary, opens the door, and I, entering, make salute, a clear, cold, stately voice greets me with : "You are Captain W. F. Hamilton, of the First Kentucky Cavalry, bre-vetted for gallantry at Shiloh, just returned from a visit to your Rebel friends and relatives in Baltimore ; what do you want with me, sir ?"

For a moment I stand, astonished at the under-sized figure of the Secretary of War ; then as I look at him he seems to become a giant. The great eyes flash through their glasses at me ; the dilated nostrils appear expanded by latent fire ; the massive forehead, which is for one moment that of a judge, contracts and be-comes that of an inquisitor. ' "Why are you not in uniform ?" is thundered at me.

I can see anger, even suspicion, in his glance.

An inspiration prompts me to speak quickly. " I am not in uniform," I say, "because the matter is so urgent."

" What is it ? "

" This ! " I unbutton my coat and place in his hands my Confederate commission.

Mr. Stanton inspects it for a moment, then chuckles grimly : "Young man, you've saved your neck."

"My neck ! " I ejaculate with a start.

"Yes. In an hour you would have been arrested, and with that in your possession, what chance would you have had before a court-martial ? "

" Arrested ? "

" Certainly. Baker's detectives report by telegraph that you, a Union officer, visited your family, all of whom are rabid Secessionists, and departed from them, not only without altercation or quarrel, but blessed and caressed by both father and sisters. Two of the Secret Service were with you on the train. Had you tried to leave it *en route*, you would have been seized. You have had a very narrow escape."

"You do not doubt my loyalty ? I, who have turned my back on home and friends for the cause ? " I gasp.

"Not *now !* But you Border-State men have so many temptations, Baker keeps his eyes on all of you."

"Then let me destroy the cursed thing !" My hand is stretched out to seize the paper and tear it up.

But the Secretary motions me off, and holding Jeff Davis' commission in his hands, remarks : "You're either a very brave or very rash young man, to have carried this with you !" Then his eyes that have always been upon me become searching. He queries : "Why did you even take it ? "

"Because some day—" I cry.

But he cuts me short. "Some day, you may do a great thing with it—for your country ? "

"YES ! "

"Then keep it, and if the chance comes, do it !" He hands the document back to me and remarks caustically : "I shall not ask you who gave it to you. I know you would not answer, and we must not press you Union men of the Border States too strongly. I can guess your agony in putting yourself apart from friends and kindred, because of your country, Captain Hamilton."

Then his tone becomes kindly. He laughs : "Going out again with that badge of treason on you ? You are taking great chances, young man. Wait till I make it innoxious to you." He hurriedly writes a few lines empowering me to bear any document whatsoever for the service of the United States, directing I shall be held harmless for having them in my possession. Signing this, he gives me his hand cordially.

Four weeks after, I find myself this night, in command of a Union picket guarding the Potomac. The river rolls silently beside me, the Stars and Stripes float over me, while my dear father and sisters are praying for me, their loved one, believing me to be fighting for the cause they adore, under the Stars and Bars of the Confederacy.

CHAPTER II.

A SWEET PRISONER.

SUDDENLY these gloomy reflections are interrupted by my first lieutenant, Harry Harrod, whispering excitedly in my ear, "Captain, they are crossing from the Virginia side."

"Are you sure?"

"I hear them!"

"Very well," I order. "Take a platoon with you; go down to the shore again and warn the sentries to be on the alert."

My first lieutenant departing on his errand, I summon my second. To him I remark, "Mr. Cartwright, is the bridge over the canal ready to fire on the instant?"

"Yes, sir. It's dry as tinder and we've soaked the timbers with two cases of coal oil to make 'em burn lively."

"Quite right! Do not light it without my personal command and order the men to mount on the instant. Don't let the bugle sound 'boots and saddles,' that might be a warning to the enemy. Direct all corporals and sergeants to see that every trooper is prepared for immediate action."

Then striding to the near-by bivouac where the loquacious Lommox is reclining on the ground, surrounded by three or four of his men, I speak rapidly: "Sergeant, are you prepared for your ride to Washington?"

"Ay, ay, sir. Though I don't like running away as soon as the Rebs show their cursed heads."

"Nevertheless, you must fly the moment I give you my report. Make straight for Frederick; if any Federal troops are in the town, warn them—then on to Washington, communicating to the commanding officers of any United States forces between Frederick and that city the intelligence of the Confederate crossing. Why is not your horse ready?" I ask sharply.

"I have me hand on the baste's bridle at this moment, Captain ; though it's too dark to see 'em," answers the Irish sergeant with a smothered guffaw.

Then hurriedly, but silently, I step down to the bank of the Potomac. One of the sentries, as I answer his challenge, mutters : "Don't you hear 'em, Captain Hamilton? By the splashing, they're wagons of some kind."

"And in a devil of a hurry too," adds Harrod.

"They can't be part of the Confederate forces," I laugh. "Lee wouldn't invade Maryland with his ammunition trains or artillery as advance guard. Besides, these fellows are running away from somebody and scared out of their boots."

This is now plainly apparent to our ears.

Over the soft ripple of the waters in the quiet night air comes vividly in excited German accents, "Dunner und blitzen, Fritz! If dat damned black mule balks vonce more agin mid himshelf, you shoot him, shust as he stands, und cut dem traces like heel! Mein Gott in himmel! does you think I'm going to be caught py my own mule? Slash 'im! Cut the hide out of 'im. I stands de beer all around, boys, ven ve strikes ze Maryland shore."

"Begorra, you bet he stands the beer all around when he strikes the Maryland shore!" chuckles sergeant Lommox, who is now by my side.

This promised beer seems to have a great effect, not only on my sentries, but on the German's own men. The cracking of whips and the swash of the waters indicate the teamsters are crossing rapidly—but not too quickly for my soldiers, who are waiting for them with mouths made thirsty by this hot night.

"We'll bag 'em all," I think, grimly, as I note from the sound there are not more than four or five wagons. "Harrod," I order my first lieutenant ; "pass the word for silence ; let them all get on shore, then not one can escape."

Two minutes after, five four-mule teams, the drivers cursing in German with great slashing of whips, holloaing and hullabalooing, dash out of the quiet ripples of the Potomac and rush up the Maryland shore.

"Dere's a bridge right along de canal here! Ve makes for it kevick!" cries the Teuton voice.

"Halt there! Advance and give the countersign!" orders the sergeant of the guard, sternly.

"Mein Himmel, it's dat damned Stuart's cavalrymen. Boys, ve are goners!" shrieks the affrighted head of the party with a German oath, and an effort is made to turn the rear team into the river.

"Stay quiet, Dutchie, or be jabers, we'll fill you full of lead," orders Lommox.

"Who are you?" I cry; for I am now sure these are not soldiers; certainly not Jackson's veterans.

"Gott in Himmel, who are *you?* That is vot is de matter mit me!" answers the excited German voice from the darkness.

"We're Troop A of the First Kentucky Union Cavalry," I shout, instinct telling me the Dutchman is too excited to explain who he is.

"Union Cavalry! Boys, ve are saved!"

"Now, who are *you?*"

"Lammersdorff! So help me Gott! August Lammersdorff! Sutler mid Bank's Corps, and pursued by Lee's whole army. Vip up de mules, Fritz! Get right avay out of here, mein frient yourshelf, odervise you is a losht man."

"Be jabers, you're a lost man," cries Lommox, "if you don't put up that beer you promised in the middle of the river when ye reached 'My Maryland.'"

"All right, de beer goes, but for God's sake let me go away. Here, Fritz, Conrad, make de Union boys comfortable mit demselves. By Shultz's ghost, I thought I vas gone up de spout."

A spigot is hastily put in a keg of beer in one of the sutler's wagons. I permit my men to accept the German's hospitality, while I inspect his sutler's permit by the light of a sulphur match.

"Hab a cigar, Cap?" Lammersdorff says in eager hospitality.

"Thank you," I respond, and lighting up one of the purveyor's best *perfectos*, I question the Teuton rapidly:

"How did you get into Lee's jaws? Banks is in Washington."

"Ven Banks falls back from Bealton, I vas left behind. Den I has to light out for meinself und vile Lee vas massacreeing Pope, by jingo, I flanks de whole Rebel army and comes behind dem. But ven I gits down vere I thinks I'se safe, mein Himmel, I finds Lee vaiting for me to gibe me hell."

"You say you were pursued by Lee's whole army. What makes you think that?"

"De Rebs comes on us so shpunky!"

"Any other reason?"

"Yes, I heard de marching of men like von ob Leettle Mac's big army corps!"

"An army corps?"

"Und de rumbling of half a dozen batteries of cannons. You don't mishtake dem for de creekings of sutlers' vagons, does it?"

"Half a dozen batteries of artillery!"

This information is so important, and Lammersdorff seems so impressed with the fact that he must hurry on, that I detain him only long enough to buy a box of his best cigars, with which I fill my pockets, cigar-case and saddle-pouch, distributing a few to my two lieutenants.

"Don't keep me here, Captain. For God's sake, let me go on or I'm a losht and a ruined sutler. I has fifty thousand in greenbacks and twenty-five thousand in a commissary's draft on my body," he whispers frightenedly, then breaks out despairingly: "How long do you think dese vagons vould last mit Stuart's hungry devils. Dey'd eat 'em up and drink 'em up and smoke 'em up before I got drew cussing 'em!"

"Very well," I answer, "you can go on!" And I give orders to let him pass the little bridge over the canal.

"For God's sake, come mit me, Captain!" begs the good-hearted German, who I can see by the light from my burning cigar, is in shirt sleeves, and the perspiration of exertion and anxiety rolling down his round Teuton face.

"No! I'm guarding this ford. Good-bye; thanks for your cigars; I hope we'll meet soon," I add.

"Gott in Himmel, I hope ve *von't!*"

"Why not?"

"Because if you shtay here another hour I vill have to go to Richmond or hell to meet you," is cried out to me, as the wagons disappear into the darkness, driven rapidly, the mules trotting as they rush over the little bridge.

The noise dies away up the Frederick pike; as not altogether pleased at the German's suggestion, I turn to my duty.

"Lommox," I order, "go to the bridge with your horse and be ready to ride like blazes the moment I give the signal!"

Leaving Harrod in charge of the bridge, I crawl to the front. At the bank of the river, quietly giving the countersign to the sentries who challenge me in low voice, I shortly encounter my seeond lieutenant. "Do you hear any noises?" I whisper.

"There is certainly no sound now of movement across the ford," he replies. "Perhaps they're waiting for a signal."

A moment after I start with surprise.

A sentry challenges sharply.

A low, sweet, delicate, feminine voice comes through the still night air, saying easily: "You are part of Stonewall Jackson's command, I presume?"

"Great goodness! A woman!" I gasp.

The next instant I have captured a very pretty prisoner. At least, I judge so by the voice. For my hand is on the bridle of her horse and the soft voice is saying to me: "Are you some of Stuart's troopers?"

"No!" I reply, with military promptness. "You are speaking to Captain Billy Hamilton, of the First Union Kentucky Cavalry."

"*Billy Hamilton!*" The tone is one of great astonishment. "Captain in the First *Union* Kentucky Cavalry?" The voice, for a second I think, indicates disdain.

"Yes! My orders are to stop any one crossing the river."

"What! Hinder me from visiting my—my aunt in Leesburg?"

"Certainly!—unless you have a pass from the General in command of this division, or the War Department at Washington."

"O-oh!" This is a sweet, low gasp of dismay. "I had supposed that you military gentlemen considered women non-combatants," adds the girl in piquant savageness; for her accents tell me she is certainly very young.

"Please give me your name," I demand with military directness.

"My—my name?"

"Certainly!"

"I—I cannot give it you!" There is a strange embarrassment in the voice.

Into this I break, ordering the sentinel sharply, "See who that is in the undergrowth. If he doesn't come out, shoot him at once!"

"Don't shoot!" screams a scared darky voice, in answer to the click of carbine-locks. "'Fore de Lawd, I'se only de missis' servant."

"Stop your men!" cries the young lady. "Don't shoot! Quashie, come here! Don't try to fly!"

A moment later a figure on horseback draws up beside her.

"Lawd-a-massy, dis niggah's most scared to death!" mutters what is apparently a darky servant. I believe him, as to his fear; for I can hear in the gloom his teeth chattering like castanets.

Then the girl orders: "Quashie, you see these men?"

"'Deed I doesn't, missie; I hears dem."

"Don't try to run away from them, and do what they tell you, or you'll be shot at once."

"Yes, missie. Am dey going to shoot you too?"

"I hope not! You wouldn't kill me, Captain Hamilton, would you?" The tone is coquettish, alluring.

The easy use of my name astonishes me; but with military gallantry I answer: "Not by the Stars and Stripes!" To this I add: "How did you get here? You could not have crossed the bridge."

"No-o," there is a slight hesitation in her answer. "We—we must have lost our way and come up the river."

"Then how did you get over the canal?" My tone is suspicious.

"Over the canal? Is there one here? O heavens! Quashie, we might have fallen in and been drowned!"

This is a bare-faced attempt to simulate feminine naïveté and female terror. I am about to speak with great severity to my sweet prisoner—for I have made up my mind that she is very sweet—when suddenly there is the rattle of dropping shots—not from the river, but from the rear of my command—and sounds of combat. Across the Baltimore and Ohio Canal, the darkness is lighted up by the flashes of carbines and revolvers.

"Damnation!" cries Harrod. "We're taken in flank —surrounded!"

A second's reflection tells me that the Confederates have crossed the Potomac at White's Ford, further down the river, and we have not been notified by the troops guarding that point.

"Mount your horse, Lommox!" I cry, struggling to the bridge. "Ride while you've time! Carry the news, the Rebs are in Maryland!"

"Faith, I'm gone!" answers the sergeant, and the sound of his horse's hoofs rings out rapidly on the little bridge and dies away smothered by distance and the noise of firearms. A moment later the flashing of Confederate carbines tells me he is running the gauntlet.

But I have no time to speculate on his fate. My own —that of my command—even that of the fair creature who is beside me—occupies my attention. I hurriedly seize the reins of the young lady's horse, for from the movement of her steed I see she is turning it and would gallop across the bridge towards the Confederate lines.

"If you go to them it is your death!" I whisper. "In the darkness they'll think you one of us. For God's sake keep on the other side of me!"

"You wish to be very sure of your prisoner," she mutters.

"I wish to do what I can to keep you alive."

"Ah, thank you! You think your body may intercept a bullet that would reach me?"

"Yes!" and I draw her back from the circle of light made by the burning bridge that has been fired by my order and is now blazing briskly.

This done, I must save my command, if possible; the weight of fire in our front indicates that at least a regiment is engaging us. However, they are coming on cautiously, thinking we are but a picket, and not knowing the meagre force that is opposed to them.

There is but one hope!—to flank them! My troop numbers scarce fifty sabres. The force opposed to them, must amount to several hundred.

Fortunately, but few casualties have yet occurred,

the darkness preventing any accuracy of aim.
"Come with me!" I whisper to my young lady
prisoner.   Passing the word for the men to hold their
fire and to follow me as silently as possible, I turn my
horse's head towards the west.   The darkness is our
only safety ; were it daylight, the paucity of our
numbers and our route of march would be discovered.
Then we would be overwhelmed in a moment ; for
though the canal is between us and the enemy—the
distance between it and the river is only a short hundred
yards and with little cover—their carbine fire would
destroy us.

I soon discover that my flank movement is not a
success, for a portion of the Confederate force is apparently moving parallel to me.   A moment after, guessing at our location from our noise, they scourge us by
a volley.   Three or four of my troopers fall from their
saddles.

Merciful heavens !   Even this portion of the rebel
force is a full regiment.   A cavalry brigade must be in
front of me.   Fortunately they have not been able to
cross the blazing canal bridge.

'Suddenly a desperate idea strikes me.   " Give them
one volley to check them," I order.   "Now, my men,
follow me ! "

" By the Lord ! " whispers Harrod, " you're not
going into the river ? "

" Yes, to the Virginia side ; it is our only chance.
We may escape that way.   Where is that poor girl ? "
I ask anxiously.

" Here, at your side, my gallant captain, who is
trying to take such good care of me," whispers the
sweet voice.

" Very well.   Please—please keep in front of me.
Sergeant, get a few files between this young lady and
the enemy."

" You do nothing but think of my safety ? Thank
you ! " And a delicate, soft, exquisitely shaped hand—I
can tell that from its feel—seizes mine, and pressing
it, sends through every vein a thrill that the danger of
death cannot destroy.

A moment later we stagger the Confederate advance
by our rapid carbine fire, and I lead my men down to
the river, to ford it.

"We must hurry," whispers Harrod. "The moon is rising. It will show our small force to them. We will be shot down before we get across."

"It is our only hope," I return. "What chance would we have, charging a brigade?"

We are scarcely half-way across the river, when two rockets rising from the Maryland side burst into red and white stars.

I shudder as they are answered from the Virginia shore. The next instant my lieutenant grasps my arm and mutters : "Good God! We're in front of a whole Rebel division!"

For in the first faint light of the rising moon, dark columns of infantry are leaving the shadows of the Virginia woods and entering the river. We can even hear the rumble of artillery and caissons.

With a muttered oath, my color-sergeant seizes our guidon, and reversing its pole, plunges the flag that will betray us under the water of the river. Obeying a wave of my hand, my troop follows me, edging down the river in an attempt to get on the flank of the enemy on the Virginia shore.

But we are too late. The advance guard and skirmishers of the Confederate division are already around us in the river, the report of firearms on the Maryland side hurrying them to the support of their cavalry.

At first they mistake us for part of their own force on the other side of the stream. This gives me a short-lived hope ; for a Rebel infantry captain laughs at me as he urges to greater speed his men, who are fording waist-deep : "Are they making it so hot for Stuart over there that you're retreating?"

"Yes," I reply. "Hurry up and support him!" as I still keep my course down the river. In the thick undergrowth of the Virginia side, we may yet escape —some of us.

But even as I do this, another column comes into sight below us.

"That's damned strange!" cries the Confederate captain after me. "You boys ain't used to run from Yankee cavalry."

The next second, the rising moon, breaking wholly from the thunder-clouds, brilliantly illuminates the scene.

" By heaven, there's something wrong here ! Their uniforms are blue ! " cries the Rebel officer.

" Hanged if they ain't Yanks, flying from Stuart ! " yells one of his men, in the easy discipline of that time.

" My God ! don't fire ! " I cry, " there's a lady riding with us."

The next second we are surrounded. With the muskets of a Confederate regiment of infantry levelled at us, and the suspicious clicking of gun-locks in another one marching on our flank, as the order comes : " Make Ready ! " to resist would be useless. I sullenly surrender.

A moment later we find ourselves deprived of our arms. To our captor's questions, I give the name of my command, and find myself a prisoner.

" I am glad you did surrender," whispers the sweet voice at my side. " For see ! " and she points down the river ; " There are miles of them ! To resist would simply have meant the slaughter of your brave fellows."

I glance, following her hand. A Confederate army corps is on the banks of the Potomac. Turning, I look at her : the moonlight shows me a form light and graceful as a sylph's, clothed in some dark riding-habit that outlines each rounded contour of beauty.

A second glance—for I give her several—shows me the young lady sits her horse perfectly and manages it with the ease and certainty of an accomplished equestrienne. Her face is too much in the shadow for me to note all its loveliness—that came to me afterwards —though I can guess it has both youth and beauty from the brightness of her eyes as they look into mine.

" Thank you," I remark. " You were very kind in not betraying us. It did no good, but, believe me, I appreciate it."

" You feared I would do *that* ? " she asks reproachfully, " when you took such good care of—of——"

" Of my fair prisoner," I murmur suggestively.

" Your prisoner no longer ! 'she laughs. " You've only had a short ten minutes' power over me. And now you're *their* prisoner. I hope they'll treat you as kindly as you did me."

" Not much chance of that," I mutter, my voice growing husky, as I think of a long imprisonment before exchange. "I suppose they'll send me to Libby Prison." Then I ask, perchance even anxiously : "And you ? "

"Oh, they'll regard me as a non-combatant ; these Southerners are very gallant. I presume now I shall be permitted to visit my mother in Leesburg." Her tone is confident.

"Your *mother ?* You said your *aunt.*"

"I meant both."

By this time we have been escorted to the Virginia side of the river, and are now brought by our guard to an officer, who, after a few words with his subordinates, inspects us by the light of a blazing pine torch.

As I am about to give him my name, the gentleman breaks out cordially and eagerly : " Permit me, Captain Hamilton, to introduce myself as Major Thornton of the First Virginia Cavalry, acting provost-marshal of Ewell's Division, Jackson's Corps, of the Army of Northern Virginia."

"George ! " I cry out, as I recognize my old West Point friend, who had been a First-classman when I entered: the George Arden Thornton, who, lured by his sweetheart's eyes, had left the ranks of the Blue, and who now is one of Stuart's dashing cavalrymen.

To this he replies: "Billy, I'm mighty glad to see you, but sorry to see you wearing that uniform."

Before I can reply to this, he whispers significantly : "By Jove, you're in luck ! I see you have a petticoat with you."

"A lady I captured, attempting to cross the Potomac," I answer quite loudly, anxious to prevent any embarrassment to the fair creature whose attitude, as well as I can see by the torchlight, indicates impatience.

"And one who would like to have your private ear for a moment, Provost-marshal," returns the beauty somewhat sternly.

At this Thornton, who is punctilio itself to the fair sex, doffs his slouched hat gallantly, as the young lady continues, a slight embarrassment in her voice : "I— I was so—so fortunate as to be captured by Captain Hamilton. Am I to be considered a non-combatant by you, or am I to have, in one night, the distinction of having been a prisoner of the Army of the Potomac on one side of the river, and of the Army of Northern Virginia on the other?"

"Be assured the Army of Northern Virginia will do its best to keep all such prisoners as *you*," returns the Confedate major gallantly, apparently impressed by the sweet tones of his captive's voice.

"Then—before you put me under guard," laughs the young lady, "permit me to whisper a word in your ear."

With this the provost marshal, taking the young lady's horse by the bridle, leads her a short distance from me, and I watch her discontentedly. As she converses apparently eagerly and impressively with him, I think, perhaps bitterly: "She, when I captured her, accorded me no such explanation."

A moment after Thornton turns to me and suggests: "What shall we do with you, my boy in blue? Eh?"

"Send me to Richmond, I suppose!" I mutter gloomily.

"No, I've better news than that!" the major says cordially. "We haven't men enough to spare to guard the prisoners we're taking. We shall carry you with us into Frederick and to-morrow parole you until you're exchanged: at least, I believe that is the order at present. Give me your word, and you can take your horse and go with us comfortably. I shall be crossing the river myself as soon as I give directions about your men, whom we shall parole at once not to serve until exchanged."

His cheery words make my heart jump; I am not to suffer confinement in Libby Prison. I go with him to sign the parole of my troop.

Returning from this, my charming ex-captive rides up to me and remarks, apparent petulance in her tones: "I am not to be permitted to visit my friends in Leesburg. Like you, *I* am a prisoner. That awful provost-marshal insists on taking me to Frederick. I shall not be released until Stonewall Jackson gives word to that effect. They—they think me a Union spy!"

"I don't imagine they'll shoot you offhand," I reply, delighted that this fair, yet rather mysterious young creature is to journey with me.

The piquancy in her manner indicates she will make a charming companion on the night ride into Frederick.

"Oh, I don't suppose they will *need* to hang me.   I shall be executed by refrigeration in this night air," laughs the girl.   "My riding-habit is wet to the knees."

"That I shall try to obviate!" cries Thornton, stepping up.   "Come with me at once; across the river we will give you a camp-fire!"

A few moments, and we find ourselves upon the Maryland side of the river.

"I see you've delayed us for an hour," remarks the major, gazing on the ruined bridge.

The Confederates are blowing out a sluice gate and closing a dam, so that the canal will soon be dry—and their engineers are hastily erecting a light bridge or two to replace the one I've destroyed.

While this is going on a big bivouac fire is rapidly built for us by Thornton's order, and my fair companion, wringing out the skirt of her riding-habit in front of it, makes as exquisite a series of silhouettes as fitful flashes ever showed to admiring eyes.   Her very occupation compels an innocent abandon that permits most charming hints of a figure as graceful as a naiad's, as she shakes the Potomac water from her clinging skirts.

But there is no air of coquetry about her, though I catch a glance or two that she steals at me, when she thinks I am not noticing her.   In them, I can only see disdain, haughtiness, perchance contempt.

A moment later I think this idea is caused by the conviction that every Southern woman hates a Union soldier; for the young lady's voice has become winning, her air disingenuous, as she queries: "I suppose after your parole you will return to Washington?"

Then her eyes become wistful and eager.   She whispers: "I believe a Southern *Union* officer like you should be in high favor with the War Department."

"I am!" I reply, with the proud assurance of youth, as I stir up the blazing brands, to get a better look at her.

"Ah!" she gazes at me wistfully, then murmurs a gracious;   "Thank you!   My habit is perfectly dry now."

As she lifts her graceful head, by the flashes of the camp-fire, which is now burning very brightly, I obtain a first thorough impression of her face; I behold youth,

beauty, vivacity, combined with a subtle yet charming fascination.

My glance is so searching a blush flies over the exquisite features. She murmurs, a bashful embarrassment in her tones : "You are satisfied with the inspection of your—your former prisoner, Billy—I mean Captain Hamilton ?"

This most easy use of my Christian name astounds
me.

"You—you have known me before ?" I gasp in surprise.

"No ; of course not ! Oh ! What was I thinking
of ! What have I said !" she stammers, growing red
as a peony in the firelight. Suddenly she cries excitedly as if to avoid further questions : "Look ! See !
Isn't it a glorious sight ! Behold the Confederate army
crossing into 'My Maryland.'"

And the girl's eyes become inspired !

From the elevation of our knoll by the river bank, I
gaze, and a sight comes to me that takes all else from
my mind.

The veterans of Jackson's advanced divisions are
fording the river, that flows waist high here—one con-
tinued stream of marching manhood : each eye bright-
ening as the bands play "My Maryland" ; each regiment cheering as it steps on the soil of the State they
think to win and add, a new sister, to the Confederacy.
Regiment after regiment of Virginia boys, brigaded
under Taliaferro, veterans of many pitched battles, victorious on many stricken fields ; their uniforms ragged,
their feet sometimes even bare, but their muskets gleaming brightly and their cartridge-boxes filled, tramp past
us.

These are followed by Stafford's Louisiana lads,
five regiments, that give the wild Rebel yell as they
touch the shores of Maryland.

Somehow, the enthusiasm gets into me. Somehow, I
remember I am a Southerner ! Somehow, I want to
yell too !

But I am recalled to my duty by the sweet voice of
my companion saying sarcastically : "Don't you wish
you could cheer with them ?" Then as if willing to
undo the effect of her words, Miss Variable quickly
adds : "Pooh ! We're two poor prisoners together.

Both Southerners, and both on the wrong side, I presume."

I do not answer this : the sight is too impressive. Silently both of us gaze, the placid river flowing past us swiftly in the soft moonlight that tinges its ripples.

From up-stream, borne to us by the breeze, come the sounds of the Confederate engineers throwing, by the light of blazing torches, a pontoon bridge across the Potomac, for the passage of the artillery. To our right, two miles away, distant explosions tell us Stuart's cavalry are blowing up culverts and destroying the Baltimore & Ohio railroad, cutting off the doomed garrison of Harper's Ferry from flight, succor or assistance.

And still we gaze, and still they come : regiment after regiment, column after column—the young manhood of the South ! Archer's Tennessee Riflemen, from the ridges of the Allegheny ; Thomas' Georgia Infantry and Pender's North Carolinians, their bayonets gleaming, their bands playing—not in the glorious panoply of war, but in the stern, dread reality of slaughter and of death.

Forgetful of dead comrades fallen in Chickahominy swamps, careless of the decimation of the Second Manassas and Chantilly, reckless of everything except that they *must win ;* triumphant and confident,—for they are marching under a leader who has never lost a battle,—Stonewall Jackson's "foot-cavalry " tramp joyously across the fair Potomac water from bloody fields they have gained to other bloodier ones to be fought. Over all this, as each regiment reaches the Maryland shore, floats one continuous Rebel yell.

Their losses, as they march, my military eye tells me, have been awful. Brigades are commanded by colonels ; captains lead battalions ; and in one instance I note a lieutenant is the ranking officer of a regiment.

"Oh Heaven ! How these darling, ragged, barefooted, light-hearted heroes have suffered to win ! " sighs my beautiful companion. "Oh mercy ! " she mutters. " Don't look at our glorious boys any more ! To-night they're full of life, hope and courage ; to-morrow how many of them will die here, right in this State." And the girl bursts out sobbing as if her heart would break.

But the men we look at, think not of death but of victory; and the wild yell of triumphant invasion drowns the sad sobs of tender womanhood,—who pities, who sorrows for these light-hearted, devil-may-care Southern boys as they pass on with merry jest and careless laugh to the shambles of South Mountain and Antietam.

CHAPTER III.

WHO THE DUCE IS SHE?

A FEW moments after, as if to brush away any Southern sentiment she has displayed, Miss Enigma whispers: "Just see to my horse's girths, my gallant cavalryman. Then you can put me in the saddle—for here's Major Thornton come to tell us, I imagine, that we must both make a long jaunt into Frederick."

"You have divined correctly," returns the gallant Southerner, and he gives directions to the troop of cavalry who are under his immediate orders.

A moment later, the prettiest foot in the world is put into my eager hand, and I swing Miss Beauty into her saddle. I call her Miss Beauty now; I have no other name for her. Once or twice I have, at odd times, by deft hints expressed my desire to know this young lady's baptismal appellation; but at these moments she has grown unusually stupid and doesn't seem to understand what I am suggesting.

She has apparently been no more explicit with the Confederate Major, for we have hardly mounted and taken a by-path to get away from the marching infantry who will delay us, when Thornton says gallantly, but decidedly: "Now I must know the name of my prisoner."

"Not this evening," answers the captive mutinously; then adds playfully: "I shall not reveal my identity to any one save General Jackson himself;" next murmurs bashfully: "As if I would have all my friends in Virginia and Maryland know I've been conducted without chaperone, by two dashing officers, on an all-night-ride. Besides what would Mrs. Thornton say?" Then she laughs into the handsome Confederate's face:

"Your marriage, more than your desertion to the enemy, brought sad hearts to many Washington beauties, I believe."

"Ah, you're acquainted in Washington?"

"A little."

With this the two go into a conversation, which I cannot catch, as they are riding side by side, and the narrow country lane compels me to keep in their rear. So I go to meditating as to whether it is only fear of scandal, or some ulterior political or military motive that makes this young lady silent as to her journey, not only to myself, but to the Confederate. Surely she could confide in one of us, I think.

Then suddenly a spasm, which I have since discovered was jealousy, flies through me. Was it in hope of meeting some particular officer of Lee's army that this girl, who from her appearance is of gentle birth and tender breeding, has taken this wild night-ride through the lines of contending armies?

But Miss Enigma who rides in front of me gives me little opportunity for further grounds of speculation at present. Thornton's questions perhaps becoming too searching, she suddenly grows so sleepy that she can answer neither of us, though I note she guides her horse as dexterously as before, as we two ride on glumly after her.

Soon after we enter the main road in advance of the infantry, but behind the cavalry that is hastening towards Frederick.

A moment later, the young lady turns in her saddle and beckons us beside her. As we ride up, she says :

"Would you like a sleepy prisoner, or a very gossipy and wide-awake captive, Major Thornton?"

"I hardly understand you," mutters the Confederate.

"Well, I mean that if you put searching military questions to me, I shall be so sleepy I cannot answer them. If you permit me to chat about the affairs of the world, I'll make myself as entertaining as I can, for the courteous manner in which you've treated me this evening."

"Anything but a silent prisoner!" laughs the major.

Whereupon she turns to us, and we enter into a conversation about general news; even going as far as Italy and Garibaldi's attempt to capture Rome, and

from this drift to Washington society and Virginia
matters and Maryland affairs, the young lady's babble
being so bright, charming and pleasant, that the ride
seems very short as we come into Frederick about daybreak.

A huge bonfire of burning commissary stores destroyed by the Federal provost-marshal, who has re-
treated with the one company under his command,
leaving only the sick in hospital behind him, shows
me that Lommox has reached here safely and given his
warning.

So chatting, we ride on into the little capital of
Maryland. Every moment this young lady's conversation gives me more potent hopes of learning her
name. Unguardedly, this beauty incognita has ad-
mitted she knows several of my Baltimore friends and
one or two of my Washington acquaintances.

"It'll be the devil's own luck if I don't find you out,
my elusive charmer, after the hints you have given
me," I think cheerily as I assist the young lady from
her horse at the entrance of the principal tavern in
Frederick Town.

This is now lighted up with its doors open, and the
proprietor is answering Thornton's hurried military
questions as to the number of the United States troops
that have been in the town, and the direction they
have taken, his darky servants going about rather
nervously in the presence of the invading Confederates.

Roused by the noise of Rebel hoofs, a number of the
townspeople in hastily-made toilets are thronging
about the advanced squadrons of Stuart's Cavalry,
gaping at their invaders, who call themselves their
friends and say they come to free them.

"Gol darned if I thought you Rebs—I—I means
Confeds—were in fifty miles of us," I hear a farmer,
who has come in with early morning vegetables and
poultry, say to one of Stuart's troopers, as the cavalry take all his supplies, and pay, to his astonishment and delight, in Yankee greenbacks, and gold,
probably gleaned from the Federal dead at Second
Manassas.

His business with the boniface finished, Thornton
turns to us and speaks with military promptness.

"Remember you are both on parole not to leave this hotel without my permit. Have I your word of honor that you will remain here ?"

"You have," I reply, " and my thanks also for your courtesy."

" Have I yours also, Miss —— ? " says the Confederate, addressing the young lady, who has not replied to him.

" And if not ? " answers the fair captive airily.

"Then I shall be compelled to place a sentry at the door of your chamber," remarks the provost-marshal sternly. " A discourtesy I am loath to be guilty of, to a young lady whom I wish to treat with every possible consideration."

" Under these circumstances you have my word, Major Thornton," replies the girl. Then, a strange eagerness coming to her voice, she says impulsively : "Only *please—please* let me see General Jackson as soon as he arrives, you—you don't know how important it is ! "

" I will try and accommodate you, but I am a very busy man," answers the Confederate officer. Then he rides hurriedly away, leaving us two captives looking in each other's face, as I give the darky groom a dollar, and tell him to see our horses are well fed and bedded.

" You wish to see General Jackson immediately ? " I query meditatively.

" Yes, of course," answers my ex-captive. " My night's experience makes me anxious to escape from between contending armies."

"Ah, yes," I reply. "Only I thought your manner indicated that it is more important for Jackson to see *you* than you to see *him.*"

"Goodness, what a suspicious creature you are ! " half laughs Miss Incognita. "Don't you see I am as much a captive as you are ? But, good-morning, I am very tired and——" Her languid manner indicates that she wishes to end the interview.

" You would like a little beauty sleep, eh ? " I suggest, as I assist my fair companion into the hotel and do what I can for her comfort.

" Of course ! " returns the young lady laughing. To this she adds : " A little would do you no harm also," and trips away attended by the hotel-keeper, leaving me chewing my moustache and gazing wonderingly after her.

Has this interesting creature been caught accident-ally between contending armies, or is she one of the "dyed-in-the-wool" Secession girls who'd risk every-thing for their cause, even life itself, and be a bearer of information to the Confederate chieftain, or is she, worse still, the affianced or the wife of some Rebel officer desperately seeking, at the risk of her own per-sonal safety, the lips she loves, the arms she longs for?

" Damn it, this last is the worst of all," I think, as my heart sinks.   "Better the lover of the Confederate cause than the sweetheart of a Rebel officer.   Curse it —how jealous I am becoming."

A moment later I conclude that Miss Incognita's suggestion as to sleep is a wise one, I have been in the saddle almost continuously for forty-eight hours.

Five minutes after I am shown into a little bed-chamber whose dormer windows open on the main thoroughfare of Frederick.   As I look out, a battery of Confederate artillery is thundering up Market Street, the stars and stripes have been hauled down from the flagpole in front of the town hall, the Rebel banner is flying in its place; the rising sun gleams on the flashing bayonets of an infantry division marching from the south—Stonewall Jackson has entered Fred-erick.

*　　*　　*　　*　　*　　*

Notwithstanding the noise of ammunition trains and the rumbling of artillery, my forty-eight hours in the saddle makes me sleep well and soundly.   Once or twice, however, I dream of a fairy figure in a dark gray riding-habit.

Some unusual and more potent noise in the street awakens me.   I spring from my bed and grasp for my absent sabre, thinking for a moment that it is the call to arms.   I glance from the window, and look out on a soft Maryland September day.   The rattle comes from the drums of a Confederate brigade marching up the street.   I see the gray uniforms; recollections of the preceding night throng upon me.   My lack of weapons brings my situation home to me—I remember I am a prisoner.

But appetite in a healthy young man is always a dominant passion. Thoughts of breakfast prevent my growing morbid over my captivity. The officer with meagre rations the night before, rejoices in the chance of a hotel breakfast.

I glance at my watch ; it is twelve o'clock in the day.

Making a hasty soldier's toilet, I step below into the main room of the hotel. This is now full of a conglomeration of Maryland citizens and Confederate officers. The faces of the invaders are full of exultant hope, the countenances of the invaded bear the impress of the mighty passions of that mighty time. All of them betray concern ; some of them indicate joy ; others, though they try to conceal it, bitter animosity and undying hate.

A few, however, display such tremendous out-spoken enthusiasm and friendship for the Rebel soldiers that I know it means recruits for Lee's invading army. Some of these gibe their neighbors of Union sentiment with vindictive speeches.

As I elbow my way through the throng, I hear one of them scoffing : "Hi, Jake, Pap Lee and his boys'll make you walk Spanish for telling on Bill Garvey when he took that band of volunteers over the river two months ago."

"Garvey's in the old Capitol prison," guffaws another. "You'll know about what his feelings are when you're in Libby yourself. Didn't reckon we knew you'd betrayed us ? Trying the sneak act, eh ? "

For this remark has produced a deathly pallor in the face of the man addressed, and he is leaving the hotel, the fear of immediate retaliation showing in his shivering limbs.

But despite the cruel passions of civil war, the nervous tension seems to have made down-hearted Union men and enthusiastic and triumphant Confederate sympathizers equally thirsty. The bar-room of the hotel is doing a great business, the chink of glasses sounding merrily, some of stuart's officers remarking that the whiskey is as good north of the Potomac as it is south. Altogether, the scene is one of great excitement, brilliancy and *élan*; there is cheering on the street, and the bands of the Southern Infantry, as they pass the house, are triumphantly playing, "My Mary-land," "Bonnie Blue Flag" and "Dixie."

In this gathering my blue uniform naturally attracts both attention and comment. A gray-coated captain, after consultation with one or two of his brother officers, steps to me and asks firmly, but politely, the reason of my presence. To him I return shortly that I am a prisoner under parole.

As I do so, we recognize each other as classmates at West Point. The Rebel's manner changes, so does mine. We forget we wear different uniforms and fight under opposing flags. The old days on the green parade-ground on the Hudson come back ; the old class feeling so often displayed during all that bloody time returns to us. Personal friendship, that even the awful animosity of that war did not destroy, when dying Armstead begged to be carried to his old chum Han-cock's tent, when Sherman and Johnson, though com-manding opposing armies, were to each other as "Bill" and "Joe," comes to us and makes us clasp hands over the bloody chasm.

Jeff Crockett, of the Twenty-second Confederate Ten-nessee Infantry, says to Billy Hamilton, of the First Union Kentucky Cavalry : "I am almighty glad to see you, though deuced sorry to see you dressed in blue. But I'll give you a hint ; if you are a prisoner and hungry, you had better feed at once—you may not have long to stay here, and your Yankee commissary is a good way off. Besides," whispers the young officer as I voice my thanks for the information, "there's a deuced pretty girl in the dining-room. Her beauty kept me from eating a few moments ago, and I had the appetite of a government mule."

"In a gray riding-habit?" I ask excitedly.

"Yes, but I did not look at her dress. It was her face, her face, Ramrod."

Jeff is calling me by my old class name ; but I hardly listen to him ; for I am turning eagerly to the dining-room with the sudden hope in my heart that I may catch my ex-captive at breakfast.

Entering, I find that fortune has been kind to me, though for a moment I hardly recognize her.

Before, her beauty had been partly concealed by the shadows of the night. At best, it had been but the suggestions of the fitful brands of a camp-fire, of flickering coal-oil lamps, and dim kerosene effects of the country hotel. This morning, under the soft summer sun that floats through the windows and halos her exquisite personality, her loveliness is a revelation.

Eyes of deepest blue, sparkling when betraying vivacity, but dark when indicating passion; forehead, low. as in all beautiful women, but still high enough to predicate brilliant man-catching mentality and that sprightly feminine intuition—instinct—divination—call it what you will—that seems so weak logically—that is so strong actually; complexion of mixed lilies and roses; mouth, kissable yet refined—even haughty; chin that would be firm were it not so womanly; a nose, patrician, with just enough retroussé in it to give it piquant witchery and alluring roguery; chestnut hair, wavy and curling about an exquisitely-formed head, and all this supported by the figure of a nineteen-year-old Venus, which is a good deal more graceful than the seven-and-twenty article.

This is what strikes my eyes as I place them on my captive of the preceding night. Altogether she is a most charming picture: the riding-habit of the night before seems somehow to have been made by some subtle art as fresh as if it had suffered no contact with Potomac water or dust of Maryland roads. A half-blown rosebud or two, tucked into its bosom, adds to the graceful effect as their perfume floats about her.

Sleep seems to have made the young lady more docile. She looks up at me archly, then a great, red, burning blush flies over her face, the reason of which I cannot guess, though it gives me a rapture which is increased by a soft, liquid Southern accent and piquant daintiness of demeanor.

"Good-morning, Captain Hamilton," she says cordially, though she has become strangely bashful. "Captivity has not destroyed your appetite, I hope."

"Nor yours either, I can see," I answer, as I inspect the depleted breaklast-table in front of her and take my seat immediately opposite.

The dining-room is nearly deserted. I felicitate myself upon chance of *tête-a-tête*.

"No trace of cold from your ducking last night?" I

question a latent anxiety in my voice that apparently impresses the young lady.

"You're concerned for my health?" she says airily; then suddenly laughs: "Oh, of course *you* should be!" and another wave of blushes flies again over her expressive face. A moment later she asks, a peculiar, embarrassed persiflage in her tone: "Why?"

"You were my captive when we forded the Potomac," I answer. "I always like to take good care of my *lady*-prisoners."

"Have you had *many?*" A sneaking, though wistful, eagerness in the inquiry delights me.

"You are my *first*," I return; "but the experience is so pleasant I am longing for many more."

"Humph! The remark is not so flattering as you intended it to be," laughs the young lady. Apparently she is growing more at her ease.

There is something familiar about the girl by daylight. Hang it! where have I seen Miss Alluring before? I rack my brain as I order from the attendant darky waiter a supply of provender which apparently astounds my *vis-à-vis*.

"Mercy! Your government rations must be very meagre, my cavalier," she says vivaciously.

"They are! This is my first civilized breakfast since I left Washington, six days ago."

"And you hope to be returning there shortly?"

"Yes; unless I'm sent to Libby Prison," I mutter glumly; then I ask eagerly: "And *your* fate? Have you seen General Jackson?"

"Pooh! That was settled early this morning. I'm afraid that great commander thinks I'm a very saucy girl," remarks the young lady piquantly.

"I hope not!" I answer gravely. "Stonewall Jackson is respected by every one, North or South."

"And why not?" cries the girl defiantly. "Why shouldn't I give him a piece of my mind, if he treats me like a prisoner and threatens to send me to Richmond under guard? Anyway, I don't care. I suppose I'll see my mother and my aunt in Leesburg some day —before I die."

"Why, I thought you were a Southerner!" I say impulsively.

"And are you not a Southerner?" she asks, "and

yet for the Union?   Are there not cold-blooded Southerners like you and me, who remain on the side that is
most convenient for them?   But come !   Let us run
over to the stable and look at our horses ?   Here's some
sugar for my Bonny Belle."   The girl has taken three
or four lumps from the bowl.

She rises and trips to a French window that opens
on the veranda at the rear of the house ; from which
steps leads to a garden, through which runs a path
apparently to the stables of the hostelry.

Standing with the sun shining on her delicate, piquant, patrician face, the green ivy leaves blowing
about her graceful figure—what man wouldn't follow
her.

Delighted to know that this beautiful creature is certainly on my side of the political fence, I spring up
from the relics of Maryland biscuits, porterhouse steak,
and corn-cakes and coffee; though I blush as I remember that I, a cavalryman, have, attracted by
woman, forgotten my steed's breakfast.

Stealing a few lumps of saccharine to make my
apology to my charger, I follow my beautiful guide
across the little garden.

" Neglected his horse's breakfast !   That's nice for a
dashing, yet sleepy dragoon," jeers the girl.

" I have been in the saddle for forty-eight hours," I
mutter shamefacedly.

" Well, *I* didn't forget your horse, if you did," laughs
the young lady.   " When I came out this morning to
see after Bonny Belle I took care that your charger—
Roderick, you call him, I believe—had everything necessary for his comfort."

We are standing beside the horses now, her pretty
little half Arab being stalled next to my heavier Ken-
tucky-bred roadster, which has carried me through my
first campaign and become a charger in several skir-
mishes in Tennessee and Kentucky, and the pitched
battle of Shiloh.   My companion has petted and given
the sweet dainties to her mare, Bonny Belle, while I
have made my amends to Roderick, who crunches the
lumps of sugar between his strong teeth, and looks at
me affectionately from his great big, honest eyes, as I
fondle his soft nozzle.

A moment later Miss Vivacity has tripped beside me

and is petting my horse also. "What a noble fellow !" she says, and inspecting Roderick's good points
with the eye of a horsewoman, whispers : "Fit to
ride for a man's life !"

Ye gods ! How a magnificent horse sets off a beautiful woman ! I can see her now, as she stands with
one hand over the shoulder of the great chestnut, the
closely fitting riding-habit outlining each exquisite
contour of her beautiful form ; its skirt, held up by a
dainty hand, displaying an equally dainty foot, in
tightly fitting, burnished riding-boot : the other little
white hand is playing with the flowing mane of my
big chestnut.

A moment later tears come into the girl's eyes. She
mutters : "Oh, if these Confederates steal our horses
from us ! It—it'll break my heart to lose Bonny
Belle !"

A glum feeling comes into mine also, as I see in
imagination some hard-riding trooper of Stuart's be-
striding my favorite war-horse.

Perchance sympathy makes us both tender to this
noble animal : we vie with each other in petting him
and caressing him. Suddenly an electric spark flies
through me. In fondling my charger's nozzle I have
unwittingly touched the beautiful hand of my companion, which is stroking it also.

A blush is on her face as she moves a little away
from me.

I step after her and say : "I hope last night's adventures have made us friends ; that, though you will
not give me your name, I may see you again." There
is a suppressed passion in my voice, that—fight it
down as I may—I can't keep out of it.

The girl's answer astounds me. "Oh, you will
doubtless see me quite often—*too* often perhaps ;" she
jeers—looks at me demurely for a moment—then
suddenly bursts into a paroxysm of roguish laughter.

A little mockery in her cadences makes me more
ardent, I mutter : "I shall live in that *hope !*" and
my voice conveys even more than my words.

Apparently the beautiful creature at my side thinks
so. She turns to me, and with flashing eyes murmurs :
"You say pretty things to many women, I suppose,
my gallant Captain." Then her voice grows deep per-

chance passionate, as she demands : " Have you the right to ? "

"Certainly ! " I answer, ardently, yet carelessly.

" *Think !* " my charmer looks me straight in the eyes. "Are you not engaged? Are you not the affianced of Miss Eva Vernon Ashley, of Virginia ? "

"Oh, that little witch ? " I laugh. "Egad ! I have not seen her since she was ten."

"Are you not betrothed to her *now ?* "

"Y-e-s," I mutter, chewing my moustache. "I suppose it's a family arrangement. But then I have not seen her for a great many years."

"And I have no doubt the girl was ugly," sneers my fair companion.

"No, on the contrary, she was as pretty a little termagant as I ever put eyes on."

"Ah—ah ! " There seems to be a triumph in my inquisitor's voice—why, I cannot for the life of me understand. "You think she may have grown more beautiful?" she queries eagerly.

"Yes; but I hardly believe she would come up to a young lady that I have met more *recently*." My accent on the last word is significant.

"Oho ! " The girl is giggling in my face ! Then she continues slowly and meditatively, "I suppose, like most young officers, you're permeated with that naughty soldier sentiment so ably voiced by fickle Tom Moore ? " And she quotes these damnable lines :

> " 'Tis sweet to think that where'er we rove
> We are sure to find something blissful and dear,
> And that when we're far from the lips we love
> We've but to make love to the lips we are near."

"On the contrary," I say, made desperate by the alluring beauty, who seems to scoff the pangs she raises in my heart, "in this case the lips that are near are also the lips that are *dear*."

"I—I will tell those words," remarks the young lady, biting her lip, "to—to your fiancée—" at the word the fair face suddenly grows as red as the roses in her habit. "You shall see what Miss Eva Vernon Ashley of Virginia, thinks of them." With this she suddenly bursts out into such an uncontrollable fit of laughter that it seems almost hysterical.

"You're a deuced curious girl," I meditate glumly, as I look at her; though there is a latent haughtiness in her manner that I cannot understand.

Just here, perhaps fortunately for me, this extraordinary interview is interrupted. Major Thornton enters the stable hurriedly and remarks: "I've been looking for you all over the hotel. Come with me, Hamilton, at once to General Jackson's headquarters." Then he bows to the young lady—rather coldly, I think.

"Has my fate been decided upon?" she asks quickly.

From her position I cannot see the face, though I note on Thornton's a kind of wary smile as he returns: "You will probably be sent South under a guard."

"To Richmond?" asks the piquant prisoner, with apparently forced anxiety.

"You will pardon me. I cannot discuss this affair with you," answers the Confederate major; it seems to me, with an affected and exaggerated brusqueness.

"Ah, you Southerners are not as gallant as Captain Hamilton, the Federal, was to me but a few moments ago." She turns on me a sweet, yet mocking smile.

Stepping to her, I whisper : "You will forgive words I couldn't help uttering?"

"I will, if Miss Eva Ashley will," returns Miss Enigma in a low voice ; then suddenly breaks out laughing again.

"You won't tell me your name?"

"*Never!*"

With this answer I am compelled to be content, for Thornton is saying impatiently: "Come quickly, Hamilton, if you would escape Libby Prison."

We walk out of the stable and cross the garden, the young lady following us, a strange merriment in her beautiful face. In the hotel I whisper to Thornton : "Tell me her name. You must have discovered it by this time."

"Not on my life, young man!" is the Confederate's jeering answer. Then he utters this ambiguous suggestion : "But you will doubtless know some day to your sorrow." And he, too, goes into an uncontrollable fit of merriment.

"Hang it! Are they both mad?" I think. Then I mutter: "Who the deuce is she?" For oh, how I want to know ! the exquisite, roguish, pathetic, sympathetic, jeering beauty of the girl I caught upon the banks of the Potomac has surely captured *me*.

CHAPTER IV.

STONEWALL JACKSON ASKS A FEW QUESTIONS.

In the main street, checking with some difficulty his merriment, which I look sternly upon, for it seems to me there is a mocking ring in it, the Confederate major, forcing his face to seriousness, remarks with military abruptness : "They have a few questions at Headquarters to ask you. If you reply to them satisfactorily, Captain Hamilton, you will probably be paroled at once."

"And if my answers are *not* satisfactory ? " I ask moodily.

"Then, perhaps, sent to Richmond under guard."

This suggestion makes me gloomy. I have a pretty shrewd idea of the kind of questions that will be asked me, and have determined not to reply to them. But present military spectacle drives from my mind visions of Libby Prison.

Evidences of the Confederate occupation are everywhere present. A brigade of A. P. Hill's Division is marching up the street, its band playing "In Dixie's Land." The faces of both officers and men are confident and enthusiastic, though their uniforms are worn and ragged.

Their reception by the inhabitants of Frederick indicates a decided variety of political sentiment. In some cases the blinds of the houses are closed, though from behind them eager eyes are scrutinizing the boys in gray as they march past. Some of the other dwellings are open, their occupants, men and women, gazing with curiosity upon the military pageant, with faces showing a sympathy they dare not more openly express. In a few others, however, Southern sentiment is vivaciously, enthusiastically and boldly displayed. One mansion is decorated with Confederate flags, the ladies and gentlemen on its veranda waving their handkerchiefs and displaying the Southern colors, while the members of the family distribute to the passing soldiers eatables and clothing such as seem most needed.

"That's Ross's residence," remarks Thornton. "He's the happiest man in Maryland. You Yanks had him in Fort McHenry for awhile, but now he is able to shout secession as much as he likes without being arrested. He is giving us a banquet this evening. I hope to make up for six months short rations at Mr. Ross's hospitable board."

"But supposing we Yanks come back," I ask.

"But you won't, my boy; we are in Maryland to stay," replies the Confederate, confidently. "Anyway, our friends here are having a good time now. The pent-up enthusiasm of two years is let loose kiting! They've just torn up and destroyed the office of the Frederick "Examiner," a red hot Black Republican paper. Scholtz, the editor, skedaddled this morning as Jeb Stuart's Cavalry came into town. But here are Jackson's headquarters."

The number of orderlies holding staff-officers' horses, an occasional brigade or division commander riding up, all indicate the military home of the Confederate chieftain. At present Bradley Johnston, who has just been appointed provost-marshal of the place, is making an address in the garden outside to a number of the citizens of Frederick who are congregated about him, assuring them that their private property will be held inviolate, and any supplies taken from them will be paid for in Confederate or Federal money, as they elect; that any soldier discovered in the slightest transgression against private rights or property will be summarily and severely punished.

Making our way through gaping farmers who have come grumblingly to headquarters to present orders for live-stock and provisions gleaned from them by Rebel foraging parties, Thornton ushers me in by a side door.

Here, after a few whispered words with an orderly, my Confederate friend remarks to me: "You'll have to wait a short time. General Jackson is now engaged with General Stuart."

With this he leads me into what is apparently the

main room of the house, where a number of Rebel officers are standing about chatting, and a few more are writing, seemingly very busy over general staff duties.

As I enter, a little conversation is wafted to me from a red-faced brigadier and a colonel of cavalry, who, in his high boots and plumed slouch hat, looks like an old-time cavalier. Apparently, they have not noticed me, and their words are by no means guarded.

"We have tried every way to get the information, for General Jackson seems to want it immediately," says the colonel. "You see, none of our command crossed into Maryland earlier than dusk last night, so no trooper or officer of ours can tell. Two of McClellan's Army Corps never crossed the Potomac to join Pope. We must know whether any of them have been sent into Harper's Ferry to strengthen that place."

"Then why the deuce don't you try the cursed Maryland farmers?" interjects the brigadier, with an oath.

"We have!" returns the cavalryman. "One half won't tell us if they can ; and the other half have been so busy harvesting their corn that their sleepy, bucolic eyes haven't noticed. Besides, the trains with rein-forcements might have passed through in the night."

"By the Lord Harry ! if I were Stuart, I'd get it out of these cursed, no-side Maryland yokels if I had to string 'em up by the thumbs !" mutters the burly general-officer, whose breath indicates Kentucky Bourbon.

"But," dissents the colonel, "you know we invade this State as friends, not enemies !"

"And the blasted Maryland farmer has by this time discovered that there's lots of Yankee greenbacks for his live stock and grain, delivered to the U. S. Commissary in Washington," mutters the brigade-command-er. "That's the reason these country louts outside scowl at us—their deliverers—as they take our Confederate currency for their farm produce."

Then his eye suddenly catches my blue uniform, which, with my lack of side-arms, now begins to attract attention from the surrounding warriors in gray. He advances irascibly towards me, and I, catch-ing his name from Thornton, remember him as a gentleman I had heard of, in old army lore, as a bully in Dragoon service on the frontier, where, after eating government pap for thirty years, he had resigned his command at the first rumor of secession, and come East, "to give the Yankees hell," as he expressed it.

Glaring at the blue uniform he had once worn, this potentate growls : "Who the devil are you ?"

After learning my rank in the Union Army and the particulars of my capture, this bluff old soldier says to me, the arrogance of authority in his voice : "Come, sir, we want the following information from you, and we must have it quick ! If your answers are satisfactory, we will parole you at once."

"Isn't that somewhat in the nature of a bribe, General?" I reply to him.

"You must be your own judge of that," answers the martinet sharply. "What is the strength of your garrison at Harper's Ferry?"

"My military honor will not permit me to answer that question, sir," I return stiffly.

"Confound it ! How many men have you at Martinsburg ?"

"I am unable to state."

"Hang it ! What is the strength of your command at Winchester ?"

"I cannot reply."

"Dash it, don't you mean to give me any information at all?"

"Yes. Permit me to be of service to you, General," I say blandly, unheeding Thornton's warning look. "You were educated at West Point—only a great many years before me—you must remember the teachings regarding military secrecy and military honor. I imagine they were just the same in your day as they were in mine."

"Damn it, sir ; do you mean to teach me my profession ?" roars the Rebel brigadier, getting very red in the face, for some of the staff officers about find great difficulty in choking down their merriment.

"Your parole is revoked !" he says to me sternly, then summons a sergeant : " Place this man under immediate close arrest ; forward him under guard to Libby Prison in Richmond by the first return wagons ! "

My heart sinks at the prospect of long confinement; perhaps during the whole war.

Here Thornton comes to my aid. He remarks: "Pardon me; I have General Jackson's orders to conduct Captain Hamilton to him immediately."

"Then why the devil didn't you say so?" growls the blustering brigadier.

A moment later I hear: "General Jackson desires to see you now."

An orderly opens the door, and Thornton beckons me into an adjoining apartment.

As I enter I catch "reinforcements—Harper's Ferry." But I am thinking more of my personal fate than anything else, and I scarce note the words.

A dashing, bronzed and free-and-easy trooper is just striding out.

I stare as I recognize, from old West Point history, the great cavalry-commander remembered at the Military Academy as "Beauty" Stuart. His brow is lofty and his eyes as flashing as a roguish boy's, and his manner as full of juvenile freshness as a Plebe's.

Can this be the man who has made himself famous as the inventor of the complete-circle-of-the-enemy-raid? Is this the cavalryman who rides all day and fights all night, and then rides on again?

But it is!

For a quiet, modest, but mathematically precise voice calls him back: "One moment, General Stuart; remember I *must* have this information!"

"General Jackson, you *shall* have the information!" says the cavalryman, confidently. "If I can't twist it out of the farmers' boys, I'll——"

"Remember—no threats, nor force! We come into this State as friends."

"I'll—I'll wheedle it out of the farmers' girls, along the Baltimore & Ohio railroad," laughs the trooper, stroking his long moustache caressingly. "General, I'm *good* with the girls!"

Apparently the dashing Confederate *is* good with the girls. For even as he speaks, some pretty little Maryland maidens are decorating with wreaths of flowers his prancing war-horse, held by an orderly, in the street outside.

Striding from the house, this rough-riding, hard-

fighting, non-drinking, never-swearing cavalry general
of boyish frankness and youthful *élan*, steps to the
street and swings his long legs, in high boots, over his
mettlesome Virginia charger.

Then leaning laughingly from his saddle, he picks
up a little tot, who unabashed offers him a sweet-smell-
ing posy. Kissing the child tenderly, he holds it in
front of him, and so surrounded by fresh blooming
flowers and with innocent childhood in his arms, the
Virginia cavalryman is for one moment a picture of
peace.

Then placing the child carefully on the ground, Jeb
Stuart becomes a man of war again, and plunging his
rowels into his steed, dashes away, singing gayly :

> " If you want to have a good time,
> J'ine the cavalry !
> J'ine the cavalry ! "

Turning from this martial, yet pastoral scene, I
anxiously place my eyes on the arbiter of my fate.

Seemingly too absorbed in thought to notice me, a
tall, raw-boned figure, in a faded, battle-worn, undress
uniform of the Confederacy, is rapidly, with a peculiar
stride, pacing the floor. The two stars on his military
collar indicate a major-general.*

" This is Captain Hamilton—the officer you wish to
see, General Jackson," remarks Thornton, saluting.

As the staff-officer retires, I will confess my view of
the Confederate chieftain astonishes me. Can this be
the man who has carried victory in his hand on so
many stricken fields ?

Though his aquiline nose and firm lips under the full
beard and moustache indicate decision, and his high
forehead and massive brows portray both gigantic,
intellectual force and power of intense concentration
of mind, still his gaze is more that of a student than a
warrior, and his manner diffident—even to bashfulness.
His smile is winning, his voice has the quiet tones
of a reticent professor rather than the sharp command
of a military chieftain, though there is a mathematical
directness in them as he says to me : " I am sorry to

---

* Jackson was not made a Lieutenant-General till after Fredericksburg.—ED.

trouble you, Captain Hamilton, with a few questions, before granting your parole. You had been scouting on the Potomac, I understand, when you were captured ?"

" Yes, sir," I answer promptly.

" Ah, guarding trains on the Baltimore & Ohio railway, I presume," he says. His eyes are meditative.

" No, sir," I reply carelessly. " There were no trains to guard."

" Thank you ! "

Suddenly his manner changes. He is no more the student ; he is the military genius—the inspired strategist—the commander who holds the forces of war within his grasp.

" Good God ! What have I carelessly told him ! "

He has sounded a bell upon his table. A staff-officer enters hurriedly. To him he whispers certain orders with great rapidity, repeating them over, I imagine, from the way he speaks and adding : " See that every division-commander in my corps gets this in duplicate by separate messengers within the hour." As I stand in the corner of the room and watch the play of his precise yet confident and enthusiastic features, and see the nostrils of the aquiline nose expanding, and the great eyes, glowing under their prominent brows that give to them such intensity of divination, I start and wonder : " Have my words produced this sudden resolution in the Confederate commander ? "

All at once it strikes me like a rifle shot. If there were *no* trains to guard on the Baltimore & Ohio railroad, the only route to Harper's Ferry, *no* reinforcements have gone into this place. Some one must have given the Confederate general exact information as to what was the strength of its garrison a few days before. If they have not been reinforced, by the two corps of McClellan's of which we have no report, he knows the exact Union forces in the doomed fortress. What Stuart's cavalry could not get for him,—what Maryland farmers could not or would not give him,—what the blustering brigadier could not bully out of me, the student, in two most politic and deftly worded sentences, has drawn from *me.*

I gaze disconcerted and chagrined out of the window,

and see staff-officers one after another galloping off hurriedly, and a division-commander and a couple of brigadiers mounting their horses and riding away in sudden haste.

A moment later, the courteous voice of the Confederate chieftain calls me to him. " There is only one thing more, which can in no way affect the military situation," he says ; "the young lady you arrested at Norton's Ford last evening—the one captured when you were taken prisoner." There is a pathetic interest in the Confederate general's tones.

" Yes, sir ; what of her ? " I ask anxiously.

" Do you know her name ? "

"No, sir ! She absolutely refused to give me any information on that subject ! "

"Have you any idea of her purpose in attempting to cross the river?"

"No, sir. "

"This is on your honor, both as an officer and a gentleman ? "

" It is, sir ! My answers are absolutely correct."

"Thank you ! Then you will be paroled as soon as possible."

A moment later the Confederate General gives directions to this effect to Thornton, who is waiting for me ; then astounds and confuses me again by ordering an aide to bring to him instantly the map of Pennsylvania, and calling the dashing cavalry colonel of the plumed hat in to him, I hear him in distinct voice and direct tones order :

"Colonel Brien, overtake General Stuart and tell him your regiment is to ride as far as Chambersburg ; I wish to know if any Pennsylvania militia or State troops are gathered at that point. You will make no attack upon them—only so far as is absolutely necessary to develop their force. Then return with the information to me."

" Is this last order intended to befog me ? " I think, as I notice the General glances towards me once or twice. Any way, this places my mind in a muddle. I had supposed General Jackson's point of attack was Harper's Ferry ; now it seems to me his eye is turned towards Harrisburg and Philadelphia. At all events, I am no more sure of his absolute intentions than when

I entered. All I know is that my hasty words have given him the information he wanted.

So we walk out from the headquarters of the man whose genius made for the first two years of the war a triumphant South.

CHAPTER V.

"FIND HER AND—MAKE LOVE TO HER."

In the street, the Confederate Major whispers to me: "What do you think of him?"

"Think of him?" I answer. "He is the greatest diplomatist I ever saw. He got out of me as an irrelevant side remark what that blustering brigadier could not by direct questions."

"Ah, but you should see the diplomatist *in battle*," answers my companion, "or on the march. Hang it, he gives us no rest! We've marched farther, fought more and eaten less than any troops in the history of the world; and would go faster, if the cursed commissariat could keep up with us!" says the major, unwittingly betraying the great weakness of the Confederate army—their commissariat.

The provisioning their men and foraging their horses was always their embarrassment.

Even this very day an effective commissariat might have made a change in the whole war. Could Stonewall Jackson have moved at once, Harper's Ferry would have fallen five days before it did. Jackson's immense Army Corps would have joined the main body of Lee's command at South Mountain. With the Confederate force so increased in power, McClellan's army might have been beaten at Turner's and Crampton's Gaps; there might have been no Antietam.

Evidences, though, of the hurried gathering together of provisions are now apparent. A cavalry troop comes up, driving a drove of cattle on the hoof. Shortly after another appears, escorting wagons laden down with forage, corn and provisions. Evidently every effort will be made to get on the march at once.

"You will have to stay here," remarks my Confederate friend as we pause in front of the hotel, "until I can escort you from the lines. That I shall be too busy to do before evening. Make yourself comfortable, and eat another square meal."

"Thank you," I reply, and hurry into the hostelry. But a square meal is not in my mind—my one thought is to again see the beautiful face I left there this morning. For some very curious speculations have come into my mind regarding Miss Illusive. Why was General Jackson so anxious to discover if I knew her name or her reasons for crossing to the Virginia side?

With this purpose I look around the hotel, for I hesitate to inquire about my charmer at the office; my questions might perhaps unpleasant produce comment upon the lady of my thoughts.

I look about the garden. She is not there!

I wander to the stables. Our horses are crunching their oats cheerily. Bonny Belle, the pretty half-Arab mare which had borne my companion so bravely the night before, is whinnying for more sugar; but her fair mistress is not there to give it.

I recross the garden and return to the hotel, to eat a moody meal. I daudle the time away, lounging about with one of Lammersdorff's cigars in my mouth. Darkness slowly comes upon the scene.

I stroll out upon the veranda. Sitting in the twilight I find at least quiet; for though the front of the house is full of customers, the garden is practically deserted. The gnats in the soft summer evening air annoy me. Hoping to escape them, I take my chair, descend to the garden and seat myself, thinking the breezes of the evening may blow them away.

In this position my head is some two feet below the flooring of the balcony. In the darkness, which is aided by some shrubs and the climbing vines of the portico, I am indiscernible from the illuminated portion of the house. A gloomy meditation upon my coming enforced inactivity until exchanged causes my cigar to die out. This is broken in upon by a soft feminine voice above me.

It is her voice; her vivacious accents! The lady of my quest is speaking apparently to a Confederate officer, by whose side she is promenading the veranda. Who is the gentleman? I know from his tones he is not Thornton.

As they walk, when near me I hear their words; when at the other end of the balcony, I miss them. It seems to me I miss those I want most, though even as it is I hear too much for my own peace of mind; for this is what comes to me in broken-up, disjointed phrases :

"Oh ! how great my joy at meeting you ! " What a pleasant walk we've had, dear Charley——"

Then they are at the other end of the veranda.

My heaven ! What a pang "*dear* Charley" gives me. My charmer has come to meet a Confederate beau ! That's the meaning of her night ride between contending armies.

They are near me again.

Suddenly my woe at this beautiful girl being the sweetheart of another is destroyed by chagrin, even rage. As she comes near me this time, the young lady is apparently merry.

"Wasn't it curious ? " she is babbling. " My being captured by *him*, and he a *Union* officer. It—it was quite embarrassing." There is a delicious naïveté and diffidence in the girl's voice.

"He made a little love to you, I presume, eh ? " says the masculine voice in bantering tones.

"He—he *might* have," is murmured in sweet yet bashful accents. " But—but I kept him in order by threatening to tell his fiancée, Miss Eva Vernon Ashley, of Virginia."

"WHAT ? " almost screams the man. "You disciplined his amorous spirit in that way ? Well, of all the cool and original things ! " and the gentleman burst into uproarious laughter.

"Yes, I've—I've had hysterics over it twice to-day," giggles the young lady. " Oh, Charley, how he looked at me when I taxed him with his engagement ! Ha, ha, ha ! He, he, he! "

The light, silvery, yet half-mocking cadences of the girl mingle with the deeper guffaws of the man, both dying away as they leave me, for they are pacing towards the further end of the veranda.

With a gesture of rage I toss away my extinguished cigar. Curse it ! they are laughing at *me !*

But greater anguish is in store. They are approaching again. She is saying very tenderly : " Fancy my

joy when I saw you, dear Charley, ride by in the street.
I'd—I'd not seen your loved face for three long months."

And then—my God!—the sound comes to me of a
tender kiss!

His affianced or his bride; I know that now! For I
feel that this girl is one who would never surrender her
lips unless she had given her heart in honor. Her pure
innocence and noble womanhood have told me that.

Thank heaven, she has turned and gone into the
hotel with her Confederate. I shall suffer no more
agony from their half-mocking laughter—from their
torturing kisses.

Permitting a few minutes to elapse, partly to overcome my agitation, and partly that by no chance the
girl may suspect I have overheard her tender interview,
I rise and stroll into the hostelry, thinking glumly how
she must love him. No wonder she doesn't care to
have her name known, for the gossip of an army.
She took the chances of war to visit her affianced, and
he—curse him!—didn't even seem over-complimented
by Miss Beauty's devotion and the risks she took to
meet him.

In the hotel I am almost immediately met by
Thornton. He says: "Come with me; I am to take
you to the provost-marshal, who will receive your formal parole, and then I'm to conduct you out of the
Confederate lines."

"Come on—*quick!*" I return savagely.

"You'd not like to see Miss—Miss Incognita—just
for one moment?" asks the Confederate major with
a grin.

"Certainly *not!*" my tone makes him start—then I
query anxiously: "My horse?"

"That you are to have. Stonewall Jackson, who
thinks of everything and every one but himself, told
me not to put you down on foot in the road."

Delighted that I have saved Roderick, I go to the
stable, saddle up hurriedly and rejoin the Confederate
major, who mounts and rides with me to the provost-
marshal's office. There my parole is formally made
out.

As this is being done I note a cavalry guard under a sergeant being told off.

An hour later I am shaking Thornton's hand and

bidding him "Good-bye and God bless you!" at the last outlying Confederate picket.

"You know the name of the young lady?" I can't help saying.

"Don't ask me any questions about her," he replies; then bursts out laughing.

"You refuse to answer for *military* reasons?" I question half-angrily.

His reply astounds me: "No; for *social* ones!"

"What mystery is there about her and *me?*" I cry, sudden inspiration coming to me. "And what are you going to do with her?"

"She is to be sent South under guard this evening," replies Thornton.

"For what reason?"

His answer almost petrifies me: "Hang it! We think her a Yankee spy. The girl has even refused to speak to General Jackson. Egad, you ought to hear some of the Secesh maidens in Frederick discuss her. A Virginia girl rude to Stonewall Jackson! They'd like to tear her eyes out."

"Impossible!" I mutter.

"Nevertheless, the sergeant's guard for her left the provost-marshal's office even as we entered it. You saw them told off. But I must bid you good-bye. Here, we've put you in the road, with a horse. Take one of my pistols; bushwhackers may be about. Good-bye; God bless you! Give my love to the Baltimore girls."

"And my regards to Mrs. Thornton," I reply, as I ride off into the darkness along the pike that leads from Frederick towards Urbana *en route* for Washington.

Roderick carries me eighteen miles that night to Clarksburg. In proof of the efficiency of the rebel patrols, I am halted on this portion of my journey by scouting parties of Stuart's command, and compelled to show my pass from Confederate headquarters no less than five times.

Judging by the talk of the innkeeper of this place that I am pretty well beyond the sphere of Rebel raiders, I sleep in Clarksburgh. Getting on my way the next morning about eleven o'clock a little adventure comes to me that has considerable effect upon my life, though at the time I think it unimportant. Some few miles beyond Middlebrook I overtake five four-mule sutlers' teams, apparently held up by a couple of men in the road.

"Hello, more Rebel raiders!" I think, but journey confidently towards them, as I have a Confederate pass in my pocket. On approaching, however, I discover the men on foot wear blue uniforms and are holding an excited discussion with a gentleman who is damning them in High Dutch and Low Dutch, with now and then a Yankee oath with German phrasing. I recognize the tones as Lammersdorff's.

"Mein Gott in Himmel, is dat you, Cap? You vas alive mit yourself?" cries the sutler who, in his shirt-sleeves, and armed only with his black-snake whip, is confronting a scoundrel who is handling a U. S. Army musket.

"Yes, but captured, as you said I would be," I answer, riding up.

"Den, kevick! prove you is alive by helping me to stand off dese damned tieving bounty-jumpers who vants to drink my beer for nutting."

"You lying Dutch huckster!" cries one of the ruffians, "Take that to keep your jaw shut!" He is a cocking and raising his gun as my revolver cracks. The Confederate had loaded his weapon properly, and the fellow screams with pain as his arm falls to his side.

Then he and his comrade jump the fence and take to the fields. Gazing after them, I discover the two men are half-drunken stragglers from one of the regiments in camp near Washington, a kind of gentry very prevalent about the capital in those days.

"Thanks for your aid and comfort," says the German gratefully. "I shan't forget dat you saves my life." Then looking at me with wondering eyes, he mutters: "And de Rebs didn't send you to Richmond?"

"No! I am on parole, but hungry."

"Vell, sit in ze vagon mit me. Von of my boys vill ride your horse, and ve'll eat a Bologna sausage und delicatessen, und crack a bottle of champagne together on your escape from ze Rebs und my escape from dese damned Union robbers. Here, Fritz, hitch ze Cap's horse alongside your offish mule; ze von dat doesn't kick mit himself."

I accept the genial sutler's offer, and together we drive towards Washington. We soon come upon scouting parties of Union cavalry, of Pleasanton's command, thrown out to mask the movement of McClellan's army corps.

As we approach Rockville, our way is blocked and our journey made tedious by the infantry of Couch's division, already on the march to attempt to save Harper's Ferry.

After passing with great difficulty these sunburnt veterans who, just returned from the battles of the Peninsula, are nearly as dirty, though not quite as ragged as "Stonewall" Jackson's boys, we come on Slocum's division, the advance of Franklin's corps, likewise dilapidated by hard service, and the First Massachusetts Battery, led by its gallant young captain, Josiah Porter, that is on its way to take its place at the apex of that fiery crown of artillery that at the Antietam hurled back Lee's last desperate charge of veterans that never had been stopped before.

"Hello, damn it !" growls Lammersdorff. "More troops, more dust und more vagons und ardtillery. I'd shust as vell go into camp myself by the road undtil dey passes."

To progress on the main high-ways is now simply impossible. They are blocked with marching infantry and rumbling artillery that is being pushed out from Washington in the attempt to relieve Harper's Ferry. The dust and heat are terrible.

Bidding adieu to Lammersdorff, I mount my horse, and taking lanes and by-roads, and passing the white tents of new regiments and the brown, weather-beaten ones of veterans still in camp, and batteries whose guns are yet parked, I reach the city that is now not only an armed fortress, but the great gathering-place of all who come to prey upon the revenues of the nation in distress and the troops engaged in its defence; from army contractors, who are here to make their millions out of the government, and gamblers who fleece high-play officers, to courtesans who prey upon the boys in blue after the paymaster has made his rounds—the Washington of the war.

Evidences of this are on every side of me, as I edge my way past a regiment of marching infantry, amid the dust of Pennsylvania Avenue, whose sidewalks are crowded by the conglomerate throng of an 1862 evening.

Women of the town, in gay dresses, are trying their allurements, jostling and jesting with the rank and file of the army. Staff, general and mounted line officers are galloping about. Civilians in plain clothes are everywhere mixed with army blue. The big gambling-houses on Pennsylvania Avenue are lighting up for their night's work with high rolling officers, who will risk and lose their money this evening as recklessly as they will risk and lose their lives a week from now at bloody South Mountain and deadly Antietam. Yet, over, all hangs a certain indiscribable air of anxiety and excitement—Lee is in Maryland.

Forcing my way through this concourse, I finally reach army headquarters to report myself and the capture of my troop.

Two hours afterwards, as I sit in Williard's smoking my after-dinner cigar and listening with one ear to a Jacobin Senator attacking Lincoln for not emancipating the slaves off-hand and putting Fremont at the head of the army, and with the other ear being edified by an Illinois army-contractor, who is busily engaged in obtaining the help of a Western Congressman for his schemes, I am hastily summoned by an orderly to the War Department.

It is dark when I arrive at the old-fashioned brick building. On hearing my name the officer in waiting tells me that the Secretary will see me shortly.

Amid hurrying officers and busy heads of departments, surrounded by the semi-panic of rebel invasion, in the midst of the mighty military preparations of the nation in its death-grapple, Edwin McMasters Stanton seems to be able to devote two minutes to *me!*

A few moments after, in his private office, he asks anxiously what I know of Lee's force and Jackson's movements, and listens eagerly, but irritably, to my account of my capture, and the information I give him in regard to the Confederate occupation of Frederick. As I look at the scowling brow, implacable countenance, and irascible figure of the head of the War Department, I do not deem it wise to tell him of the information the Confederate strategist gained from my careless answer to his astute question.

"If Jackson attacks Harper's Ferry, he will probably get it : he gets most everything !" mutters the Secretary glumly. "God ! Wouldn't I like to have him on the Union side !" And he goes into a moody meditation, stroking his long beard reflectively.

This I dare to interrupt by suggesting : "What is to be done with me until I am exchanged ?" For I don't care much to be sent out on the plains to fight Indians, or to the northern frontier to police it—a disposition that was made at that time of quite a number of Union troops under parole.

"You ?" remarks the Secretary, his deep eyes looking at me contemplatively through his glasses. "You ?" Then he suddenly takes me off my feet. He says rapidly : "There was a girl you captured at Norton's Ford, who was brought into Frederick and stayed at the same hotel as you did."

"There was," I answer, wondering where he got all this information : though Baker's spies are thick as blackberries this September in Maryland.

"Well, you—you had a little flirtation with her, I am informed. Find her out and *make love to her.*"

Here I sweep him off his feet!

"Impossible ! " I reply. "She has been sent South under guard, suspected as being a Union Spy."

"Can I have been mistaken ?" mutters the Secretary. Then he suddenly says : "If you see her in Washington, make love to her and"—his eyes light up with the fire of a Vidocq—"tell me all about her—*I want her !*"

Fortunately, I get out of his presence without his seeing my face. In front of the dimly-lighted War Department, I look up at a shadow in the Secretary's private office—I think of her sweet face and of his police-magistrate, detective, cold, merciless eyes.

"My God ! He thinks her a Rebel spy !" I mutter astounded. "This I know to be false !" Then I add savagely : "Damn you. You shall never have her ! "

But turning away, I jeer myself bitterly : "Nincom-poop ! What strange thing has come into your heart that you, a Union officer, will risk life itself—ay, perhaps even honor—to save some Confederate trooper's sweetheart from Mr. Secretary Stanton of the United States War Department?

BOOK II.

THE PROVOST MARSHAL AT BALTIMORE.

CHAPTER VI.

MAJOR ANANIAS OF STUART'S CAVALRY.

WILLARD'S HOTEL being at this time intensely noisy, excessively crowded and decidedly expensive, I move to the quieter quarters of an F Street boarding-house and remain in Washington under waiting orders, killing time.

This is not difficult to do ; the excitement would kill almost anything—even time. The general anxiety of everyone fills the place with a pent-up, compressed and latent dread. Every word you hear at Wormley's restaurant or Willard's Hotel is : "Where is Lee now?" or "Has Jackson gone into Pennsylvania?" "Do you think he'll get here and capture us ? " "What is McClellan doing?" "Why hasn't he brought on a battle ? "

The force attributed to the Confederates, makes me jeer. Once from reliable contrabands it is placed as high as 250,000 cavalry, infantry and artillery with 400 guns, and published as a *fact* by the newspapers.

Again, it is reported that Jackson has flanked McClellan and is now in a direct march for Baltimore and about to blow up the bridge over the Patapsco. On hearing this, one of the few ultra-bloodthirsty Jacobin senators summering in Washington, stops abusing the government and is heard to whisper, with white lips :

"My God ! What will Jackson do with me if I am captured?" and takes a train for the North within the hour.

Even in the great gambling-houses on Pennsylvania

Avenue at night, as Government contractors lay their money on cards, the hand of the Rebel is felt hanging over the "Goddess of Chance." In Chamberlin's, one evening when the stakes were very high, it is related that a luckless gamester, in revenge for his losses, ran in from the street, crying: "My God, gentlemen! Save yourselves and your money! Stuart's Cavalry is raiding the town!"

More curious to relate, in thirty seconds the great establishment was nearly empty, though one cold-blooded croupier coolly remarked: "I guess Jeb Stuart and Stonewall Jack won't git here till after this deal," and raked in every stake left by the fleeing gamesters.

This anecdote is related to me by young Napoleon Leonidas Finnaker, of Chicago, a clerk in Meigs the Quartermaster-General's office. Little Finnaker occupies the next room to mine at my boarding-house on F Street.

In the social republic of Mrs. Lorimer's dining-table I soon discover little Nap Finnaker is the most un-blushing braggart and most audacious liar I have ever encountered, and that for concentrated, condensed cheek and assurance he can give points to even the celebrated Beau Hickman, who is still ornamenting Pennsylvania Avenue with his perennial nosegay in his buttonhole.

Being connected with the Quartermaster-General's Department, little Napoleon thinks it necessary he should assume martial airs, and would wear a uniform if the regulations permitted. In fact, he confidently informs me that it was to keep him out of the army that he was put in General Meigs's office.

"I *would* go to the front, my dear fellah. Wild horses couldn't keep me from getting at the Johnnies' throats. The only hope of my frightened mother was a *compromise*, and so I entered the Quartermaster-General's department!" he babbles in a voice deep, bass and resonant and of such tremendous power that, looking at his little stature and slight physique, he seems to be all lungs, wind and noise.

After the first battle of Bull Run, this little swash-buckler had the audacity to bring himself in wounded, though he had spent the whole day in bed, timidly listening for the sound of the approaching Confederate cannon.

"Good gad, my boy!" he says to me in a roar. "We military men look at the present situation with extreme concern. Whenever *I* have encountered 'Stonewall' Jackson, I have found him invincible. And—damn it!—they're *not* going to move the War Department! Think of it! the imbeciles! We clerks will be butchered to a man! Stanton sits there grinding his teeth as if nothing was happening; doesn't the idiot know that they'll cut his throat? Haven't they sworn vengeance on him and us for Pope's outrageously bloodthirsty and foolish proclamation in Northern Virginia? Three hundred thousand Texas bowie-knife cut-throats in Maryland! And yet, we are staying here to be sacrificed! Four times in the last three days have I applied for leave, and it has been steadily refused me. They talk of organizing us into a militia company of home guards, for the crisis!"

Then suddenly he trembles and whispers in deep voice: "Good God! What is that *horrible* extra? Oh, curse it! What *is* McClellan doing?" and wanders out into the street, with pale face and timid air.

For the newsboys are crying outside: "Lee in full march for Baltimore! Maryland Secesh have risen to a man! Rebel Cavalry raiding to the gates of Harrisburg!—Panic in Philadelphia!—Brag threatens Ohio! Business stopped in Cincinnati!" and other pleasing war rumors of that stirring time.

Every one is on the alert, I among the rest. I run out into the street, and try and pick up news; for I feel that on this campaign, probably within the week, will be settled the fate of Washington. However, I note with pleasure, that the few soldiers left in the town are much more confident of the success of the Union arms than civilians; especially those of the troops who have served under Little Mac, as they call him, now that he is again in command.

So the time flies on.

On the twelfth of September, it is announced that the advance division of the Federal Army has reoccupied Frederick.

On the thirteenth, that Stonewall Jackson has at-

tacked Harper's Ferry. Lee has probably fallen back
to protect his lieutenant.

Early on the morning of the fifteenth comes the
news of the victory at South Mountain, and the forcing
of Turner's and Crampton's gaps by the Union forces,
with most exaggerated details ; Lee is reported
wounded and the Confederate loss seventeen thousand
men. Every military eye is on Harper's Ferry.

Will it hold out until relieved ? McClellan must be
very near to it now !

There's no more news from the front—apparently
the victory has been over-estimated. All we can learn
is that every surgeon, every ambulance, and enormous
hospital stores have been sent to Frederick. This
indicates a heavy loss to our troops.

On the morning of the sixteenth, I am again summoned to the War Department. Hoping that they
have found some employment for me that will not be
inconsistent with my parole, I hurry to the old-
fashioned brick building. There are now not so many
officers about ; most of them are at the front with
McClellan, and every man jack of them from the As-
sistant Adjutant General to Madison, Stanton's colored
factotum, is suspiciously quiet and anxious.

"Is there any news of Harper's Ferry?" I ask one
of the officials in waiting.

"No, but a courier must come from McClellan soon
to Frederick. To that point the telegraph line has been
repaired."

After some half-hour's waiting, I am ushered into the
Secretary's private office by black-faced and white-
headed Madison.

"He's powerful out of sorts this morning," whispers
the old darky. "Be careful and rub him the right
way."

As I enter, I feel a presentiment of evil come on me.
The cold blue eyes glare at me through their glasses.
Hardly recognizing my salute, the Secretary begins :

"Since our reoccupation of that town, I have had
some curious information from Frederick. It is reported to me that immediately after your interview at
Jackson's headquarters with that general, he gave instant orders for his corps to prepare to march. You
will state immediately to me what were the exact

questions he put to you and your answers to that Rebel lynx."

After a moment's pause of consideration, I answer this question truthfully and exactly.

As I give the two questions of the Confederate general and my careless reply to the last one, the Secretary starts up from his desk, and standing in front of me, breaks out viciously in low, clear-cut, incisive, yet measured tones :

"And *you*, by your imbecile answer, told him that *no* trains had gone over the Baltimore & Ohio Railroad ! Then, of course, *no* reinforcements went into Harper's Ferry. Oh ! you're a *beauty* to let the cat out of the bag ! Curse it, sir, couldn't your little brain guess that that Rebel watch-dog knew that with no reinforcements he could probably capture the place, commanded as it is, by a septuagenarian officer ? "

And pushing his eyeglasses upon his forehead he glares at me and goes shuffling vindictively about the room.

Before I can answer this invective from my superior officer, to which I have listened respectfully, fighting down indignant words upon my lips, the door is opened and old Madison makes his appearance, ushering in Colonel Hardie.

"What the devil, you infernal nigger, are you coming in here for, sir ? How dare you break into a private interview of mine ? " splutters the head of the United States dogs of war.

"You will pardon this intrusion, Mr. Secretary," interjects the colonel hurriedly. "This telegram could not wait. It is from the front."

Pulling his eyeglasses down on his nose again, Stanton reads the dispatch. As he does so, he looks up from it at me, and his face horrifies me.

It is the incarnation of the hate of the war.

"By Heaven ! " he mutters, "Harper's Ferry has surrendered and fallen with eleven thousand men. McClellan too late ; Jackson too quick ! It's always so with these Democratic generals and Border-State officers ! " and he glares at me.

Then he snarls : "It's to this young man, perhaps, I owe this dispatch. Get out of my presence ! Go to the devil ! " he thunders. "You'll hear from me !

You shall remember Harper's Ferry longer than I will.
Don't forget that, my Maryland recruit!"

As I leave the apartment, I hear him saying, his
voice low, his diction clear-cut as if quoted from the
book of fate: "By the Eternal! Give them as many
victories as they like, but I'll grind these Southern
cavaliers out under the heel of Northern infantry before I get through with them, if it takes a year! if it
takes *two*; if it takes *ten!* So long as I live, I'll pound
away at Jeff Davis and his Rebel crew!"

Two hours afterward, I am directed to proceed to
Baltimore and remain on waiting orders. I am very
glad to get away from an official whose ill-will I know
I have, and one who can certainly prevent my advancement.

While in Baltimore on waiting orders, I am not compelled to wear my uniform. I can again associate with
my old-time boyhood comrades and renew the friend-
ships of my early youth. I can again receive my dear
sister's caresses; I can once more embrace my father
that I revere and honor, despite the difference of our
political opinions, if they have not heard I wear the
blue.

A visit to our Charles Street residence soon shows
me they have not. I steal a few more kisses from my
loved ones under their misunderstanding that I wear
the gray. My father's and sisters' astonishment at
seeing me is only exceeded by their joy that I have not
fallen in the carnage of the recent battles.

To their eager inquiries, I answer in a shamefaced
way, that I have been captured near Frederick when
detailed on a scouting party, and having been paroled
until exchanged, I have naturally come home to live
until by cartel I am freed from my obligation not to
take up arms.

"Taken near Frederick?" mutters my father. "It
is curious that the Yankee papers did not mention it;
they generally magnify their slight successes, instead
of concealing them. And paroled? That is a rather
unusual complaisance to a Confederate prisoner from
Union authorities."

"Well, I've my orders from Stanton himself," I say,
growing more confident, "to live in Baltimore until
further directions."

What my governor's reply would have been I know not; for Birdie here breaks in enthusiastically: "Captured near Frederick? Billy, you must have been with Jackson!"

"I was!" I answer, the confidence of the liar growing in me. "I saw 'Stonewall' on the afternoon of the fifth. I was at his headquarters with Thornton, of the First Virginia Cavalry."

"And soon after you were captured, my poor brother?" interjects Virgie with a kiss.

"Yes! In the Federal lines the next day by noon!" I reply, staving off further inquiry by caresses. To these they all respond; even my old *régime* father unbending and telling me with tears in his eyes that their anxiety has been awful, ever since the second Battle of Manassas.

"We could get no accounts of the Southern killed and wounded. You don't guess the anxiety of those who wait here to learn of their loved ones in the Confederate ranks," he remarks. "There's Mrs. Bouvier has an only son in the Maryland Line. William, if you've any tidings of Arthur Bouvier—a lieutenant in Brockenbrough's Battery—you must go at once and give them to his mother. She's a widow now. You remember little Arthur? you used to play with him!"

"Yes, of course," I answer uneasily, "but I did not see him. He must have been in Longstreet's corps."

"And then, perhaps, you met Charley St. George; you remember Eva's half-brother, he's so handsome —in Mumford's Second Virginia?" asks Birdie, with very eager eyes.

"No! I met Stuart and saw Brien of the First Cavalry, and Thornton and Ruff Crockett of the Tennessee Infantry. But when a man's fighting and riding, and fighting again, social duties take the rear rank decidedly!" I answer.

"Then you *didn't* see Eva?" murmurs Birdie, disappointedly.

"See her? Of course not!" is my unabashed reply. "I had something more to do in Viriginia than to look up girls—even my fiancée." I wince at the term, however, as I utter it, for I am thinking of the beautiful creature who stood beside me the only few minutes I spent in Virginia while Stonewall Jackson's men crossed the Potomac.

"And the gray uniform we made for you?" whispers my elder sister. "We had rather speculated how Miss Ashley would admire you in it."

"The gray uniform is a thing of the past," I laugh. "You should have seen what was left of it after Cedar Mountain, Second Manassas and Ox Hill. I believe by that time I was as dirty and as ragged as any trooper in Stuart's."

Great powers, how I am lying; but mendacity once begun must be carried to the end. I have spoken of battles; mention compels description. My father and my sisters gather round me closer and listen to the veteran Confederate. Their eager anxiety as to my personal adventures has to be satisfied.

Fortunately, I have seen enough stricken fields, and a battle in Virginia can't be very different from a combat in Tennessee.

I give my loved ones details of Jackson's defence of the railroad embankment at Pope's big defeat. I ride with Stuart on the foray when we capture Catlett's station. With him I raid the great Federal Commissary stores at Manassas Junction, and growing vivid I tell how, after living on corn in the ear for a week, we knock off the heads of champagne bottles and drink the vintages of France and feast on canned chicken and lobster-salad, and condensed plum pudding, our meal lighted by the blaze of five million dollars worth of Union stores for Pope's hungry army.

Then both papa and sisters show their love for me by asking more questions, and Major Ananias, of Stuart's Cavalry Division, at last finds himself located definitely as an officer of the Jeff Davis' Legion, an intimate of Fitz Lee's and on speaking terms with Rosser, Robinson and even Jackson.

As I think over the matter afterwards, the only apology I can make for myself, is that if I told the truth, I lost the love of my dear ones, and that one lie leads to another, the very nature of my description requiring the endorsement of detail vivid and exciting as the scenes I described.

"I'll keep their love and their kisses as long as I can," I think desperately. "They'll hate and despise me so much after they know ; a little more delusion and exaggeration won't add to it—all but Birdie ! "

Of my younger sister I have a little hope—she is so sweet, so amiable, so affectionate to me always—she will not hate her brother *forever*, even if he is a Union officer.

Perhaps my answers might receive more critical analysis were they all not so glad to see me safe and unwounded, and were not the anxieties of the present so great that the events of to-day engross them more than the happenings of yesterday—for as yet the news of Antietam has not arrived.

In fact, even as I, in our quiet family home on Charles Street, Baltimore, am conversing with my family, the veterans of McClellan and Lee, at Sharpsburg, not a hundred miles away, are slaughtering each other on that desperate and bloody field which decided the fate of Maryland.

But no news comes to us this day ; the streets of the town are full of people desperately anxious as to the result of a campaign, which means so much for the city, many of its citzens of large property, yet Southern sympathies, apparently dreading the approach of Lee's army victorious and triumphant more even than his defeat.   This curious state of feeling is explained to me at the Maryland Club.

" Don't you know," whispers George Ransome to me, "the Federal authorities have made little preparations to defend this town from Lee ; but *ample* for its destruction in case the Confederates occupy it.   They've six mortar boats in the river under Porter, and with *bombs* from them falling in the streets and the fire of the forts, this place will be a living hell—and then our mothers, wives and women folk."

The genial club man's face grows white and long as he thinks of his handsome young wife and two pretty children.   Many talk of flying on the approach of the army they hope with all their souls will succeed and conquer.

But my father is made of sterner stuff—on my suggestion that he go to New York himself, or at least send Virgie and Birdie there, till the danger's is over, I am met with stern rebuke ; not only from him but from my sisters.

"For shame, William!" they cry. "Fly from the army we love? Avoid Lee and Jackson when they come to free us?"

"You've never seen a bombardment," I dissent; "you don't know what it's like and I pray God you never will."

But the next day, the news comes of Antietam. McClellan has saved Maryland to the Union; Lee, baffled and brought to bay, two days after gets back into Virginia as best he can.

Heavens! how I have to struggle to conceal the triumph in my face from my two pretty sisters, who go about with sad, even teary eyes, from my father, whose countenance is as long as Job's tribulations. It is more difficult to lie with the phiz than with the tongue.

"You—you don't seem downhearted, Billy—even now!" whispers Birdie.

"Oh, Lee'll be back again!" I contrive to utter.

"Yes, the Southern boys'll never give up. They'll never leave us under the heel of our oppressors!" ejaculates Virginia confidently and defiantly. Then womanhood coming up in her, she murmurs—"But how many of them have died here for us already."

But, curiously enough, the excitement of Antietam is soon over. Accustomed by two years of war to its varying chances, Baltimore to my astonishment grows gay in a social sense. I accompany my sisters to receptions and dances, and renew many old acquaintances with the *jeunesse dorée* of my native city, both male and female.

The gentlemen look at me with kindly eyes—I have battled in a gray uniform—and am even now a Federal prisoner.

The young ladies are inclined to make a hero of me; I have ridden with Stuart and Fitz Lee; for my sisters have girl's tongues, and every one hears of their dear brother who marched with the Confederates into Maryland and fought so gallantly under Jackson, though he was taken prisoner by the odious Yankees.

I am quite the rage at receptions and dances; and many a Baltimore civilian and club man has ground his teeth as I have led out his sweetheart for the german, or carried his beloved off for soft conservatory flirtation under his jealous eyes. My martial air is effective, the scar of my sabre wound most subtly potent with the female heart—for I have received it in the cause they love. Had it been acquired under the "Stars and Stripes," the wound for which they adore me would be only a badge of infamy in their bright Southern eyes.

The war has drifted back to Virginia. In the arms of my dear ones, the delights of peace seem near to me.

So, blessed by my father, loved, petted and caressed by my sisters, and flattered by the society of the Monumental City generally, I pass my time in a fool's paradise—almost forgetting that I have eaten the Northern Union apple and must some day be discovered and expelled from my present Southern Eden.

The day of my exodus comes sooner than I expect—and as, in the case of Adam—by means of a serpent.

From my social day-dream I awake with a start.

CHAPTER VII.

A BLOW IN THE DARK.

I have accompanied my sisters to a dance given by Mrs. Coleman. In the carriage going to the *fête* we have all been very merry; Birdie remarking roguishly: "You must be very careful this evening, Cyril, or I shall surely write and tell tales of you to Eva Ashley. Your conduct the other evening with Lulu Davant was outrageous."

"Indeed! What was my offence?" I return, stroking my moustache contemplatively, though I know very well to what she refers, for in the bright smiles of one of Baltimore's fairest—and my native city has many who are fairest—I have been trying to forget the charming maid in gray-riding-habit who still seems to haunt me.

"What was your offence?" remarks Virginia in stately tones. "Only this—paying too great attention to one young lady when you're engaged to another. Now, William, I know the girls here make much of you—too much."

"But then they know you're a gallant Confederate cavalry-man and can't help it," interjects Birdie getting my hand in hers.

"Still, as a man of honor, my brother," continues my elder sister, "you must remember you are bound to another."

"Yes, a young lady I'm to marry as soon as the Yanks have fled to Canada," I mutter savagely, Virgie's criticism not being very much to my liking, as Lulu Davant has as pretty blue eyes, as lovely a figure, and as plumply rounded white shoulders as you'll see in a ball-room, and waltzes like Terpsichore herself.

"You'd not sneer in that way, my brother," answers Virginia, "if you saw the beauty of the girl to whom you're engaged; if you knew her exalted mind, her exquisite womanhood."

"Pooh! That Davant girl is no more to be compared to Eva Ashley than a Union cavalry captain to you, Billy," babbles Birdie airily.

"Well, I'll try and be more circumspect," I mutter, wincing at the shot my dear little sister has unwittingly given me.

A couple of minutes later we are in hospitable Mrs. Coleman's parlors which are thronged with the best society of Baltimore, the ladies' white arms and gleaming shoulders, being set off by exquisite ball gowns, the gentlemen all in the plain black and white of evening attire *de rigueur*, for no blue uniforms ever find their way into the *haut monde* of Maryland at this epoch.

A little orchestra is playing merrily.

As I enter I note we apparently create a sensation; several near-by couples stop dancing and gaze at me; a peculiar and by no means cordial expression on their countenances, especially those of the ladies.

But I hardly appreciate this; I am a favorite with most of the girls, anyway, and my eye is upon Lulu Davant as the pretty little chick sits in a far-away corner—waiting for *me*, I fondly think.

We approach our hostess.

Mrs. Coleman, though she has a surprised look on her face, greets my sisters kindly though in a curiously sympathetic manner; to me she gives a cold haughty courtesy then turns to other guests.

Doing the old *régime* act I think placidly as I look

at the dowager. But having made my duty bow I pass on, too eager for Miss Lulu's smile to pay particular attention to any one else in the room.

A moment later, I am before this young lady who had listened to my honeyed words for a too short hour in Mrs. Gill's conservatory but the day before and seemed to think them very pleasant—to receive a shock.

"Miss Lulu," I say, bending over the fair girl whose eyes turn away from mine, "you remember your promise of yesterday evening."

But the eyes—the blue eyes that had looked into mine so languishingly scarce a day ago—now gaze at me, cold as a Greenland iceberg. Then shuddering slightly Miss Davant turns to a near-by gentleman and murmurs: "Mr. Key, this is *our* dance, I believe. Supposing we begin now; the room is a *little* cold."

"Oh, dash it," I think glumly, "some one's been telling the fair Lulu of my Virginia engagement. Hang it, if she can be rudely indifferent so can I—till I bring her to her senses. Ah, here's Miss Madeline Reeves, she's pretty enough to make any other girl jealous."

With this, I step to the piquant Miss Maddie, a brunette who has been quite partial to me ever since she was a dainty, sixteen-year-old lassie, and suggest the honor of a dance.

But if the blonde Lulu Davant has been icily indifferent, the brunette Maddie Reeves simply appears to *loathe* me. That's the only word that can express the shudder in her exquisite form, the shrinking from me as if I were a viper, as she draws herself up and remarks to a passing beau: "Mr. Jervaise, would you take pity on me and take me away. I don't like *slimy* things."

After one short stare of astonishment, I have a pretty strong suspicion of what is the cause of my tribulation. I hear a maid who within the week has been cordiality itself to me whisper to her escort something about renegade and Yankee spy, as she cuts me dead.

A very little of this sort of thing goes a good way with me; the gentlemen's glances I return, scorn for scorn, glare for glare; but the ladies—the bright eyes that have looked so caressingly on the cavalryman of Stuart's, they stab me to my youthful heart.

Not wishing to spoil my sisters' evening, I edge my way to Virginia. I have little trouble in doing this, though the room is crowded; for the fair *demoiselles* clear the way for me, drawing their crinolined jupes aside for my passage very much as if I were a rattle-snake crawling amid their dainty slippers and pretty ankles.

At my sister's side, I whisper to Virginia, who is in conversation with young Mr. Darrell and apparently has no idea there is anything the matter—"In case I should wander off, could you find somebody to take you and Birdie home?"

Virgie looks at the young and handsome Mr. Darrell and thinks she *could*.

"Then make my excuses to Mrs. Coleman," I suggest.

"You are not well, Billy?" asks my sister anxiously.

"Quite up to anything," I remark. But I want to behave myself very well and Lulu Davant looks very, very pretty this evening."

With this ambiguous excuse, I turn and pass out of the *salle de danse*, followed by vicious glances from those of the ladies who look upon my exit.

I've about made up my mind what the trouble must be. In the dressing-room I get not only evidence of what it is, but also of what has produced it.

Young Darrell, a high-spirited, kind-hearted young gentleman and great friend and admirer of my elder sister, has hastily followed me.

He had returned my bow as I had addressed Virginia. but coldly; he now comes up to me and mutters: "For God's sake, Bill, give me your authority. Let me go down and tell them all that this is a lie from Hell."

He thrusts a Baltimore evening paper into my hand. His finger is on the paragraph. Reading it, I know how I've been struck and who has struck me.

"It's all true as Heaven!" I answer.

"Good God! You came here to play the spy," mutters Darrell, his face turning white as he thinks of the treason he and his friends have spoken to me when they thought me a Confederate officer.

"No spy!" I answer sternly. "I—I concealed my rank in the Union army when I came here, so as to get a few more kind words from my dear old father, a few more sweet kisses from my beloved sisters. But now—" I look at the paper and falter : "These are lost to me forever. Believe me," I add, "no treason spoken to me when I was thought an officer of Stuart's will cost any man or woman anything." I offer him my hand.

But young Darrell mutters : "I pity you, as I do any one who loses friends and kindred, but I pity more your poor father and sisters," and does not see my hand.

Thornton of the Virginia cavalry, Ruff Crockett of the Tennessee infantry, had given me the greeting of man to man, though they wore the gray and I the blue ; but this young dandy who had never raised sword or pulled trigger draws himself away. Oh, the awful vindictive hate of the non-combatants in those war days !

But here is something tangible that I can meet, and fortunately from a *man*.

" Mr. Darrell," I remark, "if you think because I am a Union officer, my hand is not worthy your notice, I can draw it across your face. That'll at least make you *see* it."

But he mutters : "My God ! I—I can't fight you ! I—I am engaged to marry your sister. Virginia has just honored me by accepting my love. When I heard the rumor of this, I felt I must speak to your sister at once so I could be enabled to stand by her thoroughly in this misfortune."

"Very well," I say sarcastically, as he turns away. "Take my sister's hand instead of mine, Mr. Darrell. It's much prettier, softer and more Southern."

But with this jeer on my lips I know Darrell is right as to my losing friends and kindred. As I read the paragraph I am sure it has cost me that.

Curiously enough, the article is very complimentary, the newspaper printing it being a Union one and strongly supporting the Government.

It reads :

" We are happy to announce the appointment of Captain William Fairfax Hamilton of the 1st Kentucky Union Cavalry as Special Provost Marshal of Maryland.

This appointment was made under the instructions of Secretary Stanton himself, to reward Captain Hamilton for distinguished gallantry at Forts Donaldson and Henry and the Battle of Shiloh in Tennessee, when the rebels threw up their hands.

Captain Hamilton was unfortunately captured by Jackson during that Rebel general's recent raid into Maryland and being under parole is consequently not able to engage in active service until exchanged, though eligible for the office of Provost Marshal, in which he can make copperheads and secession sympathizers walk very straight in his native city of Baltimore. For the gallant captain is the son of our well-known capitalist, Carroll Lamar Hamilton of Charles Street, and as such a shining proof to the *jeunesse dorée* of Baltimore that all of them are not out and out Rebels nor secret aiders nor abettors of Jeff. Davis and his Richmond traitors."

Following this is the official order of the day :

"HEADQUARTERS DEPARTMENT OF MARYLAND,
"Baltimore, Oct. 14th, 1862.

"General Orders No. 34.

"Captain W. F. Hamilton, 1st Kentucky Cavalry, in compliance with the orders of the Secretary of War, is hereby appointed Special Provost Marshal of the Department of Maryland and assigned to duty at this headquarters.

"He will be obeyed and respected accordingly.

"By order of

"MAJOR GENERAL JOHN E. WOOL,
"Comd'g Dept. of Maryland.

"Official.

"JAMES R. BELLOW,
"Asst-Adj.-General."

"By·Heaven!" I mutter, as I stride down Mrs. Coleman's steps. That was a blow in the dark, for my unguarded words to Stonewall Jackson at Frederick.

The crafty subtlety of the attack appalls me. I am made the officer whose very duty compels me to arrest Rebel sympathizers among my old friends and numerous relations, all of them apt to get imprisonment for their Southern views. Besides, this will forever cut me off from my father's affection, my sisters' love.

Evidences of this come to me very fast.

As I enter my home my father, who has apparently been waiting up for me, meets me in the hall with an agonized face. In his hand is a copy of the evening paper, also a document that bears the War Department's brand.

I could not believe what I read in this cursed newspaper, sir," mutters the old gentleman, "though this seems to confirm it." He passes me the envelope addressed Capt. W. F. Hamilton, 1st Kentucky Cavalry, on service.

"Is this for you?" he asks falteringly.

For answer, I break the seal of the missive.

It contains the order mentioned in the paper and directs me to report at the Provost Marshal's office, Baltimore, for duty on receipt of it.

"My God, I—I can't believe it," stammers my father. Then he cries out to me, "Bill, my boy, tell me it is not true?"

"It is, sir," I answer quietly for the old gentleman's grief appalls me.

"True that you have been a Union officer, while you smuggled yourself into my heart and your sisters' caresses? Good heavens! it will break their hearts when they know that the wounds you bear upon your brow are the marks of infamy, not honor."

"Not that, sir. No scar of manly combat is dishonorable," I reply.

But he interrupts me, lashing himself in rage, "Not when received in crushing us under the heel of the Yankee? My God, my boy—that I adored—deceiving me—crawling into my home as a Confederate officer—when he's a traitor to the South—a traitor to his country."

"I may be a traitor to the South, but I am not a traitor to my country," I return stoutly. "I have received an education from this country; I have fought for this country; I'll stand by this country—the whole of it, not part of it—till I go under."

"Then out of my house, you damned Yankee scoundrel," cries my father. "Out of my house!"

No appeal of mine will he listen to, though I beg him to consider I have a right to my faith, as he has to his.

It is useless for me to expostulate with him.

My father falters: "Heaven forgive you; you've broken my heart," and the banging of his library door is answer to my last word.

Defiantly I go upstairs, don my blue uniform, and pack my trunk.

Jonas, the negro footman, with a sad look in his eyes, carries it down and mutters: "Good-bye. God bless you, Massa Bill, then whispers, "I hopes you fight de Rebs like hell," and by my direction goes in search of a cab.

As I wait for the vehicle I get another greeting.

A carriage draws hurriedly up.   I hear the patter of light slippers on the front steps, as I am about to open the door.

Virginia and Birdie fly in.   They have heard the news.

"Go back with us, Bill," cries my elder sister defiantly, "and tell them it is all a dastard lie. Tell them—— " Then she sees my Federal uniform, nad pauses petrified, but shuddering.

As for Birdie, dear little Birdie, she begins to cry as if her heart would break and implores me wildly : "Take it off !   Take it off !   Take off the horrid thing, Billy.   Why, one would think you were an Abolitionist."

"I am not an Abolitionist," I mutter sullenly.   "I am only an officer of the Government of the United States, your country."

"Our country is the South—when our brothers and sisters live," cries Virginia who is striding about with the air of Lady Macbeth.   Then she bursts out laughing in a horrid, jeering, unnatural way : "Oho !   The gallant officer of Stuart's, he who rode with Lee and fought the Yanks with Jackson."

"Forgive my deception," I cry desperately.   "I only deceived you so as to keep your love—your kisses."

"Which you have lost forever," returns my stately sister, with white face, and agonized though unforgiving eyes.   "Good-bye !   Until you repent in sackcloth and ashes ; *no !* in Confederate gray—I call you brother no more.   Come, Birdie !"   Virgie turns and walks up the stairs though once I see her falter in her step.

But Birdie, dear heart, is in my arms !   She is sobbing : "Good-bye. God bless you, Billy, though I don't suppose I'll ever see you again.   You can't fight against our Southern troops, they'll simply kill you, that is all."

Then she goes faltering on—for my only answer to the dear little girl is a caress : "What will Eva Ashley say when you fight against her friends and burn her Virginia home ? She'll despise you. You've lost not only your family but your wife ! But I forgive— I pardon you—you don't know what you're doing, you foolish fellow—my *only* brother !"

Then she screams out : "Virgie, come and give him

a kiss !—be a sister to him ! Father, come and give him your blessing before he dies ! "

But the scene is too horrible. With a hasty kiss, I break from her clinging arms and run from the house.

Truly the Secretary knew how to reach the heart of a Border-State Union officer.

CHAPTER VIII.

THE LUNCHEON AT GUY'S.

I SEND my baggage to an out-of-the-way hotel and the next morning report at the provost-marshal's office for duty. Somehow I get through my work for a miserable three weeks, that is made endurable only by the renewal of a West Point intimacy with an old classmate, Captain Arthur Vermilye, commanding one of two light batteries of the 21st Artillery.

This young officer is stationed with his regiment at Fort McHenry, and cut off, like myself, from the society of Baltimore ladies by his blue uniform. Naturally, we become even greater chums than in our days at the Academy. Arthur, however, has one advantage over me. On leave, he can run up to New York where his family occupies a distinguished social position, and being a man of large means, enjoy the delights of home, of girls' sweet voices and feminine bright eyes.

But no social happiness can come to me. The local press have made me prominent, the loyal portion of it eulogizing me as the most uncompromising out-and-out Unionist of the State, the journals of secession proclivities sneering at me as strongly as they dare, and hinting I am both a coward and time-server.

During this time my official business, thank Heaven, is almost entirely routine work, and brings me little in contact with my fellow-townsmen with whom I have been intimate before ; for since Lee's retreat from Maryland, the government authorities have little fear of Baltimore secessionists, those of them who have determined to go to the war having already gone South long ago.

Still I do my utmost to fill my office efficiently, seizing, one night, in a country house just out of Baltimore, three Confederate sympathizers who are about to cross the Potomac to join the Rebel army under Lee. This makes me all the more hated and, fortunately, feared, for it stops covert newspaper abuse.

But as a rule my provost-marshal duties are mostly gathering in drunken soldiers who have overstayed their leave of absence, apprehending a few bounty-jumpers, now becoming numerous under the new call for troops, and stopping the underground mail route to Richmond *via* Leonardstown, by means of which some medicines and supplies, as well as a few volunteers for the Rebel ranks and returning Southern soldiers who have sneaked over into Maryland to visit relatives, find their way to the South.

This places me on rather intimate terms with several of Lafayette C. Baker's Secret Service detectives, and likewise produces a long distance acquaintance, by reports I secure of them, with quite a number of Rebel blockade runners, Potomac pilots and Maryland underground post-office runners, etc., among them the celebrated Wat Bowie and the renowned Alec, the guide *par excellence* for Rebel parties crossing to Virginia.

Of the latter, I arrest none, no evidence being obtainable against them at the time, but from the former I receive some inside information one day that causes me to open my ears very wide.

I, in command of some twenty troopers, have gone down to Leonardstown, accompanied by two of Baker's detectives, by name, Rod Gibbon and Joe Shook. These two gentlemen hunt in couples, Mr. Gibbon, who is a Maryland farmer, and knows the State from one end to the other, being the "bull-dog" of the partnership; Mr. Shook, a Pennsylvania Dutchman, from the vicinity of Hanover, just over the State line, who has enough Hebrew lineage connected with his Teuton blood to make him cunning as a Judas Iscariot, acting as the terrier of the firm.

In their company I brush up Leonardstown to find our suspects as usual not *en evidence*, our local spies telling me that Bowie has crossed the Potomac, and Alec is probably at Port Tobacco.

In the Leonardstown hotel, which is a miserable one, as almost all Maryland rural taverns were in that day, over a badly cooked and worse served dinner, of which I furnish the only endurable portion in the form of a bottle of whisky from my saddle-pouch, Rod Gibbon and Joe Shook, made sociable by the liquor, go to telling me anecdotes of their war detective life, how they have arrested young ladies of the *demi-monde* travelling under passes issued by division commanders, how they have broken up Confederate mail routes, how they had even been caught in the Rebel lines during Lee's recent invasion of Maryland, and were never taken for anything but farmers and locals.

"Ye didn't git off quite so slick, Cap. I seed ye in Frederick just after the Rebs had nailed ye," remarks Mr. Shook with a grin.

"You saw me in Frederick?" I return, my eyes expressing my surprise and interest.

"Yas, I war the country farmer selling vegetables and chickens to Stuart's men, when you rode up with a Johnnie officer, and a gal on a dappled mare. Rod, here, war the countryman driving of my wagon. Gee-hosh! But I'd have guv half a month's wages to have been in yer boots!" adds the Secret Service lynx with another grin.

"You'd have liked to have been in my boots when I was a prisoner?" I ask astonished.

"Yes, siree, if the gal war the one I've since allowed she might be. Would yer mind giving me a description of her? There warn't no light in front of the house, and gol darn it, we darsn't go into the hotel with the Reb cavalrymen. Some cussed secesh local might have recognized us and guv us away. Both of us war wearing cavalry boots under our jean pants, the Rebs come on us so suddenly. We only jist got warning half an hour afore of Stuart's coming, from Kelly, the telegraph operator, before he took to the woods. Luckily, Kelly's brother war a truck farmer, and that guv us a chance to take suspicion off of us by selling the Johnnies his farm stuff."

"There warn't no show to make a run of it," interjects Mr. Gibbon. "We were both so lame we could hardly walk, and our two nags had been ruined by a darn niggah. Besides, we wanted to get a look at the gal. You couldn't give us a description of her, could yer, Cap? You must have seen her in a leetle better light than we?" he asks eagerly.

Somehow, instinct tells me to assent to this.

"Certainly, I can!' I reply. "I saw her the next morning."

And then instinct tells me to give these two government blood-hounds such a description of the girl that I captured on the Potomac, they'd look her straight in the face for a day and never dream they had heard of her.

This I do frankly and fully ; so fully that Rod Gibbon mutters, disconcertedly : "Ye say she's a brunette gal? Curse me, I thought her a blue-eyed blondy."

"Then you've had your idea of her for nothing," I reply, and growing curious in my turn, I query : "Why do you want her description ? "

"Because—I don't suppose it makes much difference in my telling you, Cap. Reckon we're mistook any way," returns Shook. "But Rod and I allowed she war a gal that Stanton had told our boss, Baker, to git at any price. Some highfalutin creature that's got a way of getting inside War Office information somehow, and then gitting it to Reb headquarters slick as grease. We'd kind o' got on her track that very night down by the Potomac. At least, we allowed we had, and were riding after her like streaks of lightning along a country lane, when, gol darn it ! suddenly both Rod and me, we were riding neck and neck, both thought we had struck Kingdom come ! The gal, or her damned niggah, who was called Massie or Quashie, or some such fool name, had stretched a rope knee-high across the lane from one tree to another. Rod and me couldn't do more than limp around for an hour, and our horses were so shook to pieces that we had to leave 'em and hire a wagon to git us to Frederick. Of course, as soon as we could, we sneaked away from Stuart's men to where we could git off our cavalry boots and make ourselves look like real Maryland jays all over. The next day Rod strolled back into Frederick to git a look at the gal in the hotel, but on Market Street we heer'd as how the gal war to be sent down South under guard for insulting of Stonewall Jack. So we reckoned she warn't our bird, but since then, I rather guess that Stonewall Jack war too smart for us Secret Service men, just as he'd been too slick for a good many Union ginerals. So, Cap, I'll give you a tactic. If you should happen to see that ere gal, just p'int her out to Baker, and it may make you a Colonel." With this, Shook winks knowingly at me with his cunning gray eyes.

Now, on my return to Baltimore, this conversation has more effect on me than I will admit to myself. I have had some thoughts of resigning my commission. It may be a year before exchange will place me in the active ranks of the army. I am pretty well aware that advancement will be very slow at best, under the negative enmity of the Secretary.

But from this moment, my views change. I have entered the army to fight for the Union. Mr. Stanton *isn't* the Union. In a day, in a week, under the quick changes of the political volcano in Washington, he may be out of office. He certainly will be if McClellan remains General-in-Chief, and everything points to little Mac's retaining his command. Since his victory at Antietam, the Democratic General is the idol of the army ; ay—even of the people, save certain Western politicians who want a Western General in command.

But underneath my outburst of patriotism, I find a lingering hope of being in some way of aid to a bright face and charming personality, about whom, it seems to me, the meshes of a net dangerous to her liberty— perhaps, even to her life—are being drawn.

Perchance *I was half-way traitor even then !* At all events, I knew that a certain young lady with blue violet eyes and nut-brown hair would receive succor from me—even in the face of the Secretary of War himself.

About the end of October, somewhat to my astonishment, I receive information that I will shortly be relieved from active duty in Baltimore and again ordered to Washington to await my exchange.

I am delighted to go—my native city has become to me the saddest spot on earth—for I am in my home, yet homeless. My brother-officers that I associate with are happy ; the Baltimore girls may scorn them, but there are awaiting sweethearts in the North. When their furloughs come, welcoming arms and sweet lips will greet them by their firesides. As for me, I am desolate beside my own roof-tree.

Fortunately, I have never encountered my father. My two sisters I meet one day in the hurrying crowd on Baltimore Street, and find I have now—only *one*.

Virginia passes me by as coldly and haughtily as if I had never existed as her brother, only I notice she shivers as she draws her dainty skirts away from my contaminating blue, for I happen to be in uniform.

Birdie, God bless her dear heart, gives me one agonized glance, and the tears well up in her soft eyes as I pass hurriedly on.

Half a block away a pleading little hand is laid upon my arm. Birdie has run after me.

"Billy!" she begs. She is almost crying now. "Passing me without a word?"

"Virginia cut me as if I were a dog," I mutter, indignantly. "Why shouldn't you do the same?"

"To my brother?" shudders the girl. "No, no! Ah! pity us! You're breaking father's heart. Please— please! Even if you won't fight for it, don't fight against the cause we love. Think of us a *little*. Virgie hangs her head in shame when she hears whispers about you. When 'spy,' and 'dough-face,' and 'traitor,' and 'coward' come to my ears, I—I can't defend you; I can only slink away and cry."

"Don't trouble yourself to defend me, dear Birdie," I whisper. "As for my flirting young lady friends of yesterday"—my voice becomes bitter—"let them say what they please. In regard to my gentleman defamers, send them to me; I can defend my good name and the uniform I wear. But—" I go on, in sarcastic voice:—"Virgie is waiting for you half a block away. The air about her Union brother is too tainted for her Southern nose."

"But not for me, Billy," sobs Birdie; and putting her arms around me right in the street, my darling little sister kisses me as tenderly as if I wore the gray and not the blue.

"No," she pouts. "I am not going to Virgie. She can stand there as long as she pleases. I haven't seen you for two weeks. Supposing you take me to lunch with you, my—my brother."

That word settles it !

"Who could refuse dear little *sister* anything ?" I answer. "Come along, Birdie, let's forget this cruel war over the *menu* at Guy's."

The 'Guy's' of that day was a fashionable restaurant, but expense was little to me. Fortunately, I had received from my mother's estate a considerable income, and now, though cut off from any assistance from my father, am, with my pay, financially very comfortable. There is only one obstacle to my sister's lunching with me at Guy's : that is, I have invited for the same meal, at the same place, the only officer I am particularly intimate with in the Baltimore garrison, Arthur Severance Vermilye of New York.

As we turn off Monument Square into Guy's, I see the handsome fellow standing waiting for me, and remembering he is of the very best family connections in the Empire City, and in every way my sister's and my social equal, I mutter to myself : "Why not ?"

Two minutes afterward, I lead my classmate to Birdie as she is sitting at table, and to her astonished glance, say : " Permit me to introduce my great friend and class chum, Captain Vermilye, of New York. Arthur, this is my sister, Miss Clara Oriole Hamilton, whom our family has called ' Birdie' since she first chirped. Captain Vermilye had my invitation to lunch."

" And if he had cut me off from the additional pleasure since he added you to the party, Miss Hamilton, I should never have forgiven Ramrod," interjects Vermilye, giving me my Academy nickname in an easy offhand manner, for the Captain of Artillery sees the embarrassment the first introduction he has ever had to a Baltimore belle brings upon her.

"I am always pleased to meet a gentleman who has been kind to my brother," remarks Birdie, forced to a cordial tone, though, in truth, she has since confessed to me she thought of running away. "Billy's letters often mentioned you when he was at that awful West Point that has made him——"

" *What ?*" asks Vermilye, bowing haughtily and

getting red in the face, for though desperately anxious to know Baltimore girls—as what young man wouldn't, seeing their beauty day after day—he had even expostulated with me when I suggested the introduction, remarking : "It will only embarrass your sister to be rude to me. Hang it ! She's pretty nearly cut your acquaintance though you're her brother, I understand. Curse it ! These Baltimore beauties have got into the habit of scorning us."

"Nonsense ! Come along," I whisper. Its a bad habit we must break them of." This last with a laugh, for I am in high spirits. At least, I have regained *one* sister, and Birdie this afternoon looks beautiful enough to make any brother proud ; so beautiful, I have little difficulty in bringing Vermilye over to our table.

A moment after, Birdie, who of course feels she can't slight his uniform unless she slights mine, finds herself seated at table with two officers in the hated blue, and one of them very handsome and very charming, for never have I seen Arthur exert himself to please as he does at this meal. Fortunately, he has not only a face that is effective with young ladies, but a bearing that, though it is punctilio itself, is veiled by that high social art which conceals it. Besides, though perfectly unassuming, and with no suspicion of familiarity in his manner, he has a frank style, and an easy honest *bonhomie* that forbids man or woman to keep him at arm's length if he wishes to get nearer.

In this case, apparently, he wishes to get very near Miss Birdie, whose piquant archness seems to be heightened by the latent embarrassment of being cheerful with her tyrants, and holding out her metaphorically manacled, though exquisitely gloved, patrician hands in fellowship to her military jailers.

Seeing Vermilye, who has been longing for feminine society,—the thing he likes and from which he has been cut off in Baltimore,—putting his best foot forward, I devote myself to my oysters, partridge and champagne, and permitting him to monopolize my sister's small talk, am delighted to see, after a little the two get to chatting, not as enemies, but as friends, perchance even as a young man and young woman who want to make a mutually good impression.

Chancing to hear that for social pleasures Captain

Vermilye runs up to New York when he can get leave, and very shortly discovering that he moves in the best set in the society of the metropolis, Miss Birdie commences to ask that gentleman of the new figures in the german at Mrs. Belmont's recent ball on Fifth Avenue.

A few minutes after they discover they have mutual friends in Manhattan, for my sister had been educated at Miss Hayne's Select Academy in Gramercy Park.

Before I realize it, the two are deep in social chat, repartee, and the polite, yet charming nothings that make young ladies and young gentlemen pleasing unto each other. The meal apparently runs along very smoothly on the pleasant lines of society, which are about the same everywhere, Captain Vermilye telling my sister of a ball he has lately been to in Washington, that of Mrs. Senator Rufus J. Bream. "By-the-by," he adds, turning to me, "a young lady there mentioned your name to me. Incidentally she had learned that I had been in the class of 1861, and I presume from that she judged I was your classmate at West Point."

"Indeed?" I answer. "A girl in Washington takes enough interest in me to talk about Billy Hamilton? What's her name anyway?"

"She is a Virginia young lady, I believe," answers Arthur carelessly; "Miss Eva Ashley."

"Eva Ashley!" cries Birdie excitedly. "Well, I should hope she *would* take an interest in Billy. She is engaged to be married to him."

"Engaged to be married to *you?*" echoes Vermilye, turning his eyes upon me with about the same expression in them as if he had heard I had just won the capital prize in the Havana lottery. "Then I can congratulate you on gaining certainly the most beautiful woman in Washington."

"Why not say Baltimore as well?" adds Birdie enthusiastically.

"I would have until this afternoon," remarks the artillery-man pointedly. "You see, I haven't had much opportunity of inspecting Baltimore *faces;* the *backs* of the young ladies have been generally turned to me when I chanced to encounter them, but now, judging by sample—"

Here I interrupt, for Birdie's face is growing very red under my comrade's impassioned glance.

"Oh! Go a little further," I say nonchalantly. "Make Miss Eva Ashley the prettiest girl in the world."

"She is!" says my sister promptly. "And you are the only man who has not enough interest in her to find out for yourself. I—I don't believe you'd walk into the next room if your affianced were there at this moment."

"This is very extraordinary," mutters Vermilye, looking at me so astonished that I hasten to explain: "You see, Arthur, I haven't seen my putative *fiancée* since we were children. Our families made the arrangement for us in our early youth. As for Miss Ashley, I expect the minute she sets eyes on me she will repudiate it, if she has not done so practically already."

Vermilye's answer startles, even horrifies me. "I don't think she has," he says slowly.

"Why not?"

"Because I heard the young lady tell an officer, who was inclined to be very attentive to her: 'I always think it right to warn gentlemen that I am already affianced.'"

This remark gives me a shock. Miss Ashley's faithfulness may seriously embarrass me. I think glumly of that girl in the gray riding-habit as I gaze on Birdie making play with Captain Vermilye.

What the deuce has got into my Rebel sister? She is flirting as if the Union officer were a cavalier of Stuart's.

As for my comrade, he apparently is doing his level best, for Miss Birdie's eyes are very bright, and her smile saucy and piquant, and her exquisite features most dangerously pretty in their dainty beauty, as the meal runs along to its close, I throwing in a word or two now and then, merely to show that I am *en evidence*.

As we rise from the table, the only embarrassing incident of the afternoon takes place. Bowing his adieu, Vermilye says,—his eyes fixed eagerly on the fair face that looks so piquant under the little hat that tops the clustering curls: "Miss Hamilton, I hope I shall see you again,"

"Indeed you shall!" cries Miss Birdie, eagerly holding out her hand to the handsome captain. "Don't fail to call soon." Then she suddenly grows red as fire; his blue uniform has made her recollect. The next instant, she adds with woman's exquisite tact: "That would be my invitation to you were not my sister and my father so averse to the cause you serve. As for *me*, I have met to-day two Union officers, one my brother, whom I love, and the other"—she looks shyly at him,—"who—who has given me a very pleasant afternoon."

"Believe me, I would not embarrass you for the world, Miss Hamilton," returns the Captain. "Under the circumstances, I shall only call by deputy."

"By *deputy?*"

"Yes, I shall take the liberty of sending a bouquet to represent me in your salon to-morrow. You need not fear," he adds hastily, for Birdie is pale now, though her eyes are very bright. "It will be anonymous. But when you see it, think Arthur Severance Vermilye is bowing before you."

Her face flames up at his words, for the gentleman's tone seems to indicate more than he expresses.

"Indeed I will," answers Birdie heartily and extends her hand, which the Captain takes with old-time deference.

Then we bid him good-bye, I escorting my sister to the neighborhood of her home. Though the girl seems in high spirits, she says but little until near her Charles Street residence.

"Don't come any further, Billy," she remarks nervously. "If papa saw you he might make a scene."

"Very well," I reply. "But where and when am I to see you again?"

"I—I don't know," she answers dubiously, prodding the toe of her little boot with one of the petite parasols ladies sported in those days. "Unless"—here she looks at me suddenly and roguishly—"unless you invite me to lunch again!"

"All right!" I answer cheerily. "Day after to-morrow. Will you come?"

"If they don't lock me up," returns Birdie laughingly, but nervously. Then she *does* grow pale as she whispers : "I suppose Virgie will scold me awfully for going with you."

"Pooh," I say, "I know her stately manner. Miss Virginia Lawrence Hamilton will say ; 'My sister, I do not presume to dictate to you, but I think you should regard papa's wishes in this matter.' But, Birdie, you'll come, even if Virgie does bully you?" I ask eagerly.

"Won't I ; with my whole heart ! "

"Very well, then ; same time, same place ! "

"Yes, Guy's—one o'clock, Monday."

"And same party?" I add, unable to restrain a little brotherly joke.

"What do you mean?"

"Arthur Severance Vermilye, of course."

"Oh! if you like. He's a—a very charming gentleman."

"Union officers are not so awfully awful?" I jeer. "Don't kiss his bouquet."

"What nonsense! Under the circumstances, that would be equivalent to kissing *him*," whispers Birdie, haughtily yet bashfully ; then runs away with a very red face, though her saucy nose is quite high in the air.

CHAPTER IX.

"GIVE ME FIVE MINUTES ALONE WITH HER?"

A few hours afterwards I meet Captain Vermilye at his quarters. Curiously enough he seems rather glum and out of spirits. But the minute he receives my invitation to a second luncheon at which my sister will be present, he brightens up immensely, accepts eagerly, and goes off to billiards with me in the very highest feather.

The consequence is that we three meet again for luncheon in Guy's Restaurant at the time appointed, but here, Miss Birdie gives *me* a start. On the previous occasion, she had been very prettily gowned, but her toilet this time is of such stunning style, *chic* and effectiveness, that I gaze at her astonished, and know the get-up is *not* for me. In addition, she wears in the bosom of her corsage, a few exquisite rosebuds.

"Souvenirs of your last call," she says, archly pointing to them, as Captain Vermilye bends over her extended hand.

So sitting down, the two seem to commence about where they left off on the previous luncheon, and with a cordial familiarity that astounds me, proceed to play the game of Adam and Eve.

"Judging by your tree-and-easy greeting, Captain Vermilye has called several times, Miss Birdie," I mutter roguishly, as I digest my oysters.

"He has, twice—by bouquet! Though that is not the most satisfactory way for a young lady to receive a gentleman's visits," she remarks coquettishly, blushing very prettily as she speaks.

"Nor the pleasantest way for a gentleman to pay them," returns Vermilye, ardently.

Then I break in : "No unpleasant social family effects from our last meeting, Birdie ? You suggested being locked up in your room," I laugh.

"Not the slightest. Virgie has never spoken to me about it. Better still, has never spoken to papa. Though doubtless angry with me, she has too noble a nature to think that her prejudice should separate me from my brother."

This gives me a pang. What will Virgie think of me if, in addition to my own offences, I add the unpardonable one of putting Birdie in the zone of Union influence, emphasized by a pair of very handsome masculine eyes, a very effective masculine moustache, and a very lover-like manner, for that is what I begin to see in Vermilye's tender tones and expressive glances.

Apparently, this idea strikes Miss Birdie at the same moment, for she grows very red, then turns very pale, and from now on doesn't seem to give much attention to her lunch ; though, perhaps, this is because she pays so much to the dashing artillery captain, whose manner is now so unmistakably gallant that it gives me a start.

But the *fête* draws to a close.

Though Birdie hasn't eaten much, nor drank much for that matter, her face seems strangely flushed and

her eyes unnaturally brilliant as she says she has had
a delightful afternoon.   This is evidently intended
more for Arthur than for me, at least she looks at him
as she makes the remark.

So Birdie and I walk home again, and this time,
instead of being silent, the young lady has a good
many roundabout questions to ask me, the drift of all
of them deftly turned toward my comrade.

Though I answer her questions, in an off-hand, big-
brother manner, still I think my eulogy of the gallant
captain is satisfactory to my pretty sister; for, as
she bids me good-bye, on Charles Street, she says:
"Thank you, thank you *so much.*"

Then she adds, a curious eagerness in her voice:
"When do we lunch again?"

"Ah, you liked the oysters; Guy's *menu* was excellent?   I say banteringly.

"Of course I did.   When do we lunch *again?*"

"Do you wish me to include the captain?"

"Cetainly!"   This is emphasized with a blush, she
adding severely: "It would hardly be polite to exclude
him *now.*"

"Very well," I say, "I'll tell Captain Vermilye of
your hospitality.   Same time, same place, four days
from now."

"That's Friday, but don't mention my suggesting his
attendance.   It's very bold my lunching with two
gentlemen even though one is my brother," murmurs
Birdie bashfully.

So I go off laughingly to tell Vermilye about the
arrangement for him.

To my astonishment the artilleryman has grown
more gloomy than ever.   More curiously, when I again
suggest the proposed entertainment to my brother-
officer, he appears about to decline my invitation.

"Why? What's the matter?" I ask, astonished.
"You've nothing to do, and surely have no other
social engagements with ladies in Baltimore!"

"No; that's the reason I hesitate to accept your
very kind invitation," remarks the captain, chewing
his moustache and puffing his cigar in an uneasy and
nervous manner very unusual in him.

"Indeed!" I say haughtily, and turn away rather
inclined to be angry.

But he stops me. Laying his hand on my arm he says impulsively and impressively : "For God's sake, don't misunderstand me, Bill, and answer me this question : Do you believe in love at first sight?"

"Of course I do! What man of twenty-three doesn't?"

"*Lasting* love?"

"Yes ; the *strongest* kind. I am a victim of it my-self."

"Oho!" he laughs lightly, then goes on anxiously : "Then you will appreciate *my* position. To meet your sister at any time would be one of the greatest pleasures of my life, so great a joy that I hesitate to take it. To be very candid with you, Miss Birdie Hamilton"—he lingers quite tenderly over the "Birdie"—"has made a greater and much more positive impres-sion upon me than any young lady I have ever met. Set apart from her by the passions of this damned war, and unable on account of sectional hate and prejudice to visit her father's house, would it be honorable in me to continue meeting this young lady? Now, as her brother, if you repeat your invitation to me"—his eyes are very eager—"Hang me if I don't accept it, and you may know what to expect!"

"Come!" I say cheerily. "If Miss Birdie is the same girl she was yesterday, the minute she doesn't want to see you she'll let you know."

"Done!" cries Arthur, and his jaws shut together with a click like the sound of one of his own battery trace snaps. Then our hands clasp; mine, I think, tending to give encouragement, for Vermilye goes off and plays billiards with me and seems in great spirits the whole evening.

Naturally, I get meditating on this matter. Once or twice I find myself thinking : "Hang it! If Arthur should hold a winning card with my pretty sister, that would be a beautiful revenge upon the governor for turning his back upon me. *Two* blue uniforms in the family!" Then I mutter : "Why not? Vermilye is an honorable gentleman, a man of fine family, first-rate position, and large fortune. A much better match for Miss Birdie in every way than some of these Balti-more young gentlemen of long pedigree and impetuous chivalry, but slender means, and no particular manner of improving them. Why should I discredit my own uniform? Miss Birdie must take her chances in this matter." Here I chuckle to myself, "And hang me, if the dear little girl seems to be very much averse to taking them on her own account!"

Still, on consideration I conclude it is hardly fair for my sister to enter upon a defensive campaign without warning. Therefore, by means of one of our old footmen, Jonas, I smuggle a note to her, and, Miss Birdie meeting me the next day in Monument Square, we go off on a stroll together.

During this I tell her, by means of masculine hints and brotherly jeers, as indirectly as I can, the impression I think she has made upon my comrade.

Then, Miss Clara Oriole Hamilton astounds *me*. Though she is sometimes a mass of blushes, and at others her cheeks grow pale, her questions are very straight and to the point.

"Do you think, Billy," she asks with white lips and anxious eyes, "that aside from all sectional prejudice, Captain Vermilye would not only be a suitable match for your sister, but a man in whose hand you would be happy to place mine and call yourself his brother?"

"I do!" I reply earnestly and frankly. There is something in the girl's face—something in the girl's voice that tells me it is my duty to answer her with a brother's frankness.

"Thank you," she says, looking at me gratefully; then astounds me, for she murmurs: "You have made me very happy, but"—here she grows very bashful— "I will think about coming to the lunch. If I do come, you may know that a blue uniform makes no difference to me." Then suddenly she mutters, "Papa and Virgie!" and bursts out crying as if her heart would break.

To her I falter: "I should not have let you meet him."

"Don't say that," she whispers impulsively. "God bless you for doing so!" then runs away from me.

Of this interview, I say nothing to Arthur. Consequently he sits down to lunch with me the next time at Guy's, not guessing that I have given a hint of his passion to my sister. As the hands of the clock move round he glances eagerly and anxiously at the door of the restaurant each time it opens, and grows more and more gloomy, for no Birdie comes to brighten our conclave with her smiles.

I grow gloomy also; though thinking of the mangled state of my own affections I mutter grimly : "The course of true love never did run smooth."

Suddenly, I see a change in Vermilye's face. It has become radiant as the sun which is streaming through the windows.

I need not ask the reason. Light footsteps are bringing my sweet sister towards us, though there is a peculiar set expression in her face as she murmurs : "You will excuse my being late, Billy. I have had a little trouble at home."

"Was it with the governor?" I question uneasily.

"No, with Virgie. She has discovered that I—I take lunch with *two* blue uniforms." And the girl's face grows red as fire.

As I look upon Vermilye I know that he has determined that no more embarrassment of this kind shall come to my pretty sister. Drawing me a step aside he whispers to me : "For God's sake, give me just five minutes alone with Miss Birdie! You owe it to me now !"

"All right ! But first give me a few minutes interview with these oysters, partridge and champagne, "I whisper in his ear.

I had always known Vermilye to be a man of exceeding grit ; but his resolution of formally asking the hand of a Baltimore belle of ultra-secession proclivities and family, at third time of meeting, and he a Union officer, excites my admiration for his social nerve.

I glance at Miss Birdie, and notice that my sister's pretty features have an air of agitated bashfulness that is foreign to them, likewise a suspicion of humility that is most unusual in her. She looks to me like the bird in the snare of the fowler.

"Egad," I think grimly, "some citadels are taken by sudden assault more surely than by slow sap and approach."

Accordingly the meal runs along, I doing the high spirits for the party ; for though Arthur's conversation is easy and unaffected, still there is a tinge of anxiety in his voice, and his tones are mostly low and deep—very much like those I have noticed in men just before they head a desperate charge, where defeat means probably annihilation. At proper opportunity, I stroll out after a light for my cigar, and contrive to occupy myself with the weed for a few minutes, then return—to be astounded !

Birdie is sitting alone, with the palest face and brightest eyes.

Has Miss Rebel given Captain Yankee his *congé* in short order? "So you sent poor Captain Vermilye away," I suggest, chewing my moustache glumly.

"No. He went of his own accord, to—to buy the engagement ring, I believe," falters Birdie, her face a mass of color now. Then she says quite haughtily : "You knew what my answer must be, the moment I came under these circumstances to lunch with Arthur. You needn't look surprised at my using his first name ; I've been thinking of him as Arthur for the last day or two."

"God bless you !" I say huskily, and hold out my hand. "I know you have selected a gentleman who will make you happy, if you love him."

"*If* I love him !" says the girl. "Am I not proving that now?" Then she falters : "Good heavens ! Papa and Virgie—how shall I tell *them?*"

Gazing at her, I determine that though Vermilye's social nerve is very good, my pretty little sister, with her soft voice and butterfly manner, has even perchance a higher social courage than his, in accepting the hand of a man who wears the uniform her father and her sister hate ; holding herself up to the rage, scorn and hate of every one who has been a companion of her childhood.

"There's only one thing that I'd like changed in the affair," Birdie whispers pathetically to me.

"His blue uniform ?" I suggest.

"Pooh ! I don't think of Arthur in any clothes at all !" says Birdie defiantly. "No, no, of course, I don't mean that. I—Billy, you—you sha'n't laugh at me !" She is red as fire now and very savage. "I—I wish Arthur were not so extremely rich. They'll say that I was false to my Southern birth, not for love but for money."

"Pshaw !" I return in cynic tones. "Don't let that trouble you. You'll find a very much better chance of winning love's battle with plenty of money behind you than without it."

"Nonsense!" answers the girl sharply. "You're trying to make me think you are not romantic ; when, Billy, I know you're the most inflammable piece of masculine material on earth."

"Even more than the clothesless Arthur?" I say, regarding her with the eye of a brother, privileged to joke on such occasions. At which she blushes hotly, and, despite herself, commences to laugh in an hysterical, nervous way.

Fortunately, this is broken in upon by the return of the ardent one. "I've got the prettiest ring," he whispers to her eagerly, "that I could find on Baltimore Street. But we'll not put it on *here.*" He looks at me suggestively as we shake hands and I congratulate him, then remarks in the coolest manner : " I say, Bill, supposing I escort Birdie home this afternoon."

"Certainly," I reply, for Birdie has given me an imploring glance ; though I feel perchance a little pang of jealousy at the thought that when the lover comes, the brother steps quickly to the rear.

Two or three minutes after I hear them say something about Druid Hill Park, and conclude that Miss Birdie's jaunt will be a much longer one on her way home than it had been with me.

"Any way," I cogitate, as I look at the two departing together : "they'll make a very handsome couple. Arthur is the best fellow in the world, and Birdie the best girl I know—*except one !*"

BOOK III.

A BEAUTIFUL ENIGMA.

CHAPTER X.

An hour afterwards, at my quarters, a despatch from Washington, ordering me to report forthwith at that city, turns my thoughts for the moment to my own position.

While I am pondering over this, Vermilye joins me, looking a little happier, if possible, than when he left me.

"Put on the engagement-ring?" I say laughingly.

"Didn't I! Bill, I'm the happiest man on earth!"

"No fear of facing papa, eh?"

"Not a bit! I have settled the whole matter with Birdie; no embarrassment must come to her from which I can relieve her. She shall wear my engagement-ring openly in the light of day."

"To-morrow I call upon your father—I introduce myself in the full uniform of a Captain in the United States artillery—I prove to him that aside from differences of political opinion, I am perfectly fitted to be his son-in-law; that I have ample fortune to support your sister in every ease, elegance and distinction in life; that as my wife, she'll move in the very best set of metropolitan society."

"With your uniform on, you may count on my governor showing you the door—he did me without mine, in very quick order."

"Then I shall bow myself out," returns the Captain, "but not until I distinctly inform him that I consider the shoulder-straps I sport no bar to my wedding anybody! I shall also suggest to him that though I may not enter his house again, there will always be a seat at my fireside for papa, when he changes his mind,—after I

marry his daughter!   For that I am going to do,—war
or no war—South or no South—North or no North!"

"But supposing Miss Birdie is restrained?"

"That she shall not be!" answers Vermilye, his eyes
cold but glinting.   "Trust me to hold what my sweetheart's sweet lips have given unto me.   And trust your
sister also for keeping her troth."

"Well, I rather imagine you and the guv'nor will
have a decidedly exciting, though perhaps not an entirely pleasant interview," I remark grimly.   Then I
ask: "And Birdie—what does she say about it?"

"Oh, Birdie, I hope, is happy, though I'm sure she's
palpitating," laughs the captain.

"Well, I'm sorry I shall not be here to see it, and
aid you," and I show Arthur my order to Washington.

Then, convinced of the necessity of an adviser as
regards my own affairs, and having very much of a
brother's feeling for Vermilye, I take him into my confidence, explaining the whole of my troubles with the
Secretary of War and most of my adventures in Frederick—omitting only that of my young lady captive
with a gray riding-habit; I having an extreme diffidence about confessing I have fallen in love at almost
first sight with a girl whom I am convinced is at least
the betrothed, if not the bride, of some Confederate
officer.

To my astonishment, Captain Vermilye, who has a
mathematical mind, entirely disagrees with me.   He
says: "You'll get no promotion.   Your chances in the
army are naught.   You'd better resign at once, Bill."

"McClellan has the love and confidence of his army.
Stanton will not remain Secretary of War," I reply.

"I beg your pardon, for that very reason McClellan
will not remain in command."   Here Vermilye's voice
grows low and cautious.   "There is no wish in Washington to build up a Democratic fetish for the people to
vote for at the next presidential election.   For that
reason McClellan—all the more so because he has
lately been victorious—will be deposed from command.
Do you suppose Mr. Secretary Stanton will let a general remain who has branded him with the sentence:
"You have done your best to sacrifice this army!" *

* See *The Army in the Civil War*, Vol. V., *Antietam and Freder-
icksburgh*, by General Francis Winthrop Palfry.—ED.

"But McClellan has the army behind him."

"That would count for everything were Little Mac a man like Bonaparte. McClellan now is in the position to play the Cæsar. Quite curiously, the Abolition Republicans—and a lot of the Jacobin press—have made it possible for him to play that role, and play it as a patriot.* Let him walk into Washington and say: 'Thou art weighed in the balance and found wanting, I proclaim a provisional government,'—he has the power to do so, for the moment any way; what the country at large would do afterwards I don't propose to speculate upon. But I have heard such whispers from the officers of the Army of the Potomac that I know that McClellan has only to hint—nay more, not to restrain them—and they will follow him to Washington the moment he has been deposed from command, to ask, with the loud and potent voice of a hundred thousand veterans : 'What is the matter with our victorious general?'† He could pose as a patriot, and if he wins the war, be considered the saviour of his country, not only against the politicians in the capital, but against the Southern Confederacy. But if I know anything of the man," adds Vermilye, "Little Mac is too good a soldier, too great a patriot, and too conservative a gentleman to take by the force of bayonets what the gods have given to a Cæsar. Therefore he will be deposed ; therefore he will resign his command ; therefore he'll be crushed ! Were Stanton, McClellan, and McClellan, Stanton, I might predict a different ending. Consequently, I say to you, if you have been so unfortunate as to have incurred the displeasure of the Secretary of War, the sooner for your own success in life you take off your shoulder-straps and go to work at something else than soldiering the better for you.

* See New York Republican journals of that time (1862) ; note the hints in Harper's Weekly, about a provisional government being necessary ; read the editorials of Horace Greeley. Unless these were the ravings of lunatics, they meant that the government in Washington was so inefficient, so absolutely incapable of fighting a victorious war, that it should be deposed by somebody.—ED.

† It has been creditably reported that immediately on McClellan's removal from command after Antietam there was a meeting of the officers of the Army of the Potomac, called to do this very thing, and had it not been for McClellan's own personal entreaties and influence, it would have been done.—ED.

Of course this is confidential," whispers the artillery-man.

"As one brother to another," I say, and make him happy with the speech, though I add glumly : "I do not think I shall take your advice ; at all events, not till I have gone to Washington and seen what is before me."

"Very well, every one makes his own bed," returns my chum philosophically, "and I've got to see about making mine now."

So Vermilye goes with me to the Baltimore depot and bids me *bon voyage*.

Two hours after I am in Washington, and taking up my quarters in my F Street boarding-house, discover that my provost-marshal fame has preceded me, and I am regarded not only as an intense Union man, but as a tremendous cut-the-throat hater of all Southerners.

Mrs. Lorimer, my landlady, as she greets me at the front door, whispers : "We read in the papers about you, my noble boy, in that hot-bed of secession. I was afraid from what the *Baltimore Comet* said, you might be assassinated on the streets of that town for your intense loyalty."

Mrs. Lorimer poses as the widow of a dead diplo-matist and declares she has been ruined by the aboli-tion of slavery in the District of Columbia ; though as she has been engaged in the boarding-house business for twenty years, this measure of the government can hardly have affected her social status. At all events, it hasn't affected her patriotism, as noting on which side her bread is buttered, her best front parlor being rented to Miss Lucy Albemarle, the beauty of the Treas-ury office and putative niece of the sturdy Union Con-gressman Cobblestone, whose influence has obtaned for Miss Albemarle that appointment, and her other guests being mostly of northern proclivities and senti-ments, Mrs. Imogene Lorimer is now shouting for the Star Spangled Banner as loudly as any boarding-house-keeper in Washington.

Further evidences of my fame as an intense Unionist come to me at the supper table that evening. Two New England girls, clerks in the Interior department, congratulate me upon my war-record, and a fascinating widow, whose chief occupation is lobbying contractor's bills through congress by her smiles upon its members, glances at me and suggests, rather flirtatiously: "I suppose, now that the Baltimore girls have turned their backs on you, you will *thoroughly* enjoy feminine Washington society." This is emphasized by a look of her lustrous and drooping eyes that have been very effective upon legislators during the last session.

But little Napoleon Finnaker, of the Quartermaster-General's office, perchance thinking to add to his own military splendor and glory by my patriotism, rises from his place at the dining-table, and walking over, taps me on the shoulder, and says loudly and patronizingly: "We've been talking about you in the War Department, Captain Hamilton."

"Indeed!" I say surprised.

"Yes! You've been doing great things in that secession haunt, and doing them nobly. Provost-Marshal in Baltimore!" His voice is a roar. "By the stars and stripes, how your secession relatives must have ground their Rebel teeth when you captured those three Confederate sympathizers! How all your Baltimore friends must love you! Oh, Yankee Doodle! I think I see papa's glance, and also hear Miss Virgie's and Miss Birdie's kind words to their Union brother. The papers here state that you were requested to leave Mrs. Coleman's dance the night your appointment was published. I hope you insulted a few of those damned blue-blood copperheads. I would, you bet! You see, there's a kindred feeling between us two, both out-and-out fighters and both cut off from active service. You, by your parole; I, by the tears of a widowed mother. By John Brown's body! I never get down to the Long Bridge but I have a terrible struggle to hold myself from going over into Virginia and having another crack at the Rebs."

"Yes, you haven't had that pleasure lately," I remark sarcastically, Mr. Finnaker's suggestions about Baltimore friends and relatives making me inclined to be surly with him.

"Yes! Not since Pope's Second Battle of Bull Run. Then, I rode to the front and as usual had a horse shot under me. Didn't I. Mrs. Lorimer?"

This last is in savage interrogation to the landlady who is indulging in a quiet feeble snicker, having surreptitiously served Mr. Finnaker's breakfast to him in bed on the morning of the Second Bull Run, that hero having spent that day quivering between bed-clothes.

But no matter what the opinions of Mrs. Lorimer and her guests are in regard to Mr. Finnaker's war-record, there apparently is none in regard to mine, when I report at Secretary Stanton's office on Saturday morning, for I am very warmly received by the officers in waiting and congratulated on my Baltimore record.

After dawdling away my time among reporting staff officers, eager army contractors and people with grievances of all kinds, from the mother of a deserter who has been sentenced by court-martial to be shot, to a congressman who is kicking about a transportation contract, for my affair now seems to be routine business, old Madison shows me in once more to the office from which I had departed pursued by official anathema.

In reply to my salute, Mr. Secretary Stanton, who had reviled me on my departure, receives me quite affably upon my return to Washington.

"Having proved you, I know I can trust you now, Captain Hamilton," he says, regarding me quite benignly through his glasses and stroking his long beard contemplatively.

"Proved me?" I stammer. "I do not understand. Why trust me more now, Mr. Secretary, than you did before?"

"Because I have put you through the furnace, and you have come out molten gold. When I signed the order making you Special Provost-Marshal of Maryland, where your father and your family and the friends of your youth—all rabid secessionists—were living and plotting, I said: "If he stands this, there's no further doubt of the unhesitating loyalty of Captain William Hamilton.""

"And you," I mutter, "have cut me off from my family—my friends? They hate me worse than if I were a Northern soldier."

There is a desperation in my voice that seems to please him.

"And made you all the better Union man for it," he laughs. "If you could resist their entreaties to lean to the Rebel cause, and have stood up under their contempt and contumely for not doing so, I can trust you in the middle of Lee's Rebel army. They hate you—you hate them : that is the proper kind of war feeling : the better hater, the better warrior. Apropos of that, until you're exchanged, I want a man who can resist bright eyes, for a certain purpose. You will remain in Washington, under full pay."

"And my duties ?"

"They will be explained to you when the time comes. Do them well, and I forget your indiscreet answers to Stonewall Jackson's questions before he captured Harper's Ferry."

Wondering what the deuce he wants of me, I half laugh : "Thank you for a very pleasant way of spending the days of my parole," and turn to leave him.

But he calls me back to him and remarks : "You must look to me for promotion. He who stands by me, I stand by him."

"Thank you once more, Mr. Secretary," I reply, saluting ; and leave him gazing affably after me.

As why should not he ? For in his pocket he has a document that brought a shriek of discontent, a muttering of rage, from a hundred thousand veterans encamped in Virginia—the order for his enemy's, but their beloved general's official head.

Getting out from this interview, I stand for a moment on the lawn in front of the old three-story brick building, with its white facings and semicircular window heads, which at that time was known as "The War Department," the white columns in front of it contrasting strongly with the prevailing gray of its time-worn brick, and wonder what the devil Mr. Stanton wants me to do that will require me to resist bright eyes.

Suddenly a shudder goes through me. Can it be anything connected with the subject about which he spoke to me before—my captive of that night on the Potomac?

Then I speculate ; "Shall I meet her ?" and look round at this great city of the war—this capital surrounded by an armed encampment—this place where the delights of peace, the *fêtes* of fashion, the beauty of ladies, mingle with the rumbling of artillery wagons, the tramp of marching regiments, and the rattle of ambulances as they glide to the military hospitals?

Standing where I am, the city makes a beautiful but

varied panorama, Immediately to my right, set back
in its grounds, is the White House, seeming very bright
this sunny day—where Abraham Lincoln, with all the
cares of a nation in its death-grapple upon his shoulders, still maintains that calm serenity, that pleasant
bonhomie, that enable him to give tears and sympathy to the suffering soldier, jovial Western anecdotes
and backwoods' parables to besieging politicians, and
ofttimes sound military advice, told with homely common sense, to his erring generals. Beyond that, looms
the Treasury Department.

Directly in front of me across Pennsylvania Avenue
stands the building that is now known as Corcoran's
Art Gallery, but at this time is occupied by the Quartermaster-General of the United States Army. To the
right of this is Lafayette Square, with its colossal Jackson statue amid pretty plants and parterres.

Just across Seventeenth Street, on the corner immediately to the west of the War Department, is that well-
known old brick bar-room that we used to call Mulloy's,
I think, a resort celebrated in those days as being the
drinking-place of generals—chiefly political brigadiers.

Adjoining this, further to the West, in the direction
of Georgetown, are a number of small cigar-stores, low
groggeries and places of disreputable savor gradually
growing more disreputable as they approach the low
flats towards the Potomac, until they reach their apogee
of disrepute, crime, drunkenness and lewdness in the
district immediately surrounding the great Quartermaster's stores on Twenty-second and G Streets, whose
immense warerooms run pretty close to the Potomac,
where they join the extensive yards upon the river-
bank filled with the lumber and marine supplies of the
Quartermaster's Department. Back of these is the
Potomac, and beyond its muddy stream the Virginia
hills, crowned with their outlying forts and decorated
with the white encampments of protecting Union troops.

On my right hand, in great contrast to the squalor
of the low grounds towards the West, runs the same
great avenue, but it leads to fashion, wealth, and the
struggling concourse of the better half of the inhabitants of this war-time capital—the great centre of the
hive—from the White House to the Halls of Congress.

Carriages roll about ; in them beautiful women,

fashionably gowned, and sometimes more sober equipages carrying cabinet-officers or foreign ministers. Generals and staff officers prance about on horseback, though most of these are political warriors, who have never yet smelt powder, and never will if they can help it.

Along the sidewalks throng the crowds of a great military capital. Officers and soldiers, of the local garrison or called here by military business, contrast greatly with the hurrying civilians, though their uniforms of dark blue mostly show the signs of hard service and actual war. Government contractors, who are nearly all very bloodthirsty, crying for Southern gore with their mouths, and fleecing with both hands the public purse, each of them doing the damage of a Rebel regiment, jostle with applicants for office of all kinds and the general political bummers and hangers-on of a great nation which is giving with lavish hand for its protection and its existence—the scavengers of the treasury. Secession-sympathizers, slyly glorying at each victory of Lee or defeat of the Federals, are mixed with the Union masses, the great, strong arms which upheld this country in her travail, and Jacobin politicians, calling every man " copper-head," but themselves.

These are now leavened with numerous department clerks, both male and female, for the beauties of the Treasury Department, sometimes yclept its " courtesans," many of them being protégés and *chères amies* of Congressmen and Senators, or those high in political power, have come out this lovely afternoon to give life, beauty, vivacity and wickedness to Pennsylvania Avenue.

And each and every one upon those crowded streets, is dominated by the awful war-time passions of civil contest.

Among the gentlemen-attachés of the various offices, I note little Napoleon Finnaker strolling from the Quartermaster-General's counting-rooms opposite.

As I walk down the avenue he joins me, linking his arm in mine with his usual assurance. There is an air of mystery about the dapper creature as he remarks, with a furtive gesture toward the War Department : " We did a great thing in there to-day."

"And what was that ? " I ask laughingly.

His answer stuns me.

" We deposed McClellan from command of the Army of the Potomac and put in Burnside."

" Impossible ! " I gasp.

" Fact, just the same. Nobody knows it but a few of us, who are the inside clique. Keep it dark ! "

" De—deposed from his command ! " I stammer, as the thought flies through me that I am fortunate in having regained Stanton's favor.

" Yes, deposed—for absolute military incapacity. Let Lee escape from him after Antietam. By the Star-Spangled Banner, if I had been in his line of battle, I'd have shown Little Mac a wrinkle or two ! Why didn't he press Lee ?—*press him !* That's the tactic—PRESS HIM ! Between ourselves, we suspect him of dis-loyalty."

At this news I give a sigh—as over one hundred thousand other veterans do this day ;—perchance guessing at the military incapacity that is going to doom fourteen thousand of them to useless death and wounds in that great Fredericksburg slaughter-house blunder.

Whereupon little Finnaker looks at me sternly. He says : " A word of advice to you, my cavalry buck. If you want to get in out of the wet, drop all McClellan sentiment. No Democrat is going to get very far in this army, without a pull-down. Listen to me—I'm on the inside ! "

And so he seems to be ; for in the course of the next week or two I discover that Napoleon Finnaker seems to be on the inside of everything. War Department secrets in some way drift in to him ; social news is at his finger-ends. For he is quite a dandy at all local balls and parties, dancing in a volunteer uniform that throws a brigadier-general's into the shade. For this very purpose he has formed and recruited, all by him-self, *on paper* in distant Illinois, a military company—of which he is the sole member—and having elected himself captain of the same, Napoleon has naturally selected his own uniform, which is gorgeous beyond compare. With this he flourishes at social functions, doing the heavy military swell in a very languid, finnicky, yet at times ferocious manner, especially after battles fought near the capital.

His babble makes the stroll down the avenue a short one, for he knows every one, and our walk is a running comment from him on passers-by.

"Look there! Do you see that gal? She's Treasury—Division C, Room Number 21. Ah, how do you do, Miss Albemarle?" and he takes off his hat and bows to the department beauty. "Our star boarder," he babbles. "You see, I had something to do with her appointment," he whispers. "Lucy Albemarle's particular friend, Congressman Cobblestone, implored me to use my influence. If you want to get on Cobblestone's right side, show her attention, but for the Lord's sake don't make him jealous; the aged Congressman's like a sultan when the boys get round his putative niece!" and the little fellow goes into a hideous guffaw. Suddenly he cries: "Oh, by George! there's Mrs. Senator Rufus J. Bream! Her equipage—that one dashing up the avenue—two white horses. I selected them for her: I am said to be the best judge of horseflesh in Washington. Rufus is a great chum of mine; has supported me for promotion twice with the Quartermaster-General. I back him up when he makes his great war speeches. He's the man we war officials like; he has demanded that the quota of troops from every State, except his *own*, be increased. You should listen to his eloquence! after I hear him I feel like cutting Southern throats, cursed if I don't."

Under this gentleman's tutelage, I stroll down the avenue, being introduced by him right and left, and chancing to meet a crony of his, one Henri Dubois Arago, a handsome young Creole, we step into Willard's for a game of billiards.

"Mr. Arago, besides holding an important clerkship in our office," Napoleon whispers to me between shots, "represents a syndicate that has a permit from *us*, to buy seized and confiscated rebel cotton in Louisiana. Arago's as black a Republican as Horace Greeley," he adds vivaciously, "and as liberal as a gold-broker with his cash."

This intense Republicanism in a man from Louisiana seems to me a little curious, though this is easily apparent, as Arago dispenses lavish patriotism with a

loud yet melodiously sensuous voice to his surrounding friends and liberal tips to the billiard attachés during our hour's exercise with cue and balls.

Getting away from this, however, I at last find myself at my. F Street boarding-house, to be surprised by
a card requesting the pleasure of my company at a
soirée dansante at Mrs. Rufus J. Bream's, on Wednesday,
the twelfth of November.

That evening, on his invitation, in company with
Mr. Finnaker, who acts as guide, and Mr. Arago, who
joins us, I kill time in the Capitol, seeing a play at
Ford's Theatre and afterwards dropping a treasury note
in Chamberlin's great gambling-house, where at last
McClellan's deposition has got noised about late at
night. Here Napoleon swells around, among congressmen and army contractors, remarking : "We of the
War Department did it," and introducing me as a
staunch Maryland Unionist who as provost-marshal
at Baltimore had made the gilded secesh youth of that
place toe the loyal line and sing the "Star-Spangled
Banner" and "Yankee Doodle" instead of "Dixie."

To my astonishment, I discover that nearly every
one I meet seems to think me not only a Union man,
but a personal hater of every Southerner from Jeff Davis
down to his lowest rebel private.

I am too down-hearted over my loss of boyhood's
friends and my father's and my sisters' love to take
the trouble to deny this, and go about in a gloomy and
morose manner which seems to add to the impression
that I am a stern and most determined loyalist.

Leaving Arago, who seems an inveterate and eager
gambler, still engaged over the board of green cloth,
where his eyes sparkle with love of gain and his black
frizzly hair and jet moustache seem to bristle with excitement, little Nap Finnaker and I, about two on Sunday
morning, stroll out of the brilliantly lighted rooms on
our way to our boarding-house.

On our walk home, probably some recollection of
Mrs. Bream's invitation turns my mind to my shadowy
fiancée. How will Miss Eva Vernon Ashley regard my
vindictive Unionism ? Perhaps this may give the girl
an opportunity she may have been longing for, an excuse to break off the slight bond that connects us, and
leave me free—free to follow the girl in the gray riding-

habit.   Pshaw ! what good will that do me ? Is not
the girl in the gray riding-habit the sweetheart of a
Confederate trooper ?   As we stride along, I ask a few
questions of Mr. Finnaker.

"You're as much *au fait* with society as you are with
the War Department ? "

"Well, rather, my boy ! "

"You're an intimate friend of Mrs. Senator Rufus J.
Bream ? "

"You bet !   Why do you ask ? "

"I have an invitation from that lady for a dance at
her house next Wednesday."

"Yes.   My mention of your name probably got it
for you, my boy.   I was telling her last night of your
provost-marshal adventure," is the confident answer.

"You remember a ball Mrs. Bream gave some two
or three weeks since ? "

"Well, I should ejaculate ! "   His deep voice is
strident will pride.   "What I don't know about that
ball isn't worth knowing ! "

"Do you recollect meeting there a young lady, Miss
Eva Ashley ? "

"Eva Ashley, the belle of the army ? Tra la la la !
I danced with her two or three times ! " and little Finnaker skips about humming the latest waltz ; then goes
on :   "I tell you what, my cavalry buck ! she'd suit
you ! Miss Eva is as pretty as a new Government
ten-thousand-dollar bond, and as good a Unionist as
the Goddess of Liberty on it ! "

"As good a—a Unionist ? " I stammer.

"Well, rather ! She's Mrs. Rufus J. Bream's *niece !*
When she first came to Washington a few months ago,
Miss Pocahontas—she comes from Virginia you know
—was inclined to be a leetle offish to shoulder-straps,
but we boys in blue soon brought her up.   Besides,
living in his family, who could resist the inspired eloquence of our great war orator, the Senator himself ?
Bream's voice is almost as good a one as mine.   Miss
Eva is now the belle of the Quartermaster's Department."

"Ah, and flirts with every brigadier of you, I presume ! " I mutter rather savagely.   What dog, even if
he doesn't want the bone, but objects to any other cur
having it !

"Well! Hm—that is—hm—hm—a little. She's always so excited about our army movements, you know. Lord! any time, I will talk army to her, I can get half an hour's tête-à-tête. She is so interested in *contemplated* movements, the disposition of our army corps and plans of our generals, don't you see. In a few days I have promised to take her through our Quartermaster-General's Department and let her see its inner workings. Mrs. Bream will act as her chaperone."

But I make no answer to these remarks; I am too astonished by them! That Miss Eva Ashley, the daughter of an old Virginia house, connected with half the leading families across the Potomac, should have become a dyed-in-the-wool Unionist astounds me.

Finally, I conclude philosophically, if I am a Union officer why shouldn't she be a loyal girl? Then mutter disconsolately: "Egad! My Baltimore provost-marshalship may make her even more faithful to the vows of her early youth than before. By the Lord Harry, at Mrs. Bream's dance I'll see this army belle and—and settle my matter with her!"

With this rather grim reflection, I turn in and go to sleep, even amid the all-night bustle of this war-time capital, for several new batteries of light artillery, apparently ordered to reinforce the army, are rumbling through the streets on their way to the Long Bridge to cross into Virginia.

CHAPTER XI.

MR. ARAGO'S TREASURY GIRL.

On Sunday, arising late in the day, I spend most of my time in unpacking my baggage and arranging for a prolonged stay in Washington, engaging for this purpose a little private parlor in addition to my bed-room.

This done, I stroll to Willard's, to find the town excited over the news of McClellan's removal from command, such reports coming of the rage and anguish of his army at being deprived of their beloved chief as make a good many high in authority, in Washington this day, bear very white and anxious faces.

Early on Monday morning, however, I discover I have an affair on my hands that for the moment drives all else out of my thoughts.

Coming down to a languid and late breakfast, I find on my plate several letters, bearing the Baltimore post-mark.

Noting these, little Finnaker, whose eyes seem every-where, forgets his omelette and coffee, and remarks joyously yet jeeringly: "Good news from home, eh?" and rubs his hands gleefully. "Papa sends his bless-ing and the young ladies their kindest wishes to the Union Provost-Marshal, eh?"

But I am too busy over my correspondence to break his cursed head, which is my first impulse.

As I read, I discover a crisis has come in my family, and that Arthur Vermilye and Birdie Hamilton will very shortly elope.

In the afternoon, trying to get out of my head this matter, in which I can do no good by personal inter-ference, and may do much harm, I saunter down to see Lieutenant Harrod, of my troop. This young officer, during his parole, is employed as Under-Quarter-master in the great Government Storehouse on twenty-second and G Streets.

As I pass the office of the War Deparment, I can't help wondering what curious mission Mr. Secretary Stanton intends to employ me upon. Somehow I grow eager to discover it.

A moment later, passing Malloy's Generals' Bar-Room at the corner, I observe Mr. Henri Arago saunter out of the cigar store just beyond it. This place has been pointed out to me as frequented by secession-sym-pathizers, probably on account of its immediate prox-imity to Mulloy's bar-room ; its hangers-on hoping to pick up stray bits of military information from the con-vivial chat of Union officers over their whisky, most of which will drift across the Potomac by underground mail-routes to Lee and other Southern generals.

Mr. Arago has apparently been in the place buying a cigar, for he is lighting one as he comes out. As he encounters me, he seems to give a start of annoyance, though a moment after his face becomes cordial.

With effusive greeting he offers me a Havana from his case, remarking : "Captain Hamilton, these are the finest *Bouquets Especiales* in Washington. Permit me to give you a local hint ; if you want a good cigar, Bermudas in there will sell it you, especially if you mention my name. I don't give this information to many people, otherwise the thieving Don would raise the price on me."

Accepting and lighting up, I find the cigar a magnificent one.

"You passed a very pleasant Sunday, I hope, Mr. Arago," I say carelessly.

"Yes ; but a curious one for me. I went to church in the evening."

"I presume you had an attraction ?"

"Well, yes ; I escorted Mrs. Senator Bream and her niece."

"Ah, Miss Ashley! I believe, is very pretty!" I remark.

At my words, for one moment, a peculiar startled and agitated look flies over Arago's sensitive Creole features. Then suddenly his eyes glow, with the light, I think, of passion.

"Miss Ashley is very beau-ti-ful," he says softly and lingeringly, as a ring of blue vapor floats out from his rather sensuous lips; "but *au revoir*. I am behind my time already at the Quartermaster-General's," and suddenly bidding me good-bye, he hastily crosses the street to take his place, I presume, at his desk in the Government office.

I carelessly wonder if Arago is smitten by the charms of Miss Ashley ; for several passing expressions I have caught from other officers and gentlemen in the last day or two have conveyed to me the idea that my putative *fiancée* is very popular in Washington society.

A few minutes afterward I turn off the avenue, and going down Twenty-second Street make my way through long trains of army wagons, even now loading with supplies for the front, many of them driven by half-drunken teamsters, and approach the Quartermaster's immense storehouses.

In this vicinity I am impressed by two things : first, the generous provision of the Government for the wants of its great army ; second, the enormous preparations to despoil, of both virtue and money, the eight thousand attachés, clerks, laborers and enlisted men that toil in this Government hive, in surrounding debauchery, prepared for them in the numerous low haunts of drink and women that are entrenched about Uncle Sam's depot; two sides of a great square being one mass of the lowest kind of army groggeries and camp women's houses.*

In the Depot Quartermaster's office I am heartily greeted by my first lieutenant. Campaigning together has made us strong friends. In answer to my inquiries, Harrod informs me that Cartwright, the Junior Lieutenant of the troop, has a desk in the Quartermaster General's main offices during his parole; that most of the members of the troop until exchanged are being employed on various duties in the great army depots of Washington, and that Sergeant Lommox, who had escaped with despatches from me the night I had been captured, is now acting as mounted orderly at the Quartermaster-General's office.

With most of this I am already acquainted, as the powers that be have already informed me that they wish to keep my troop intact until exchanged; then add it in a body to our regiment, which is now at the front, minus Troop A.

Even while they are talking, among the various orderlies arriving with the numerous requisitions for supplies, Lommox comes riding up, and pulling from his waist-belt an order from the Quartermaster-General, goes in with it to the Depot-Quartermaster.

Two minutes afterward the gallant Irishman joins me and Harrod, and saluting, says: "Begorra! Happy I am to see you alive, Cap, though I had a close shave of it meself after I left the little bridge. A hull Rebel regiment let loose on me an' I had to jump the fences and take to the fields. Musha, I think I must have flanked a hull brigade of Rebs. When I saw their force I gave you and the rest of the boys up for lost."

* Near Twenty-second and G Streets, Headquarters of the Depot Quartermaster, two sides of an entire square were occupied by the lowest groggeries, wherein at all hours of the night could be seen the common soldier, the teamster and the mechanic.—Lafayette C. Baker's *Secret Service.*—ED.

"Well, we were captured while you escaped," I remark.

"Sure, an' it's little good that did me. I'd jist as well be paroled as the rest of yez. Instead of riding down Rebels, I am only using a fine charger to gallop up and down F Strate with requisitions for supplies and transportation, whin, after Antietam, I hoped to be fighting under Little Mac. But divil a chance I'll get now, they've—they've cut poor Mac's head off." And tears came in the honest trooper's eyes.

"Well, we'll be exchanged soon," says Harrod cheerily.

"That's what I am hoping," remarks Lommox. "for it comes hard on to me to take orders from little upshtart Government clerks who have never raised sabre or pulled trigger, and I could baste the life out of 'em with one little hand." He extends an enormous paw and goes on savagely, "Ther's that little Napoleon Finniky ! Some day when he puts on style wid me, I'll be knocking his head against the side of the War Office !"

"For God's sake, don't do that !" I say, laughing. "There's the guard-house here as well as a guard-tent at the front."

"Divil take me ! Don't I know that as well as any of yez ? Begorra, it's always full here !" remarks the Sergeant, as, with a grin, he mounts his horse and gallops on his way to headquarters.

A few minutes after, Harrod getting leave of absence, anxious to get away from the interminable din of this Government beehive, we stroll out from it, and saunter down towards the Potomac through the great piles of lumber, pontoons, rigging and marine army stores, which have been accumulated for Government use.

"I imagine we'll be sending a lot of these to the front soon," remarks Harrod, tapping one of the pontoons.

"Indeed ! Why ?" I ask carelessly.

"There's a rumor somehow got round here that the army under Burnside is going to Richmond by way of Fredericksburg."

But I pay little heed to this, as we very shortly get to discussing the various members of my troop, whether they can all be got together in a hurry, for both of us have a latent hope of quick exchange and active work at the front. I ask individually after the members of my command, for an officer who does not take a personal interest in his men will never get efficient service out of them. Finally, I leave Harrod, after inviting him to join me and Cartwright, our Junior Lieutenant, at a supper at Wormley's the next evening.

With this idea in my mind, I return to the Quartermaster-General's, to find Cartwright at work at a Government desk. In answer to my inquiry as to how he likes clerking, my young fighting lieutenant smiles grimly and dashes his pen away. "By Kentucky Tom-cats," he snarls, "I feel like a rooster with his head cut off. What's a fellow good for without a sword in his hand now? Do you reckon that dandy Cock-a-doodle would do much towards helping us lick Jeff Davis?" and he points to little Finnaker who is pushing his way to me and calling out: "How are you, Provost-Marshal?" Then Cartwright asks eagerly about our chances of early exchange, and accepts my invitation to meet Harrod and myself the next evening.

It is growing dark as I leave the Quartermaster-General's Office and go to Wormley's to make my arrangement for a convival evening with my two subalterns. Finding I am late for supper at Mrs. Lorimer's, I remain in the restaurant and dine there, and coming out from this, it being now dusk, receive an extraordinary surprise.

I have turned from Pennsylvania Avenue and am walking on one of the more quiet streets. Striding rapidly along, I overtake a lady and gentleman walking in front of me. The gloom prevents my noticing anything except that the lady is very graceful, and the man apparently young and vigorous. Evidently too interested in their conversation, for they are speaking very earnestly together, to notice anybody else, their ears do not catch my overtaking footsteps.

Hesitating to jostle them, as the sidewalk is narrow, I turn out and cross the street. As I do so, a few words in a familiar voice catch my ear. They are: "Make sure I will give the despatch to Lommox." The name of my old sergeant attracts my attention. The voice is that of Mr. Arago of the Quartermaster-General's Office.

Arrived on the opposite sidewalk, I happen to glance at them again. They are just passing under the gas-light.

My heart gives a jump. The lady he is speaking to, as well as I can discern by the flickering light, is my ex-captive of the Potomac. For a moment I stand uncertain. Then I am sure! Have I not seen that bright face and those blue eyes lighted up dimly by camp-fire on the Potomac; by coal-oil lamp in the hotel at Frederick? After a moment's consideration, I make a step or two to overtake her, to greet her, but they have passed on into the gloom. The rencontre might embarrass her.

I go to my boarding-house wondering what the deuce she is doing here in Washington? How is it she's talking to Mr. Arago of the Quartermaster-General's Office? Why has he mentioned to her the name of my sergeant? Anyway, I can now discover her name. Arago will at least be able to tell me that.

I go to Willard's, that evening, but he is not there, then later to Chamberlin's. Here Mr. Arago is losing some of the booty of his cotton ventures in Louisiana, for he seems to be in a very bad humor. It is rather difficult to get much opportunity for conversation with a man deep in the mysteries of practical Faro. Besides, in the heterogeneous crowd of even the best Washington gambling-house, any mention of a lady's name would be almost an insult to her.

However, curiosity drags me on, and, waiting im-patiently, when Mr. Arago ceases play for a few minutes and seats himself at the magnificent supper-table, where a feast fit for Lucullus is served to the votaries of chance each night, I contrive to occupy the chair next him.

Over our meal, I incidentally remark: "That was a very pretty girl I saw on your arm this evening."

For a moment he looks at me surprised, and returns uneasily: "I only remember meeting you this morn-ing, Captain Hamilton."

"No, it was too dark, and you were too interested to see me," I whisper laughingly. "It was on the corner of Thirteenth and F. Streets."

For half a second his moustache twitches; then he mutters: "You saw her face?"

"Only sufficiently to know that she is beautiful."

"Ah, yes! *diable!* I remember now," he laughs; then sneers, showing his white teeth: "Most of the young ladies in Clark's Printing Department of the Treasury are pretty—*very* pretty."

A suggestive laugh that comes up from one or two near-by gamesters, who are discussing their terrapin and canvas-backs, at the name of Clark's Printing Department young ladies, closes my lips, for at this time there are some curious and horrible rumors floating about Washington in regard to the ladies of that particular department of the Treasury. Many an innocent girl being unjustly judged for the light conduct of her sisters in office.*

With a shudder, I think: "Can it be possible? Can she be—?" But here something comes into my heart that tells me that either I have not seen my lovely ex-captive of the Potomac in his company, or that Henri Dubois Arago is an infernal cur and liar!"

If the first, all right!

If the second, I will shove his cursed insinuation down his throat at the first convenient opportunity.

But going home, just the same I have an unpleasant night of it.

---

* The minority report presented in Congress, in 1864, presents the following picture of the immoralities which prevailed in the Treasury Department at that time:

"These affidavits disclose a mass of immorality and profligacy, the more atrocious as these women were employees of Clark, hired and paid by him with the public money. These women seem to have been selected, in the Printing Bureau, for their youth and personal attractions. Neither the laws of God, nor of man, the institution of the Sabbath nor common decencies of life seem to have been respected by Clark in his conduct with these women. A Treasury Bureau—there, where is printed the money—representative, or expressive of all the property and of all the industry of the country,—there, where the wages of labor are more or less regulated, and upon the faith and good conduct of which depends, more or less, every man's prosperity—is converted into a place for debauchery and drinking, the very recital of which is impossible without violating decency. Letters go thence, to clothe females in male attire to visit the 'Canterbury' (a notorious dance-hall). Assignations are made from thence." *Sights and Secrets of the National Capital*, by Dr. John B. Ellis.

This report was supported by numerous affidavits.—ED.

CHAPTER XII.

BAKER'S SECRET SERVICE.

THE next day, filled with a desire to be sure in the matter of the girl I saw with Arago, I use the acquaintance of a Treasury official whom I know slightly, and under his auspices visit that department, paying particular attention to Mr. Clark's Printing Bureau young ladies, and though I discover many lovely faces and graceful figures in the Treasury building, none of them are the beautiful face and exquisite form for which I am looking. To be as certain as possible I spend the day with this gentleman, taking him to lunch with me at Willard's, and contriving to drop with him into the Bureau several times, and by the evening have made up my mind that it is practically impossible that the young lady in the gray riding habit, with whom I spent those pleasant two hours at Frederick, is one of the employees of Uncle Sam's Printing Bureau. *Ergo*, Henri Dubois Arago is a liar, but after a little consideration I conclude the present is not the time to shove his lie down his throat.

Concluding my investigation, I find it is the hour of my appointment with my two lieutenants at Wormley's. In that well-known restaurant, we three ex-warriors, whose sword arms have been cut off by our parole, fight our battles of the Tennessee campaign over again. Our closing toast is : " May we soon get to the front."

The next morning I receive an envelope, the contents of which give me a start. Coming direct from the War Department, it directs me to report to Lafayette C. Baker, head of the United States Secret Service, at his office forthwith. With this comes into my mind a presentiment of the duty expected of me.

Less than an hour afterwards I enter that place of *mouchards*, which at that time was generally despised by military men for its arrogant authority and frequent violation of constitutional liberty and the rights of the citizen, even in extreme Northern states far removed from actual war.   There, closeted with the head of the spy bureau and general dirty-work department of the Secret Service I find to my disgust that I have too truly guessed the mission for which they want me.

After congratulating me upon the staunch Unionism I have shown as provost-marshal of Baltimore, that official, I believe his rank was Major, goes on rapidly : "Captain Hamilton !   You arrested a girl at the crossing of the Potomac on September 4th, the night you and your command were captured by Stonewall Jackson."

"Yes, sir," I answer.

"That young woman was brought to the hotel at Frederick with you ?"

"Certainly !   We were both held as prisoners by the Confederates."

"Two of my detectives, Joe Shook and Rod Gibbon, reported to me afterwards that they had reason to think that girl was a rebel spy whom they were in pursuit of that very night.   Do you know the woman's name ?"

"I do not," I answer.   "As my captive she refused to give it to me."

"Ah !"

"She also declined to disclose it to the Confederate officer who had charge of us both after I was captured by the Rebels," I add.

"Humph !   That's a little curious !" mutters my inquisitor.

"It would be !" I reply.   "But I have reason to believe that she was travelling with the intention of visiting her sweetheart, some officer of Jeb Stuart's, and I presume didn't care for army gossip to make too free with her name."

"Shucks !   What reason did she give you for wishing to cross to the Virginia side ?"

"She said she was going to visit her aunt and mother in Leesburg."

"You must have seen her in Frederick, she stopped at the same hotel.   Give me a description of her.

I don't like his blunt manner.   He is addressing me very much as he would one of his own spies ; but I answer giving him promptly the same false description of the young lady as I gave his emissaries, Shook and Gibbon.

"Curse it! A brunette!" he mutters, a disappointed look in his face; then asks eagerly: "You would know her again?"

"Certainly!"

"Well! I'll be candid with you," he says. "For months we had have reason to believe that in some mighty smart way *inside*-secrets of the War Department have been conveyed to the Confederate leaders. Now, there are some pretty big difficulties in doing this thing, I flatter myself. First, it's mighty difficult to get the secrets of the War Department, and second, its rather hard to get them out of Washington; but somebody who hasn't cared very much for their neck has been doing it, and we think this girl is about the brightest, cutest, tarnationest, smartest critter on earth, and has had something to do with it. We're surrounded here by any quantity of half-way Rebel spies. A good portion of the locals of this town are secesh. Half the market-men that travel in with produce from the surrounding country try to take out information with them, and so on from that up. The wives of a few of the Union officers we can't trust; they are Southerners.*

"But this makes little difference to us. It is *general* information, and Stonewall Jackson and Lee can guess at it pretty near as accurately as it is given to them, but the information that has been sent across the Potomac by means of the person I am speaking of has been *inside vital* points and contemplated movements that have been very valuable to the Rebel generals. If she isn't the party, we *don't* want her; but if she *is*—!" he snaps his great jaws together and looks the unutterable!

"I don't think she can be the one you want," I reply.

* In Richmond, after its capture and occupation by the Federal troops, accurate tracing-drawings of all the forts and fortifications about Washington, taken from the absolute military maps of same made by the Federal engineers, were found among the Rebel documents. They were supposed to have been made by the wife of a prominent U. S. engineer officer, taken secretly in his private office at dead of night, and transmitted out of Washington by means of her brother. This lady was a noted secessionist, though her husband was one of the staunchest Federal officers that helped Uncle Sam put down the Rebellion.—ED.

"The young lady herself acknowledged to me that she had been saucy to Stonewall Jackson."

"For what reason ?"

"Well, for holding her a prisoner in Frederick, and not permitting her to go and see her aunt and her mother. She was afterwards sent South under guard, it was creditably reported to me, suspected of being a Union spy."

"Who told you that?"

"An officer of Stuart's command."

"Cock-a-doodle ! of course they'd say anything to save their emissary." Then the head of the Detective Bureau goes on with a grim smile :

"Some of these things don't go very well together, young man ! Virginia girls are not in the *habit* of being saucy to Stonewall Jackson, and if she was in love with the Confederate officer, the chances are she is a thundering big Rebel anyway. At all events, we have a suspicion that some one moving in the very highest society here, by means of personal influence, or some other damnable art, gets hold of War Office *secrets* and sends them across the Potomac, and whether it is man or woman we intend to have 'em. Now what I want you to do is to look about Washington society—your old blue-blood Baltimore family will give you entrée to all kinds of society here, both Union and Rebel. You're thundering good-looking. Hang it, I think a good many gals 'd look sweet on a cavalry fellow like you!" he mutters with a chuckle. "And if you see this young lady—I notice you speak of her as a young lady of birth, education and breeding."

"I do !" I reply, "of the highest."

"Well, if you see her make a *leetle* love to her—a few conservatory flirtations ; arm around the waist, head on shoulder, fountain playing softly, band music coming faintly—you young army chaps understand," he chuckled in grim suggestiveness, " and—and tell me what you find out from her. Girls in sentimental moments sometimes let the cat out of the bag, even the cutest of 'em show a bit of its tail ! "

This cold-blooded proposition to me that I should obtain a young lady's confidence, perhaps even win her affections, in order to turn her over to his brutal **hands and stern military punishment, makes my blood**

fly into my face. I am about to answer hotly, indignantly. Suddenly I become cool as ice ; I think of *her !*
The art of a diplomatist comes into me. I reply : "I
understand perfectly. If I meet the young lady I will
report to you everything I can discover about her."

"Very well ! go to work at once. There is a party
at Mrs. Rufus J. Bream's this evening. Would you
like me to get you an invite from the Senator ? He is
with us body and soul."

"I have one already," I respond.

"Very well, then ! Good-bye; I've got a heap of
business to take care of, young man !—half a dozen
bounty-jumpers, three or four deserters, two or three
Potomac mail-route chaps, and an English officer
who has been trying to get over the river to join Lee's
army in Virginia, to attend to this morning. Good-bye,
let me know all that you can discover, and *quickly !*"

But as I am leaving, he steps up to me and whispers :

"Efficiency in this matter won't hurt your promotion in the army ! "

Getting out of his office I walk down the street, and
going to one of the squares, take a breath of purer air.
The ineffable insult of asking me, an army officer, to
be a spy upon a young and lovely girl ! For a quarter
of an hour I have thoughts of throwing up my commission.

Suddenly I mutter : " Resign ? NEVER ! You have
made me a spy. Damn you, I will be a spy, not to aid
you but to defeat you : not to destroy her, but to save
her ! "

The thought of a pair of blue eyes, and the recollection of the soft brown hair and pretty hand of the
girl as she played with Roderick's mane that day in
Frederick, the sun shining on her and outlining her exquisite figure in its natty gray riding-habit, comes back
to me, and somehow I determine, even if it carries
with it disgrace, perhaps ruin to me, to stand between
that charming personality, whether she's another
man's sweetheart or my own, and try to save her
from the web being drawn about her pretty self that
is dangerous to her liberty, perhaps even to her life.

My first step in this matter must evidently be to find
her. My most direct means of communicating with
her, if my suspicious are true, is through Arago. He has

evidently lied to me in regard to her being one of the Treasury courtesans.   Was this intended as a slur upon her, I meditate?

Suddenly it comes to me: "No! it was to prevent my making further inquiry about her.   Arago doesn't wish attention attracted to whatever relations he may bear to this young lady."

I determine to investigate this.   Somehow a detective feeling is getting into my veins.

Two hours afterward, at Willard's, I have the chance of making my test, though it compels me to open my hand quite freely to Mr. Henri Dubois Arago, of the Quartermaster General's office.

That gentleman and young Mr. Finnaker are playing a game of billiards with disastrous results to little Nap, for Arago has a facile Creole touch with his cue that produces many French caroms, but as usual, young Napoleon is trying to bluff things through. They are gambling on the game, Finnaker betting high that Arago will miss his shot, thinking to test that gentleman's nerve, and losing his money doing it.

I stroll up to their table, and indulge in general billiard-table conversation, making side-bets myself on some shots.

Soon little Napoleon, whose losses have made him desperate, offers to wager a twenty dollar bill that Arago cannot make his next point.   The carom is one of considerable difficulty, but easily within the Creole's powers.   I have seen him on the previous afternoon make similar ones, accurately and certainly.

"You will lose your money," I laugh, but as I speak I see the chance of testing the Creole's interest in the young lady about whom he has lied to me.   As he is preparing for the effort, little Finnaker fortunately gives me the opportunity.

"By-the-bye, Hamilton, where have you been all day?" he cries, rubbing his hands and looking at me. "You've missed it! You might have come in and bet against Henri before."

"Oh! I had some personal business with Baker's Secret Service office."

"Ah! look out for them, my boy!" laughs little Nap, chalking his cue.   "But then you are on the inside!"

"Yes! *very much* on the inside."

" Your Provost-Marshal business, I presume," remarks Arago, looking up from his cue ball.

"No," I answer. " I was so fortunate as to capture a very pretty girl on the Maryland bank of the Potomac one night. They wish me to hunt her up and tell them if I see her in Washington society ! "

I time this speech to strike Arago just as he attempts the shot.

At my words a slight but convulsive twitch in his arm makes his billiard essay a fiasco.

" By Jove, your twenty is mine ! " laughs Finnaker.

" Here, take it ! " mutters the Creole, in a half-startled half-dazed tone. Then looking at me, he partly opens his lips as if about to speak, but suddenly turns to the billiard table and continues the game ; though from now on I note his skill seems to have left him, and little Nap Finnaker ends the contest in triumph.

" You've a very good nerve, Mr. Arago ! " I cogitate glumly, "but I gave your ganglions a little pinch that surprised them."

On my way home to Mrs. Lorimer's I meditate on this matter. Even as I dress for Mrs. Bream's thoughts of meeting my putative *fiancée*—Miss Ashley—for reports of her beauty, loveliness, *chic* and general fascination have come to me from so many lips that I can't help having a latent curiosity about her—do not drive Arago and the fleeting vision I saw under the gas-light in Thirteenth and E Streets from my head.

My reasoning upon this subject brings to me the following startling conclusions : First, Arago must have reasons for wishing his relations to the young lady—whatever they are—to be private and unobserved. Hence his enormous lie about her being one of the Treasury beauties.

To this is now added my suspicion that he is aware of the young lady being my captive of that night on the Potomac—otherwise, why did my remarks about her and Baker's Secret Service so jar his nerves, that from being an expert with the cue, he became in one second the veriest amateur. She must have told him of that meeting.

To this suddenly comes with an awful, dismaying bang into my brain—My God, if Baker's suspicions are *true !*

CHAPTER XIII.

But my meditations on the unknown girl are here broken in upon. Little Finnaker comes striding into my parlor, in his militia uniform. This is a Turko-Zouave dress, of Oriental ferocity.

"I have a question or two I want to ask you, my son of Mars," he says, trying to bring his enormous voice down to a whisper. "But this must be private!"

"Certainly."

"I know I can trust you ; your intense loyalty shows me *that!* So I want a hint from you. Though you're in the cavalry, I presume you studied engineering at West Point?"

"I did, till my head ached!" I laugh.

"Now, this is *very* dark!" he steps up to me, and speaks in my ear, his deep voice making my tympanum ring : "Orders came from the front to-day to prepare a pontoon train with eighty pontoons and two thousand feet of wooden bridge, with extra anchors and lashings, and forward it to Aquia Creek. Arago sent the requisition down to the Depot-quartermaster, special order 1410, by that cursed insolent Irish orderly Lommox, not two hours ago. As a military engineer, what does it mean?"

I glance at an elaborate map of Virginia that I have hung on the wall of my parlor, for convenience in following the movements of the army. After a minute or two's inspection of this, I reply sharply : "Fredericksburg!"

"Ah, you think it means a pontoon bridge to cross the Rappahannock at that point?"

"No," I reply. "I think it means two, perhaps three, pontoon bridges—for Burnside's army to cross at Fredericksburg. If you've reported your orders correctly to me, I should judge that is the route the new commander of the army intends to take to Richmond."

"You bet! What do you think of it?" asks Finnaker eagerly.

"Humph! If he gets over before Lee can entrench himself back of the city," I remark, "it might not be a bad plan."

"Well, I think Ambrose understands that; for the orders have come to expedite getting together that pontoon train and start it as fast as possible. We sent the requisition off like a shot; that insolent beast Lommox was back in five or six minutes, though I think his horse must have thrown him, he was dusty as a badger when he reported back. Now, you must take your oath not to whisper this to anybody!" he adds warily. "I tell too many things now. Some day I may get into trouble over them."

"Some day you may!" I think grimly; but not wishing to cut off my inside information, I do not voice this.

While we have been talking, I have finished a most elaborate, and I hope effective, military toilet, for—shall I confess it?—the benefit of Miss Eva Ashley. What man does not wish to look his best in the eyes of a beautiful and fascinating girl to whom he has been a childhood sweetheart—at the first meeting after mutual maturity? Whether he wants her love or not—no matter how attenuated Cupid's ribbon that once joined them has grown—he wishes the little girl to see that her boy beau, in manhood has not deteriorated.

So with my heart beating at the thought of meeting for the first time in seven years my putative *fiancée*, and rather wondering what will be the precise nature of her greeting—whether she has not practically forgotten me—but still with my heart fluttering slightly about the affair, accompanied by Finnaker, I step over to Mrs. Bream's old-fashioned but handsome residence on the north of Lafayette Square.

The distance is a short one, the night pleasant; though even as we arrive, quite a string of carriages are putting down various ladies and gentlemen at the wide-open, hospitable portals. Most of the gentlemen, from clanking sabres under their cloaks, and spurs flashing in the gaslight, I discover are in uniform.

"Yes; it's going to be quite a military affair," remarks little Napoleon to me. "We let in a few Congressmen ; some foreign attachés wander in ; but this evening it's mostly the 'boys in blue' and the girls who love 'em. It is one of four that Mrs. Bream's going to give ; not big crushes like her grand ball, but jolly, happy frolics, where every one knows everybody else—and the prettiest girls in Washington to dance with, flirt with, and make 'em love you."

Most of this is whispered while we are divesting ourselves of our outer wrappings in the gentlemen's dressing-room.   Around us I note, among lots of blue uniforms, a few dress coats, worn mostly by foreign legation attachés ; beside me is Señor Rafael Ortegas, the Spanish first-secretary, also Rupert Schuyler and Jack Totten, old West Point friends ; General Broughton of the Engineers reminds me he is also near me, by doing me the honor of treading on my toes.

I deliver my cavalry cloak and helmet to the inevitable attendant darky of all Washington residences, though little Napoleon refuses to surrender his Turko headgear to that functionary, probably thinking that it gives him greater martial ferocity.

"All of us boys from the front !" remarks Napoleon, who seems to know everybody, looking round at several officers, on temporary leave from the Army of the Potomac—"to-morrow we go out and get at the Rebs again—don't we, comrades ?"

"By Jove ! how I sympathize with your martial ardor, Mr. Finnaker," laughs young Totten of the infantry. "Penned up here, with never a chance to shed your blood."

"Yes, it is sad !" cries Napoleon unabashed. "Though I'll bet I have had more horses shot under me than any man present ! And at First Bull Run— damn me !—acting as a volunteer-aide, I was wounded ! If you don't believe me ask Colonel Cameron of the 79th New York ! But then he's dead, poor fellow—fell at my side and died in my arms ! Good God ! don't talk of it here ; it might frighten the girls." And the little liar brushes actual tears out of his ferocious eyes.

Finnaker has told this story so often that it has become a reality to him ; and so strongly was this fiction embedded in his mind that after the war he applied for a pension on it—by special legislation.

A moment later, I step downstairs to pay my respects to my hostess, followed by the little hero, who suggests : "The girls are waiting for *us*."

I had seen Mrs. Senator Bream several times when she visited West Point during my cadetship. At midsummer hops I had had the honor of dancing with the wife of the distinguished Senator, who is as lovely, pleasant, and hospitable a young matron as ever forgot old husband,—though only for a moment—in the arms of a dashing lieutenant. For Lucy Bream was always the *Bona Dea* of us cadets ; her happy face, her bright smile, had enlivened many a dress-parade for us, and made charming many a graduation hop.

As I enter the fête, I observe that the double house is a roomy mansion, old-fashionedly spacious, with rather low ceilings. Its ample parlors are of sufficient extent to give dancing-room to a hundred couples. In the large hall, surrounded by potted plants, a portion of one of the bands of a garrison regiment is playing vigorously, as many dashing fellows are doing the *deux temps*, each one with a pretty partner, to the dreamy music of Godfrey's "Mabel" waltz, that is just now very popular.

Elbowing my way discreetly between one or two surrounding wives of Senators and Congressmen, I find myself bowing over the fair hand of Lucy Bream.

Thirty odd years have fallen lightly on her dimpled shoulders, her soft, brown Virginia eyes are as charming and her voice is as sweet, as when, some twelve years before, she enchanted cadets as pretty Lucy Warrington. She is the youngest sister of Miss Ashley's mother. "The baby of the family," I have heard her called in the old time, before she married the rising Border-State politician who afterwards threw away his Democracy and became the great Republican war-horse.

That political luminary is not in the room.

Noting my glance, Mrs. Bream remarks : " I'm exceedingly glad to learn that you've escaped from your secession relatives in Baltimore, Captain Hamilton. But you needn't expect the Senator until later ; at present he is occupied on committee business at the capitol. I never see him now until eleven o'clock." This last with a little sigh ; as she loves her old spouse very tenderly—though perhaps not in a Juliet fashion.

"And—and Miss Ashley?" I ask, gazing about curiously.

"Oh, Eva will be down presently—she complained of a slight headache after dinner but finally went out for a walk and fresh air, this beautiful afternoon, and did not return till quite late." To this Mrs. Bream adds significantly, "You and Eve used to be quite friends in the *old* days;" and asks me after my father and my sisters.

"I don't know very much about them at present," I return glumly.

"No, I presume not," she laughs suggestively; then murmurs, with the tact of the hostess: "Ah, Mr. Finnaker—as usual here when the pretty girls *come!*" and greets Miss Sallie Bridger, a dashing frontier amazon from the plains, and the Misses Alice and Laura Cushing of New York, metropolitan beauties, who are spending a month or two in Washington.

I turn from my hostess and glance round the room at as pretty a war-time frolic as I have ever seen.

For Mrs. Bream's party, though it has not all the redundant paraphernalia that have come to later American social functions and its young ladies are not all decked in imported Parisian gowns, though the favors in its german will not be made of silver and gold and decked with jewels, has an informal jollity about it that is missing from so many of the more elaborate affairs of the next few decades.

The girls all look as pretty and happy as wood-nymphs, though half of them have probably made their own simple dancing frocks; but in them they are a merry lot of open-hearted, whole-souled damsels, many very beautiful, and all very well pleased with the gentlemen in attendance upon them, who are mostly of the younger and fighting blood of the army —dashing fellows on short leave from the front.

For in those days it was flirting, dancing and loving one day, and shooting, fighting and dying, the next! Some of the officers about me, even now, are giving their young eyes their last earthly feast of beautiful women, though they do not know it; and are making love as persistently to the pretty maidens in their way

as if they will live to be centenarians and die with
four generations around their bedsides.

Upon this scene I took philosophically. The strains
of the " Mabel " waltz are floating in my ears.

Mr. Finnaker is saying : " Miss Ashley, let me present my friend, the ex-Provost-Marshal of Baltimore and
gallant Union officer, Captain Hamilton."

Turning, I bow to a radiant mixture of arch smiles
and blushing embarrassment, and murmur : "I have
known Miss Ashley before."

Suddenly the room seems to revolve around me
with jiggling dancers ; the music seems to give a
mashing crash upon my brain. I see standing before
me, as piquantly lovely, as exquisitely beautiful as
when she wore the gray riding-habit, my ex-captive of
that Potomac night—my charmer of those two happy
hours in Frederick.

Cavalry officers don't faint. Therefore I do not reel
and utter a smothered cry, but, chewing my moustache,
look sheepishly at her as she says—for women always
have social presence of mind :—"No need of an introduction, Mr. Finnaker ; Captain Hamilton and I are—
are old friends." Then she makes my heart beat with :
" Billy, will you give me your arm and take me out on
the veranda ? It—it's a little warm here, and as sub-
hostess I have been dancing continuously."

Remembering Mrs. Bream's remark I know the
young lady has told a little fib—but it makes me very
happy.

"Yes ; very old friends," I contrive to mutter.
"Though I've not seen you for *several* years."

At my omission of the Frederick meeting she gives
me a grateful glance.

Again I notice Miss Ashley's tact.

She says : " *Captain* Finnaker, you won't mind losing
me for a few minutes. I'll give you a dance later in the
evening—two of them, if you like"—and sends little
Napoleon away very happy both for her dance and
his military title. Then placing upon my arm a light
hand, the touch of which thrills me from heart to
brain, she almost whispers in my ear : "Thank you
for not remembering *too much*."

In a dazed way, I lead her through circling dancers,
and happily get her to a window opening on the bal-

cony without accident to her light muslin skirts and lacy draperies.

For she is all in white—diaphanous white. The only color about her—except her cheeks, which are roses and lilies by turns, with varying emotions—is a broad scarf of light pink satin or silk or some other glistening texture that girdles her fairy waist and floats off over the fluttering little flounces of her crinolined skirt to petite pink slippers that come peeping out from under it.

The gown is very simple ; perhaps it has been made by her own pretty fingers. But—heavens and earth ! —what a magnificent pair of shoulders and arms spring out of it, superb in sculptured beauty, gleaming like ivory and white as driven snow.

As I draw the curtains back for her to exit in advance of me, I feel as if I could kiss every dimple in them.

Glancing archly over her shoulder as she passes, out, perhaps the girl catches the spark of proprietorship in my eyes, as I am looking proudly at her and thinking *"My fiancée!"* for her fair cheeks grow redder even than they were before. The next instant the blushes leave her face, which grows deathly pale, her eyes blaze, her delicate nostrils expand in haughty coldness ; Miss Eva Ashley is no more the bashful maiden, but the self-possessed beauty of society.

On the broad veranda, which fortunately is occupied by but few of the ladies and gentlemen of the fête, I silently place a chair for her in a retired nook and another for myself.

A moment later she glances at me shyly, then laughs archly : "Why are you so glum ? One would think meeting me after childhood's hours, was not pleasant to Sir Galahad."

To this I do not immediately reply ; I am gazing on all this loveliness surlily. For, curiously, just at this moment, the memory of the accursed kiss I heard on the Frederick hotel balcony, and the "Dear Charley !" that brought misery to me as I sat in the gloom of the tavern garden, have made me tremendously jealous. "What right has she—my *fiancée*," I am thinking, "to dare to let another man salute those lips that should be for me and me only ?"

Oh! how constant I have suddenly become to our childhood's engagement. Into my mind has flown with all a Romeo's ardor, "She is my betrothed, and by the Eternal, she shall be no other man's!"

Still, as I look at her radiant beauty, softened by the subdued lights that stream from the curtained windows upon Miss Ashley, a sudden and unpleasant reflection intrudes itself upon me: "How will she *now* regard the engagement made for us by papa and by mamma?"

Evidences of this do not come to me immediately, as I seat myself beside her, for the young lady looks at me merrily, though graciously, and murmurs gratefully: "Thank you again for not being *too* explanatory before Mr. Finnaker. I do not care," she whispers, "for my harum-scarum, fly-away escapade that night you were so kind as to—to save my life, Billy, to be common gossip."

"What makes you think I saved your life?"

"Why, one of your poor troopers you ordered to ride behind me was shot down. And you—did you not have a bullet through your clothes as you kept so carefully between me and the Confederate fire?"

"Yes, I believe I did lose a button," I murmur; then go on, in a tone whose gloom is deeper than the night: "No wonder you wish it to be a secret, Miss Ashley, when you visited the Confederate Army to meet a handsome young officer!"

"I beg your pardon, sir." The blushing girl has become a statue of ice and as haughty as Lucifer.

"Oh, you need not dèny it," I mutter savagely. "Sitting on a chair in the garden at Frederick—in the early evening—as I might be sitting down below this veranda now—I heard you call a gentleman 'Dear Charley!' And then—God help me!—I heard you—"

"Kiss him?" she laughs. "Why certainly! My half-brother, Charley St. George, of Munford's Second Virginia Cavalry. Of course I kissed him, when I hadn't seen him for months!" then adds slyly: "And you were—" But she checks herself, biting off the word she is about to utter, next a sudden eagerness, perhaps anxiety, coming into her voice, she asks uneasily: "Tell me *all* you heard that evening?"

"Nothing more!" I reply, and mutter glumly, "Wasn't that *enough?* Didn't I suffer so much misery that I couldn't bid you good-bye in Frederick that night?"

At this she breaks out laughing but remarks in common-sense tone : "Don't be foolish, Billy ! What right would you have had to complain if Miss Ashley had kissed any man? You've paid so much attention to her since you left West Point." There is a haughty sneer in the patrician face, her nostrils are dilated with lady-like contempt.

Here despair and Cupid give me a crafty suggestion. I murmur : "*Miss Ashley's* kisses made little difference to me then, but that one of *my ex-captive* in the gray riding-habit did mightily."

"Ah, yes, I perceive !" says the young lady slowly, and breaks into a slight laugh, in which I can't help joining.

Then I whisper : "You told Miss Eva Vernon Ashley, that you disciplined Captain Billy Hamilton with threats of his *fiancée,*"—she grows rosy at the appellation—"when he was about to make a little love to you? You remember you threatened to tell her of my perfidy," I laugh ; I am so happy now. "How did Miss Ashley receive your communication?"

"Oh, she knew you were fickle without my telling her," giggles the young lady. Then suddenly she grows, I think, cruelly cold ; she remarks haughtily "You have already taken a tone with me, Captain Hamilton, that years of attention should not allow a gentleman to assume to a lady."

"Yes, I was jealous, I'll admit it," I say, my voice growing very tender. And carried away by her glorious beauty, which is as tantalizing to me, as the forbidden fruit was to the serpent, I whisper : "Will you not permit me the pleasure of being jealous of you, Eve?"

It is the first time I have used her Christian name. As it strikes her ear she grows very red, but answers firmly, though laughingly : "Not until you have earned the right, by months and months of devotion."

Here inspiration comes to me. I answer : "I have already two months to my credit !"

"Two months? I—I hardly understand you."

"From the night of September 4th to November 14th, this evening," I whisper, "I have been devoted to

you—not perhaps as Miss Eva Vernon Ashley, but as
the beauty of the gray riding-habit. Permit me to
unite the two young ladies in one. It is not always we
can combine love and duty. You know your mother
and my father wish it. I always like to please my
governor," I add nonchalantly—thinking I've played a
master stroke.

But I haven't!

"Yes; you are *always* anxious to please your father!"
she sneers half-laughingly, "Union soldier and ex-
Provost-Marshal of Baltimore. Oh, yes, you always
enjoy making your governor *happy.*" She rises, as if
shaking some insect from her dress, and remarks in
icy hauteur: "But please take me in to the dancers;
our absence will be noticed, Captain Hamilton."

"Hang it! what have I done to displease you now?"
I say, hurriedly rising after her.

"Nothing; only it is cold here." Her white shoulders shiver slightly. "If you prefer the moonlight,
stay outside; but I must go into the ball-room."

Silently I open the window for her, and she passes
into the throng; and I, gazing after her, see her
face, which had been cold to me, light up with gay
smiles as she is surrounded by half-a-dozen blue uniforms and one or two black dress-coats. A moment
after she is whirled away into the dance by young
Schuyler, a lieutenant of engineers.

On my charmer's last vagary I look with gloomy eyes,
and stand speculating in the moonlight: "Is it because
she thinks me an undutiful son? or is it because I, a
Southerner, am a Union officer?"

A moment later I speculate again: "Is she devoted
to the Union as little Finnaker so proudly asserts? Has
the great War-Senator's eloquence converted her?"
Somehow, it seems to me it would take a good deal more
than eloquence to make most Virginia girls anything
but the most pestilent of Rebel maidens. I know *my*
eloquence has never converted any of them. "The
only thing that has ever seemed to soften them has
been making love to them," I chuckle grimly to myself, as I think of my dear little sister Birdie's icy
hauteur growing soft and pliable and sunshiny under
handsome Arthur Vermilye's ardent glances.

Suddenly all speculation of this kind is knocked out of my brain with another battering crash !

I see Miss Ashley, beautiful as a sylph, come floating through the crowd of dancers, steered by the arm of Henri Dubois Arago, who in plain, civilian, faultless evening dress, is guiding her through the throng with Creole grace and suppleness.

"She *was* the girl Henri Arago talked to that night !" flashes through my mind. "She—Eva Ashley—my *fiancée*—was the girl he scoffed at as a Treasury wanton !"

But noting him, I see his bearing to the young lady is punctilio itself; though as he looks upon her there is something in his eyes that makes me hate him.

Then with a little gasp I remember what the Chief Detective of the Secret Service Bureau said to me this day. "My heaven ! Can he be right ? Is Eva Ashley the woman Lafayette C. Baker and Edmund McMasters Stanton want ?"

That I must discover—for her sake—for my sake: to defend her properly—to keep her from military punishment ! That I must know, and know quickly !"

***

CHAPTER XIV.

THE BELLE OF THE ARMY.

To do this I must have not only the talent of a Vidocq and the astuteness of a diplomatist, but the cold-blooded *savoir faire* of an indifferent. Can I be that to a woman whom I have *loved* for two months— whom I have ADORED for ten minutes ?

Schooling myself to my *role*, which is not an easy one for a dashing. whole-hearted, up-and-down, cut-and-thrust, hit-or-miss cavalry officer, I step into the ball-room and do my *devoir*, in what would be, under ordinary circumstances, one of the jolliest dances I have ever seen.

I waltz with Miss Molly Bent, a fascinating little witch from Iowa, flirt with Miss Georgie Langdon of Hartford, have a very charming *tête-à-tête* with the sprightly Alice Cushing of New York. Sitting on the stairs, a little distance below us, is her brother, Jim Cushing of the infantry, paying his court to the piquant French beauty and soft Southern eyes of Grace Choteau, a St. Louis girl whose ancestors were great in the fur-trading line.

But none of these demoiselles, pretty as they are, sparkling as they are, can keep my glance from following the exquisite loveliness of Eva Ashley, as she floats about, first with one cavalier, then with another, apparently dispensing the favors of her hand quite impartially among the gentlemen about her.

Though, noting her time and again, I shortly discover that Mr. Arago somehow contrives to have a little the best of any of her attendants. Something in her manner to him makes me grind my teeth ; there seems some indescribable, common interest in both this young lady and gentleman—illusive, intangible— but still a bond of some kind between them. Once or twice, as she almost whispers to her Creole beau, I think it is some secret that is theirs and theirs only.

Determined I will not go near Eve, I still am not able to get her out of my head, and perhaps make rather indifferent company to the young ladies with whom I am talking.

So, strolling a little further, I get into conversation with our hostess. "By Jove, I'll pump her about her niece !" I think, and, chatting with Mrs. Bream, I tell her the story of my sister Birdie and her love affair with Captain Vermilye of the artillery.

"Yes ; the captain was here at my ball," remarks my hostess. "I thought him a very distinguished gentleman, besides being very rich. Your little secession sister's made a good Union match," laughs Lucy, "and I have no doubt your father in his heart of hearts blesses you for it."

"Indeed he doesn't ! You should have seen the letter he wrote me ! " I reply glumly.

"Well, it's a good thing, you young people of *opposite* sides getting together. It won't make you hate each other so much after the war is over. Now there is my niece," she looks at Eve who is standing at a little distance, talking to a couple of oldish brigadier-generals, "when she came here from Virginia, she was quite a vicious little Rebel. But though she says it was my husband's eloquence and argument that have softened her sectional animosity, I rather think you handsome young officers have had more to do with her conversion than the Senator's fiery speeches. By-the-bye," my hostess remarks, "when you were quite young was not it rumored that you were engaged—a kind of boy-and-girl affair—to Eve?"

"The rumor was true," I say determinedly, "it was *a fact*."

"But you have not been with her much this evening?"

"Why not?" I reply, knowingly. "We had a pleasant little chat out on the back veranda."

Suddenly Lucy Bream startles me. She says in American common-sense tones:

"Why not renew the affair?"

"You mean it?"

"Certainly!" To this, the matron adds, a tone of anxiety in her voice: "Step up to her now, she is speaking to Mr. Arago. Between ourselves—this must be confidential—even if you only flirt with her, do me the favor of destroying Mr. Arago's chances. I—I don't like the way Eve is carrying on with that young New Orleans man; I have spoken to her about it, but my niece laughs it off."

"I have your good wishes?" I ask anxiously.

"Yes! to the fullest extent." Lucy Bream's hand meets mine with hearty grasp; her frank eyes look into mine encouragingly: I know I have a friend in the camp of my sweetheart.

Still, something in the matron's eyes makes me whisper: "You think I have a difficult task before me?"

Her answer is not assuring. "Very! At least, it would be, young man, if I were Eva Ashley. Engaged to her as a boy, and neglecting her as a man! In addition, Eve's natural pride has been augmented by her poverty. You see, she is very sensitive now; her family's losses by this war in the Valley of Virginia have made her poor. And let me tell you, my gallant captain, if she thinks for one moment your neglect of her came from the knowledge of her poverty, good-bye to any hope of her! I'm not altogether pleased with your conduct in this matter, Billy," adds the aunt, looking at me rather savagely.

"Then for God's sake, let me atone for it!"

"Ah! Now that you see Eve's about the prettiest thing in the world——"

"You do not understand. I—I cannot explain— only believe me, I have loved her ever since I saw her as a woman!"

"Pish! For an hour?"

"No; for much longer."

"Tell me!" Woman's curiosity is blazing in the eyes of the matron. But this shows me Eve has not made her aunt her confidant of her night ride between the armies. Under the circumstances, I must keep my lips closed.

"Tell you," I laugh, "when I'm *married* to your niece."

This last is a whisper that makes Lucy Bream give a little startled, "Oh!"

But though my words are confident, my heart is not equally so. I sit apart and inspect glumly Miss Eva's radiant beauty, from the brown, sunny curls that crown her graceful head to her exquisite feet and ankles disclosed to me in the dance, by her fashionable crinoline, as she waltzes with young Burbank of the cavalry, or Ortegas, the Legation attaché, and exchanges military confidences in out-of-the-way nooks with several old general officers.

But suddenly I find my indifference is rewarded. Why is it that women are so apt to run after the cold shoulder? Seeing I will not go to her, Miss Ashley, to my astonishment, comes to me.

"You got tired of the moonlight, I presume, Billy," she says, apparently as if she had left me on the best of terms; then adds, as she drops languidly into a seat beside me: "Found another young lady who likes the moonlit piazza?"

"No," I growl. "There is only one here I'd care to share it with. You know who *she* is." I gaze straight in her face, though I have great difficulty in keeping my lip from twitching.

"Oho! Trying to make up by present ardor for past indifference?"

"My heaven, how you misjudge me! My devotion

to the girl in the gray riding-habit kept me away from
my—my *fiancée*." I rub the title into Eve till her
cheeks blaze—and get a great big hope from it, for she
doesn't command me not to use the term.

"Yes ; that is a redeeming point in your favor," she
observes in icy tones. "I don't suppose I should be
very angry at any compliment for the young lady you
have just mentioned." Then suddenly she whispers ·
"But no more of this *here*," a tinge of anxiety in her
voice ; for the music has ceased, and our words are now
quite distinct to those standing near us.

Then the girl gives me another hope, though this
time it is tinctured by rage. She remarks : "No, Mr.
Arago, I don't think I can give you the next dance.
You see, I haven't seen my old playmate, Captain
Hamilton, for several years. We are indulging in rem-
inisences."

"Pleasant ones, I hope," mutters the Creole, bowing ;
though his tone indicates he would prefer that they
were unpleasant.

"Very pleasant ones ! " I interject. "So pleasant
that I think I shall have to take Miss Ashley in to
supper."

"That honor has been already accorded to me ! " replies the clerk in the Quartermaster-General's.   ·

"Has it, Eve ? " I ask, in old-friend tones, a little
emphasis on the young lady's Christian name that
makes the gentleman standing before us turn angry,
though inquiring eyes on me.

But here consternation comes to me. Miss Ashley
says, an indescribable something in her voice : "Mr.
Arago is correct : I have already promised him that he
may look after my appetite this evening ;" then adds
to him : "I shall be waiting for you here ; it is after
the next dance, I believe."

And the Creole leaves us, with triumph on his face,
while I cogitate dejectedly : "What is it that makes
Miss Ashley so complaisant to this gentleman ?"
Though now she is trying to show me it is only good
breeding, for she is saying : "I had already made the
engagement with Mr. Arago, so don't wrinkle your
brow so savagely, Billy."

"Curse it ! Is the poor little thing trying to palliate
to me her acceptance of the Creole's attentions ? Hang

it! is she frightened of him? Still, as I look at the high-bred face, courageous eyes, the haughty and clear-cut nostrils of the girl sitting beside me, it is very difficult to think Eva Vernon Ashley is afraid of anything—much less a half-French gentleman from New Orleans, with suave voice and oily smile.

I must be hating Arago! I thought him a handsome fellow but yesterday : now he seems to be repulsive.

But schooling myself to society manners, and determining to make the best use of my time, I do drift into reminiscences with the charming creature at my side. It is : "Billy, don't you remember that——" "Eva, do you recollect when——" But these are broken in upon by half-a-dozen gentlemen coming and begging for a turn, and finally, to get away from these, I suggest : "Dance with me?"

"With pleasure!" says the girl, and putting a dainty hand, light as a falling snowflake on my shoulder, my arm goes round her waist—the first time I have clasped it since she has become a woman—and I feel the heart of Eva Ashley beat against my own. Somehow, its throbbing seems to tell me that she loves me—that she *has* loved me ; somehow, it is as if she felt confidence in my supporting arm—that peace has come to her. In my soul I swear : "She shall never regret it!" as with the music of that soft, sweet "Olga" waltz floating in our ears, her little feet keep perfect time to my West Point step. For one sweet moment I forget I have a Secret Service suspect in my arms, and think my love can be a happy one.

Suddenly her heart gives two grand throbbing, wave-like beats against mine. Mr. Arago is saying over my shoulder in happy tones : "I am waiting for my recompense. The next is supper."

Afraid of him? Hang it, her eyes blaze with triumph and success!

As she leaves my arm and puts her hand upon the black sleeve of the Creole beau, it seems to me that Miss Eva Vernon Ashley wants to be very kind this evening to Henri Dubois Arago, Chief Clerk in the Quartermaster-General's office.

Is it for some mighty service he has rendered to her? Meditating gloomily on this, I follow them to supper.

With terrapin and champagne, come in Senator Bream and two or three more politicians, bringing with them the awful passions of the war, into our mirth and revelry. Our soldiers fought and forgave; our politicians never fought and never forgave, and always kept talking about it.

The conversation which had been that of any joyous fête and festivity far from the noise of cannon, now becomes that of an entrenched camp, the enemy not very far away.

A Jacobin congressman, even as we eat and drink, commences to attack McClellan. Finally young Captain Totten, who is just from the front, with tears in his eyes turns to him and says : "You have never fought under that general—I have! But if you will join me and stand with me in the next battle—by Heaven, sir I think you'll wish we had him back! I know *I* will ! "

Prophetic words! Already the advance divisions are in motion for the awful mistake at Fredericksburg where handsome Jack Totten fell.

Premonitions of this movement commence even now to permeate army circles; for I hear an engineer officer near me whisper to a young lady : "Mabel, I'm ordered to the front to-morrow morning; I suppose there'll be some bridge-building."

"Oh, Heavens, George ! " gasps his sweetheart, who is looking anxiously in his face; then she falters : "Why ? "

"Because I take with me all the reserves of the engineer battalion especially equipped as pontoniers." The last of this speech is quite loud.

At the young officer's words, my jealous eyes, that have never left them, note that Mr. Arago pauses as he is drinking his champagne and gazes, a strange look of ecstatic joy in his face, at the beautiful girl sitting beside him who is playing with oysters *à la* Maryland, for this evening Miss Ashley doesn't seem to have much appetite—perhaps some reminiscences of her headache that had taken her out walking in the afternoon, affecting her. Then her eyes meet his—no love in them, thank God—only some enormous glory—Eva Ashley has the look of a general who has won a battle.

Just about here Mrs. Bream comes and takes a seat

beside me, remarking with a hostess's anxiety : "You are not eating, Captain Hamilton."

"No ; but I'm drinking," I laugh savagely, and toast the charming matron in another glass of her champagne.

"You're not getting along as well as you expected?" she whispers, glancing across the room towards her beautiful niece.

"Oh, yes ; I'm doing pretty well," I say, with a confidence that seems to astonish her.

"Indeed ! How ?"

"I have discovered the reason of Eva's interest in Mr. Arago."

"What is it ?" Again feminine curiosity lights the eyes of pretty Lucy Bream.

Again I disappoint it. "Tell you—after I'm married to Eve," I whisper.

"Pooh !" You're the most disappointing creature I ever saw !" she laughs, as she rises from my side and goes over to her husband, to make him happy with her wifely attentions.

And the Senator is very happy ! He is now in the midst of what he thinks a good anecdote. His strident voice, that has lately filled the halls of the Senate, fills the dining-room, and would bring confusion upon little Finnaker, if anything could.

The conversation has fallen upon Abraham Lincoln, who occupied not only the hearts, but the attention, of the people ; his stories, *bons mots* and backwoods repartee amusing the army at the front and even the copperheads, as they plotted his political downfall at the rear.

"I've got a new one of Abe's," chuckles the Senator. "To-day, the President and I visited the Quartermaster-General's office. While we were there, the greatest patriotic chatter we either of us had ever heard came resounding in to us.

"'Good Lord !' says old Abe to me. 'Do you know that reminds me of the explosion of the *Belle of Alton* on the Wabash in 1842.'

"'How, so Mr. President?' replied I, preparing to laugh, for I could see the twinkle in Abraham's eye.

"'Well, when the *Belle of Alton* blew up I heard the darndest, biggest, most horrible noise on earth, and looking round for the cause of it, darn me, if I could see anything left—the whole thing was nothing but *noise and wind!* Little Napoleon Finnaker reminds me of that explosion.'"

A roar of laughter breaks out from every man and woman of us, and looking about I expect to see Nap crushed and broken.

But rising with his champagne glass in his hand, the Zouave uniform making him ferocious, the little hero cries : "Thank you, Mr. Senator! Our honored chief knew that the explosion of the *Belle of Alton* killed one hundred men. By Jove, sir! he knew I was equally *deadly!* Phil Kearney saw me shoot six rebels before he died in my arms at the battle of Chantilly, while I soothed his last anguish. Ask *him* if you don't believe *me!*" And the little fellow gazes at the laughing crowd.

Then suddenly tears come into his eyes, and he mutters, his voice unsteady with champagne : "But Phil —poor Phil Kearney—is dead! Another comrade gone. Soon perhaps the Rebel bullets will give me my quietus also."

Curiously, Finnaker's eloquence, tears and champagne grief carry conviction to some. Pretty Ethel Davenport, who has just come from the West, whispers to me : "Is he so *awful* brave ?"

"Captain Finnaker is as brave as he looks," I answer laughingly.

By this time the fiddlers have got to playing again, and the younger contingent saunter out from the jolly supper-room to dance the german. Taking opportunity of the cotillion, I lead out several times Miss Ashley, and once tossing me a flower favor she gives me floral invitation to tread a turn with her. But all the time I see Arago has the best of it ; he gets most of the dances : though once, as I guide her to the strains of the Faust waltz, Eve adds to the brightness of its music one ray of sunshine. Her lips whisper : "Come and see me to-morrow, Billy,"

"And why?" I mutter savagely.

"We've not *half* finished our reminiscences."

"What time?" I ask eagerly.

"About three o'clock." This is said consideringly.

I consider also, and remember Arago's hours of duty

must keep him at the Quartermaster-General's all the next afternoon.

" Very well," I answer briskly, and leave her, not wishing to commence the campaign with too much ardor; though I cannot stand and see her dancing every other figure with that cursed Creole, who seems so ineffably pleased with his success over me. As for the young lady, she is now making play with two or three old general officers in a way that surprises me.

As I bid Mrs. Bream a hasty adieu, my hostess whispers : "A little more difficult than you reckoned ? eh, my captain ? My niece is not picked up again as easily as you imagined." And she casts a significant glance towards the fairylike creature, who is now chatting with old Broughton of the engineers.

Strolling from the *fête* in the early morning light, as I walk to my F Street boarding-house I hear the rattle of drums and the tramp of boys in blue. A regiment of infantry, on its march through the city to cross the Long Bridge, and join contending armies in Virginia, blocks my path. Waiting for this to pass, I am joined by old Broughton, that old engineering authority having tramped after me from Mrs. Bream's.

" Awfully jolly shindig, young man ; regular Kentucky frolic !" he babbles to me, made loquacious by champagne. " Yankee Doodle! how the girls danced that Virginia reel ! Did you see me foot it with that little Ashley witch? Hang me, sir, I made a hit with her ! Nothing would do, but old Broughton must take her out on the balcony ; her bright eyes wanted a little more of him. What she doesn't know about pontoon bridges now—ain't worth knowing. She's smart and cute as a vivandiere, and beautiful as a topographical map, sir. By heaven, you should have seen her pretty lips as she lisped : ' Dear General, how long a bridge will cross the Rappahannock ? ' Guessed Burnside's movement—guessed it like a major-general ! And my God, what shoulders and arms ! Reminds me of Dolly Madison, sir, when I was a plebe—the belle of the army, sir ! "

But Broughton's remarks don't make much impression upon me at the time, though as I watch the venerable military scientist turn up Pennsylvania

Avenue, it seems to me curious that Miss Ashley should be interested in pontoon bridges,

Then I go home; but *not* to sleep. My soft couch is harder than any bivouac ground I have ever lain upon. I toss about my pillows. A Secret Service suspect! Good heavens, what curious bond is there between Eva Ashley and Henri Dubois Arago? Why is she grateful to *him* ?

CHAPTER XV.

THE CIGAR STORE NEAR THE WAR-DEPARTMENT.

I DETERMINE to investigate him. Making inquiries in a casual way, so as not to attract attention, I discover that Mr. Arago has been representing his cotton syndicate in Washington ever since General Butler captured New Orleans—that is, for something over six months—having arrived at the capital bringing strong letters of recommendation on account of his activity in disclosing concealed Rebel arms in New Orleans, and Rebel cotton in the surrounding parishes. In the course of the next two months,—by political influence that the cotton-stealers who have grown rich out of this business have brought to bear,—Mr. Arago has received appointment as a clerk in the Quartermaster-General's office, and rapidly risen in that department on account of executive ability as well as general attention to his duties.

He has no funds of the government in his hands, therefore no attention is paid to his conspicuous pursuit of the goddess of chance in the great gambling-rooms of Washington, it being generally considered that the Creole's wad of greenbacks comes from his portion of the profits of the cotton-stealing gang.

He has apparently been on visiting terms at Mrs. Bream's for four or five months, and probably made Miss Ashley's acquaintance at the home of her aunt. Aside from his love of play, nobody has anything to say against him; and his faro and poker everybody seems to think is his business, not theirs.

From all accounts he is well in favor with the powers

that be, one gentleman giving me a start by remarking : "By Jingo I think he's even in touch with Baker's Secret Service Department."

"What makes you think that?" I ask.

"Why, I'm inclined to imagine that he kept them from pulling, one evening, Jake Burner's second class gambling-house, that has brought a few paymasters to ruin."

If this is so, I reflect, Arago must have a good deal of influence with Baker's Secret Service, for that officer generally does his work with grim severity, whenever he gets a chance at gambling-houses that rob Uncle Sam's boys of their money, the houses of ladies who steal virtue from the soldiers, and the general vices of the capital, doing this with the same haughty disregard of constitutional rights that pervades his treatment of copperhead newspapers, democratic politicians and any other persons or things the government desires to squelch.

But in the afternoon my thoughts of Mr. Arago are practically driven out of my mind by the charms, witcheries and allurements of Miss Ashley.

At the time appointed, I call at the Lafayette Square residence, and find I have one tremendous advantage over my rival. My entire time is my own ; his is naturally circumscribed by the duties of his office. While he is making out quartermaster's requisitions, I can fight Cupid's battle, and, thanks to Lucy Bream, have the delights of *tête-à-tête* in which to do it.

Miss Ashley receives me with unaffected ease. Still, all this day there is a latent air of triumph about her. Sometimes I wonder if it is not triumph over me ; for she must know that, no matter how remiss I had been as a lover to Eva Ashley, I am a regular Romeo to my ex-captive of that Potomac night. This I practically suggest to her, though not in direct words.

To this she remarks, blushing a little : "Yes ; that is a very pleasant way of excusing yourself. But do you know, I like to think of you best as the little boy——"

"Great Scott! In pinafores?" I laugh.

"Yes ; the little boy who guarded me, though he did it in a very lordly way."

"Guarded *you*?" I say, astonished.

"Why, yes. Don't you remember when at school I got into trouble, who assumed my woe? Billy Hamilton! When by accident I tore Webster's dictionary, who got up and lied for me and said *he* did it? Who took from the awful Miss Priscilla Sturgess, the austere Yankee schoolmarm, the whacking that should have fallen on my shoulders? Billy Hamilton! Who trounced Sammy Jones, because he teased me? Billy Hamilton!" And her eyes look more gratefully at me than they had done the evening before; but not so gratefully, I think, as they had gazed upon Arago once or twice the preceding night.

Still, if she wants to make a hero of me, though I've forgotten about it, I'm agreeable.

Then *I* commence to remember also. What a darling little witch Eva was at school—how I had, in the conceited manner of the *big* boy, extended my protection over the *little* girl—how I had *permitted* her to love me. With this comes the disconcerting thought: "Hang it, *I'm* doing the loving now!"

One reminiscence leads to another. We get to chatting of old times, and finally I lead her to Frederick Town, and that night on the Potomac.

But here she stops me with low voice: "As a great favor to me, I beg you to forget that, and never to speak of it." There is a nervousness in her manner that frightens me, linked as it comes into my mind with the request of the Secret Service Department.

"Certainly, your wishes are my command," I murmur, though I cannot help wondering if she didn't visit a Confederate sweetheart, why does Eva Ashley care so much to have that episode in her life obliterated? "You know, of course," I add, "I shall never mention this again."

"Please, never do."

"Though I can't help thinking of you," I whisper, "with the sunshine playing about you, as you stroked Roderick's mane."

"Roderick? Ah, your handsome charger!" Her eyes have lighted with the fire of the Southern horsewoman. "Where is he now?"

"Eating his oats, I presume, comfortably in the stable. And Bonny Belle, your pretty half-Arab mare?"

With twitching lips, the girl mutters : "I have sold her—sold my Bonny Belle," and her beautiful eyes grow full of unshed tears.

"Sold her ! " I ejaculate.   "Why ? "

"Because—can't you guess it—we, in Virginia, are so very poor ! You do not know what the troops whose uniform you wear have done to us ; how they have oppressed us ! " And the fire in her eyes burns up their tears.

Then she checks herself and mutters, wringing her hands slightly : "But I must not think of our wrongs. I am here—far away from troubles of that kind. I might be rich—God bless Aunt Lucy's kind heart !—but my pride won't let me accept too much, even from her. Though this little gown is her present to me." And she glances at the pretty but unpretentious dress she is wearing, that, decking her exquisite figure, becomes as beautiful as any robe invented by French modiste.

"'Though we won't speak of Bonny Belle," I remark "I cannot help thinking of you and Roderick, when you played with my charger's mane, and my hand accidentally touched yours." I look at her dimpled member with its delicate, white, patrician fingers, and think I have played a master-stroke.

But I have not !

" Ah, but then I reminded you," the young lady says, "that you had a betrothed you had *forgotten*," and her glance grows stern and haughty. Here she falters, her face ablaze with blushes : "No—no ; I don't mean that."

"Ah yes, you do. Betrothed—that is the word between you and me."

"Yes," she says sarcastically. "The betrothed you had forgotten."

" But still *betrothed !* "

" Not *at present !* " She draws herself up haughtily, then looks at me, I think, savagely and sadly.

" You will not let me use that term to you ? "

" Not until you have done a good deal more to earn it than you have so far. Do you think it has been pleasant to my pride to think you had tossed me from even your memory ? "

" But I had not forgotten you, I was always thinking of the girl in the gray riding-habit."

This touch perchance makes her slightly more com-plaisant to me ; but as I look at her I can see I am go-ing to have no favored lover's privileges. Those lips that are so tempting, seem a thousand miles away.

Just at this moment, Lucy Bream comes in and startles me by saying : "Good gracious, you here yet, Billy ? "

"Holy poker, do you begrudge me a few minutes ! You're not as hospitable as you were last night," I laugh.

"Is n't two hours long enough for a *first* interview ? " she laughs. "Have you persuaded Eva that she once loved a little boy ? "

Then, oh, the blushes on the face I am gazing at !

But the girl says lightly : "It is of such little conse-quence—loving *little* boys. Loving men is the more important matter."

But here perhaps a little of the coquette coming into her pansy eyes, Miss Eve gives me one ray of hope. She whispers to the matron : "Can I invite him ? "

"Certainly."

"To-morrow evening we're going to the theatre, Billy. Would you like to join us in our box at Ford's ? "

"Wouldn't I? I could sit through a whole perform-ance, only looking at your shoulders."

At this the two ladies burst into merriment, as I, a latent hope in my heart, glancing at my watch, find I have been there two hours.

Shaking both ladies by the hand, I note Lucy Bream's clasp is cordial and Miss Ashley's but an endured salu-tation.

Out in the avenue, I mutter to myself : " A long siege, much strategy, and then a desperate assault, before that citadel can be retaken."

Ah, Billy Hamilton ! When you let a child's love pass away from you, you did not know how precious the woman's would become !

During half an hour's walk, I decide upon my plan of campaign. First and foremost, I must make Eve love me—if I can? Second, I must destroy Arago's influence over her, whatever it is—if possible?

I continue my investigations in regard to that gentleman, but with unsatisfactory results. True, he is a gambler, but many dashing, high-spirited young men of that day were votaries of cards and chance, and nobody thought the worse of them for it.

Still, I think I will see a little more of the gentleman than I have lately ; but during the day this is difficult to do, for Arago, and for that matter Finnaker and all in the Quartermaster-General's office, are very busy.

Late on Friday night, however, I discover him at Chamberlin's. Arago is playing as usual, and to my astonishment seems to feel the strain of the game. At least he is nervous—an emotion he has never displayed at faro before, though I have seen him play for higher stakes.

On seeing me, however, he seems to become jovial, and giving up the green table, we two take a drink together. During this he jokes : " Been to see your old friend Baker again, eh ? "

" No," I laugh ; " you need not miss another shot at billiards on his account ; " and rather think I may startle him.

But to my dismay, the Creole's eyes light up with a triumph he cannot conceal. He becomes extraordinarily happy and jovial, even laughs with me at his losing his money at billiards to such a duffer as Finnaker. Then producing his cigar-case, he proffers in his light, elegant and winning Southern manner, one of his famous *Bouquets Especiales*, in fact, presses two or three upon me, saying : " You looked a little surly, my dear fellow, when I took her away from you to supper the other evening ; but you must get accustomed to that." His eyes grow luminous, and sensuous ; in his imagination I am sure he sees the girl I love and *sees her as his own*.

" I am not accustomed to getting used to anything I don't like, Mr. Arago, and I object to your tone to me," I remark coolly but imperiously.

" Ah then, please accept my apologies. I beg your pardon," he murmurs, so humbly that I am compelled to receive his *amende*. Anyway, I can't quarrel about her in a gambling-house. But even as I do so, I catch his Creole glance once more, and it shocks me. Into his eyes has come a look of pity, perhaps even contempt ; he seems to think me but a poor opponent in the game he is playing. For somehow it strikes me that the triumph in his eyes comes not alto-

gether from his success over me in the ball-room with
Eva Ashley.   He seems to have suddenly taken upon
himself a renewed and most buoyant confidence entirely unwarranted by the slight advantages of escorting Miss Ashley to supper and getting the most of her
dances at Mrs. Bream's *soirée*.

As I leave him, for now he seems to waste but little
attention upon me, having returned to his faro game,
crying vivaciously: "I put fifty on the queen, and
copper the jack with twenty!"   I know that Henri
Dubois Arago and I are enemies.

Going home I turn the matter over in my mind, and
this curious suggestion strikes me like a rifle-shot.   The
Creole knew I had instructions from the Secret Service
office in regard to the young lady I had captured at
Norton's Ford ; my foolhardy information to him as I
made my billiard test has shown Arago that !   In some
way he knows that Eva Ashley is the girl I captured
on the Potomac ; furthermore, he must be aware I
have recognized her at Mrs. Bream's as my ex-captive.
I have told him I have not seen Baker ; *ergo*, I have
not reported my discovery.   Perhaps my negligence
in this makes him think he has a hold upon me.

This view of the matter seems a very serious one,
as I reflect that every day I fail to report my discovery
of the girl I met at Frederick to Uncle Sam's detective
bureau, the greater chance Arago has of placing me
under the suspicion and condemnation of the War
Office, who have made me their spy.

"By Jove, they may put me in the old Capital prison—that *would* give him a fair field," I cogitate rue-
fully.   But dissecting this idea the second time, I
throw away any thought of immediate annoyance to
Miss Ashley or danger to myself on this point, as Arago
has seemed as anxious as I to shield the young lady
from scrutiny or surveillance, if his remark about the
Treasury young lady indicates anything.

Anyway, though the concealment of her identity
may bring annoyance, perhaps condemnation upon
me, she, standing under the very wings of the great
War Senator, who I know is truckled to for his vote,
eloquence and influence by the government itself, who
is regarded as strong a Union man as any War-Senator
or War-Governor in the land—the niece of his wife, an

inmate of his household—the most that can come to Eva Vernon Ashley will be a most polite request to kindly visit Mr. Stanton in company with her aunt and tell him of her movements during that September evening. "Dash it!" I laugh, "she's as safe as if she lived in the White House! Besides—egad!" I continue, "I can shield myself under her wing. I have but to mention that though I discovered the young lady, I found that she was of such loyal standing, so intimately connected with the patriotic Senator Bream, that I did not wish to bring his family under any slur that might come to them from Baker's too alert detectives."

"By Jove, with the Senator standing by me, I can rout every government spy from here to Michigan!" I laugh, and grow rather merry over this matter.

Smoking the last of Arago's fine cigars the next morning, it suddenly occurs to me I'll have a box or two of these for myself, and incidentally see what Mr. Bermudas says about his customer.

Consequently, about eleven o'clock on Saturday morning, I wander into the cigar store next to Mulloy's Generals' Bar-room. This has not so many brigadiers in it as on previous occasions. Some of them have gone to the front, for the army is now in motion; the rest of them are mighty busy in forwarding supplies to it and on general staff duties.

The little cigar-store is very much like any other little cigar-store. It has the inevitable wooden figure of the Indian chief in front of it and, apparently to reduce the rent, a bootblack's stand in the back portion of the shop, at which a darkey, as I make my purchases, is polishing boots at five cents a shine. I am waited upon by Señor Bermudas himself. To him I mention my name, stating Mr. Arago had advised me to try his particular brand of cigars.

"*Caspita!* he's a very good customer," says Bermudas, a genial-mannered Cuban, with a voice soft and soothing as the smoke of his own cigars.

"Here are the *Bouquets Especiales*—Colorado you wish, Señor Capitan?" he remarks.

Making my selections, I take from a box I purchase, a few cigars for my case. With one in my mouth, I turn about for a light.

"Here, Quashie," cries Bermudas. "Fire for the Señor."

At his word the boot-black, who has just finished shining an under-Treasury clerk's shoes, steps to me. As I light my cigar nonchalantly I gaze at him. "By the Lord, Cuffy," I cry, in the careless tone of one addressing a nigger, "You have got a smashed eye!" For the appearance of one side of the black's face is something terrific.

"'Deed I has, Massa," mutters the black promptly. "Yo'd t'ink yo' had one too, if a damn U. S. Guberment mule smacked you in de jaw wid his behind hoof. Ef yo' don't believe me, yo' jest get behind one of Massa Linkum's teams down near Twenty-secon' an' G Streets."

"Yes, we must all look out for Uncle Sam. He kicks hard and strong," I laugh, thinking perhaps to give Señor Bermudas, who is suspected of secession proclivities, a timely warning.

So, followed by a little laugh from two or three lounging purchasers or bystanders, I take my way, carrying two boxes of cigars, smoking which I shall spend some of the most terrific hours that ever came to any man.

One of these comes to me this very night!

About eight o'clock in the evening I stroll down F Street, and turning along Tenth come to Ford's Theatre, a plain stuccoed building, which nearly three years afterwards was brought into most melancholy prominence by the assassination of our nation's President after he had done his work upon the earth.

At present this little theatre is a scene of happy merriment and boisterous laughter.

Though Saturday is technically called "Niggers' night" in the South, a good-sized audience is present, many of them officers ; the enormous local garrison, which generally numbers twenty-five thousand men, assuring that.

Among the blue uniforms and black coats are scattered a good many ladies, quite a contingent of them young, charming and beautiful, but none so lovely as the fair girl who sits beside pretty Mrs. Bream in stage-box A, the two ladies being well backgrounded by the massive form of the truculent War-Senator, who is behind them in black broadcloth coat, cut rather too big for him, his low velvet vest displaying a border-state expanse of rumpled and crumpled shirt-front.

As I enter, a burst of laughter greets me. Every one is enjoying John E. Owen in his marvellous role of "Solon Shingle" in *The People's Lawyer*. The next moment I join the box party, greet Mrs. Bream and her niece, shake hands with the Senator, and seat myself behind Miss Ashley's statuesque shoulders. But get little attention from her, for all through the piece she is laughing till the tears run down her fair cheeks—as for that matter, so are the whole of us, the Senator swallowing a chew of tobacco in his uproarious merriment.

Between the acts we all get to chatting together—for a moment on the play ; afterwards on other matters. Glancing at the audience, Mr. Senator Bream remarks : "I think I'll go down and see poor General Braxton."

"Yes," titters his spouse. "*Poor* General Braxton is getting up to go out. But why do you call him *poor ?*"

"Well, the unfortunate fellow's got a secesh wife. She drives him to drink."

"And how about the unfortunate secesh wife ?" remarks Miss Ashley suddenly and sarcastically ; then laughs : "I hope, Uncle Rufus, that you don't make Aunt Lucy's having been born in Virginia an excuse for visiting bar-rooms."

"Not the slightest, my dear. I visit them *without* excuse," chuckles the Senator ; then whispers, laying an affectionate hand upon his spouse's shoulder : "I have perfect confidence in the patriotism of my wife and the unfaltering loyal Unionism of my dear little niece." With this the political magnate strolls out of the box, leaving Miss Ashley with very red cheeks and a kind of spasm of anguish in her eyes.

Suddenly she breaks out upon me, as if to get something out of her mind : "You have not told me, my Union Provost-Marshal, how you left your father, and dear Virginia, and sweet little Birdie in Baltimore."

"Oh, they're quite well, I believe, especially Birdie. I haven't seen much of them since I became sponsor for their loyalty," I mutter.

"Why *especially* Birdie ?" asks the girl astonished.

Thus adjured, I recklessly run into a narrative of my return to my family, my posing as trooper in the Jeff Davis' Confederate Legion, my stories of Major Ananias's dashing rides with Stuart's cavalry, the awful catastrophe that came upon me when it was announced that I had been appointed Union Provost-Marshal, and from this I pass into a description of handsome Arthur Vermilye, of the artillery, one of my brother officers, winning, with my connivance, sweet little Birdie's love.

During this, Mrs. Bream has laughed heartily several times, but here her niece startles and horrifies me. I *think* I hear her sigh out : "What an ineffable apostate ?"

"Oh, you needn't look so severe, Miss," laughs the aunt. "Supposing Miss Birdie does elope, it's an awfully good match for her."

But the girl, tapping the rail of the box with her fan, nervously, murmurs : "Dear, *weak* little Birdie."

"*Weak*, in gaining handsome Captain Vermilye for a husband?" ejaculates Lucy Bream.

Here the girl astounds us both. She swings round on us, her eyes blazing, and remarks : "Weak, in not making Captain Vermilye jump over to *her* side of the fence to woo her, instead of her crawling through the hedge to *his* political pasture." Then she goes on, her face seeming inspired by some subtle emotion : "Every girl in this war should at least make one convert."

"What convert?" I ask.

"*The man who loves her!* Every girl should at least do that. Her arms should only go round the man whose heart throbs with her heart—whose triumph is her joy!"

"Humph!" I jeer. "That depends upon who loves the strongest."

"Ah! Who—loves—the—strongest." This is sighed out. Then, looking into my face, she half sneers : "Who loves the strongest will be the weakest in patriotism, eh, Captain Hamilton?"

But I have no chance to answer this. The Senator comes in, wiping his moustache, the curtain goes up, the house breaks into screams of laughter at John E. Owens in that roaring farce, *The Live Indian.*

But after this is over, as the green curtain falls, Miss Ashley turns to me, and, with curious change in her manner, permits me to cloak her. As my hands tremble arranging the draperies about the beautiful shoulders, she gazes at me with a look that makes my heart beat very fast. "Thank you, Billy," she murmurs. "Now you remind me of the little boy that took such good care of the little girl."

It is not the speech, but the manner of it that causes me to walk on air ; that makes the theatre, half empty now, its plain seats and benches in full view, seem Elysium, as I offer my arm to Eva Ashley and follow Mrs. Bream and her husband from the box. For there is a confiding clutch in the little hand that is on my arm, and the graceful head seems to nestle very close to my shoulder, as we come down the few stairs and step out into the lobby.

A moment later I put her into the carriage, and she gives me another joy. Mrs. Bream suggests : "We are to have a little quiet supper at home ; won't you join us ?"

"Yes, won't you, Captain Hamilton ?" comes to me in Eve's voice pleadingly.

For answer, I step in beside her and am, for a short hour, the happiest man in Washington ; for at the little supper-party my goddess seems to have become like the girl that morning at Frederick—free, unaffected, sweet to me.

I bid them good-bye, and she, running out in the hall after me, whispers : "To-morrow, take me to church—won't you, Billy?"

"With Mrs. Bream ?"

"No ; all by ourselves. I am an Episcopalian."

"Then if you're an Episcopalian, so am I," I answer. "What is *your* church is *my* church."

"Ah—then what is *my*——" but whatever is in her mind, she checks herself, and extending a gracious hand, says shortly : "Good-night."

This time it is not an endured salutation. Her soft white fingers clasp mine as I look into her eyes ; but these droop under my glance ; her beautiful head is turned slightly away, in graceful bashfulness.

"Good-night," she murmurs, and as if afraid of herself, runs from me.

· "Good-night," I say, my eyes on fire, my soul in heaven ; and though the night is dark, I walk home amid sunshine.

As I stride along Lafayette Square, I cogitate : "What the devil has caused this change in her?" But whatever it is, I don't care ; it makes me happy.

Arriving at my F Street boarding-house, I sit down, and over one of Arago's exquisite *Bouquets Espéciales* I chuckle : "By hookey, my Quartermaster-General's clerk, you haven't much chance when you run against a cavalry boy. Anyway, I'm in heaven ! "

CHAPTER XVI.

SPECIAL ORDER NO. 1410.

INTO this heaven suddenly comes the roll of war !

Little Finnaker, hardly waiting for my cheery "Come in," enters the room, his face pale, his eyes excited. "I—I couldn't sleep, I'm so flabbergasted," he whispers. "There's the devil to pay with *us !* "

"What is it ? "

"This is *dark*—but it's hell ! "

"Well, what's the row now ? "

"This is most strictly private ! "

"Have I ever blabbed of your pontoon order? "

"It's about *that !* My God, there's the devil to pay ! You heard me tell you that we sent down a special requisition number 1410, to the Depot Quartermaster, calling for eighty pontoons and two thousand feet of bridge, to be got ready at once ? "

"Yes, certainly."

"Well, special order 1410 to Depot Quartermaster has been forged or altered. Lee'll get to Fredericksburg before our pontoon trains—and then God help Burnside ! "

"A special order of the Quartermaster-General's forged or altered ! " I gasp. "Impossible ! I know their checks and routine."

"Don't fly off ; listen to me ! " breaks in Finnaker. "This evening—only an hour ago—we sent down to ask Depot Quartermaster when he would have requisition 1410 ready. Curse it, he knocked us off our feet. He replied that requisition No. 1410 had been filled and ready to start for two days. This astounded *us*, eighty pontoons and two thousand feet of bridge got ready in a few hours. Meigs sent me down to see about it. At the depot I found there were only *eight* pontoons and *two hundred feet* of bridge—good Lord, just a tenth of the order. What use is that to bridge the Rappahannock at Fredericksburg?"

"Then it *is* Fredericksburg?" I say, chewing the end of my cigar.

"Yes, we know it now in the department."

"But how did the mistake occur?"

"That's the devilish part of it. Our order-book copy reads eighty pontoons in both letters and figures, and two thousand feet of bridge in both letters and figures; and the requisition received and on file at the Depot Quartermaster's reads eight, in both letters and figures, of pontoons, and two hundred feet, in both letters and figures, of bridge. Those eighty pontoons should have moved to-morrow; at the latest, on Monday. You know, Burnside has started his command to-day; the pontoons were to have met his advanced divisions at Fredericksburg, and Sumner's army corps was to have *immediately* crossed and instantly entrenched itself in the heights beyond; then the crossing of the rest of the army would have been assured. Now, if Lee gets there before the pontoons, Burnside is blocked."

"But how did the mistake occur?" I ask, running through my mind the usual military formula of the Quartermaster-General's office, which would certainly prevent it.

"The order left us all right; of that we're certain! I myself and two other clerks saw Arago give it to Lommox. That damned Irish traitor is under arrest now, for just as sure as Lommox delivered the requisition that is now at the Depot Quartermaster's it reads *eight* pontoons and *two hundred* feet of bridge."

"Lommax a traitor?" I cry. "Nonsense! He is as blundering and honest an Irishman as ever lived! How long did he take to deliver the order?"

"He reported back in ten minutes; six going and four returning."

"That's quick enough; five good long blocks each way, after dark, in streets crowded as they are round the Quartermaster's depot."

"Yes," remarks Finnaker. "That's the devil of it! The orderly made about the right time, and it's certain that requisition could not have been changed or forged in a moment. The order reads,—so they tell me—all right, as regards penmanship, at the Depot-Quarter-master's office."

"What does Lommax say?"

"He says nothing, but curses low and deep, and repeats that he received the order at 6 : 45 and delivered it at 6 : 51 P. M. as shown by the receipts."

"Then the trouble is with Arago," I cry, anxious to make things hard for my Creole rival.

"Nonsense! I and another clerk stood by Arago as he copied it. While it was drying, he went off to wash his hands and ran over to Bermudas's for a few cigars. When he came back we had it sealed in the envelope and I walked out with him and saw him deliver it to Lommax. We were chatting together about something else at the time."

"Did Arago call your attention to his folding up the order?"

"Hang it. He didn't fold the order. I folded it in the presence of Wilkins, the other clerk. My eyes never left the envelope till I saw Arago deliver it to Lommox. I can swear to it; Arago's all right; it's that damned Irish traitor *certain!*" He always looks saucily at me when I boss him; he's a disloyal scoundrel sure as poor Colonel Ellsworth died in my arms."

"Pooh," I mutter, "Lommox has risked his life on too many battlefields to be called traitor now. How does Arago take it?"

"Beautifully! He's cool as a julep! It is the big guns that are raging. Stanton's over at our office, giving us all fury. Meigs is raising the deuce with his assistants—and they are giving their clerks glory halle-lujah! As for the Depot-Quartermaster, he says stiffly he obeyed orders as he got 'em and he don't care a cuss for anybody."

"What are they doing?"

" Working like beavers—they'll get the pontoon train off by the 20th, and it may get there in time, but I doubt it—especially if it rains and makes the roads bad—you know Virginia mud."

"Where's Lommox?"

"At his quarters, under arrest and cautioned to say nothing about it. That's the cue of all of us. Good lord, if the newspapers get hold of it—flaming head-lines "ANOTHER BLUNDER!"—"PROVISIONAL GOVERN-MENT," and all that, don't you see! As for Stanton, I heard him say, ' By the God of Heaven, when I catch the traitor who did this I'll hang him high enough for the whole Army to see him, and Lee's Army too! My lord! the way he looked make my blood run cold, and I've been in four pitched battles, I have. So keep it *dark*. Keep it *close*. But then I know I can trust you as I would myself!"

"Better!" I say grimly as Finnaker goes off ex-citedly.

The affair, though it interests me, doesn't excite me very much. If the pontoons don't reach Burnside in time and he finds Lee ahead of him and intrenched, he must turn back and try another way to Richmond. I reflect as I puff cigar smoke about me. For at this time, I did not guess the tremendous political and popular pressure that would be brought to bear on that doomed commander to force him on to the awful disaster of Fredericksburg—when, on that dread night of the thirteenth of December, had Stonewall Jackson's advice been followed Lee would probably have made an end of the Army of the Potomac and perhaps the American Union also.*

As it is, my mind chiefly turns to the predicament of the honest Irish sergeant. "Poor devil Lommox," I mutter. "Lommox!" What were the words I heard Arago whisper that evening to the girl at the corner of Thirteenth & E Streets? "*Make sure I shall give the despatch to Lommox!*" The lady on the corner of Thir-teenth & E Streets was Miss Eva Ashley!

My God, the girl I love!"

Then suddenly Mr. Arago's exquisite *Bouquet Espé-ciale* becomes bitter as gall in my mouth—the room grows dark to me! O powers of Heaven! what a

* See Appendix.—ED.

night I spend !   What can I do—if my half-formed
fears are correct?

Nothing !—at all events, nothing for the present.

I try to sleep but cannot, and the next morning going
desperately to the Lafayette Square mansion have my
anxieties practically knocked out of me.

In answer to my card, Miss Eve floats down to the
parlor looking beautiful as a Venus, fresh as a wood
nymph and innocent as an angel.   Dressed in some
light walking dress, for this Indian-summer day is
warm and balmy, she seems to me a fairy, beneficent
and charming.   "She might carry a little information
between lines," I reflect as I look her over with lover's
eyes : "many a Southern maid has done that !   But
block the march of the Army of the Potomac?—*Never !*"

Comforting myself with this conclusion, I address
myself to the object of my fears who stands before me,
a delicately-gloved hand extended cordially, but a
piquant pout on her coral lips, murmuring reproach-
fully : "Captain Brown-Study, you haven't said good-
morning."

"Haven't I ?" I say, with a start.

"No, and you haven't told me how you liked my
dress.   I made it myself," she goes on with that most
charming, subtle, and deadly coquetry to the masculine
heart—that I-lean-on-you business.—What you think
is right, *goes.*—You are so strong and I am so de-
pendent.

Ah, the power of woman through her very weakness !

Thus adjured I give the little hand a tender squeeze,
cast my eyes over the garment, and taking advantage
of my opportunity enjoy a beauty feast.

But perchance lingering too long over this, my enchantress bursts out laughing : "What do you know
about hoops, ruffles and flounces?   Oh, mercy, the
dragoon is trying to talk like Monsieur Worth, that
man-milliner in Paris."

Suddenly she brings to bear upon me another most
artful, yet potent feminine witchery.   She shows she
takes a profound *personal* interest in me ; she cries :
"Good Heavens, Billy !   You look as if you had been
up all night."

"No, I went home straight from you."

"Well, you look fearfully dissipated any way—I—"

here she grows bashful and diffidently suggests : "I hope you haven't been gambling at your own rooms," then sighs, "So many young men ruin themselves in that way."

Catching a glimpse of my face in a neighboring mirror, I perceive that a sleepless and intensely anxious night has given me a decidedly *roué* appearance this morning.

I can't tell her what caused it—at all events not until I have to speak to her to save her—so I mutter, with a little yellow laugh, "Well, take me to church, Miss Angel, and let the minister, exhort the dissipation out of me."

"Come !" and the girl leads the way out of the house towards St. John's.

It is scarcely a step, but in that moment Eva Ashley changes. Before, the bright girl of earth, she now becomes the protégée of Heaven.

As we enter the portals of the house of God, I know I love a truly good girl ; one who believes in her religion—one who loves her Redeemer. As the soft strains of the organ come to our ears, the beautiful eyes beam devoutly, the exquisite face grows more lovely because it grows more holy. Eva Ashley sinks down kneeling in the pew and whispers her petition to heaven and seems to pass away from earth's troubles and earth's passions. Throughout both service and sermon, I, and all other temporal things, seem apart from her. What sinner could fail to be impressed with such a saint ? And I—rough-riding cavalryman, curiously careless of spiritual things, as most of us were in those days, when death was so near to us—can't help praying with her and feeling in my heart I am not worthy of her. As most men do in the presence of women who are truly good.

But once in all that holy ceremonial I notice that a thought of the passions of the awful struggle of the outside world come to her and I observe her very closely. Though I pray with my devotee, I can't keep my eyes off her earthly loveliness. I note the graceful head crowned with its clustering curls, the superb contours of her gracefully developed figure ; every movement, as she kneels, displaying new beauty lines.

As I do this, my glance catches a little foot, highinstepped and perfect in outline and proportion, that has stolen out in its tight-fitting boot from beneath the crinolined skirt. For the life of me I can't keep my eyes off its beauties. The rector is praying for the success of the Union arms. Suddenly the little foot, that has been quiescent, for one moment taps nervously upon the church floor—then with a sudden shiver grows quiet again ; but Eva's body has drawn itself up from very force of emotion. I can see each beauty curve, extend itself, and her clasped hands clench themselves, —the girl is praying with all her heart and all her soul to the God of Battles. Do her petitions ascend to heaven in unison with her pastor's—or is she imploring heaven for victory of the Boys in Gray over the Boys in Blue, as many another Southern maiden prays this November Sunday?

She rises, and there is a new look in the beautiful face. The corners of the eyes have become drawn— the curves of the chiselled mouth are rigid—an unearthly self-devotion is in those delicate features.

Where have I seen that inspired radiance before? A shiver runs through me as I remember it was in an old picture of the Maid of Orleans.

That day, as we come out in the whispering crowd from the portals of the House of the God of Peace and Love into the presence of cruel war and the emblems of mighty contest—never absent in those dread days from the nation's capital, for orderlies are holding officer's chargers at the entrance of St. John's Church, and ambulances are waiting for the wives and daughters of generals in the field, and across the square an infantry regiment is tramping to the front, its band playing "John Brown's Body"—I catch a little nervous flutter of the graceful hands that hold the prayer-book.

Gazing on the beauty at my side, I meditate : "My Heaven ! Is Eva Ashley a 'Joan of Arc?'" My mind suddenly opens. I see that here is a girl who has the soul to do great things.

A platoon of cavalry comes galloping up as we descend the steps. They halt, the lieutenant springs off his horse and advances toward us.

My fears for her make me a coward. I think it is a Provost guard. The little hand on my arm seems to clench itself, but the face is calm as a martyr's.

Dashing Molly Bent comes laughing down the steps behind us. She speaks to Eva. I give a start. My Maid of Orleans is discussing with her friend the latest fashions.

The Lieutenant has just saluted a Major-General, The cavalry is only the escort of some corps or division commander, to guard him on his ride to histroops in Virginia.

For the first time in my life I feel I have nerves. But I must know—for her safety I *must* know.

After a few salutations to some legation chaps and one or two young officers who will have word with her, Miss Ashley, getting out of the throng, walks blithely by my side. We are near Senator Bream's front door. the girl remarks casually : " Not so many gentlemen at church as ladies ? "

" No," I reply. " Were it not for you women the minister might shut up shop."

"That indicates you would *not* have come, had I not invited you, Billy."

"Certainly not ! This is the first time I have been to church for a year. Have you made many other other proselytes ? "

" A few," she half laughs. " Mr. Finnaker and Mr. Arago come sometimes at my solicitation."

"Ah, yes ; but the Quartermaster-General's Office is too busy to-day."

"Indeed ? "

" Yes ! " I see my chance and play my card desperately. " You know they got off that great pontoon train last night and this morning."

As my lie strikes the girl ; for one instant, a shivery shudder runs through her limbs ; her face grows pale and drawn, she passes her hand over her eyes as if the sun blinded them. Then drawing herself up as if to bear a blow, Eve, for one second, looks me straight in the face. What she sees there, I don't know—but her lips and cheeks regain their color, her eyes grow sunny, she innocently asks : " What pontoons ? " then not waiting for my answer, laughs : " You military men always think women are interested in your tactics. Are they going to build a bridge over in Virginia ? "

Great powers ! Am I so poor a liar ?—or is her glance into my heart deeper than I have guessed ?—or

is her information so *sure* on the subject, that she knows
I haven't told the truth?

I don't have much time to speculate on this, we are
already at Mrs. Bream's door.

"Can I take you out walking this afternoon," I ven-
ture.

For a moment the young lady looks as if she would
accept, then says, slightly embarrassed : "I—I would,
but unfortunately I—I have a prior engagement."

"With Mr. Arago?" I ask, both fear and jealousy
flying up in me.

"Y-e-s—I'm sorry." Then she gives me a crumb of
consolation. "You are going to Mrs. Judge Burton's
dance on Tuesday, I presume?" she asks, smiling at
me.

"No—I have not heard of it!"

"If I get you an invitation, will you take me?"

"With pleasure. Does Mrs. Bream go?"

"Perhaps yes—will you take *me* anyway?"

"Won't I!"

"Thank you." She extends her hand to bid me
good-bye, but I seize it and hold it, and whisper words
to her that I can't control as I look into the dear face.
"For God's sake, take good care of yourself."

"What do you *mean ?*" Her cheeks are pale and
eyes inquiring.

"What *don't* I mean!"

"And why?" A spasm of agony runs over her delicate features. Perhaps I am squeezing her little fingers
too hard.

"Because you're so dear to me—darling —! Forgive me—I can't help it—I *wouldn't* if I could—I *couldn't*
if I would."

"Oh mercy, what an ambiguous creature you are,
Billy!" laughs my enchantress mockingly, pulling her
hand away. "Goodness gracious, every one is look-
at you ; the street is crowded. Tuesday evening, nine
o'clock : I will get Mrs. Burton's invitation card for
you. Good-bye."

Then she frightens me.

I have made two steps down the vestibule stairs. A
hand is suddenly laid upon my arm, light as a feather.
A soft voice whispers in my ear very sadly, very tenderly : "You wouldn't care *too* much if anything

happened? You would forgive me—wouldn't you, Billy?"

I turn and catch the eyes, laden with unshed tears. Joy and rapture—in them is *love!* Despair and misery —in them is *agony!* But she flies from me; the door closes on the figure of my divinity.

I stagger down the steps and mutter: "God help me—I'm half sure now! What shall I do to save her?"

BOOK IV.

THE BATTLE FOR HER LIFE.

CHAPTER XVII.

I KNOW I won't get the facts out of her. God bless her dear heart, she wouldn't tell me; that would implicate me.

My one chance is Arago, and from what I have discovered of this gentleman's coolness, it would take the torture to open his lips. Still I will further investigate him.

All the afternoon I do this, though not effectively, for I dare not ask directly; everything must be insinuation, suggestion. I can only discover the Quartermaster-General's clerk has lots of money, which he says comes to him in gold drafts sent from England. This is perfectly in accord with his connection with the cotton syndicate; the market for that commodity is England; there they are paying enormous prices for the white fleece to keep their Manchester operatives from starving. Naturally Arago's profits would come from England. In addition I learn his luck at faro has lately been very bad.

Suddenly—it is astonishing what slight things a man grasps at when he is falling into an abyss—I am smoking gloomily—suddenly into my throbbing head flies a name, "Quashie?" Something connects "Quashie" with the girl I love.

"Quashie" gave me the light for the first of these *Bouquets Espéciales* I am smoking. Quashie, whose face had been half kicked off by a government mule; Quashie who—I have it! Quashie—that's the name of the darky servant who rode by Miss Ashley's side that night on the Potomac. It's a common enough cog-

nomen among plantation darkies ; still, I'll investigate
Quashie.

Though it is evening, I tramp over to Bermudas's
cigar-store and buy another box of the famed weeds.
Casually inquiring, I find that Quashie finished up his
boot-blacking early in the afternoon, and can discover
nothing more about him.

Returning gloomily to my room, but slight comfort
is brought to me by Mr. Finnaker. That little hero
comes bustling in, closes my door mysteriously, locks
it, sits down by my side and says : " I've stopped here
to smoke a cigar and talk things over with you." He
lights up one of my *Bouquets Espéciales*. " You know,
you're the only one we *dare* consult. We haven't got
any further in that altered special order No. 1410 business."

"Oh, the pontoons?" I remark, affecting a nonchalance I do not feel. "What are you doing about
it?"

"Well," he says, "we're shoving the work on 'em
day and night. We'll have the trains ready to start by
Thursday, the 20th ; we may get 'em to Burnside in
time, and—*we're keeping the matter very dark*. You
see, we're afraid of the infernal newspapers. If the
New York Herald knew of it, wouldn't Stanton tear his
beard—oh, my!" The little patriot gives a grimace of
disgust.

"Have you found the traitor who forged the false
requisition?" I ask, with apparent unconcern, though
my teeth meet in the end of my cigar.

"No, we have put that into Baker's hands; the
Secret Service is nosing that out," he whispered. "Let
Baker alone ; he'll smash the infernal rebel spy like a
mosquito."

"Yes, Baker is very acute," I mutter, with a shiver,
as Finnaker, having finished my cigar, leaves me.

"Too infernally acute!" I think, an hour afterwards, as I still smoke and ponder.

"No. 1410—special requisition—altered or forged
while passing from the Quartermaster-General's office
to the Depot-Quartermaster—the envelope in charge of
a trusty and true cavalry sergeant—and delivered over
five long city blocks in *six* minutes ! By heaven,
Lommox couldn't have got drunk and sober again in

that time ! It was no art of liquor that did this. Pish !
no delicate girl could have executed such superb strategy. Arago must be the guilty one !" I laugh to myself half hysterically. "Still, why her anguish, her
anxiety ?"

I cannot sleep ; it is no use to go to bed. I step out
and pace the streets, and my steps will lead me towards
one house in Washington. As I stride past on the opposite side of the street, there are lights in the parlors
of Senator Bream's mansion. It is too late to call,
otherwise I would go in. Round Lafayette Square I
go half a dozen times.

On my sixth circuit, on Fifteenth Street, somewhere
between H and G, I think it is, I encounter Arago.
He is apparently on his way from Eva Ashley ; he has
doubtless heard her voice within the minute. Jealousy, hatred and distrust flame up in me.

"Taking a walk, Captain ?" he says, after a few
words of polite greeting.

"Yes," I reply.

"Where are you going, this fine night ?"

"Anywhere."

"Oh, very well, come with me, and we'll have supper at Chamberlin's and a dash of faro."

"I'm your man !" I answer.

Perhaps in his company some of my vague, yet torturing, suspicions will take more definite form. Anyway, in the excitement of play, I may forget—for a
minute.

We stroll towards Chamberlin's together. "Are
you going to Mrs. Judge Burton's hop on Tuesday
evening ?" I ask for want of other topics.

"I think so," he remarks nonchalantly. "And you ?"

"Oh, certainly. I have the pleasure of escorting
Miss Eva Ashley."

This touches him ! He has not heard this before, I
can see by the angry expression of his face. He is
about to burst out—perhaps I shall get a better hint
from his rage than his suavity—but he suddenly checks
himself, and murmurs, in rather sarcastic tones : "Then
I congratulate you upon the prospect of a very *pleasant* evening."

"Will **you** try a cigar ?" I say, in equally polite
voice.

"No! *Diable, yes!* That is what I have been wanting. Thank you. I see you are smoking my brand."

"Yes; I took your hint." Then some despairing inspiration flying into me, I continue: "I went to Bermudas's and selected my cigars yesterday. By-the-bye, they've got a darky boot-black over there who, I should think, was a terrible fighter."

"Indeed?"

"Yes, Mr. Quashie has got the most fearful eye I ever saw on any nigger. Curious name too: I don't suppose I should remember it, if I hadn't met a darky of the same cognomen, one September night on the Potomac under rather peculiar circumstances."

Have I struck a rift in his armor? The Creole's hands tremble as he lights his cigar. But he steadies himself, and remarks nonchalantly: "Yes, Quashie is rather a common name among our contrabands, I believe."

We are at the door of the great gambling-house. "On second thoughts I don't think I'll go in," I say.

"Ah, changed your mind about playing?"

"Yes, I feel a little done up to-day."

"Very well; good-bye. I wish you a pleasant evening at Mrs. Judge Burton's." There is a nasty and sarcastic sneer on his face as he says this and steps into the brilliantly lighted rooms. I turn away, walk home and think of "Quashie"—and her danger.

I go to bed and try to sleep, to keep my mind calm for the morrow. But when I sleep, I dream horrible things.

Early the next morning, rising unrefreshed, I bolt a hasty meal and walk over to Bermudas's cigar-store, thinking to find the darky, but Quashie is no more blacking boots, in fact his stand is gone. I am told Quashie has got tired of his job and gone off and joined an army sutler. To hunt for him, among the hundred thousand contrabands that loaf about the forts and camps and thoroughfares of the capital is a practical impossibility.

Early in the day I receive Mrs. Judge Burton's card of invitation. I think I will go up and thank Eva for it. That's the idea! Perhaps in her extremity she may confide in me.

To my concern Miss Ashley is not in, though I find

Mrs. Bream looking fresh and pretty, notwithstanding there is an air of latent anxiety about her.

"Eva's gone to visit Mrs. Rignold," she remarks.

"Ah! Far from here?"

"Yes, quite a distance, over towards the capitol, Massachusetts Avenue, near E Street."

"Don't you think I might stroll over and bring Miss Eve home?"

"Yes, if she'll let you?" smiles Lucy; then suddenly she breaks out on me: "What is the matter with the girl? Do *you* know?"

"No," I reply, summoning the arts of a diplomat. "Nothing serious, I hope. She—she isn't sick?"

"No, but there's some gimcrack on her mind."

"Since when?"

"Since last evening."

"What makes you think so?"

"She walked the floor of her chamber half the night. You've had nothing to do with it? You have not been playing fast and loose with her again?"

"On the contrary, she's been playing fast and loose with me," I say bitterly.

"Yes, you don't look over chipper yourself?" remarks the matron contemplatively. Then she makes my heart jump by saying: "These lover's quarrels!"

"O God, if that were all!" I think.

"Very well, run off and find her!" laughs Lucy. "I see you're anxious to bring her home."

With this I walk off; but at Mrs. Rignold's on Massachusetts Avenue, discover to my concern that Miss Ashley is not there and furthermore *has not been there*. At least, so the servant states at the door. My peace of mind is not added to by learning my sweetheart has some appointment she does not wish her aunt to know of—something she will even deceive her about.

I go back to Senator Bream's; Lucy has gone out; the young lady has not returned.

I call later in the evening. The Senator, his wife and niece, are away at dinner. I wander about aimlessly, but can do nothing.

The strain is commencing to tell upon me. Finnaker remarks it, as he strolls into my rooms late in the evening, when I am pacing the floor.

"You look seedy, my cavalryman," he observes.

"What you and I need is to be at *the front.* This absence from whizzing Minie balls and bursting shells is killing both of us;" then he suddenly breaks out : " By Bunker Hill, are you in love? I hear from Arago you took Miss Ashley to church yesterday. Very fetchy girl—very patriotic—very susceptible to the Quartermaster-General's office. If you don't believe me ask Arago."

" That's the first witness you have cited who hasn't been *dead*," I mutter savagely.

" Well, Arago may be soon—if work can do it; we're being ragged to death. That damned order !"

"Anything more about its miscarriage?"

"Nothing! Only we keep it close, sir : close as a percussion on the nipple of an Enfield. We've even released Lommox."

" Has the sergeant said anything further?"

"Not a word, I understand; simply sticks to his story—received the order at 6:45 and delivered it 6:51 P. M. as per receipts. Sometimes I think the Depot-quartermaster must be the disloyal villain. There's a traitor somewhere, but Baker'll have him—Baker'll have him !" With this he goes away, leaving me more miserable than ever. Jealousy is in my mind, as well as love and anxiety.

The next morning I discover that Baker is engaged in the matter.

A note is brought to me, directing my immediate presence at the Secret Service office. I go there; fortunately, my nerves are already braced for any blow.

I get one !

" I haven't got much time to give you, Captain Hamilton," says the head of Uncle Sam's spies. " But I thought I'd ask you if you had seen anywhere in Washington the young woman for whom I told you to keep your eye peeled."

" No," I reply ; " I don't think she is here. At all events, not in fashionable society."

" All right ; but there's been hell raised here lately."

" How?"

" That's my business. However, I think if the girl's here we'll surely find her; though I reckon she didn't have anything to do with this ; this is a little too gigantic for a woman. But still we want to see that girl; if she should be mixed up in this accursed treason, there's ten thousand dollars for all of us. So we've another society buck looking up things also. By-the-bye, it might be as well to consult with him; he's already landed *sub rosa* one or two lady Rebels in the Old Capitol prison. He may give you a point."

"Of course," I mutter. "We—we might hunt in couples."

"Quite right! I think you know him already."

Then the words that come to me from the chief of the Secret Service make my head buzz. "He is Henri Dubois Arago, one of the head-clerks in the Quartermaster General's office," says the detective. "By your face I see you know him."

"Don't I!" I contrive to stammer. "He—he plays a devil of a game of poker."

"Yes; too much for you, I can see by your phiz, Captain Hamilton."

"All right; I'll—I'll meet him at Mrs. Judge Burton's dance to-night, if not earlier."

"Very well; only look alive."

Then I walk out. The sun was shining as I stepped in—it seems dark as an eclipse now.

Ten thousand dollars for the life of my love! Arago an agent of the Secret Service! He has already delivered up to Uncle Sam's Justice some fair culprits! Good God, why is he sparing *her?* Anyway, he has me in his grip. He knows I have seen the girl for whom they are looking and recognized her; he knows that I have *not* reported my discovery to the Secret Service Bureau—furthermore, I have denied having seen her. But what do I care for *myself?* It is she for whom I tremble.

Still, in my confused mind struggles one ray of hope. Evidently the War Department wishes to keep this awful mistake, or accident, or blunder about the pontoons as quiet as possible for the present: that may be one element of her safety.

I look around the great city. I think of its encircling forts, its vast garrison, each bridge patrolled, every avenue of escape guarded with military discipline and martial rigidity, and mutter to myself: "Oh God, I am helpless!"

My almost aimless steps have taken me back to my boarding-house. Here another pang, another surprise of that awful day, comes to me. A letter in an unknown lady's hand is delivered.

I open it, and turn at once to the signature; it is from Miss Ashley: then I read, in rather trembling characters:

" MY DEAR BILLY :

" Pray heaven you don't misjudge me ! When I asked you to take me to Mrs. Burton's dance this evening, I had forgetton that I had made a previous engagement for the escort of Mr. Arago. He insists that I fulfil it; therefore I beg you don't come to my house for me.

" Still, for the love of heaven, don't let any pique, indignation or just anger at my inexcusable forgetfulness keep you from being at Mrs. Burton's to-night. Come, if you only come to quarrel with me —but *come!* It is vital to both of us, if you meant your few wild words when you last clasped my hand ! *Come if you mean them !*

" Yours,

" EVA.

" Don't try to see me this afternoon ; but *come to-night !* "

First, rage fills me. What hold has this cursed Creole that he should compel the girl I love to cancel her own request to me. By the Lord, is he threatening her? Why does she beg me not to come to her this afternoon? I clench my fist in jealous rage, as I reflect these are Arago's off-duty hours.

Then suddenly comes—over all my doubt and misery—one great joy. If the last part of Eva Ashley's letter means anything, it means *she loves me.* Can I be faithless to her in her extremity? Shall I prove to her that I *am* dastard, that I *was* liar, when I whispered in her ear last Sunday morning?

The climax is approaching. To save her I must be ready to act like lightning. What are the sinews of war—of love? Money ! I overhaul my funds available ; then go down to my bankers, and by pledging certain securities, have placed to my credit cash sufficient for almost any emergency.

This done, feeling I must regard my sweetheart's request and, fighting with myself, I keep away from Mrs. Bream's big house on Lafayette Square but write Eve, asking her to give me her confidence, her love, —to renew the engagement of our youth—telling her

I adore her—telling her I know she is in trouble—begging her to let me bear it for her.

This despatched, I go down to Willard's and try and kill time knocking the billiard balls about; but time won't be killed, and goes very slowly. I stride to my F Street boarding-house. Here I pack a valise. In a campaign always be ready for quick movement.

This done, Finnaker comes bustling in from his clerical duties.

"By-the-bye, here's a note for you, I got in the hall," he says.

I tear it open. It is only a line from Durant, the colonel of my regiment, to say he has come in on some regimental business and asking me to call on him at Willard's. "Anything new?" I ask, as I hand him a cigar. Finnaker always tells me more when he is smoking.

"Nothing; only *we've* released Lommox from arrest, though we haven't put him on duty. We're keeping this thing bottled up, sir—*bottled up like champagne !* * Wait till the cork pops—then I pity the traitor."

" Have a bottle with me—this evening."

" Won't I—Munn's Extra-Dry ! "

With him I go down to Mrs. Lorimer's tea, and eat nothing, but drink something to strengthen me for my fate. Finally, I make my toilet and walk to Mrs. Burton's dance about ten o'clock this evening. Fortunately, Finnaker is busy with War Department duties, and I am relieved from that little hero's chatter on the way.

In Mrs. Burton's parlors I find my advent has been deftly heralded. My hostess greeting me, says : "I'm sorry that you were prevented from coming with Mrs.

---

* It is a curious fact that the War Department have *never* explained that, though Burnside sent his order for pontoons on the 9th of November originally and both Halleck and Meigs telegraphed about them on the 11th and 12th of November, still the Depot Quartermaster at Washington never heard of the pontoon order until the 14th of November. *Vide* Burnside's testimony, Appendix.

No elucidation of this matter was attempted even after Fredericksburg was fought and lost, though the press of the country were denouncing Stanton and Lincoln for the disaster : *See* Appendix ; Editorials, New York Herald, etc., and Harper's Weekly Cartoon, January 3d, 1863—Columbia demanding her 15000 sons murdered at Fredericksburg from Lincoln, Stanton, and Halleck.—Ed.

Senator Bream and her party; but better late than never, Captain Hamilton."

Therefore I know Miss Ashley must be here.

At first opportunity I look about for her. She is not in the parlor where Mrs. Burton is receiving; but I see Lucy Bream, looking very pretty and placid, a few chairs away.

As I greet her she says: "You missed Eva at Mrs. Rignold's the other afternoon; she returned almost immediately after you had left."

"How is she?" I ask uneasily. "Any more gimcracks on the mind and all-night séances with herself?"

"Oh, no; entirely normal once more. Look!"

I follow her glance, through the folding doors. And what a picture!

Amid the crowd of circling dancers, brave men, and lovely girls in *robes de bal*, each one meant to be seductive to masculine eyes; their white arms flashing and shining shoulders gleaming, I see but one!

A goddess of beauty, in a toilette made to pull the heart out of a man, is floating with fairy steps to the soft "Dream of the Ocean" waltz.

Floating; that's what she is doing! for all this night the loveliness of Eva Ashley seems to me more of the air than of the earth.

From the white camellia stuck in her waving curls to the light tulle skirts, flounces and furbelows that wave like billows over her swaying crinoline, beneath which scintillate and gleam superb ankles and petite feet, she has no speck of color, save hot burning blushes vibrating over cheeks that grow pale as lilies as she looks on me.

Then suddenly into her eyes fly two sparks of emotion. In them I see what makes me happy—in all my anxiety—ay—even though the arm of that accursed Creole tyrant circles that lithe waist and presses her to him.

I know he is her *tyrant* now! For catching her glance at me, Arago whispers to her. Eve turns her eyes from me—the beautiful orbs grow dim with tears behind them, her proud head droops. I can see her white, sculptured bosom throb tumultuously with the short, rapid beats of some supreme emotion. In my soul I

know it is fear, not love that causes Eva Vernon Ashley to accept the attentions of Henri Dubois Arago.

What immense motive, what intense strain makes
this high-bred Virginia girl, a descendant of one of
Rupert's cavaliers, tremble as she looks into the face
of the New Orleans drift-away? Her ancestors were
not wont to have their hearts beat in panic-terror
as they faced Frenchmen at Crecy, Poitiers or Azin-
court. And from the way Stuart's cavalry are fighting
across the Potomac now, their blood doesn't seem to
have deteriorated.

Is it the terror of the victim for the mouchard?
Shades of Vidocq ! give me a mouchard's cunning to
defeat him !

No ! better still, give me American pluck to save my
love from his two-faced clutch. For if she is guilty in
this thing—he must be guilty *also*.

Made strong by this idea, I step towards Eve. The
dance has ended—she is escorted by another cavalier
now—for in all this evening I note Arago treats Miss
Ashley, in public, with the punctilio of a Creole and
the etiquette of a gentleman.

The girl, though she is on the arm of one officer is
chatting to several others. Into this coterie I insinuate
myself. A moment later I am bowing before her and
asking for a dance. She extends her programme ; I perceive Arago has confiscated half her dances, and the
cotillion also.

"I have come !" I whisper. "You know what that
means. You received my note ?"

Her eyes answer mine, then droop, and despite a struggle, for I can see Eva is fighting to keep down emotion,
her heart throbs wildly. A blush, beginning gradually
with pale pink, that makes her face like chiselled coral,
grows into a flaming, ruby glow.

"For heaven's sake, take only one," she falters in
my ear. "The one marked with a big cross—yes, that
one just before supper—quick, don't linger, he is watching me. Thank you—God bless you."

I bow and move away, swearing for this humiliation
of my love to reckon, at proper time, with him who
causes it.

Then I try to act as other men at fêtes and revels. I
dance, I flirt, I even laugh.

The dances drift away.

Ours comes at last!

As she puts her hand upon my arm, Eva Ashley's words startle me. "Waltz with me," she whispers. "Don't talk to me. He's watching."

This I do, clutching her to my heart in a desperate way, for I know the crisis of our fate is upon us.

"The dance is ending. I have not had one word with you," I mutter.

"Wait!"

Then I see with what subtle feminine art Miss Ashley has arranged her manœuvre. By very force of being the escort of their party, Mr. Arago is compelled by ballroom etiquette and courtesy to take Mrs. Bream to supper. The refreshment-room is in the basement of the house, reached by a somewhat narrow stairway. Though he looks back lingeringly, longingly, even I think threateningly at the girl, the Creole is compelled to offer his arm and escort Mrs. Bream down, among the first hungry ones, in company with her hostess and several *passée* dowagers.

A moment after comes the rush to supper. The stairs are blocked with a crowd of eager matrons, hurrying girls and their escorts, civil and military; shoulder-straps elbow dress-coats, and gilded spurs play havoc with lace flounces. Henri Arago is cut off from us by the living crush.

The supper-room not being large enough, the over-flow now seat themselves on the stairway, in one solid phalanx.

Politeness would keep any gentleman from tramping over silk dresses, delicate feet, extended crinolines and flounces, if the other cavaliers would permit him.

The dancing-salons are empty; though the musicians are still fiddling the march to supper.

"Come!" directs my enchantress hurriedly, nervously, bashfully.

At her word I follow her, to endure the most astounding interview perchance woman has ever given to man.

In a little room of boudoir effects, cut off from the main salons of the house, the girl turns desperately to me and says: "I received your letter, Billy."

There is a directness in her tones that makes me

start. Her beautiful face, clear-cut as a cameo, is very pale, though the nostrils are dilated and the eyes of unnatural brightness. There is a shrinking modesty about her attitude that makes me pity her though they add to her ethereal beauty.

"Ah! You understood what I wrote?—that I love you?" I murmur.

"Y-e-s!"

"That I wish you to revive our engagement?"

Her answer disheartens me.

"Yes; but I do not think it wise to renew it at this time—under these circumstances."

"You don't love me?"

"I do!—with my heart—my soul!" This is sighed out with bashful voice and averted head.

"Prove it!" I say desperately.

"I will! I will marry you to-morrow morning—quietly, secretly."

"Why not openly?"

"I—I dare not."

"Anyway, *I marry you!*" There is unutterable joy in my face. I am taking her into my arms to seize a lover's recompense from the lips that have kept me waiting so long.

But she, retreating a step, whispers: "Not yet; there is one condition!"

"With *any* condition, *I marry you!*"

"Then don't look me in the face. Turn your head away,—Billy, please turn your head away."

Half sulkily, I do so. I hate to take my eyes from off the loveliness that now I feel is *mine.*

Is it?

To my ears, that can't believe them as I listen, dazed and petrified, come these words, faltered out to me in lowest whisper, as if each fibre of Eve's maiden heart rebelled against them,—as if each word was an agony of virgin modesty, as if she were ashamed the air should catch them : "You—you must promise me—dear one, you must promise me—on your word of honor as a gentleman—nay, on your oath as a man—not to con-sider me your—your—*absolute* wife until one week has passed from the day I take your name and ring."

"What do you mean?" I turn upon her.

She has faced me desperately. Our eyes meet. She

gasps : "You know what I mean ! For God's sake, don't make me explain again !" and turns away. Wave after wave of blushes flies over her face, each deeper than before. That lovely neck, those shining shoulders, that gleaming bosom, grow crimson.

The beautiful head droops.

She convulsively hides her eyes with her hands. She is sighing : "You—you make it too hard for me. You do not love me !"

Flesh and blood cannot withstand such despairing loveliness. "By the oath you wish me to take—by my word of honor as a gentleman, and a man and an officer, I take it !" I mutter, "Good God, I love you well enough to endure even this torture, this degradation ! But for *only* one week !" I have got her in my arms now. "Remember that ! One week, then my wife, my *true* wife !"

"Your *true* wife, Billy." Our lips meet in one long clinging kiss. Then she struggles from me and whispers rapidly and anxiously : "Meet me at the fountain in Franklin Square at ten o'clock to-morrow morning. I cannot get away before. Have everything ready."

"You mean the minister and the ring and the license ?"

"Yes, everything. I will meet you."

"And after the ceremony that has made you mine in law and honor, I suppose you will give me the cold shoulder for Monsieur Arago—for a week," I remark grimly.

"I am compelled to."

"Ah, for a week you will break my heart with jealousy—you will give me no wife's respect and honor —because I am dastard enough to make such ar ignoble bargain."

"No—no. Every wifely respect and honor to a gentleman who has aided me in my extremity."

"Your extremity ? What extremity ?" My fears for her make me stern to her. "Tell me, I demand."

"To—to save my life !"

"Impossible ! Explain !"

"I cannot now. There is no time. I must go back to my jailer."

"Your *what* ?"

Her words take away my breath.

"*I—I have been under arrest for twenty-four hours.*"

"Good Lord!"

"Yesterday afternoon Mr. Arago exhibited his secret service United States Deputy Marshal's badge and threatened to handcuff me and take me to the Old Capitol Prison at once, if I didn't consent to marry him."

My muttered curse startles her, but she goes on: "I am under my parole now not to leave this house without his escort or permission."

"But your uncle, the great War Senator!"

"He daren't help me even if he would. I'm too deep in this time."

"And to-morrow?"

"I will break my parole for your sake to-morrow!"

But here a soft suave voice comes floating in to us: "Have you seen Miss Ashley about, Major Hughes? Mrs. Bream is anxious for her to join us at supper. The crowd is so great on the stairs I had to come by the front door."

With finger on her lips, my sweetheart, my love, my traitor, my Rebel, my spy, floats out from me to the touch of the *mouchard;* and I, half believing this is a dream, want to go after her and take his Creole throat within my hands and wring the life out of his dastard body.

———

CHAPTER XVIII.

THE NUPTIALS OF DAMOCLES.

But brute force is not the weapon to employ against finesse. I cannot interfere now, though I have to hold myself in my chair; as I catch his voice speaking commandingly to her. It may be but a suspicion: I think I hear him say: "Be careful; your fate hangs upon your obedience and acquiescence to my rule."

It dies away; and some time after, the parlors beginning to fill with dancers, I stroll out of the little room and see my adoration seated with Mrs. Bream and looking very sweetly at her Creole captor as he stands before the ladies.

I am compelled to act as other men. If Eve can finesse, I must also.

I stroll up to the party and suggest: "Have you

had supper enough, Miss Ashley?" and would offer her my arm to take her downstairs.

But obeying a look from the Creole, who stands beside her, Eve says to me coldly: "Thank you, Captain Hamilton; Mr. Arago always takes such good care of me at supper that I never need a second bite."

He leads her off to the dance again, and Lucy Bream looking at me, sneers sarcastically: "A little harder work than you thought, picking up the old love—eh, Billy?"

"Rather," I reply, and meditate upon the aunt's deep insight into human character. "Oh, yes; her niece is perfectly *normal?*"

But *I* am not normal. After making pretence of doing a cavalier's duty a little while longer this evening, chatting with Miss Laura Cushing of New York, pretending to flirt with dashing Mollie Bent, I get away from this fête scene; its laugh is bitter, its gayety distracting to me. I cannot bear to see my promised bride bullied by this damned Creole; besides, the coming bridegroom has lots to do by to-morrow morning at ten o'clock.

I hurry to my F Street boarding-house. The sleepy negro servant-girl who opens the door informs me; "Dere was an Irish soldier to see you twice dis evening—late at night, sah."

"Did he leave his name?"

"'Deed he did, sah; it war Lummox," replies the wench. "He said he'd rouse you to-morrow mornin'."

"Oh, Lommox," I laugh. Then suddenly I want to see Lommox; he may elucidate this matter that is still an enigma to me. If my sweetheart is guilty in regard to that pontoon order, Arago must be guilty also.

Slipping a dollar into the girl's hand, I say: "When the Irish sergeant calls again, if I'm out, show him to my room and tell him to wait for me. It is important I see him at once."

"Yes, sah."

"If you remember, there's five dollars more for you."

"Den I'se suoo I'll neber miss 'um, sah!"

With this I go to my room to think the matter over. If Eve is guilty of the pontoons, her only safety is behind the Rebel lines, or in some far-away country; for I know well enough, in every state of America where the Star Spangled Banner floats, Uncle Sam's Secret Service sooner or later will get her, and I don't marry to become a widower at once.

But this brings to my mind the infernal oath my coming bride has exacted from me, and I tramp my room with rage in my soul and bitterness in my heart.

I wake from uneasy slumbers early the next morning. It is seven o'clock by my watch when I arise. A license is necessary, with two witnesses as to my identity. If my nuptials are to be kept secret I can ask no intimate friend. "To trust Finnaker is to proclaim it far and wide. Though I can depend on their silence, I dare not call upon my two lieutenants : if this thing comes to an awful ending, they might be ruined as well as I. Some out-of-the-way Treasury clerk, some buried-alive attaché of the Public Library," I think.

So about half-past eight o'clock I tramp down Pennsylvania Avenue, racking my brains for proper witnesses. In front of a beer-saloon about Seventh Street, yclept *König Wilhelm*, a genial German voice breaks in upon my meditations. With a start I wake up, and find August Lammersdorff, the sutler, is calling to me.

" *Wie geht's*, Captain Hamilton ; is your parole lifted yet ? Come in und drink a glass of beer mid me. I'm shust in from der front, und I'm shust going out again."

Suddenly it flies through me : " Lammersdorff—witness number one. Best in the world ; everybody knows him. He can get me another."

"With pleasure," I answer. In the saloon I join him in a glass of beer, and over it tell him my wishes."

"Going to be married, eh? Dat's a fine way of spending your parole ; dat will make you vant to be von of the home-guards," he laughs, as we sip our lager. "Von't I be your vitness ? Vill I get you anodder vitness ? I vill get you half a dozen vitnesses. Here's mein friend, Herr Schloss, vat is sutler mid Birney's division ; he vill step over mid me."

So, after another glass of beer, in which Lammersdorff winking at me says : "To the health of de **fust baby**," we go down together. The proper declarations being made, I receive the necessary license to make Miss Evelyn Vernon Ashley my wife.

Coming out with this in my pocket, I am still conversing with the genial Lammersdorff. "Have you had a good trip?" I ask.

"Vell, fifteen t'ousand dollars talks."

"You'll have a lively time if it rains. It looks threatening, too."

"Vell, I dodges Virginia mud dis time. I goes de odder way."

"How's that?"

"Vell, de army dey goes to Falmouth, opposite Fredericksburg. I goes down de Maryland side to Port Tobacco, den it's only a few miles ferry across to Aquia Creek, und a short haul to Falmouth."

"Then a pleasant trip to you," I say. "What time do you leave?"

"Some time dis afternoon. If it look like rains I starts early. I goes mid four vagoons."

I shake hands with him once more and get on my way. I must find some church where our names will not excite comment or gossip. St. John's won't do. After a little consideration, I select out-of-the-way Christ's Church, down towards the Navy Yard.

Catching the minister at home, I make arrangements with him for half-past ten o'clock. Looking at my watch, I find I have no time to lose. I pick up the first decent-looking cab I meet, and from a little conversation with the driver, judge that his beat being about the Capitol, he has probably never seen Miss Ashley. I get in the carriage and pull down the blinds. I don't care for outside eyes to see me and my bride on our trip about Washington. Inspired by the promise of extra fee, my jehu whips up his horses and I reach Franklin Square in time; in fact, I'm five minutes ahead of my appointment by my watch.

Directing the driver to wait for me on I street, I stroll into the grounds, almost deserted at this early hour, for the sun gets up late these November mornings, and the day is threatening. Walking to the fountain, I stand beside it, and for five minutes smoke an uneasy cigar.

Then she comes! Were it under other circumstances and were not my heart full of anxiety and terror for her, I would be the happiest man on earth; for this morning my bride is as piquant and lovely a darling as ever gave joy to heart of groom.

Her cheeks are full of maiden blushes.   A stray curl of hair is floating in the breeze beneath her piquant turban.   Her eyes are bright with excitement ; her bearing brisk with the energy of determined action ; her dress captivating and *chic*, for the day being threatening, she wears a gay Balmoral petticoat that is displayed by looped up skirt, after the fashion of that day, from beneath which two dainty feet in tight-laced, high-heeled bottines show themselves occasionally.

For a moment Eve's delicate fingers falter in my grasp as she asks eagerly : " Is everything ready ? "

"Quite, darling," I answer.   "Come with me." And placing her hand in pretty confidence on my arm, she trips by my side as I lead her across the square to where my jehu is waiting.   This worthy I have already informed of my destination, charging him to avoid the main thoroughfares and crowded streets.

I deferentially open the door of the cab ; Eve is about to get in.

But even as her foot is on the step she turns fluttering to me, looks me straight in the face and whispers : " It is not too late.   Billy, it isn't pity that makes you do this ? "

" It is *love !* " I answer, gazing into her eyes.

She knows I tell the truth.   "Thank you ! " she says, then murmurs : "You do not regret ? "

"I regret nothing," I say, "except my unmanly promise—my accursed oath."

"O-o-oh ! "   With a bashful flutter, my bride is in the cab, turning from me one of the reddest faces I have ever seen.

Stepping in after her, I close the door.   "You have every confidence in me ? "   I whisper into her ear, which seems to me like a ruby-tinted shell.

"Yes ! "   A little hand exquisitely gloved is placed in mine trustfully.

"Then don't you think I deserve a kiss ? "

"Two of them, Billy."

Her lips meet mine confidingly, lovingly ; my arm goes round the lithe waist that trembles beneath the pressure of my hand.   I am caressing her as an everyday lover does an everyday sweetheart.   I take great care to say nothing to add to her agitation, though I am determined that after the ceremony Eve shall give me every explanation it is a wife's duty to accord her husband.

We get to the minister's sooner than I expect. "Oh mercy, we are there!" flutters the girl piquantly, as I assist her out.

The ceremony takes scarcely a moment. Though Eve falters a little when she promises to obey me; as I place the ring upon her finger and look into her dear eyes, I know she means to be a loyal wife to me. We sign the register; the minister delivers to my bride, the certificate that proves Evelyn Vernon Ashley is now Evelyn Vernon Hamilton, she folds it up carefully and whispers: "Billy, even if you should hate me for this, I shall always treasure it."

"Hate you?" I whisper. "Love you! *Love you! Love you!*"

My ardor makes her extremely bashful. She trips down the steps, half laughing, half crying, while the worthy rector, with a goodly fee in his pocket, looks kindly after us as I step down the stairs to the carriage in which Eve is already seated.

"You can drive back to Franklin Square," I say to the driver—"slowly."

"Bedad, I understand, yer honor!" answers the hackman cocking his eye at me jovially. Guessing he has been on a bridal outing, he evidently expects a handsome douceur.

Then I turn my eyes on my bride. She is in a corner of the carriage, looking as agitatedly diffident as her namesake at interview with the serpent and holding the forbidden fruit in her hand.

"But it is *I* who am forbidden to eat!" I reflect grimly.

Looking on her exquisite loveliness, something in my face frightens her as I step in beside her. She mutters: "For God's sake, remember, Billy!"

"I remember my *oath*—you remember your *vows*! Two kisses," I say cheerily, "and I'm your obedient servant."

"As many as you want; I love you."

"Now," I go on, "at least I can command from you wifely obedience and wifely frankness. Tell me your

exact relations with that cursed villain of the United
States Secret Service."

"I—I do not want to give them to you.   I will *not*
give them to you !   The knowledge might compromise
you."

"You must !   I am compromised already."

"How ? oh Heaven, how ?"

"By my love for you.   I am going to save you.   If
not, why did I marry you ?—why did you marry me ?"

"Because—" here the girl frightens me.   "Because,
Billy," she whispers in my ear, "I feared that in some
weak moment I might become poltroon enough to
marry him."

"You—you love him ?"

"Love *him*—that dastard, who sells himself for money
and then betrays his purchaser?   I loathe—I despise
him !   But in some weak moment, Billy, I feared I
might, to save my life, promise to marry him.   It is
not pleasant to die so young, and for what I have done
they'd hang me high as Haman.   I—I bribed him ; I
sold Bonny Belle to give him the money.   He now
says he did it for love of me."

"The *pontoons* for Burnside?"   I whisper, so low she
catches it only from the formation of my lips.

"Yes."

"Then he's as guilty as you are !"

"No ; Arago only did it to trick me.   The forged
order was never sent.   He told me that yesterday afternoon, and laughed at me."

"Then he lies !   That forged order *was* sent.   The
pontoons have been delayed four days."

Then, oh the glory that comes into that girl's face !
"Have I given my dear country, the Confederacy,
another chance ?" she whispers.   "Have I stayed
Burnside till Lee has time ?   What do I care now if
they give me a shameful death ?   It will be my glory !"
Then the sunshine in her eyes seems to fill the carriage with radiance.

Shuddering for myself—I, the Union officer, who have
been made faithless to my cause by love, gaze on this
Rebel girl who can love but can't forget her people's
battle.

She has risen in the carriage. But I draw her back to
me and mutter : "For God's sake, think of me, who
love you—think of the husband who will save you."

"Yes, it would be pleasant to live—to see my South free! Pleasant—" She looks at me, puts her arms round my neck of her own free will and kisses me.

"Now tell me everything!" I mutter.

"I will. When I first came here, anxious to do a little for the South; full of vengeance—General Milroy had burned the house over my dear mother's head. From some hints I received in Washington, I judged Arago, clerk in the Quartermaster-General's Office, was in the pay of the Confederacy; that he received his money in drafts sent him from England. I met him in society; sounded him: he gave me some secrets, *important* ones, one of which I succeeded in delivering the morning after the night you arrested me."

"Ah! that was the reason Stonewall Jackson would not have paroled me if I had known your name!"

"When I returned here, Arago was glad to again assist me. He said, my being the niece of the patriotic Senator, one of the pillars of the Republican party, made it safer for him to be intimate at our house. A few days ago, he told me his suspicions that Fredericksburg would be Burnside's route to Richmond.

"Before leaving our Southern lines, I had held consultation with a General of the Confederate Army, who had told me carefully what thing would most cripple the Federal advance by the various routes to Richmond, the Shenandoah, the Peninsula, the line of the Rappahannock, either at Fredericksburg or above. At Fredericksburg it was the necessity of *pontoons*, to bridge the river. 'Keep them from crossing,' he said to me, 'till Lee gets ready for them and if the Yanks cross, by Dixie, there won't many of them get back again.' And I have done it!" she ejaculates in triumph, then falters: "O Heaven! what a blow it was to me, when that dastard told me I had failed—that he had trapped me. It was not the dread of imprisonment, though, my gentleman, even as he wooed me, jingled the handcuffs—it wasn't the fear of the gallows, though I saw it over me; it was the thought that I had failed that crushed me and made me coward with Arago. But now! *now!* now! Her eyes blaze up and glow. Suddenly she laughs hysterically: "O Billy! What a Rebel I am!" and sinks sobbing into my arms while I gaze on her with only one thought in my mind —how to

save her ! That's all I think of now ! How to save
her ! God help me—I have forgotten my duty to my
uniform, to my flag, to my country—all but her
safety ! "

The scoundrel Arago is equally guilty with her. I
must spare *him*—to shield *her*. Oh, I am a fine Union
man on my marriage day ! *Her* safety depends on *his*
—then *his* depends on *hers*. He dare not denounce her.
He has only tried to frighten her to gain her. He's
been partially true to his Confederate paymasters—he's
been somewhat true to his Union employers. He has
been wholly faithless and pitiless to the girl whose
beauty has driven him mad to win her—as it has me ?

As I think, my bride recovers herself and whispers :
" I should like to live now. You think you can save
me ? Her kisses make me strong enough traitor, to
swear : " " By Heaven ! No Government spies shall
ever take my wife ! "

We are at Franklin Square. Eve, after her nervous
spasm has grown calm again. Her pretty head is held
high. She whispers " That is the only break-down
of my life. And it was because I thought of you."

"Very well," I answer, as with a last kiss, I help
her from the carriage, " go quietly to your aunt's.
But be sure to be at home in an hour from now. By
that time I shall call on you ; then I shall have determined what I shall do with you ! "

My tone is that of dominant husband. She looks at
me anxiously but lovingly ; then suddenly whispers :
"You—you are going to send me from Washington ? "

"Probably ! In any event I shall do what I deem
best for my *wife's* safety ! If your only danger came
from Arago you might stay here forever. Good-bye.
Are you going to tell Aunt Lucy what we've been
doing ? "

"Oh, Heaven ! I—I couldn't—I—good-bye, my—
my—*husband !* "

Whispering this with a blush she runs lightly from
me and I, following her graceful figure with my eye,
shudder as I think of the danger that is upon my love
—not from Arago—but from others who must have
been connected with the successful execution of this
plot against our nation.

Then, dismissing the hackman with a liberal fee, I go back to my rooms on F Street, to find another and immediate element of danger to her.

As I enter my parlor, Lommox stands erect before me and salutes, his Irish brogue greeting me : "Bedad, Cap., I was afraid you were niver coming."

"Ah, they asked you to wait for me?" I remark, attempting nonchalance, though my heart is beating wildly, for here is a man who should be able to tell me much. "I supposed you were anxious to see me, and so instructed the servant to tell you to wait."

"Faith, an' I do want to see ye. Begob, Cap'n, I'm in a divil of a schrape."

"Not been drunk again, I hope?" I say severely.

"Wirrah, if it was only that ! Bad luck to it, if it was *only* that ! But it's a thing I've got to have advice upon, so I thought I'd come to ye, me ould captain. Tare an' ages, hasn't it been tearing me inside out iver since I've been under arrest !"

"Ah, you wish to speak to me confidentially, as if I were your counsel before a court-martial," I suggest.

"Faith, an' I do."

"Very well ; open your heart to me." I close my door and lock it.

"It's about them damned pontoons ! " says the sergeant in low voice, getting near me.

"What pontoons ?"

"Sure of course ye don't know anything about 'em. Nobody does ; it's a sacret of the War Department. Eighty pontoons and two thousan' fate of bridge ordered from the Depot-Quartermaster last Wednesday evening—just a week ago this cursed day. Ye know I'm one of the orderlies at the Quartermaster gineral's ? "

"Certainly."

" Well, Arago, one of the head clerks, at 6 : 45 in the avening—it was dark thin—comes out with a requisition, number 1410 they calls it." That bastely Finnaker was with him. He hands it to me and says : ' Deliver it to the Depot-Quartermaster at once.'"

"I slip the cursed envelope in my sidebelt. Yeknow they niver tell ye the importance of an order ; it's all damned official routine ; they send a requisition for a box of tacks just the same as if were a requisition that'll send a hundred thousand men to the divil—that carries the lives of an army in it," the sergeant mutters, with tears in his honest eyes.   "Bad luck to 'em ! not a word did the sons of guns tell me it was any extr*ee* importance ; just handed it and said : 'Take it !'

"With it in my side-belt, I jumps on my horse and turns from Seventeenth Strate into F. Down I goes straight for Twenty-second Strate, aisy trot. The night was as black as a dark-lantern ; there was only a few people in the strate ; not so crowded on the rise as it is further down.

"Suddenly, out of the darkness, comes to me the swatest voice I iver heard ; a poor girl shrieking, 'Oh, God, assist me ; a man is insulting me !' By heaven, I'm a soldier and an Irishman ! Bedad, there was a woman, apparently struggling with a niggah. I reined up my charger. What did I think of a damned quartermaster's order, that might be for a pace of rope or a box of tacks. I jumps off me horse to the girl's assistance, and as I jumps off, damned if the niggah didn't butt me in the stomach ; I thought a battering-ram had struck me. Then I up and at him. *Biff !*— God save us, how he squealed ! Biff !—I chased him for a block.

"When I came back the girl was holding my charger. 'Thank ye,' she said, 'sergeant.' Sure, how did she know I was sergeant ? 'I think you've dropped something.' She handed me a cursed official envelope.

"'Can I do anything more for you, me darlint?' I asked.

"'No ;' and she fled into the darkness.

"I mounted me horse, and found somehow my side-belt had been cut ; the order must have dropped from it when the niggah butted me. With the envelope in my hand, I gallop down to the Depot-Quartermaster's. I wasn't behind time more than a minute, and delivered it."

"Well ?" I say.

"Well, *murder !* That's what it is—murder ! The damned order had been changed from eighty pontoons to eight pontoons, and from two thousand fate of roadway to two hundred fate—damn it !—hardly enough to bridge a trout strame ; and, begob, they meant it for the whole Army of the Potomac to cross the Rappahannock. They didn't find out about it for four days ;

then, *whirr !*—how things ripped, up at the Quarter-master-Giniral's.

"They had me up and questioned me. 'Lommox,' said I to meself, 'stick to yer instructions. Ye received it at **6.45**, ye delivered it at **6.51**, by yer receipts; not much over time in the crowded strate between the Quartermaster-Giniral's office and the depot.' So I stuck to that story through thick and thin, and that's *all* I told 'em. They put me under arrest. But if they bring me up agin, if they go cross-questioning me, if they make make me tell 'em everything I did from the toime I jumped on me charger in front of the Quartermaster-Giniral's office to the toime I raiched the Depot-Quartermaster's—tare an' ages, they'll hang me! What do ye advise? Captain, for the love of God, what do ye advise?"

"Stick to your first story," I answer sharply. "Don't say another word, no matter what questions they ask you. Received the order at 6.45 P.M., delivered it at 6.51 P.M.

"You think that's the best way out of a bad affair?"

"Yes, I *know* it is! Besides, the Government won't want to make this too public. They don't care about army blunders being criticised in the newspapers just at present. We make too many of them."

"Well, then, it's a close mouth I'll have."

Here I ask anxiously: "What kind of a looking creature was the girl who stopped you?"

"How could I tell? She was muffled up; it was too dark. Ye know what those gas-lamps down there are; there wasn't one within half a block of us."

"Billy, Mrs. Bream and I have come to see you," strikes my ear through the closed door.

It is the voice of my wife; she has come with her aunt.

But, before I can recollect for what reason, the sergeant startles me by whispering: "I said I couldn't tell the face, but——" He has his hand upon his heart; his eyes are blazing.

"Billy, are you in? Open the door! Mrs. Bream and I are here."

"Who is that?" asks Lommox hoarsely.

"My sweetheart—my affianced—with her aunt, the wife of a United States Senator. Why do you ask?"

"Because if that was not the voice of your swate-heart, a high-bred Union young lady, Cap'n Hamilton, I'd say that was the voice of the girl who called me to her help one wake ago and swiped the true order and handed the false requisition back to me."

"Oh, nonsense!" I break out, though my face is white. Then I cry: "I'll open the door and be with you in a moment, Eve!" For I must keep her soft tones from betraying her again.

With this I turn to the sergeant and mutter: "Remember, Lommox, as you value your own safety, stick to your first story, if you don't want to drag a ball and chain all your natural life. 6 : 45—6 : 51 ! Chivalry wouldn't save you before a court-martial. Good-bye." I open the door. "If you want any further advice in the matter, call on me; I'm your friend. If you want any money in the matter, call on me; I'm your captain, I stand by you. You're a gallant fellow anyway."

"God bless you; you give comfort unto me," and stepping out, gallant Irishman that he is, Lommox doffs his forage cap politely to the two beautiful ladies and his eyes light up at the loveliness of the girl who has betrayed him—though he knows it not.

"Bedad, Cap., I wish ye and your young lady joy," he says. "Good luck. God bless your swate face, Miss. I've been your captain's sergeant for many a day." And with military salute, the sergeant strides down the stairs, while I, with the unutterable on my face, motion my wife and her aunt into my parlor; thinking grimly: "Verily, these are the nuptials of Damocles —to both bride and groom."

CHAPTER XIX.

LAMMERSDORFF, THE SUTLER.

As they come in and I close the door on them; Lucy Bream's speech tells me that she knows at least of our wedding. "Billy! Billy! how could you do it?" she breaks out.

"Then Eve has told you that I married her this morning?"

"Yes, you naughty fellow."

"Well, isn't that excuse enough?" And I point to the beautiful creature who is standing regarding us, with blushes upon her face, her eyes very bright, her head erect, her nostrils dilated, her pretty nose a little in the air.

"My husband," she says, "I thought it best, on account of a social complication, to tell my aunt I had become your wife. We have come here to consult you about this." She hands me a little note.

"I cannot understand, that wretch Arago's having the audacity to write such a nasty note ;" says Lucy Bream, savagely. Evidently Eve has told her of nothing but our marriage.

I glance over the *billet.* It is a communication from Arago, and demands that Eve promise to marry him this evening. To me, reading between the lines, knowing the circumstances, every sentence is a covert threat.

"He even writes as if he had power over her!" cries Lucy, angrily, "William, the impertinent scamp should be horsewhipped!"

"I agree with you," I say, "and I'm just the man to do it—but this is not the proper time. We have a certain young lady's name to keep above scandal, above gossip. Will you help me to do it, Aunt Lucy?"

"*Aunt* Lucy?—Oh, yes, you *have* become one of the family, haven't you?" laughs the pretty matron. "Of course, I'll do anything to keep a naughty girl like Eve, whom I dearly love, out of any trouble whatsoever."

Looking at her, I conclude that I dare not trust Lucy Bream with the awful nature of the real trouble. In justice to her, and her husband, the Senator, I must keep them out of this matter, if possible. "Very well," I say ; "will you excuse me if I ask you to permit me a few minutes' private conversation with my wife, in order that we may settle what is best to be done in an affair in which I do not wish you to be any more interested than you can help—being our aunt."

"Of course," says Lucy. "I'll go into the next room." But at the door she turns, and suggests, roguishly, "I imagine it's kisses, not words, you want with that naughty girl, Billy."

"Perhaps I'll have a little of both." I reply, as lightly as I can.

" Well, I shan't give you too many kisses," laughs Eve, trying to veil her anxiety by piquancy, "if you question me too savagely about my anti-nupital beaux —Mr. Arago, for instance."

But as Aunt Lucy closes the door, my heroine's face— great jingo, I'm commencing to regard her in that way ! —loses its lightness, though it doesn't lose its courage.

I step towards my bride and whisper : " I have but a few hours to save your life ! "

" Why ? "

" Lommox ! "

" Ah ! " her tone tells she understands.

" If Mr. Stanton questions him, under that lawyer's shrewd examination the sergeant may tell a little about the beautiful voice he recognized in this room—the tones of the girl who substituted a false order for Special Requisition No. 1410 on G Street a week ago."

" Ah, you know ? "   But her face is still corageous.

" Everything ! Where's Quashie ? "   I question hurriedly.

" Outside the lines, I hope, by this time.   Privileged contrabands roam everywhere."

" Yes ; but you—I must get you out of Uncle Sam's grip in time.   I think I shall send you to England or Europe."   I add contemptalively.

" I won't go there ! "

" Ah, rebellious already ! "

" No, my husband ; but I don't want to be too far away from my mother in all the trouble this war has brought upon Virginia and *you !* Send me across the lines—get me across the lines."

" That would be almost a miracle now."

" Yes, I know that.   At first it was easy ; then it grew difficult ; now it is next to impossible.   But still, I've had a little experience in this business *already*. And you—your knowledge of the Secret Service as provost-marshal should help you."

" It doesn't ; it only makes me despair.   Every conductor on the Baltimore & Ohio Railroad is a member of Baker's organization.   Every ticket-seller at the Washington Railroad Offices notes where you are going.   If you take tickets for Baltimore, and you get off at Leonardstown, or any other route to the Lower Potomac that might lead you into Virginia, you will be shadowed from that moment—perhaps arrested at once."

"Yes, I have reason to think that too," she says, poking her pretty foot with the end of her parasol ; then breaks out in self-reproach : "I should never have let you marry me ! I was mad—crazy—to permit you to wed me and sacrifice yourself. Forget I'm your wife. I stay here ! I take my chances ! I'm not afraid of Arago—now that I have triumphed !"

"No ; he'll never dare denounce you. But others may ; and then——" I shudder. "No, you're my wife. Never for one moment forget that ; never for one moment forget that I will save you." She answers me with her eyes and I go on with military promptness : "Have everything ready to move within two hours. Pack your riding-habit—you've got the dear old gray one," I say, a lover's tones in my voice. "Take the few things you want for such a trip in a very small valise. Be sure to wear a good waterproof and hood ; it's going to rain now. Dress very plainly ; the long rubber cloak will protect you from the weather and serve to hide the beauties of a figure that would attract the eyes of every one. Will you obey me ?"

"Yes, Billy !"

"God bless you !"

"That is what I want you to do—take me to Viginia !" She puts her arms around my neck and kisses me and murmurs : "Take me to Virginia."

There seems to be a latent meaning in her words, but I don't analyze it ; her lips make me too much in love with her to think of aught else but the beautiful creature who is my wife.

I go to the door and opening it say : "Aunt Lucy, our interview didn't take as long as you expected."

"No ; I thought you'd keep me an hour," answers the matron, adding laughingly as she enters : "Didn't even have a lover's quarrel."

"No time for that," I reply. "We've made up our minds. I'm going to send Eve to her relatives in Virginia ; that will at least stop any immediate complication with Mr. Arago. You can tell him, and it'll be best for you to announce to your friends, generally, that Miss Ashley has taken a trip North. Have you no relatives there she might visit ? "

"Yes; the Doubledays, in Southern Illinois; first cousins; Eve knows them, though they're on my husband's side. It's an out-of-the-way place; hasn't got a telegraph station."

"So much the better. Just quietly circulate this among Washington society."

"Would it not be better that Eve stayed here?"

"No," I reply, "for in that case I should have to horsewhip Mr. Arago the first time I met him."

"Very well; anything to avoid scandal."

"Thank you, dear auntie," I say, and give her a nephew's kiss. "To avoid my name being mentioned in the matter, Eve had better meet me—not at your house but Franklin Square, the place from which we eloped this morning. Then I will join her and take her away—at two o'clock."

"And can you get her through the lines?" queries Mrs. Bream doubtfully.

"I can try."

"And Eve, what do you say?" asks the aunt.

"This morning I—I promised to obey him," mutters the young lady bashfully. My bride's words give me a throb of joy.

"Very well, then. Take her, Billy, but oh! if you're not good to her—if you're not good to her!" And the Senator's wife shakes a little fist in my face determinedly.

"Ah, yes; an *aunt*-in-law, instead of a *mother*-in-law," I laugh, and give Lucy another kiss.

They are at the door. But Eve comes to me once again, and putting her arms round my neck, kisses me, whispering: "Take me to Virginia!" There is a fire in her eye, there's a latent suggestion in her voice, that makes my heart jump.

Then she leaves me, with the most difficult problem of my life on my hands. My very knowledge of provost-marshal affairs makes me appreciate the tremendous obstacles in my path. I might take my *bride* North easily; but at no point in the United States would she be safe from Baker's sleuthhounds. To get through the lines has gradually become more and more difficult since the beginning of the war; and now with Secret Service officers teeming everywhere, with each ford or ferry on the Potomac guarded, from the Cumberland mountains down to its very mouth, while small gunboats and steam launches are patrolling its navigable waters, to cross it seems to me well-nigh impossible.

My first difficulty is to get Eve out of Washington. I could take a train to the North with her and run unquestioned to New York; but if we bought tickets for Baltimore and got off at any way-point, we should certainly be watched, probably apprehended.

How to get her out of Washington?

Suddenly it strikes me. Lammersdorff!—in a sutler's wagon. Then I think of myself: though on waiting orders I cannot depart from the city without leave of absence. To ask at the provost-marshal's may cause questions.

In a flash I remember the note from my colonel that arrived the night before. For seven days' leave his signature is perfectly good. I hurry over to my commander. Fortunately he is still at Willard's. Colonel Durant is happy to see me; I had always been a favorite of his.

"I only sent for you, Hamilton, just to sympathize with you on your parole and ask if I could do anything for you."

"Only one thing," I reply. "It will save me a visit to the Provost-Marshal-General's office. I want leave of absence for seven days. My troop is not detached from your regiment."

"To visit your family in Baltimore? I thought they had spurned their Union son."

"Yes, but that's the reason. My sister Birdie has fallen in love with a Union officer, Captain Vermilye of the artillery, I want to help his suit with her."

"Oh, a good Union girl in the family?"

"No," I laugh; "but a girl who loves a good Union officer."

"Very well; seven days, with permission to apply to the War Department for thirty days more; you won't be exchanged within that time," he says glumly as he dashes off the paper.

"No," I reply; "I'm afraid not." And with a clasp of his hand I leave him, for Durant is in a hurry now; he is going to the front again.

Now Lammersdorff! I hurry to the *König Wilhelm.* The sutler is not there, but I learn where his wagons are—at least, where they should be if he has not already gone. Springing on my charger, for I have Roderick in action now, I gallop off to one of the outlying sutlers' camps of the city, and fortunately find Lammersdorff not yet departed; though he is very nearly ready for the road.

As I have been riding I have been thinking how to approach this man. A sutler's privilege is a very valuable concession; Lammersdorff will hesitate, even though he thinks I saved his life, to do anything to violate it.

"Hello, Mein Herr Bridegroom! Are your running away from your wife already?" he laughs, as I come galloping to him.

"No," I reply. But I'm running away from my mother-in-law!"

"*Mein Himmel!* I did dat meinself vonce!"

"You are a little too smart," I continue, "not to suspect that my marriage this morning was a kind of secret affair."

"Ya, I guessed you vas doing it on de sly."

"Well, my bride's mother is looking for her daughter. You see, the young lady's a little under age. Now I want to get my wife quietly out of Washington without going to the railroad depot."

"Sure! So you can get on your vedding tour vidout having your hair taken out by the roots."

"Yes, something of that kind. I have the necessary leave of absence from my colonel, but I don't want to take my wife on my arm and go to the Baltimore & Ohio depot, where I think her mother is waiting for us."

"Just so. Vell, vat can I do mid you?"

"You can put me and my wife in one of your sutler's wagons and drive us out of Washington."

"But dey vill ask me qvestions crossing the Union bridge, down mid der Navy Yard."

"Well they needn't *see* us."

"Dat es so! Dey needn't see you if I put you in ze back of von of dose vhite covered wagons and t'rows a tarpaulin over you. You von't mind riding that vay mid your pretty wife?"

On second thoughts, I say, "I will only let my wife go with you; I will ride out on my charger with my leave of absence in my pocket, and who will stop a Union officer?"

"Quite right! Ve'll do eberyting to make ze lady commonfortable."

"Where shall I put her on board?"

"Round back of dat blacksmith's shop. I drive von of de vagons round dere to get de mules shoed. I'll keep it dere; no von shall know I put any one in dere; specially as it's getting dark. Good-bye, Captain. Don't be ober un hour in bringing your frau down; don't stop too long for kisses on de way. Von't youse stop und have anodder drink in Herr Rosen's over dere? De finest beer in Washington—Sutlers' Lager."

"No," I reply; "I haven't time for that; though I thank you all the same." As I clasp his hand, I am thanking him for a good deal more than a glass of beer. Then I ride away in much more buoyant spirits than I had come to meet the genial German, who seems utterly unsuspicious of anything but a lovers' escapade. I gallop for my stable, and leave Roderick there saddled.

Taking a cab, I bolt for the bank and draw five hundred dollars. From there I hurry to my boarding-house, slip into a loose undress cavalry uniform, arm myself with sabre and revolvers, and write my holograph will, leaving everything I possess to my wife. I hastily tell my landlady I am called to Baltimore, jump into my cab and find myself at Franklin Square in time. Here I am met by Mrs. Bream and Eve, both ladies in waterproofs, as heavy clouds are gathering.

"I came to bid Eva good-bye and see the last of her." Aunt Lucy kisses her niece lovingly then whispers anxiously; "You think you can get her through the lines?"

"Certainly!" I say confidently.

"Very well, then; good-bye."

There are no onlookers this dark day, and Eve giving her aunt a tender squeeze and loving kiss, which I supplement, my wife puts her hand upon my arm to walk out of the square to the cab.

"Hello! Where's your valise?" I ask.

"I haven't got any."

"You must take one."

"Not on this trip. I've travelled enough between the lines to know I can't make this journey with baggage.　We would have to leave my valise somewhere ; it might be our ruin, if they tracked us."

As Eve speaks I feel she knows her business ; and all through this journey I find she is much more *au fait* at the finesse, the arts, the subterfuges of a contraband of war, than I.

"You needn't worry for me," she whispers, "Billy. I'm perfectly comfortable.　I have on my riding-habit, its skirts looped up over my petticoat.　See!" she pokes out diffidently an exquisite foot and ankle, and I inspecting, find that though prettily shod, she has useful, high-laced, substantial boots.　"If we have to ride," she goes on, "it won't take me a minute to prepare myself for horseback."

"What else have you got?"

"A six-shooting Colt's."

"Any money?"

"Yes ; dear Aunt Lucy gave me fifty dollars.　She wanted to press more upon me, but I wouldn't take it."

By this time I have put Eve in the cab and told the hackman where to drive.　We have plenty of time, so I don't hurry the fellow ; I want to have all of my wife s company I can get till I part from her and leave her— God help her !—to the care of Lammersdorff and fate.

"Here are two hundred dollars more," I whisper.

"No, no!"

"You must!　You're my wife : my property is your property.　Here is my will ; keep it, if anything should happen to me."

"I didn't marry you, Billy, for money or property. I married you for——"

"Love?"

"Yes, dear.　Take me to Virginia."

"Well, the property and money goes with me," I whisper, my heart beating fast ; for I have given her a kiss at her sweet words, and I press the greenbacks into her hand.　"You must !—you may need them.　You *will* need them.　I command you to take them."

"O-o-oh!　Yes Billy, of course, I promised to obey you, didn't I?" she remarks, and blushingly tucks away the money under her waterproof.

Then masculine curiosity coming up in me, I ask hurriedly : "Tell me one thing.　How did you know the exact trip on which the sergeant would carry that order?" This is under my breath.

Her answer comes in equally low tones.

"We knew about the time the requisition ought to come from the front. All that afternoon Quashie waited in Bermudas's cigar-store. It was understood, when Arago went into the place and came out with a lighted cigar in his mouth, Lommox would carry the requisition the next time he rode down G Street. Arago went into the cigar-store and came out with a lighted cigar a 6 : 40 P. M. I was in a room near by and Quashie and I had just time to get ready."

" You can trust Quashie ?"

"With my life. He fondled me in his arms when I was a little girl ; his wife was my mammee. You can trust him with your life, if he knows you're my husband."

Significant words ; that don't seem to me so significant as I hear them.

Then she says suddenly : "Tell me how you're going to get me out of Washington."

I hurriedly explain every detail to her.

"I think you've found the only way," she murmurs. "You can trust Lammersdorff?"

"Yes ; as long as he thinks I'm only fleeing from my mother-in-law."

At this, even in her anxiety, Eve bursts out laughing ; then adds : "I'll—I'll prove your story to the sutler, by looking very timid and juvenile, eh ?"

"What do you mean ?" I ask astonished.

Here to my young husband's eyes comes a very beautiful display. Eve throws off her hat ; with a few quick movements she pulls out hairpin after hairpin, then shakes her head vivaciously, and a cloud of soft brown hair, in great locks and tresses, descends from her pretty head in cascades and waves far below her waist. With deft hands she ties a bow of ribbon about her tresses. "Now," she laughs, " I'm a school-girl, and sweet seventeen !—and have a stern mother from whom I've run away with an eloping trooper."

"Sixteen, rather," I laugh. For school-girls dressed their hair in that way in those days, and the perfumed locks that fall all about Eve's fair face give her a most juvenile expression.

"So I look young and timid enough to be frightened of my awful mamma—eh, Billy?—and my husband too," she murmurs.

For my arms are around her. I am squeeezing the pliant waist that seems to throb under my hand and kissing the exquisite lips that appear to return my salutes very tenderly.

We are near the place where we must part. Eve throws both arms about me and pleads : "Be very careful of yourself. Remember you—you have a wife to look after," and blushes very prettily ; a mass of charming naivete, bashfulness and I think—love.

A moment after I assist her from the cab, pay the driver and he disappears in the gloom, for the day is now growing very dark ; a few rain-drops are coming down.

We are a short square from the sutler's camp, and soon stand beside his big, white-covered wagon, drawn by four mules. Inspecting this, I notice that it is well-springed and will travel easily.

"Lammersdorff, let me introduce you to Mrs. Hamilton," I say to the German sutler, who is waiting for us.

"Ha Ya ! running away from *mudder*, eh ? Vell, mein liddle frau I'll take care she don't catches you."

"Yes—please--please, Herr Lammersdorff, keep mamma from seeing me," falters Eve in pretended terror. "She—she might spank me !"

"Mein Himmel, your mudder must be a tough old woman !" laughs the sutler. "But I've got eberyting very commonfortable now in ze back of ze vagoon ; jush step in kevick."

With a hurried caress I lift Eve in, and she looking out says : "Thank you, Herr Lammersdorff; you've made everything very nice for me.

"The heavy covering of the wagon will keep the rain and wind from you," I whisper to her ; "I shall overtake you on the road in about two hours." Then I wring Lammersdorff's hand and question : "Your men don't know of this ? "

"Only the driver of dis team, that is, mein head man Fritz, and he's confidential. I has to let him know. See ? "

It is beginning to rain very heavily, so I change my

plan somewhat. "I don't want my wife exposed to such a storm as this will be, Lammersdorff," I say.

"Ya, it vill be a scrouger! But your liddle *frau* vill be as cosy in dat vagoon as if she was on her liddle bed!"

"I understand that," I answer, "and for that reason shall let her go as far as Port Tobacco with you. From there—to-morrow morning—it may be fine then—I'll drive her back to the railroad. I can hire a buggy there?"

"Sure! Dere's a hotel der also," he says with a grin, "but de Brawner House is not de most common-for-table for a veddin' tour—mid a bride."

"All right. That's settled," I remark and putting my head under the covering of the wagon, I hastily explain the change to Eve, saying: "Don't expect me before Port Tobacco; that will give me a chance to make a longer détour, to throw any one off my track before I join you!"

"Very well, Billy," whispers Eve, "though if any danger comes, I have an idea it will be soon after I leave Washington."

"Pish, nonsense! Arago's busy in the Quarter-master General's office. He can't suspect. Good bye!"

Then two sweet, clinging lips meet mine and,—"Be very careful, Billy," is whispered to me.

I stride off into the gloomy day. In a few minutes I am at my livery stable and mounting Roderick whom I have prepared for this journey, I ride back towards the sutler's camp. I must see she gets out of Washington safe.

Overtaking Lammersdorff's wagons just as they reach Union Bridge, with my heart in my mouth I watch them cross. They are scarce questioned by the guard.

In the rain I stand and gaze till the last wagon has crossed the Eastern Branch, then give a sigh of relief. My bride has at least escaped from Washington.

CHAPTER XX.

DEAD MEN TELL NO TALES.

CHIRPING cheerily to my gallant horse, I turn from Union Bridge, the most direct route to Port Tobacco, to pass through the city and make my exit by another outlet. That will perhaps delay pursuit if we are followed.

As I ride through the streets, a jeweller's shop catches my eye.

"By George!" I think, "my poor bride never had an engagement ring." I dismount, and a few minutes after straddle Roderick again with a glittering bauble in my pocket.

Then, coming out of the city to the north on the Bladensburg pike, I shortly get past the circle of outlying forts.

I keep along this road as far as the little town of Bladensburg before I change my direction ; then I turn Roderick's head towards the southeast.

Journeying through country roads, and gradually circling more and to the south, I strike the main pike to Port Tobacco, near Piscataway.

I have been delayed at the jeweller's so long and have made so extended a détour, that I know my wife must be many miles ahead of me, for, like a careful campaigner I have not pressed my charger.

Meeting, soon after this, a couple of negroes on the road I learn that four sutler's wagons have passed this point nearly two hours ago and a single buggy something over an hour after them.

But I don't give much thought to this buggy. I am only anxious about the vehicle that carries my bride.

The rain is falling ; the roads are getting heavy. I ride on, gloomily pondering upon what may come to me and *her*, in this debatable land that is before us.

Southeast of Washington are four fertile counties running from the capital to Point Lookout, bounded on the west and south by the Potomac on the east by

the Chesapeake Bay, no towns in them of more than a
few hundred inhabitants; they are called the Western
shore of Maryland.

It is towards this land my face is turned. I know a
good portion of the country is covered with swamps,
for as a boy I have hunted over it. I am aware the
land has been ruined by tobacco-planting, my family
has owned some of it from the days of Lord Baltimore. I am sure most of the inhabitants are Catho-
lics, that nearly all of them are Rebels, that a good
portion of its population are of comparatively little education though acute intelligence; that a great
many of them, especially at Port Tobacco, had been
engaged before the war in kidnapping and running
negro-slaves across the Potomac. But I know they
are all a hardy, sturdy crew, and nine-tenths of them
would be willing to risk even their lives to give safety
to a Confederate spy.

At this thought my spirits rise. Eve is approaching a
land of which the inhabitants are the friends, not the
enemies of her cause. Though the country is overrun
with Baker's Secret Service detectives, and the river
between us and Virginia is patrolled day and night by
armed barges, and sometimes by small gunboats;
though even across the Potomac, judging by the movements of the Federal armies, will be the Union lines,
not the Rebel outposts; which we can only hope to
reach beyond the Rappahannock—I am commencing
to have hope.

So, through Maryland mud Roderick plods, the
rain falling on me. But I am well wrapped up, wearing
a heavy army coat, and being accustomed to campaigning, I think little of it for myself. My whole concern
is for my wife; she may be exposed to the storm
that is gradually gathering; still the sutler's wagon
will give her some protection. I light one of my
Bouquets Espéciales and smoke quite contentedly.

About nine o'clock in the evening, some miles this
side of Port Tobacco, I overtake the four white-coated
sulter's wagons and raise a shout of joyous greeting.

It is answered by a white-faced, savage-eyed German,
who comes dashing towards me. "*Gott in Himmel*,
Capt'n Hamilton, I didn't egspect such treatment from
youse!" cries Lammersdorff.

"What treatment?"

"Putting a government spy in mein vagoons to get her out of Vashington. O giminy crackies, I loses mein sutler's certification for dis!"

"A government spy? Nonsense! A girl escaping from her mother. Where is she?"

"Dey have taken her away mit demselves."

"Taken her away? Where? How? Tell me!"

"Oh vell, I tells you quicker den you likes to hear it. I tells you all about it at court-martial, ven dey puts de ball and chain on me and takes avay my position as sutler mid Sumner's grand army corps."

"Damn Sumner's grand army corps! Tell we where is she! Quick!" I cry, half crazy with apprehension.

"Vell, shust about a mile off here, up comes a man riding a buggy. He says: 'I vant dot girl hiding in your rear behind vagoon.'

"'Vat girl?' says I.

"'A Rebel spy,' shouts he.

"'You're a liar!' cries I. *Dat is ausgespielt!* She's de wife of mein friend Captain Hamilton of the United States cavalry."

"At dis he gives a shriek of rage and despair, and yells: 'You damned disloyal cub of a German, sneaking out under sutler's privileges contrabands of war, look at me!' He shows me Baker's Secret Service and a United States deputy-marshal's badge, and I faints almost—I knows I am sutler mid Sumner no more!"

"Bring her out, Dutchy!" he cries.

"But I doesn't have to bring dot gal oout; for at his words she jumps from de vagoon, cool as an ice-house and lebels a revolver straight for de Secret Service man's heart, which has jumped from his buggy. 'You dastard, die mit yourself!' she cries, and she'd have plumped him sure as Forth of July isn't New Year's.

"But knowing I vas fighting for my sutler's comish, I knocks up her arm; de bullet goes mid de air, und before she has time to do anyd'ings more, de Secret Service man jumps at her and claps a pair of handcuffs on her lekdle white wrists, and pops her into his buggy, und says: 'I arrest you in de name of the United States,' and drives avay mid her. She doesn't scream; she only gave one little gasp: 'Billy!'

"Oh, yes; she's de girl vat might have been spanked

by her mudder, she is! She's de girl vat vas afraid of her mumma, she is! She vas as brave as George Vashington himself ven he cut down de cherry tree," the German mutters derisively; then shrieks out: "But God help Lammersdorff! Dat's vat I am crying! God help Lammersdorff vat has secreted a Rebel spy!"

"God help *me!*" I moan. Then I whisper to him: "Keep a close mouth about this thing. She's *not* a Rebel spy; she's my wife. That villain is the emissary of her mother, though he is a Secret Service man. I know this Arago."

"Oh, you knows his cursed name?"

"Yes, I know his damned heart. Which way did he go?"

"Ahead of us, mid de buggy, towards Port Tobacco."

"How far is he in advance?"

"About a mile or two."

"Then keep your mouth shut!" And driving the rowels into Roderick, I dash through the mud and storm.

As I ride, I think Arago has doubtless watched Eve, seen her with her aunt join me, observed us take the cab, and noticed her get into the sutler's wagon. We didn't think—I didn't think—of being tracked at the very outset. Then he has come after her, hoping to frighten Eve into listening to his suit. And, if it hadn't been for the foolish sutler, would have got his quietus from the brave girl. But now Arago has her manacled. As I think of the irons on my wife's white wrists I dash the spurs into my steed.

Fortunately I know this part of the country pretty well. I have shot over it, and a boy's recollections are generally vivid. Besides, I have a horse that in this mud will overtake any buggy that ever wheeled.

But I must be sure of Arago's course. He will hardly go through Port Tobacco; still he may not think that I am following at all; my long détour must have given him confidence. Perhaps he believes I am yet in Washington; if so, my task will be easier.

Three or four sutler's wagons are ahead of me; these I overtake. To my hurried questions one of their drivers replies: "Yes, a buggy passed him five minutes before." Another half-drunken one jeers: "Hurry up,

Cap, and you'll catch your gal, I heard her squeal as she went by me!"

By this I know Arago must have gone to Port Tobacco; there are no side-roads from this point on. Made desperate by the teamster's last remark, I put the steel into Roderick.

Into the miserable little town I gallop, 'mid numerous sutler's teams and provision wagons, on their way to be ferried across the Potomac to Aquia Creek and Burnside.

Dashing up to the Brawner House, without dismounting, I call to the proprietor, who comes upon the portico in his shirt-sleeves to greet me. "Get me a drink, quick!" I order.

Over his bad whiskey I pump him. A buggy has gone through the town four minutes ago; it went north towards Baltimore, though it may have turned off towards Allan's Fresh.

"Damn the scoundrel! he didn't stop here even for a drink," remarks the hotel proprietor. "But he will have a lively time getting anywhere in the mud to-night."

"Was any one with him?" I ask eagerly.

"How could I know, stranger? His buggy-top war up, his apron war raised, too. 'Taint likely it would be down in this ar storm!"

"Did you hear any voices?" I mutter.

"Well, I thought I heerd a woman's, but what she war a-saying I couldn't tell. Seemed to me it was kind of plaintive-like."

This urges me on. "Good-bye," I cry.

"Aren't ye're a-gowin' to stay to-night?"

"Can't!" I dash the spurs into Roderick. The hotel man turns away, and I think I hear him mutter: "Some damned Secret Service galoot."

As I plunge on in the mud, I inspect my revolvers. The holsters have kept them dry, but to be sure I carefully re-cap them both and put a little powder into each nipple of the six-shooting dragoon pistols. Good Lord! I dare not fire at Arago, with my wife beside him in the buggy! As this strikes me, I loosen my sabre in its scabbard; it is ground to a razor-blade, like those of the rest of my regiment, for this had now come to be a fashion in our cavalry. The blade has done me true service on the battle-field ; may it not do me equal good in private rencontre?

" Besides "—I am talking to myself now, I am so excited—"it is my duty to arrest the fellow. Hang it ! " I chuckle, "he's a greater traitor than I ! It is my *duty* to kill him ! " With this, into my heart comes that awful maxim : " Dead men tell no tales." *Dead*— that will be her safety—that will be my safety ! A *dead* traitor is the glory of a loyal provost-marshal."

All this time Roderick plunges along the miserable, rutty, muddy, unkept road. Suddenly a problem meets me, which must be decided on the instant. Did Arago turn off to go to Allan's Fresh, or did he skirt the great swamps drained by that stream, and keep the pike towards the Baltimore and Washington railway. I am at the junction of the two roads.

I spring to the ground. The rain blinds me ; the darkness defeats me : I cannot see his buggy tracks. Suddenly a dazzling flash of lightning illuminates all ; the rickety Virginia rail fence, the low, stunted, swamp foliage , the junction of the two roads.

By its light, thank God ! I see the plain marks of buggy wheels going north—towards the railroad—towards Baltimore or Washington, whichever way Arago chooses to travel. No doubt now ! There are five miles in which he can't leave this road, and I will have my prey before the end of it.

I use my spurs again, and Roderick, answering me, shows he is a good mud horse by getting over this infernal road at tremendous pace. I speak to him, I urge him on : "Good steed," I whisper, "you are racing for my love's safety."

Isn't there a noise in front of me ? By heaven ! —the sound of wheels and a man lashing a horse. He knows he is pursued now.

Another flash of lightning. By it I see a top-buggy but thirty yards ahead of me.

A moment later I am by its side. "Surrender, you dog ! I arrest you," I cry.

To me comes Eve's sweet voice warning me "Look out, Billy ; he is going to shoot ! "

In proof of her words Arago answers only by a pistol-shot that, in the darkness, goes wide of me. This fire I dare not return, for my wife is by his side.

"Jump out, Eve, spring from the buggy, so I dare shoot him," I shout.

Again comes Arago's pistol-shot. His bullet whistles close over my head.

"Hang you, don't knock up my pistol again!" I hear him cry to Eve.

No more chances will I take. In this game Arago has the advantage of me, so I put a heavy Colt's dragoon bullet through his horse, and the poor creature falling down in the mud, leaves my enemy stalled in the road —compelled to fight it out with me.

And on fair terms too. For with a sudden deft movement, as the horse has fallen prostrate, Eve, manacled as she is, has jumped from the buggy.

Arago has sprung after her, for he would have been at my mercy alone in the wagon. So, I leaping from my horse in pursuit of him, we meet together in equal combat; the girl standing in the darkness with manacled hands, gazing on the battle for her safety—ay, even for her life, —for I know this accursed brute will sacrifice her in some way by his subtle arts—because she can't marry him—because she is my wife.

But, thank God, I have a gallant adversary. The Creole, turns upon me. "Captain Hamilton, surrender!" he cries. "I believe you to be a traitor."

"I *know you* are!" I answer grimly. "Your pontoon treachery has been found out. Stanton has sent me to catch and hang you!" For I want to make the scoundrel so desperate that, like the trapped fox, he will fight me until I kill him.

With a snarl of rage, Arago flies at me. Our sabres cross, for he is armed like me. As our blades meet, I know a swordman's steel is crossing mine.

So we battle, fitful flashes of lightning almost dazzling our eyes. Then the gloom coming on us, we engage from feel of blade, as masters of the weapon fight.

But at each cut and guard, each lunge and parry, I grow confident. Arago has more the art of the rapier in his wrist than of the broadsword. Beside, my muscles, toughened by actual battle and campaign, will last longer than the Creole's, made effete by dainty suppers and faro table exercise and playing dandy mid Washington's fair ladies. He knows it too, for his attack becomes desperate. He feels he must end the contest quickly, or it will end against him.

But I, growing cooler with each pass and my West Point training coming to me, parry, and parry, and guard and guard, with just enough of feint and *riposte* to weary his sword arm.

As I grow cooler, he grows despairing. My God, I fear he'll surrender before I kill him !

"Dead men tell no tales," is in my heart. "Dead men tell no tales," is in my arm.

The lightning flashes. Growing desperate now, he is making play with blade, not giving point, and at that I have him. As he gives full front cut, I turn it off quickly, by a firm high guard, disengage my sabre and giving point *en carte*, put it through as black a heart as ever beat—straight, strong, full to the hilt—and draw it out with a twist, because the lightning shows me white wrists that I love, *her* wrists, with his accursed manacles upon them.

And my bride looking at this dead thing murmurs, "It was dancing with me at this time last night," then shudders : "O Billy this is a ghastly wedding-day of ours !" and sinks down in the mud, wringing her shackled hands.

CHAPTER XX.

A NIGHT AT PORT TOBACCO.

BUT my bride must be free at once.

Scarce waiting for his dying quivers, I hurriedly search with my hand the dead man's clothes and find the key of the little handcuffs that hold the dainty wrists. As I release the delicate hands, I kiss and caress them, and with a vicious fling throw the bands of steel over the fence into the swamp, cursing the dead man's indignity to this creature that I love—that now I must protect.

"Yes, they were pretty little bracelets, weren't they, Billy ?" she sneers. "Mr. Arago was kind enough to inform me he had had them made for me."

"What else did he tell you ?" I whisper savagely.

"That if I did not marry him this very night, he'd

have me in the Old Capitol Prison to-morrow morning."

"And then?"

"I showed him my wedding ring, and it seemed to drive him half-crazy; for he swore he'd have you punished as a traitor also, for concealing my identity from Baker's Secret Service."

"And after that?"

"He tried to work upon my fears for you. Arago said: 'You were only married this morning; forget the ring upon your finger. The vows you made this morning are but an empty form.' He promised to spare you, my husband, if I would get divorced from you and marry him. Arago said you would not dare contest, because he had your life as he had mine within his grip. He treated us as if we were both cowards, Billy. But I struck him in his cruel face with my manacled hands, and you ran your sword through his treacherous heart, and—our enemy is gone." By the lightning I see Eve shudder, as she gazes on the recumbent form. Then she asks eagerly: "And now what are you going to do?"

While she has been talking I have hurriedly but effectively searched the clothes of my dead adversary, taking from them a bulky pocket-book, a purse full of money, some knick-knacks and a case of his beloved *Bouquets Especiales*.

I toss his cigars away, but light philosophically one of my own, and place the rest of my plunder in Arago's overcoat, which I take from him, together with his United States Deputy Marshal's badge. In the buggy I discover nothing except Arago's pistols. Turning to Eve, I would place the overcoat upon her.

But she falters: "No—no! not the dead man's coat!"

"Then I'll don it myself." This I do; putting my army overcoat on the fair form that is standing in the unceasing rain.

"And now?" she questions.

"Now!" I pick up Arago's body and throw it over the fence into a dense growth of dogwood and alder. "If they find it," I remark grimly, "it won't amount to much. Dead men, in this debatable

Western shore of Maryland, are common enough at present."

Here the girl, who has apparently recovered herself entirely, says sharply : "Give me one of his revolvers. He took mine from me and threw it away. If it hadn't been for that foolish German, there would have been no need of your killing him, Billy. But we must be moving," she exclaims ; then queries eagerly : "You think Roderick, if we harnessed him, would draw that buggy ?"

"No ; but he will carry *you*."

"Of course he will—the lovely fellow !" and the girl goes to my charger, who, being well trained, has hardly moved from his position in the road, puts her arms round his neck and pets him, while I shorten one stirrup and sling the other one upon the pommel of the saddle.

"Can you ride that way, darling ?" I ask.

"I can ride any way ; bareback, if necessary," returns Eve confidently, "like a boy if you want. I did it when I was a little girl in Virginia. But to-night your McClellan tree there will do well enough for my side-saddle."

She has turned from me, and with one or two deft movements let down the skirt of her riding-habit.

"Now," she says, putting her little foot in my hand. Then I swing her to the saddle.

"Are you comfortable ?"

"Yes. But you—you will have to walk, my poor, dismounted trooper."

"What do I care, as long as *you* are by my side ?"

"Well, you can't trudge very far in this storm."

"Do you know the country ?" I ask anxiously.

"Pretty well ! We've got to go back to Port Tobacco. Were you mounted, we might try Allan's Fresh—a disreputable little hole, but I have friends there. To-morrow you must take me there," she whispers, as I tramp along through the mud and rain by her side. "We must leave early in the morning."

"Yes," I answer. "If Arago hadn't leave of absence the Secret Service will be looking for him. His disappearance from Washington will be noted ; on his failure to return they will suspect him of the pontoon business ; they will think he has fled.

"Arago did that work very well," she says pensively.

"Yes, lured by your beauty," I mutter savagely; for, with man's inconsistency, I am angry at the effect of my wife's supreme loveliness, though I would not have her lose a tittle of it for all the world.

"And, perhaps, my coquetry," she returns sadly, then breaks out : "But, no ; I don't repent. If he had not loved me, he might not have dared. In this storm the pontoons will never get to Burnside in time." And she would go on in her cursed Rebel style, that makes me furious, for it brings my treachery home to me.

"I forbid you to talk in that way !" I say sternly.

"Oho, a *husband's* commands !"

"Yes ; you must remember you are the wife of a Union officer,"

"I have never forgotten that, Billy, and I never will."

Then I almost curse myself for the words ; for Eve, who had been loving to me before, now seems to grow colder. But the girl throws this off after a little, and goes to discussing hurriedly with me the arrangements we must make early in the morning to transfer her across the Potomac into Virginia. In this she shows herself much more an adept than I. She seems to know those who can be trusted in this part of the country. "If we can find Wat Bowie," she remarks, "he will surely get me across the Potomac."

"And me across the Potomac, also."

"Yes, of course, *you* are going with me ? " There is a lurking joy in her voice. "Aren't you, Billy ? "

"Certainly, until I put you beyond the reach of contending armies, until I see you safe among your friends, my wife." I whisper determinedly to Eve as we tramp into the muddy street of Port Tobacco.

This seems to make her very tender to me. She murmurs : "Take me to Virginia ! I can protect you in the Confederate lines. I know that, or I'd go back to Stanton's mercy rather than let you pass beyond this State." With her words, she suddenly leans down from her saddle and puts two dripping arms around my neck, faltering : "What an ungrateful wretch you must think me, Billy."

In her tones there is love, there is even reproach unto herself ; but they make my heart ache. They show me my bride has not forgotten my accursed oath ; they indicate that my wife will hold me to it, when I had thought, with Arago dead, she might forego it.

But I haven't time to dwell on this. Even as I lift her from Roderick's back in front of the Brawner House, new and embarrassing complications come upon us.

The hotel-keeper, stepping out, says cheerfully : "I thought you'd be back, Cap," then pauses, astonished, and whispers : "You've got the gal, but where did you leave *him* ?"

Suddenly the query seems to choke in his throat, as Eve, lifting the hood from her lips, whispers a few words into his whiskey-scented face.

"By Dixie," he gasps in astonishment—then mutters anxiously, "Kin *he* be trusted?" looking uneasily at me.

"Certainly ! He is my husband."

"Then I want to warn you both, there are two Union deputies inside—Baker's Secret Service men : Joe Shook and Rod Gibbon." This last is very much under his breath.

These words carry concern to me. Shook and Gibbon, the detectives who had spoken to me about the girl Stanton wanted ! Eve is wearing the same gray riding-habit in which they saw her at Frederick. This is in plain view for she has already thrown off my rain-soaked overcoat and her dripping waterproof. What interrogations to me—what complications to her —may this not produce ?

I hurriedly whisper to her : "Be careful. Those are the two men who followed you that night on the Potomac—the night I arrested you. They saw me lift you from your horse in front of the hotel at Frederick. If they recognize you, or think they do, keep your wits."

But her words reassure me. She laughs : "Oh, I've been in more difficult places than this before." Then suddenly stepping into the lighted hotel hall, she cries loud enough for Shook and Gibbon, who are there, to hear : "Come along, Billy. Thank goodness, we're out of the storm."

At my entrance, the two detectives springing up, say cordially : "Hello, Captain Hamilton !" Then Shook,

placing his eyes upon Eve's beautiful face, chuckles :
"Crackey!   Who's yer gal?"

"My wife, of course," I answer.   "I brought her
down with me as I have to look after some sutlers,
in whose business I have an interest.   We expected to
drive back to Washington to-night."

"That's a good long jaunt!"

"Only thirty miles, but too much in this weather.
Eve," I call to me my bride, who is lingering a little
bashfully in the background.   And she coming to me,
I say : "Mrs. Hamilton, let me present to you Joe
Shook and Rod Gibbon, who hunted secesh with me
when I was Provost Marshal."

"Pleased to know ye, missus!" remarks Rod,
and then goes on in hayseed humor : "Ye know at
fust I kinder reckoned the Cap was taking an outing
with——"

"No one else, sir, I hope," interjects Eve severely.
"You don't suppose I'd let my husband go driving
about the country with any *other* young lady."

"No—of course not," mutters the detective ; then
laughs, "By gum, Cap'n Hamilton, you've got a
tight hand over yer.   Perhaps she won't even let you
go down and take a glass with us in the bar-room?"
But in this speech he suddenly pauses and gazes with
inquisitive eyes at the gray riding-habit.

"Well, what's the matter?" I ask anxiously.

"By Jove!" cries Rod Gibbon.   "Darned if Mrs.
Hamilton doesn't look like the gal, as well as I kin tell
in the darkness, you had with you in Frederick at the
hotel thar."

"Had a girl with him at Frederick—at *the hotel!* Oh!
Billy, Billy!" shudders Eve, then her eyes flash—she
cries : "Don't presume to come near me!" for I have
approached her.   "May Heaven forgive you—I never
will!" and in a flash she steps to the stairs.   "No, no!
don't *dare* to follow me!" she says in wild and tearful
indignation, then flies up to the second story where
I hear her order : "Give me a private room, hotel-
keeper!" while the two detectives do their best to
conceal their merriment.   What henpecked husband
ever receives sympathy from fellow men?

"Hang you!" I say savagely ; "you've put me in
a devil of a hole.   I'll try and make my peace with

her.   You swear that girl was only my prisoner, if my
wife asks you."

"Great gosh, Cap, we didn't guess your lady was
such a high-flyer," mutters Shook apologetically, as I
rush upstairs after Eve.

I find her standing in an old-fashioned and rather
dilapidated chamber.

Going to her I think she is sobbing, but as she
turns her face to me tears of laughter are running down
her pretty cheeks.   "Didn't I play the jealous wife
well?" she asks merrily.

"By Jove! you nearly frightened me," I chuckle;
but a moment after whisper tenderly: "You wouldn't
laugh, dear, if it had been another girl?"

"No!"   Her eyes flame up—thank Heaven, with
real passion.   "No, Billy!   That would have broken
my heart."

"Ah, you love me!"   My arm goes round her lithe
waist, and I kiss her rapturously.

"Yes, I love you.   God knows how I love you.
God knows—God knows——" and she is crying now.

"Crying when I love you—when you are my wife—
when we may be happy?"

But here she draws herself away from me, gently
but uncompromisingly, and says : "Now, you must go
away.   I'm dripping wet and faint with hunger.   Send
me something to eat.   Let me see if I can't get some
dry clothes from some woman about the house."

"Suppose I sup with you?" I insinuate.

"Oh, that will be delightful!   Have the meal sent
up here."

"What do you want?"

"Anything—everything—I'm awful hungry!   It's
ten o'clock at night.   Hurry, Billy, send some woman
to me quick!   Don't you see I'm dripping wet and you
are too?   But I'm better provided than you."

"How?" I laugh.

"Well, just as I left Aunt Lucy's house, I suddenly
remembered I was going to a land minus *les modes de
Paris*, so I clapped two pairs of silk stockings in one
pocket and my best ball slippers in the other."   And
she produces, from under her waterproof, a pair of tiny
slippers and some dainty hosiery.   "Now run away;
tell them to get a fire built in this room, quick!   Take

care of your wife," she laughs coquettishly; "that's your duty *now*—take care of your wife." As I turn away, two soft arms are thrown lovingly around me, and Eve's piquant face is against mine, as she whispers: "Hurry the supper, and don't fail to come up with it."

So I run downstairs and give the necessary orders, and furthermore see they are executed.

There is no white woman in the house, but a mulatto girl of pleasant face and willing manner acts as chambermaid; I send her to Mrs. Hamilton.

Then I go down into the bar-room, and dry myself before a rousing fire, in company with Joe Shook and Rod Gibbon.

"Got out of your trouble with your high-flyer, Cap?" whispers the first, as we take a glass of whisky together.

"Only partially." My face grows so glum that they thoroughly believe me.

Something like half an hour after this, the mulatto girl puts her head in the doorway and says: "I'se got some supper for you, sah."

"Very well," I answer; "I'll go with you," and turn to follow her.

"Comin' down ag'in?" remarks Rod.

"I shouldn't wonder," I reply. "If you fellows have got any more good stories to tell me, I'll make a night with you."

A moment after I'm upstairs again, and gaze astonished. The tumble-down room looks cheerful, hickory logs are blazing in the old-fashioned fire-place, and Eve is flitting about over a supper-table, looking as dainty a maiden as ever tripped, in a simple, light, calico dress, very clean, but worn so piquantly she seems like a nymph.

"Now keep away, Billy," she flutters, as I approach her. "Sit down! It is our first meal together. How many lumps in your cup?" for she is presiding over the teapot.

"None at all," I laugh. "Kiss the cup."

"Now, don't be foolish. My lips are for better purposes. Oh, I knew you'd kiss me when I said that. But, Billy please—please sit down and behave yourself." No, not beside me; opposite me."

And I, obeying instructions, find myself looking for the first time over the family table at my wife.

There is not much variety to eat; there's nothing but tea to drink; but we make a merry meal of it. We have country sausages and spare ribs and some Maryland biscuits, fresh butter and fresh milk, and a pair of wild ducks; very plentiful in those regions in that day, but cooked with onions and baked till a gourmand would roll his eyes in horror at them. But of these dainties I make a tremendous repast. And for that matter, Eve plies her knife and fork quite diligently herself.

This being over, I look at her and produce my cigar-case and say: "Can I?"

"Why, certainly! You know, in all *little* things I'm going to be awfully obedient to you, Billy."

So while I smoke, I examine Arago's pocketbook. The rest of his articles are of slight consequence: a pen-knife, money, some old gold and silver coins; . among them, a faro chip shows the gambler.

But the pocketbook! In it there are two drafts for considerable amounts upon English bankers, and among other endorsements on one of them is that of "Frazer, Trenholm & Co.," of Liverpool, a firm notorious for its dealings with the Rebel government, at Richmond, and at one time understood to be its agent for putting Confederate bonds and Confederate cotton on the English market. Though apparently shielded by numerous other endorsements, one of these drafts has "Frazer, Trenholm & Co.," upon it.

"Arago must have been taking big chances," I say, as I show these to Eve, and whisper: "Money just received from England. When Baker investigates, he'll find the Rebel gold that bought my enemy!"

"You—you are going to show these to the War Department!" she gasps.

"Certainly! When I return to Washington. Hang it, I shall be the efficient Union officer—who killed the Rebel spy—who pursued him. Half a dozen teamsters will swear they saw me riding after him in hot pursuit."

"No, no," she mutters. "Leave the dead alone." To impress me, Eve has approached me.

"Nonsense!" I reply. "He was faithless to both

parties, took his money from either side, and would have made your beauty, also, part of his bribe. The Rebel Government need grieve for him no more than the Federal. "Were it not for Lommox and your part in this accursed pontoon business, I think I'd dare to take you back with me to Washington."

"Don't talk of that," Eve whispers hurriedly. "I dare not. I—I *will* not go now!" Her eyes seek mine with curious, pathetic, appealing intensity.

There is some motive aside from terror in her voice, that at this moment I cannot fathom, though later on I know.

"I can't bear to lose you." I speak into the little ear: "I *won't* be parted from you." I have got my arm round her exquisite waist now, that unprotected by corset seems to thrill under my embrace.

"You must—to save my life, Billy," she falters, her heart beating wildly, her beauty enchanting enough to make a hermit writhe within his cell.

The sleeves of her dress float back to her dimpled elbows, showing arms of fairest form dazzling and snowy as she strives to unclasp my hand.

The light cotton gown outlines a figure superb as that of Venus, but bedecked by fairy graces from gleaming neck to petite foot and ankle.

Her face as she turns it to me is covered with maiden blushes, but piquant, alluring and *loving*, as if she would bind me forever to her by a thousand charms; despite the cruelty with which she means to treat me— for there is a determination in her eyes that makes my heart sink.

I have drawn her down upon my knee. The pretty slippers are flashing as she struggles in piquant rebellion. "Sit here; be quiet, you alluring little witch!" I mutter. "You are going to be an obedient wife?"

"Yes, yes! Take me to Virginia! Take me to Virginia, Billy. Until then, as you are a gentleman, remember your *oath*, as I in all my life shall remember my vows." Somehow she has slipped from me. Turning she gazes at me sadly and, looking as immaculate as a Madonna, murmurs: "Now good-night, loved one. I shall pray for you this evening."

"Good-night," I mutter surlily, and turn to the door. But her arms are round me and she is sobbing: "What an ingrate I am. You are risking your honor, your life, to save mine! But don't, don't think me an unresponsive wife, Billy. Know that I love you."

"Love *me?* Ha, ha! Ho, ho!" I laugh, her beauty driving me to a sarcastic despair.

"Love *you!*" Her lips quiver, she murmurs brokenly: "Can't you see! Don't you know, I—I have loved you ever since I was a little girl."

"Pish! I have killed the man you feared would betray you if he guessed you were my wife! And yet——"

"And yet I shall hold you to your oath!" she whispers.

"An oath you'll love me better if I break!"

"No, no!"

She has fled from me, then turned at bay for I have followed her. Her eyes shine like stars, her tresses that were banded up have come unbound and fall about her, the soft light of the room tinting them till their brown becomes like floating gold.

Her beauty makes me forget all else save that I am her husband, and she my wife, whose lips have told me that she loves me. These lips I seek with mine, and to my touch they answer soft, clinging and dewy with a passion that from my eyes has flamed into hers.

"My own, my bride." I whisper.

"Billy!" she sighs to me.

My hand caressing her white neck, touches a little golden chain from which depends a bauble. I stoop to kiss the gleaming bosom on which it lies. In rounded maiden beauty it throbs to my caress.

As my lips touch the bauble, my wife cries, a strange triumph in her voice: "Darling, you are kissing the Confederate flag!"

"Not *my* flag!" I say sternly, starting back, my hand half raised to take the traitorous emblem of enamelled gold and diamond stars, from its sweet resting-place.

But now she is pressing the disloyal thing to her lips and murmuring what seems like a prayer to it and crying: "O happy omen!"

"Forget your fetich, dear," I whisper. "There are other uses for those sweet lips to-night."

But suddenly Eve seems to become another being, some other passion dominates her heart. She draws herself up and mutters hoarsely: "Your oath! I hold you to it, as you are a gentleman! Ay—even as you are my husband; for without it I would not have wed you—dearly as I love you! No, no!"

She tears herself from my arms and stands like a priestess making sacrifice, her eyes flash, she cries: "I have a *duty* to my cause!"

Then some kind of martyrdom flies over her face, she pleads: "Take me to Virginia, Billy! take me to Virginia! No, no, please don't kiss me—forgive me—let me go—your oath—good-night—go."

For a moment I gaze indignant, but smite her with: "You dare say that to me, your husband?"

"Yes—because I love you—because I adore you—because I will have you *truly mine!*" She wrings her hands, but her eyes gleam with indomitable resolve. She throws open the door, and begs: "Remember your oath? You swore it by all that is sacred. I'll hold you to it if it breaks my heart! Then shudders pathetically: "Go!—forgive me! GO!"

Stricken and dazed, yet forced from her by her words, I stagger from the room and stride savagely down the stairs and join Messrs. Shook and Gibbon, and play a game of poker with them and drink whisky with them till almost morning. As we rise from the gaming table, Shook says: "Haven't got squared yit, with your lady, about that Frederick gal, eh Cap?"

"No," I mutter, and my tone is so gloomy and my face so savage, that the two believe I have the most jealous spouse on earth.

As they go away from me, I think I hear Gibbon jeer: "Fired!" and the two guffaw uproarously.

But I am too miserable to resent their mirth and sit and ponder over the day that has brought to me a wife who is not a wife, and a homicide that is not a murder. Anyway, I don't repent either. Eve loves me, I'll swear to that! Arago deserved his death at the hands of any loyal man, I'll take my oath to that! And what do I deserve? I'm technically a traitor—aiding a Rebel spy to escape—but hang me if any man won't save the woman he loves—if he don't, he may be Union he may be Secesh, but he's not a human being!

CHAPTER XXII.

QUASHIE, THE SECESH NEGRO.

THE roosters are crowing ; the morning light is coming as I think this last.

Her safety starts me up.   Though I first look to her comfort.

Partially dried underclothes will be neither pleasant nor healthful for my dainty darling.

I rack my brain to find Eve others.   If there is any store in this broken-down village it will hardly be open now, and we must be getting on our way very quickly.

The mulatto wench make her appearance—telling her my wants she suggests : "Sutlers."

"Lammersdorff's my man," I think.   Telling the girl to hurry up breakfast, and rewarding her with a dollar for her trouble of the night before, I set out to find the German.

This does not take long in the circumscribed limits of Port Tobacco, which looks even more dilapidated in the sunlight—for, I thank heaven, for Eve's sake, there are indications of clearing in the sky—than the night before shrouded by gloom and obscured by falling rain.

Passing from the hotel, I wander by the old Court-House in the centre of its unkept square, and in a paddock some few hundred yards from this, among a lot of other sutlers' wagons—these purveyors to the army, for their own protection, keeping in this part of the country pretty well together—I find Lammersdorff.

That worthy German who is just making his toilet beside one of his own teams, on seeing me, looks very mysterious and leading me aside asks cautiously :

" Did you git her ? "

" My wife," I answer carelessly.   " Of course I did ! she's up at the Brawner House now—has been all night."

" Vell, for a bridegroom you is an early riser, young

man, but in dat Brawner House dey has insects dot would make a gobernment mule rise up and shake himself. Now ver did you leave dat U. S. Marshal chap? Ven you left me you looks like assassinating."

"Oh," I answer as lightly as I can, "after I took my wife from him, he didn't have any more business about here. You put that matter out of your head ; you'll never hear of it *from him* again."

"So! Dat is good! Dat Secret Serbice man won't say nutten," remarks the sutler, apparently much relieved. Then, I telling him my wants, he adds : "Jake Conrade is your man. He takes drygoods to de young ladies dat follows de army—mid de camp."

I don't ask what kind of young ladies, but following Lammersdorff to Conrade's wagon, soon find myself supplied with a few pairs of good, strong, ladies' stockings and some feminine underclothes that I hope may be of service to replace Eve's soaked garments that can hardly be more than half dry by this time.

With these in my hand, I seek the Brawner House, and running upstairs knock at the door of my wife's bedroom.

"Who is it ?" comes to me in her sweet voice.

"Billy, of course ! "

"Well, ' Billy-of-course,' run downstairs at once and tell them to hurry breakfast."

"Are you nearly ready ? "

"Certainly, but I—I don't know what to do for stockings. Ball-room hosiery won't suit Maryland roads, and the ones I wore on the journey are simply caked with mud."

"Well, open the door and see what hubby sends you. I have been out shopping for you."

"What have you got?" There is feminine curiosity in the voice, and loud rustling in the room ; the door is opened a very little, and an arm white as purest marble and symmetrical as the lost ones of the Venus of Praxiteles, is extended diffidently groping in the air. It is the left arm. I seize its wrist, and selecting the second finger, press my lips upon the golden circlet that binds her to me.

Then I quickly add to the wedding ring the bauble I had purchased in Washington, slipping it upon the pretty finger.

"What—what are you doing?" she whispers.

"Putting on your engagement-ring," I say. "The one we forgot before our hurried nuptials."

"You—you are killing me with kindness," is faltered out to me.

"Then here's some more kindness!" With this I draw the superb limb to me, and despite a bewitching little scream and slight struggle, I kiss rapturously the dimpled shoulder, and am rewarded by a soft lingering sigh from the other side of the door. Next I place in the little hand the package I have bought from the sutler, and as I run downstairs hear her cry: "You good hubby! you've got just what your wife wanted.

A few minutes after, as I sit at the Brawner breakfast table, a natty maid in gray riding-habit trips in to my side.

Fortunately we are alone, Shook and Gibbon being engaged in sleeping off the whisky of the night before, and I get as sweet a kiss as ever man received.

"That's for being a good boy, hubby," she says.

"Ah, the engagement-ring," I laugh.

She gazes at the two little circlets upon her finger, the one gleaming with a diamond, the other the simple symbol of her vows; then blushes hotly and laughs: "You—you can give me another one for that, Billy."

"Certainly!"

"Now stop making love to me. Quick, let us eat our breakfast and get under way. I've spoken to our landlord, and a lady's nag and side-saddle will be brought round together with Roderick in ten minutes. Eat in a hurry."

With this we both address ourselves to very indifferent coffee, but good corn cakes, bacon, and fresh fish, my bride explaining hurriedly to me: "I've found out where Wat Bowie is. With his assistance, half our troubles will be over."

As we finish the meal, there is a sound of horses' hoofs at the door, and settling our bill, I lead my bride out to where a darky is holding Roderick and a half-bred, rather gaunt, but apparently active mare. This nag has upon her back a dilapidated side-saddle. Behind it I carefully pack Eve's waterproof and my soldier overcoat for her use in case the rain should come again, though the sun is at present shining brightly.

I arrange the stirrup for her, and a moment after, she placing her little foot confidently in my hand, I swing her into the saddle. Then giving the dark stable boy a dollar, I jump on my charger and we canter off, passing a platoon of cavalry that have apparently come down to guard the sutlers' teams. But these pay little attention to us, the lieutenant in command simply saluting my shoulder-straps as I pass him.

Returning this, I follow Eve—for she is guide now —along the road over which we had returned the night before, but after a half mile we turn out of this, following the track that leads towards the hamlet called Allan's Fresh. On one side of us are the great swamp drained by the waters of Allan's Creek, which run into the Wicomico River, that joins the Potomac to the south of us.

"I'm glad we didn't have to go past that awful place," remarks Eve with a shudder as we take this turn. Then suddenly she starts and ejaculates : "Oh Billy, how horrible you look ! You haven't washed your face nor combed your hair. I'm sure you've not slept. You've—you've not been thinking of—of the man in the road?"

"No ; that doesn't trouble me very much. I've seen better men than he fall by the thousands in battle, I mutter. "I played poker all night to kill time."

Then perhaps catching some reproach in my face Eve gasps : "How sternly you look at me ; " and shudders : "You're—you're beginning to—to *hate* me !" Suddenly her eyes fill with tears, her coral lips tremble, she begins to cry as if her heart would break.

What man could resist the sorrow of so beautiful a creature? I swing my horse close to the side of her mare, my arm goes round her slight waist. I draw the supple figure, in all its rounded beauty, to me, and whisper : "No ; I love you. Despite your cruelty —I love you !"

"And it is because you love me," she whispers, "and because *I* love you, that I feel I am so despicable ! Forgive me, Billy !" Then even as she rides, superb horsewoman that she is, she throws a soft arm round my neck and gives me a kiss that makes my heart throb. Next, dashing her hand across her eyes, she calls cheerily : "Come on, Billy ; let's get to Virginia."

But during this ride, the young lady seems to require a good many little delicate attentions from her cavalier. Soon I have to shorten her stirrup. To do this I lift her from the saddle, and even as I hold her beautiful form in my arms she gives me another kiss and says : "That's for being so good to *me.*"

So the all the time she seems to be trying to make her peace with me by the delicate arts and subtle fascinations of a woman who feels that she is doing me a wrong. Sometimes, I have thought since, she was appealing to me to forgive her for the greater wrong she did me afterwards.

The ride goes along very pleasantly, and a few minutes after this Eve draws up her nag sharply, takes a quick look about her, as if to be sure of her surroundings, then gallops up the road about fifty yards, and turning her mare deftly sends her, in fox-hunting style, over the snake-rail fence into some swamp land.

A moment after I put Roderick to his leap, and am beside her. "What did you do that for?" I ask. "Why couldn't you let me open that tumble-down gate for you?" I point to some bars about fifty yards away.

"Of course not!" she answers. "To have opened the gate would indicate some one had come in here, and I don't imagine that Lieutenant Wat Bowie wants visitors."

"Oh, he's in the Confederate service?"

"Yes ; the partisan service. He was a Maryland lawyer ; I think now he is connected with a gentleman named Mosby, over in Virginia."

"Mosby! Who is he?" I ask. For at that time the name of the great guerrilla was just beginning to be known.

"Oh, he's one of our gallant, dashing fellows. If this war lasts much longer, you'll hear of Mosby," Eve laughs. "A Virginia boy, from Fauquier County. He has been riding with Stuart, but lately has been detached ; I believe, at his own request. Lieutenant Bowie, I presume, has come over for information."

While she is saying this, we are passing along a

half effaced trail, the swamp with its low thickets of
alder and dogwood, its bigger trees of gum and beach,
and scrub swamp oak, enclosing it. So we go winding
about, Eve seeming to know the path perfectly. Some
half a mile further on we emerge into a little clearing
in which is a Virginia shake cabin, with a chimney of
mud and stones running up its gable end.

As we come out of the timber, a couple of curs commence to bark savagely, a negro flies out yelling, and
two men, springing from the cabin rifle in hand,
cover me with their pieces.

"For God's sake, stop where you are, Billy !" cries
Eve to me, then rides towards the cabin, waving her
white handkerchief and calling : "Put down your
guns ! Watt Bowie, Jim Wiltshire, don't you know
Eva Ashley?" Suddenly she laughs. "Why, there's
Quashie also ! "

And the darky gives a yell of delight : " Missie Ebe—
Missie Ebe ! You'se got out of de Yanks' clutches.
Praise de Lawdy ! Praise de Lawdy ! " and fairly dances
with joy.

A moment later, at her beckoning, I ride up. The
two white men look suspiciously at my blue uniform.
They still have their rifles in their hands, cocked and
ready for action. · The negro turns evil eyes on me, for
he is one of the curiosities of the war—a Secesh darky ;
one whose love for his mistress makes him the enemy
of the army that comes to give him freedom. The
negro guide who betrayed Ulrick Dahlgren in his raid
on Richmond, was one ; Quashie was another ; but,
fortunately for the Union arms, there were very few
of these black-skinned anomalies.

"Well, Miss Ashley," remarks the Confederate apparently in command, "this *is* a rather curious
visitor you bring us."

"*No!* Miss Ashley," remarks Eve sharply, "but
Mrs. Hamilton. The gentleman with me is my
husband."

"Your husband ! " ejaculates one of the men.

"What ! " cries the other Confederate ; as if they
can hardly believe their ears.

But the darky mutters : "Oh, golly Goliah ! She's
married de Yank ; " then astounds us by guffawing :
'Clar' to goodness, Miss Ebe, I'se been a-fearin' dis.

I knowed you was gone on de Yank cap'n eber since he captured you at Frederick."

"You're quite right, Quashie," laughs my bride blushing vividly ; and continues : "Captain Hamilton, let me introduce Lieutenant Walter Bowie and Sergeant Jim Wiltshire."

"Then let me congratulate you, sir," remarks Bowie, his manner growing cordial, "on being the most fortunate man I know."

But the other cries out sharply : "Captain *Billy* Hamilton ?"

"Certainly," I reply.

"And you come as a *friend ?*"

"I don't come as an enemy."

"No enemy ?" chuckles Bowie. "when Provost-Marshal of Baltimore you hunted me through three counties ! "

"At that time I would have very much liked to see you," I reply.

"And now that you see me, what do you want with me ? "

"Well, my wife is too good a Rebel for me to dare to trust her in Washington ; therefore I have brought her to you to ask your assistance in getting her through to the Confederate lines."

"You guarantee this to be a fact, Miss Ashley—I mean Mrs. Hamilton ?" queries Bowie earnestly.

"Certainly ! I guarantee that my husband comes here as a friend ; and that he will leave you as a friend," answers Eve decidedly.

"All right ; it is a flag of truce till this affair is over," laughs the lieutenant pleasantly, "though you could never have escaped from me." And Bowie points to two men who have just shown themselves in the entrance of the clearing, apparently following behind us on the path that we came.

A moment later these scouts join us, and receiving orders from the lieutenant, again glide into the undergrowth and disappear. "I always like to be sure against surprise," remarks this Maryland lawyer, who has grown into an enterprising and desperate partisan

"You think you can get us across the Potomac tonight ?" I ask eagerly.

"That all depends upon the weather. We want to

cross ourselves.   And I believe a storm is blowing up,"
he points to some clouds that are now gathering.   "If
it's a black and nasty night, we'll make the attempt.
You'll have to leave your horses here ; you can't get
them across : but we've good nags on the other
side."

"Where do you intend to cross ? " I ask.

"We'll have to go pretty well down the river.   Mat-
tias Point, with two Yankee Army Corps at Aquia Creek
and Falmouth, wouldn't do.   We'd just run into Burnside's whole army."

The accuracy of his information surprises me, but I
make no comment upon it.

"I think we'll have to go as far down as Baynesville
at least," he continues.   "Then we can probably get
over to the Rappahannock near Leedstown, and across
that river you'll find your own beloved Dixie's land,
Mrs. Hamilton."

During this conversation, Quashie has been looking
me over ; several affectionate little gestures from his
loved mistress to me, have gradually changed his
manner from animosity and suspicion to respect and
regard.   Noting this, I laugh : "Quashie how about
that black eye? Was it an *Irish* government mule,
gave it to you ? "

At this he gazes at me suspiciously again, but Eve
whispering to him, "You may trust your new master,
Quashie," the black guffaws !   "Fo' de Lawd, Massa,
Capt'n !   It was a U. S. army mule wid sergeant stripes
on him arm."

Into this colloquy Bowie breaks, saying cordially.
"Now, just bring your lady, Captain Hamilton, and
we'll have lunch.   I gathered in a sutler two days
ago, Quashie is a first-rate cook, and we're in the land
of plenty.   Jim and I were just sitting down when the
dogs announced your arrival."

So we all go into the cabin, and there find a generous
meal of canned provisions, fried ham, good coffee
and some biscuit baked in a Dutch oven, and made of
United States Army flour, I notice.   So, with a bottle
of whisky of excellent quality, we gentlemen contrive
to pass the time, I adding to the store of good things
some of the famous *Bouquets Espéciales* from the
pouches on Roderick's saddle.

"By Jove, these *are* beautiful cigars!" remarks Bowie. "Do you know, Captain, about the only hardship that I really suffer is the loss of good cigars regularly. When I was practising at the Maryland bar it was twelve or fifteen a day; now it is one in twelve or fifteen days."

Here he is interrupted by the return of the two scouts, who come in to their dinner, their places being immediately taken by Bowie and Wiltshire. These men, Mr. Smith and Mr. Jake Brown, look upon my uniform with considerable distrust.

"It's kinder lucky you had a lady wid ye, Cap," remarks Jake. "I'm a sure shot, and you'd a-never got through that ar path a living man, if it hadn't been for that ar riding-habit alongside of you uns."

"And I saved your life?" cries Eve with affrighted eyes; then she suddenly mutters: "Some time perhaps I will save it again, Billy," and looks at me pathetically and all this day seems to cling to me as if she feared what the morrow might bring to us. For Bowie, as he has stepped out, rifle in hand, after scanning the sky has remarked: "It's pretty nearly certain we cross the Potomac, or drown in it to-night."

Following him from the cabin, I find the clouds are gathering fast; the wind rustling among the swamp foliage is growing stronger.

Here a little hand is placed upon my shoulder, and Eve whispers: "It's going to storm; it's getting blacker every minute. They'll never get those pontoons to Frederickburgs in time!"

While she is making this remark, I look glumly at her. Every exclamation on this subject shows she is an unrepentant Confederate and the awful political gulf there is between my wife and myself.

But perhaps catching reproach in my glance, she says coaxingly, taking my big hand in her two little ones: "Forgive me, Billy, for being a Rebel," then bursts out in a tone that startles me: "Pray God you forgive me *to-morrow*, for being a Rebel!"

"What do you mean?"

"I'll—I'll tell you in Virginia—but—not now," she falters; then begs piteously: "Don't—don't let us part *twice*," and nestles to me in a way that makes me very tender to her.

I look round, we are alone, at the back of the cabin ; the busy clatter of knives and forks from the scouts in-side denotes they will not interrupt us immediately.

I sit down upon an old settee and draw my bride upon my knee. Her plumed hat has fallen off her graceful head ; a few stray nut-brown curls blowing about, caress my lips ; the tight fitting riding-habit outlines a form of superb symmetry and rounded beauty ; from beneath the skirt looped up for walking peep two little feet and exquisite ankles. I gaze on this my bride's beauty sadly and sternly.

She looks at me archly, coquettishly, but noting my glance, her eyes grow full of tears, she murmurs pa-thetically "You—you forgive me ? "

"For what ?" I ask savagely.

"You *know !* " and she hides her face bashfully upon my breast.

Suddenly she cries : "Billy, I—I musn't love you too much ! " springs from my knee and walking about com-mences to chat with me quite merrily, telling me I ought to wash my face and hands, if not before din-ner, at least after dinner. "Don't look such an awful unkempt trooper," she half laughs, half cries. "Why, one would think you didn't have a wife to take care of you."

"For God's sake, don't torture me ! " I mutter, and stride glumly off ; but taking her advice, wash my face, and, borrowing a razor from Bowie, who returns about this time and seems to be more of a dandy than the rest of his command, I succeed in shaving myself before a broken piece of mirror.

Returning the barber's implement to the Rebel lieu-tenant, I suggest : "You're quite a Beau Brummel, aren't you ? "

"Oh, you mean because I keep this shaving tool ? " he laughs. "Not at all ; though I used to be some-thing of the kind before my trooper days. Three times have I saved myself from Federal troops seek-ing for me by disguising myself as a nigger-wench, and found it convenient to have a clean face on such occasions. It's a matter of business with me, not beauty. Though I don't mind looking my best when we get up a dance in the hills of Fauquier County, and the belles of Upperville trip the measure with us cavalry lads. Some handsome girls in Virginia, eh, Captain ? "

"Yes, I think I've shown that I appreciate their beauty," I reply, casting a longing glance at my wife, who is outside the cabin, apparently in a brown study.

"She's a little down in the mouth, isn't she, Captain Hamilton ? " remarks the Lieutenant sympathetically. "But you can be sure that I'll do my best to take care of her, and there's no girl more popular in Virginia than the young lady you've stolen from us. Why, even Carrie Barton of Fredericksburg, to my mind is not quite as pretty, and she's the toast of Richmond. You —you haven't got another of those cigars ? " he asks longingly.

"Yes, half a dozen of them ! Help yourself. God bless you, my generous fellow ! " I say, and shake his hand warmly. In fact, all of them now, from enemies seem to have become comrades to me—for this trip.

Stepping out to my wife, I note there are tears in her eyes, but she brushes them away as I sit down beside her. "You are grieving at leaving the delights and comforts of Washington ? " I suggest.

"Oh, no, for I'm going to my own people."

"Ah, but my people are now your people," I say.

"Not yet," she answers ; then whispers in sudden self-reproach : "What will you think of me, Billy, at this time to-morrow ? WHAT ? "

"Always as my wife—my beloved wife."

"I hope so ; and yet——" She wrings her hands, then murmurs : "Don't let us think of that ; let us try to be happy now ; " and charms me by her coquetries of manner, her exquisite graces of body, intellect and soul, and I love her even more as the storm breaks upon us and we have to retreat to the house.

But now darkness is coming upon Maryland. The wind is howling through the trees. The scouts have come, in ; Bowie has made all his preparations ; Quashie has cooked for us another good meal.

"Eat hearty, everybody," Jake, our guide chuckles, " our next feed'll be in ole Virginia, or——" he claps his big jaws together with a suggestive snap.

"Yes, be sure and drink lots of strong coffee, Mrs. Hamilton, the night will be bitter cold upon the water," adds Bowie to my wife.

As we eat the Lieutenant remarks : "You've got to leave the horses here.   You can perhaps pick them up when you come back, Captain.   Let's go out and make 'em comfortable while you're away."

I go with him to a broken-down barn some hundred yards from the cabin, where we do everything possible for Roderick and the mare, leaving them food and water for a week, but not closing the stable door, though putting up the bars in the paddock.

Returning from this, I am met by Eve and her darky henchman.   "Quashie," she says to him in pleading impressiveness, "remember this gentleman is my husband and your master ; that I love him as my life— better than my life—obey his words as you would mine ; love him, as you do me."

"I can't do de last, Missie," answers the negro ; "but I can do de rest, you kin bet yo' life on it. Dough I nebber 'spected yo'd say dis of a Yankee offisah.   Nebber, so help me Gawd ! "

"Thank you, Quashie," I mutter, and give the black my hand.

A greeting that apparently astounds him, for he hesitates to take it ; then suddenly seizes it and mutters: "Lawd bless yo' Massa Hamilton ! You do de right t'ing by her an' I do de right t'ing by you'. I'se yo' man from dis time on !" and goes off to gather his mistress's few belongings.

"You can trust Quashie now, my Billy," says Eva earnestly.   "He is yours as he is mine, with every beat of his true negro heart."

Little words these, but carrying life and death with them, though I know it not.

CHAPTER XXIII.

"I HAVE BEEN TRAITOR ENOUGH ! "

"Dear one, you have everything you need for the journey ?"   I ask anxiously of the beautiful creature at my side, for her charge to Quashie about me has made me even more tender than before.

"Everything, my husband, thanks to your purchases this morning. Though you made an awful fit of those stockings ; three sizes too large for my feet."

"Well, better luck next time," I say, and give her a mighty squeeze.

Here, Eve starts from me, for Bowie coming out of the cabin laughs : "Stop flirting with your wife, Captain Hamilton, and tramp along after me. We must get under way for Dixie."

A moment later we follow him, as do the whole party. Guided by Jake Brown, we tramp a long mile, half of it through a swamp trail, the other portion along an unused wood-road ; I supporting Eve and doing the best I can for her in this weary part of the journey.

At the end of the wood-road we come to a little creek that at low tide would probably be a mud flat, but is now full of water. Moored in this is a light-draught, but good-sized skiff or boat. It holds our party easily ; in fact, it would hold three or four more. Making my wife as comfortable as possible in the stern sheets of this, and shielding her with a tarpaulin that is in the boat as well as some blankets we have brought for her, and every one—God bless them !—doing as much as possible for my darling's comfort, the boat is shoved off out on the waters, into the darkness.

But it is guided by skilful hands and rowed by strong arms, and the out-going tide is with us. An hour afterwards we have come out of the Wicomico River, and are on the bosom of the Potomac, which is several miles wide at this point. The night is dark ; the rain is falling heavily.

"If the lightning doesn't show us to them, we're pretty safe from Yankee patrol boats," whispers Bowie as he steers the craft.

And the night grows darker, and the rain falls heavier, but fortunately there is little lightning. Though the wind makes a nasty, choppy sea of the Potomac, which is here practically an estuary.

After dodging one steam launch, the noise of her machinery and sparks from her smoke-stack disclosing her to us, at four o'clock in the morning, some two hours before daylight, we strike the Virginia shore, and running carefully and cautiously down it, make landing somewhere about six in the morning in a little cove which is apparently well known to Bowie, about a mile below Baynesville.

Part of this trip, under the tarpaulin and the blankets, I think Eve has slept, for she has spoken little to me except to assure me that she is perfectly comfortable—that she has made one or two such passages before—that she doesn't mind it in the least, except for my sake; snuggling her little hand into mine.

Leaving the boat by the first light of the morning, we soon reach a farmer's house.

"One of the right kind!" remarks Wiltshire, and we find it very much of the right kind, for everything that hospitality can suggest is done for us, the daughter of the house giving my wife dry underclothes and making a great deal of her.

Though, did not Eve assure them that I was her husband, my uniform would probably receive a cold welcome, as the Virginia husbandman and his wife look upon it with by no means cordial eyes.

In fact, at breakfast, the farmer's daughter, a buxom, chirpy lassie of about eighteen, remarks laughingly: "'Deed I couldn't marry a man dressed in that nasty Yankee blue! You just get Cap'n Hamilton into nice Confederate gray, and your fellow'll look twice as purty to you—'deed he will, Miss Ashley!"

During the laugh that follows this remark, Eve droops her exquisite head, as if ashamed; though as I lead her down to put her on the horse, her manner is coquettishly alluring and charmingly tender to me. Still, once or twice, as I speak tenderly to her, she hangs her head and turns away her glance, as if in some great, though latent, distress. "It is the thought that we must part soon," I conclude, and that idea makes my heart heavy also.

The party is soon on horseback—for information has been brought that there are no Federal forces in the neighborhood, all of these having been drawn into the Union army some thirty miles above us, and Bowie thinks we must start at once.

So this morning we gallop through Virginia mud from the Potomac to the Rappahannock. The sun has got out again and is shining, and it seems to be a pleasant jaunt to my wife, for the nearer we get to the Confederate lines, the brighter becomes her face, the more buoyant her air, the more loving her manner to me. Though sometimes, as she looks on me, strange spasms of agony seem to run over her sensitive features, that ripple with each passion of her enthusiastic soul, each thought in her vivacious mind.

These eccentricities of her face, grow more numerous and more vivid as we cross the Rappahannock on a flat-boat ferry, near Leedstown landing on the opposite bank, a few miles below Port Royal.

A quarter of an hour after this, we see the Southern flag, and are challenged by a scouting party of the Fifteenth Virginia Cavalry, and Eve cries, a mighty joy in her voice:

"Here are *my* boys in gray! Hurrah! the Confederate colors."

Then Bowie and Wiltshire answering the challenge, after a short conference we are passed through the Rebel picket line, and I find myself in the presence of Major Robinson, who is in command of a squadron of his regiment that are patrolling this bank of the river, to see no divisions of the Federals attempt to cross unobserved below Fredericksburg.

Gazing on my uniform, this officer orders me under guard. But, after a few minutes' conference with Eve and Bowie, he returns to me accompanied by my wife.

"Major Robinson," she says, "permit me to introduce my husband—Captain Hamilton of the United States Cavalry."

"You've not come under a flag of truce, Captain," remarks the Virginia major."

"Not unless my wife is one."

"Well, sir, she's better than any flag of truce," answers the Confederate officer gallantly. "Both sides surrender to beauty. As I understand from her, you've brought Mrs. Hamilton into our lines to save her from a very serious complication in Washington, brought about by her devotion to our cause."

"Yes," cries the girl ecstatically. "I have learnt that Longstreet's whole division is entrenched on the heights at Fredericksburg. I kept the Federals back, Billy; I kept them back! I did the work of an army corps!"

"Better than an army corps!" remarks the Confederate major. "Before the Yanks can cross, Jackson will have time to join."

"They're beaten ! They're beaten before the battle is begun ! " cries Eve in half-delirious joy.

"Yes ; if Burnside is foolish enough to make the attempt now," I think gloomily ; then look at my wife with indignation. For she is commencing to make me thoroughly realize that I am a traitor, that in shielding her I have been false to my army—my comrades. For I have saved one who has committed a military crime and doomed brave men to death—even though she is my bride.

But the girl doesn't seem to think so. Her manner is buoyant, her eye proud, her step elated ; and all this tends to make me very firm against the allurements of a beauty that now she turns on my sad heart and brings to bear upon my senses, with every subtle art a girl can use to make a man turn traitor.

The Confederate officer and my companions of the journey between lines, have, with the instincts of gentlemen, moved away from us and left my bride and me alone in a pretty sylvan glade that runs down towards the Rappahannock, which is now muddy with coming torrent, though the sun is bright in the heavens and shines upon the girl, to give her an ethereal loveliness for she has thrown off wraps and waterproof and stands, her eyes ablaze, her fair hair floating in the soft breeze, with every beauty line of her superb figure made apparent by the tight-fitting bodice and draping folds of her soft, clinging riding-habit—*to tempt me*.

Despite my anger, at her, my tone grows very sad as I say ! "We part here ; Eve, we *must* part here."

Suddenly, I start and gaze at her astounded ; for now, as she speaks to me, I begin to have a glimmering of the horrible thing she meant by saying : "Take me to Virginia."

"Part *here ?* " Do you suppose I could have been so cruel to you my loved one, had I ever intended to part from you again?" She has come to me and put her arms round me : her voice is soft with passion, her eyes dewy with love, she puts her sweet lips up to mine and kisses me with all her soul and whispers bashfully : "*Here* is where we *begin* to live together as husband and wife ! "

"What do you mean?"

"I mean *this!* As I told you one night in Washington, every girl should give to the cause she loves the man she loves. You I want to give to my country, for I love you; it's the greatest sacrifice I can make to it. The more I adore you, the grander my offering! The more your heroism, the greater will be my glory in you!"

"What do you mean?" I repeat. For even now I cannot understand, I *will not* understand the devilish bribe she is proposing.

"I mean, here is *my* flag! The one you kissed that night upon my bosom. As you love me, come under it, and *fight* under it, and I will be the most loving wife to you that ever blessed a man. You shall have my soul, Billy, my soul! I love you now! Oh, how I love you, or I would not beg you to do this thing for me." Then she suddenly screams, "Don't look at me that way!" for I have turned awful eyes on her.

"And this is your price," I whisper to her. "My honor, for your love. This is a good wife's maxim! this is a *true* wife's maxim! I have risked my life to save you—I have tainted my honor to save you—but, damn it, I've been traitor enough!"

"Ah, you give me up?" She is pleading now, her blue eyes soft and dark as violets with passion.

"*Never!*" I say fiercely, as I look upon her beauty.

"Never! God bless you for those words Billy! she sighs.

"NEVER! I made an oath to you; I have kept it. For three torturing days I, your husband, have walked by a wife who is not a wife. Every beauty, every charm of your manner, every kiss of your lips, has been to me a temptation, an agony. I have kept *my* vow; you keep *yours!* For seven days I swore; three days have passed; only four remain, then do *you* keep your vows! I go with you into the Confederate lines, but not as a Confederate soldier; I accompany you as your husband, to put you in a place of safety. I go with you into the Rebel lines as a Confederate prisoner."

Running from her, I call out hoarsely to the Southern officer, who is standing some fifty yards away, busy with his men: "Major Robinson, I wish to see you!"

"At your service, captain," he answers, coming towards me.

"You know I've been paroled until exchanged," I cry to him. "I demand to rescind my parole. Here is my sword and my side-arms. Send me as a prisoner to Richmond with my wife." Then looking at Eve, who is gasping by my side, I laugh hoarsely: "You, my bride, don't escape from me, your husband!"

But the Confederate major, stepping to us, says: "I hardly understand you. You say you wish to rescind your parole, to surrender yourself as my prisoner?"

"I do!"

That I refuse to accept, Captain Hamilton. Your parole, once given, is sacred. We have enough to support in our impoverished country, without taking a paroled prisoner there."

"You refuse to take me?"

"Certainly. A military compact once made is good, and cannot be made void at the wish of one party to the agreement without the consent of the other. I refuse to accept the surrender of your parole. You have a quarter of an hour here, under your wife's protection, which acts as a flag of truce; after that time, Lieutenant Bowie and an escort will take you back to the shore of the Potomac. Your wife is too high in our esteem for me to permit you to take any unnecessary risks in escorting her to the safety of our lines." With this the Confederate major walks away, and I see him giving orders to Bowie and Wiltshire and Brown.

"You see," whispers Eve desperately, "you can come with me in only one way—as a Confederate soldier. Think how I love you! Don't break both our hearts. Come! No wife shall be so loving. Come!" and her soft arms go round me tight and clinging, and her dewy lips give kisses unto mine that might be the foretaste of a paradise.

"Never!" I whisper doggedly. "Never! I have been traitor enough, and I know it better now than I did when I saved you. You have had your way; you will part from me, a wife who has never had a husband. I will leave you, a husband who is wedded to the memory of a beautiful, a noble, girl, in all but one thing; she thinks naught of her husband's honor."

"My God! Don't reproach me that way! Others

have left the United States service for my flag, and
hold their heads high enough."

"But not as you propose—not as military outcasts
and deserters. Besides, I am not one of them. Thank
God, not one of them!"

"Then you refuse to accept my obedience as your
wife?"

"No, on the contrary, I hold you to it," I whisper
firmly. "You are mine, my wife, and whether it takes
days, or months, or years, you are still mine, my wife!
Here!—you are going to a land of poverty. Take
what money I have about me—take it *all!*"

"No—no! If you won't accept my wifely devotion,
do you suppose I'm so mean a thing as to take support
from you. *Here!*" And with this cry she throws the
money I had given her in Washington down at my
feet. "I will not accept support from you," she
says proudly, "though I, for my part, will give you
honor and obedience and love as my husband. I will
be your true wife, though parted from you. Your name
shall be borne and held and honored by me. That is
the only expiation I can give you for my crime."
There are tears in her voice. "That's what it is, Billy;
I know it now—an awful crime against love, against
you. Had I adored you less, I would have sinned
against our love less! But I wanted you and I to have
one soul—one heart, dear one! That my joy would
be your joy; my triumph, your triumph! But now, I
—O God I've made you hate me. Forgive me—forgive
me—forgive me!"

"No; love you—*love you*—LOVE YOU;" I whisper;
for her beauty, in her despair, in *my* despair, seems to
me greater than ever. "I love you—I love you—and
even the Confederate lines shall not keep me from you."

"My God, you'll lose your life!"

"But I will win your love. When I pluck that accursed banner down, I'll clutch you to my heart."

"No—no. Don't hate that flag."

"I will! For it stands between you and me. Remember!—look on those rings that bind you to me,
and know that I *will* have you. Good-bye." I seize
her in my arms.

Then how she clings to me! How she begs, how
she sobs, how she implores me to forgive her—to love

her—to go with her.   And her caresses are as entrancing, as if she were the Goddess of love, and her lips
are sweet as an angel's, and her voice pleading as
Delilah's, and her witcheries as alluring as a siren's.

But of a sudden, with a smothered moan, I break
from her embraces and run from her—for if I stay, I
know my love will destroy the little honor of a soldier
that I feel she has left in me.

Behind me I hear a scream, and soft cries of love;
but I *dare* not look back.

I hurry to the Confederate picket, and noting my
haggard eyes, the Rebel major says huskily: "These
partings with our war-brides are cruel things, Captain
Hamilton.   I have a girl-wife in Richmond," and his
brown moustache twitches.   "But good-bye; she's
coming after you," he whispers nervously.   "Mount
your horse!   Get away quick!   Don't give her a *second* agony."

He salutes me, and Bowie and Wilshire and I pass
out of the Confederate lines.

Then I hear Robinson cry: "Good God, she's
fainted!" and something seems to crack in my head;
but I still go forward I—I *dare* not turn back.

Bowie's arm is round me for I am reeling in my
saddle.

But I stagger on, benumbed with misery and made
half comatose by despair, till four hours afterwards I
find myself and the Rebel lieutenant afloat on the Potomac.

BOOK V.

THE BATTLE FOR HER LOVE.

CHAPTER XXIV.

"I WILL GO TO THE REBEL CAPITAL."

Two days after this, I awake in the little cabin in the Maryland swamps to which Eve had taken me before we crossed to Virginia. Bowie, who is cooking his breakfast, remarks to me: "You've been out of your head a little, old man; but you'll pick up soon now."

"Was I delirious?" I question.

"Well, if you weren't," he half laughs, "you had an exciting wedding-day of it. Yesterday I thought I'd see if your delirious notions were *facts*, and rode over to where you raved about killing a United States Deputy-Marshal, and found if you had not slain him, somebody else had done his business just as you described it. A straight thrust *en carte*, eh, my boy?"

"Did I rave of anything else?" I ask anxiously.

"Well, *rather!*" He looks at me grimly. "I'm inclined to think, if some of your hallucinations were true, you had a very close call of putting on a gray uniform over in Virginia." Then he turns to me, and the laugh goes out of his voice as he whispers: "I'll take any message, anything you write, anything you wish to send to Mrs. Hamilton. And by the Lord Harry, if you want to go back to your wife, we'll make the trip together!"

But I mutter despairingly: "No; I have been traitor enough!" and try to stagger to my feet.

But I am scarce able to stand, and it is two days after this before I mount Roderick.

"You won't change your mind and go back to Virginia?" says Bowie in kindly voice to me, as he stands by my charger's side.

"No,—don't tempt me," I whisper hoarsely.

"You'd better remain here another day. You're not very strong yet, old man."

"No ; I will not put any further danger upon you. Besides, my leave of absence expires to-morrow ; I must go to Washington."

"Then this is all you want me to give Mrs. Hamilton ?" remarks the Confederate. And he holds up a note I have written in lead pencil, telling my wife to address any letters for me to the care of my sisters in Baltimore, that I will be true to my vows to her, as she must be true to her vows to me, reminding her of her promise and swearing that I will hold her in my arms soon, war or no war.

"Well, we all follow our own lights in this contest," says the partisan philosophically ; "and the next time you and I meet, I suppose, Captain Hamilton, we'll be enemies."

"Not enemies ! " I return ; "though we may be opposed to each other. For I know what you have done for me, Wat Bowie. You have taken care of a man unable, from misery, to take care of himself. You've got me through the lines, and risked your own life again to watch over me as a brother."

"Don't thank me too much," answers the gallant fellow kindly. "There's a girl over in Virginia who is a little sweet on you, I imagine ; and we think a mighty sight of her. A heap of my philanthropy was on your bride's account. So good-bye ; present my compliments to Mr. Secretary Stanton and tell him he won't get me again in the Old Capitol Prison where he once had me." Then he laughs. "By Jove, they ought to promote you for slaying that deputy United State marshal, if half you said of him was true."

But the thought of Arago and what I have to tell the War Department makes me wish to hurry on ; and so one of those curious partings of Border-State war takes place. Men who may have to fight each other in an hour, grip hands as friends, and I see the last of genial, whole-souled, dashing Wat Bowie—the hate and terror of the Secret Service. For the gallant chap falls, six months afterwards, in his foolhardy raid into Maryland to capture the Union governor of that State, potted from the roadside by a farmer with a bird-gun full of buckshot.

Five hours afterwards, just as it is getting dark, I ride up to my F Street boarding-house in Washington, in a most miserable and despairing frame of mind. I had left it braced by excitement and buoyant with bridegroom's hopes ; I come back to it bereft.

But I have not much time to meditate on my lost love. Little Mr. Finnaker comes in to me : "By Yankee Doodle," he cries, "I've been wanting to see you for the last day. Where have you been ?"

"In Baltimore most of the time—on leave of absence."

"Well, we've got the scoundrel ! *I* found him ! Arago was the traitor ! I always said so—you remember that. I always said so. For three days I tracked the double-dyed Rebel through Maryland swamps. If you don't believe me, ask Arago—but of course you can't ; he's dead !"

"Did *you* kill him ?" I ask, a curious smile coming over my countenance.

"Well, not exactly ; but I was instrumental in it. His body was brought in yesterday. Two of Baker's detectives, Shook and Gibbon, have just claimed the ten thousand dollars reward for killing him."

That evening I call on Mrs. Bream, and whisper to her of the safe arrival of her niece in the Confederate lines ; telling the aunt that I have placed my wife where she can easily get to her mother and family.

"I'm very glad you did send Eve away," remarks Lucy to me, "though I suppose her absence is a great loss to a suddenly ardent bridegroom ; your face shows that, my poor boy. But some rumors the Senator has picked up from some of the War Department officials make him also glad she's gone. The war will soon be over. Burnside is bound to get to Richmond this time ; he is already opposite Fredericksburg. And after we have whipped our Southern friends again into the Union, we'll take young Mrs. Repentant Rebel back to our arms, eh, Billy ?" she laughs good-naturedly.

It would have been wise of me to have thrown Arago's pocket-book away and never mentioned the subject to any one. But, thinking that some of the data of the traitor may be of use to the War Department in detecting other spies and traitors, the next morning I go up to the War Office and make my report, not to

Mr. Stanton in person but to one of his assistants, and deposit the pocket-book with him, telling of my having, in an investigation put into my hands by Colonel Baker, become suspicious of Arago—for I dare not mention that I know anything about the pontoon business—and discovering the traitor flying from Washington, I had pursued him and overtaken him, and on his refusing to surrender, killed him in personal combat while attempting to make the arrest.

My pursuit of Arago is not difficult to prove. Upon investigation, the War Department discover half a dozen teamsters and sutlers who saw me galloping after the Quartermaster-General's clerk's buggy on the wild and stormy night of the 19th of November. This, together with my surrender of the pocket-book and other personal belongings of Arago absolutely defeats Messrs. Shook and Gibbon's claim for the reward for killing the Rebel agent and makes them my eternal and undying enemies.

Joe Shook, meeting me on one of the streets of Washington, voices his ideas on this subject in the following words : "Darn yer eyes ! Ye've busted us, Cap Hamilton, but look out that we don't bust you. Rod Gibbon and me knows a thing or two, and we're working on it like mice on pie—we are. So look out fur us, you cursed, low-lived, henpecked husband."

"Keep your insolent tongue to yourself," I reply. "I simply prevented two scoundrels from robbing the Government ! "

"And ye'll regret that little biz to yer death—which may come sooner than ye reckon, Cap," snarls the detective at me, the look of a devil in his cold gray eyes. "For Rod Gibbon and I are sworn to do ye ! If one of us don't git ye, 'tother will, sure as pickles is sour, yer grinning cavalry buck ! "

For I am laughing in the fellow's face a yellow guffaw, his jeer about my wife making me too miserable to care about his rage.

Besides, just about this time I become so famous as a dyed-in-the-wool, loyal-to-the-death Union man, that I think a couple of Secret Service detectives, already caught in one fraud, can do me little damage.

For my sister Birdie elopes with gallant Arthur Vermilye of the New York Artillery, and this *enlèvement* of

a high-bred Baltimore "secesh" belle of prominent
Southern family by an officer wearing Uncle Sam's
uniform is heralded far and wide by the loyal press
of America and *attributed to my staunch Unionism ;*
one article stating that when Provost-Marshal of
Baltimore I had used my utmost endeavors to bring
about the nuptials of my beautiful sister to her Northern
lover.   It ends : "Long life and strong arm to the
most loyal officer, Captain William Fairfax Hamilton,
who has taught the Rebs a social lesson."

As I glumly meditate on this veracious statement, I
receive a telegram.   It reads :

> "BALTIMORE, December 2, 1862.
>
> "To CAPT'N W. F. HAMILTON :
>
> "Meet us at the Baltimore & Ohio depot at 4 P. M., to-day.
>
> "BIRDIE AND ARTHUR."

Arriving at the station on time, an archly beautiful
and bashfully blushing bride comes tripping to me,
proudly hanging on the arm of the stalwart artillery
man.   Amid her kisses, my congratulations and
Arthur's hearty handshaking, I learn the following :

Papa, acting the old-time father, *had* locked Birdie
up.   By means of the old-time darky footman, Jonas,
letters had passed between her and her lover, and the
elopement had been planned.   Miss Birdie had fled
from her home and had been privately married to the
man she loves ; who now has her as his war bride.   A
quick wedding, a short honeymoon ; perhaps the bridegroom will be hastily ordered to the front, I meditate
gloomily as I look upon a diamond tear and a ruby
drop of blood sparkling and gleaming in the betrothal
ring on Birdie's pretty finger.

Even my sister's enthusiastic and vivacious joy
doesn't elevate my spirits.   When Vermilye, slapping
me on the back with a brother's hand, whispers, "Bill,
you should go and do likewise !   Where's that pretty
Miss Ashley, eh ? " I only answer him with a hollow
groan.   I don't deem it wise to confide to him my secret ;   the fewer that know of it, the fewer that can be
compromised by my having loved, wedded and saved
a Rebel spy, whose damage to the Union arms is now
shortly to become awfully apparent.

But though news of impending operations and battle comes from the army scarce fifty miles away, Washington society goes on as gayly and as merrily as if the Angel of Death were not sharpening his sword upon the banks of the Rappahannock. At present, well born, aristocratic Vermilye of the Artillery, on thirty days' leave of absence, with his beautiful bride, is the centre of attraction at fêtes and dances.

Lucy Bream gives a magnificent dinner-party in their honor, at which the great War-Senator toasts me as the most loyal Union Border-State man—except himself—in America.

"By John Brown's body!" he remarks jovially holding up his glass of wine. "If I could have kept my Virginia niece here, I believe Billy Hamilton would have completed my conversion of her and made beautiful Eva Ashley as absolutely Union, as his brother-officer has made the pretty little flower he has stolen from the ranks of lovely secessionists."

"Yankee Doodle!" cries Finnaker, who is sitting near me with dashing Molly Bent, "that was not necessary, Senator. *I* had converted Miss Ashley before either of you. I don't like to tell tales;" he strokes his moustache calmly and simpers: "But if it hadn't been for her mother in Virginia, she might have been here now—and a bride also."

He looks so very cunning and knowing as he makes his soft insinuation that Aunt Lucy catching my savage eyes bursts out laughing till she chokes.

While I glare at him in a way that causes the pretty girl at my elbow to giggle: "What makes you look so savagely at Mr. Finnaker, Captain Hamilton? Do you want to convert *all* the Rebel maids yourself?"

"No," I reply gallantly; "there are enough Union beauties near me, without going South for any more." And I gaze at Miss Sallie Reynolds's sweet face and snowy neck and shoulders; a society compliment in my eyes, though my heart is as heavy as the plum-pudding which has just been brought on the table.

But into this whirl of fashion, gayety, frivolity and patriotism, suddenly, on the 13th of December, comes the report that Burnside has bombarded and captured Fredericksburg, and crossed his army to the South side of the Rappahannock on four pontoon bridges, these having at last arrived at Falmouth. Marvellous to relate, this walking into the trap which Lee, Jackson and Longstreet have been preparing for him quietly on the hills behind the town, for three long weeks, making a strong position, practically unassailable, and absolutely impregnable when manned by sixty-five thousand Confederate veterans under their trusted leaders *is heralded as a Union victory.* *

The next day comes the report that Burnside has attacked, and from that officer's telegrams and despatches, if he has not won, at least he has gained a decided advantage over his opponents. And the journals are full of happy comment, the capital being deliriously wild with the excitement and joy of victory. But I note that one or two high officials of the War Office, have decidedly anxious, not to say affrighted, faces.

Then comes the next day. "Disaster" is on everybody's lips; "Defeat" on everybody's tongue. "A gallant army sent to ruin!" is placarded on newspaper bulletin boards, and Fredericksburg is known to have been, if not a military crime, at least a military madness.

And I, reading the long lists of killed and wounded brave men, feel more than ever that I am a traitor; for I have saved the being whose stratagem had delayed the army and caused this holocaust. Impressed by this, I long to get to the front and put my life in the balance of actual conflict. I mutter, as I clasp my forehead with my hands : " Let me make sacrifice for her ! "

But my parole still hangs over me, and paralyzes my sword-arm.

About this time suddenly comes the first whisper of delayed pontoons ; a little ripple in the press, which, gradually growing stronger, bursts into a howl of denunciation against the War Office, special attention being given and special venom poured out upon the Secretary of War.†

Under these circumstances, Mr. Stanton is probably

* *Vide*, New York Herald, Tribune, and all other Northern newspapers of Dec. 13th and 14th of 1862.—ED.

† *Vide :* Editorials of N. Y. Herald, also the celebrated cartoon of Columbia demanding her 15,000 sons murdered at Fredericksburg, from Lincoln, Stanton and Halleck, in Appendix.—ED.

in not the best of spirits or temper. At all events, *I* find it so ; for one morning a provost guard, directed by Messrs. Shook and Gibbon, calls on me at F Street and I find myself, without explanation, removed from the social amenities of my boarding-house to a cell in the Old Capitol prison ; one of my detective friends remarking jovially : "Now, by thunder ! we've got ye where we want ye, my meddling captain !"

From the seclusion of this government Bastille, I write to the proper authorities, asking for the charges made against me, but my letter receives no answer.

Again I write, demanding to be tried by court-martial on whatever charge is preferred. This appeal produces no greater result than my former letter.

I send for Senator Bream. He comes to see me, and gives me very cold comfort by saying : "I'd do anything for you, but I can't. Martial law exists, and you'd better make a clean breast of it."

"Of what ?"

"I don't know ; the War Department keep their mouths very close on your case. But whatever it is, you'd better make a clean breast of it ; then I'll see if I can't get you pardoned. Anyway, they've got you, as they have hundreds of others all over the country ; they'll try you when they want to,—or they won't try you. But under martial law, some one has to give up something, sir, for the salvation of the country. If you are a true patriot, you should be willing to suffer for the cause."

All the time Vermilye sticks by me like a brother, and brings every social influence to bear in my behalf —and he has plenty—but in those days everything was answered by the one plea, "Military necessity."

So the long months drag away. Paroled by the Rebels, I am imprisoned by the Federals.

My incarceration is however not particularly rigid. Lucy Bream occasionally, and Birdie quite often, visits me, and newspapers are sent to me. I have my meals forwarded from a first-class hotel. Physically I am comfortable ; mentally I am in Hades ; for I am in an agony of fear about my wife—I dread that Eve will come to deliver herself to Federal mercy—to make me free. And under the circumstances, fear it might even mean her life.

For during the time, a letter has been brought to me by my eldest sister, who has come from Baltimore to see me. She looks at me and half sneers : "See to what your loyalty has brought you—imprisonment from the Yankees and the contempt of those who love you !"

"Are you here for nothing else except to make me more wretched, Virgie ?" I say.

"No ; were it not for a matter of duty, I should have never looked upon your face again." Then she whispers : "This letter arrived from Richmond."

With a smothered cry I seize and open it, and for one moment my prison becomes a palace ; then I shudder as I read ; for it runs thus :

"MY DARLING HUSBAND:

"I have written to you three times, but I suppose my letters have gone astray, or been lost in the forwarding.

"So I again write to you, for lately word has been brought to me that you have been imprisoned in Washington, and I fear it is because you have loved me and saved me. If it is for me that you have lost your liberty, I beg you to say to the War Department of the United States that I will come through the lines and surrender myself to them, rather than that you should suffer for loving too much

"Your wife—your true wife—your devoted wife,

"EVA VERNON HAMILTON."

Though this puts me into a rapture, it sends a thrill of fear through me. I cannot write to my wife from the jail, but I tell my sister—in whose honor I can trust whether she loves me or doesn't love me—of my marriage, and beg her to write my bride for God's sake not to come, no matter what happens to me ; that my only happiness in life is in knowing that she is safe. And Virginia goes away from me with a very white and astounded face, though she has promised to do my bidding.

Soon after this Birdie comes to me in the despair of many other young brides of that day, to tell me that her husband's battery has been detached from Fort McHenry and ordered to active service.

"I know he's going to be killed, Billy !" she sobs brokenly. "I know this diamond on my ring means my tear—this ruby on my ring means his blood. That's what it means, Billy. The awful Rebels are marching North !" for this is just before Gettysburg. "They're going to kill my husband !" then she cries savagely, clenching her little fist, "Oh, how I hate them!" and goes from me to weep, as Arthur Vermilye's light battery rolls out of Fort McHenry and up the long dusty roads to join the crown of artillery that at Round Top and Cemetery Ridge checked the highest rolling tide of the Confederacy, when Pickett's Division made their fatal, yet immortal, charge.

So the summer of 1863 rolls away, the winter passes, and the spring campaign opens, while I am wearing my heart out against the bars of the Old Capitol prison.

About this time comes Grant from the West, and the great campaign of 1864 begins with the Wilderness. But some three months before this the military hand that has seized me relaxes its grasp. One morning, to my astonishment, a couple of deputy United States marshals—for I have been held by the Secret Service, not by the military arm, as that would have been impossible without court-martial—convey me in a carriage to the War Department.

After some formalities and waiting, I am shown into Secretary Stanton's private office.

He looks at me very much as a cat does a mouse, stroking his long beard reflectively, and remarks, in suave but incisive tones: "Captain Hamilton, I can *hang* you!"

"Not without trial, Mr. Secretary," I reply, and then ask : "For what?"

"You escorted a female Rebel spy out of Washington—the very one you were charged to deliver over to Baker of the Secret Service."

"I escorted my wife out of Washington, I will admit," I say firmly.

"Who?"

"My *wife!*"

"But I am referring to Miss Ashley!"

"So am I. I married her, the day I escorted her out of Washington!"

"The devil!" he mutters, and stares at me astonished as I add :"

"You can put me on court-martial for that—if you like, Mr. Secretary."

"But I don't wish to. I don't want any of that matter gone over ; it has passed away now. I wish to spare you. I desire to promote you," he goes on persuasively. "I wish to give you a chance to distinguish yourself. *I have use for you!*"

"How?" I cry. "Have I been exchanged? Am I free to go to the front?"

"You have been exchanged for six months, and I want you to go *further than the front.*"

"What do you mean, sir?"

"You recollect, nearly two years ago you brought me a commission made out to William Fairfax Hamilton, as major in the Confederate army and signed by Jefferson Davis, and his secretary-of-war."

"Certainly, sir!"

"You told me that you had kept it in order that some day you might do with it for your country a great thing. That time has now come."

"Please be more explicit, Mr. Secretary."

"Well, I mean this. I want to know exactly the strength of the Rebel garrison of Richmond and its fortifications, and what are the chances of capturing it by a *coup de main.* They are sending every man they can spare, and lots they can't spare, to Lee's army to oppose Grant's spring campaign. Richmond must soon be pretty well denuded of troops. I want to know the chances of a quick cavalry command reaching Belle Isle prison, releasing the prisoners there and raiding Richmond, before I dare order the movement. I am very explicit with you. Captain Hamilton, I want to know the chances of its success."

"I will go!" I whisper, with a suddenness and eagerness that astounds him. "If in return for my risk of life and military honor, you agree to grant me the full and free pardon of my wife."

"The girl that delayed the pont——" he checked himself and replies sharply. "No, no! Impossible, sir.'"

"Then, Mr. Secretary, I lift no hand to destroy the Southern Confederacy and place my wife in your power."

"What's that!"

He stares at me savagely, then his blue eyes light up, —he mutters considerately. "It does seem hard for a man to fight to put a halter on his loved one." Next with incisive voice he says quickly : "Though I had sworn never to forgive her—you know the awful thing

she did—I'll—I'll pardon your wife if she takes the oath
of allegiance !—*and you succeed.*"

"Mr. Secretary," I cry, "I will go to the Rebel
Capital ! "

For into my mind has suddenly sprung : "My wife
is in Richmond. Though I go there as a spy, Eve
cannot betray me ; for I saved her when she was in a
strait as dread and as cruel as mine will be. When
next I see her—my oath has passed—then she cannot deny me the love of a wife."

And my face, made gaunt and haggard by the misery
of nearly fourteen months' imprisonment, has such a
glow of rapture, such a spark of hope in it that the
Secretary says : "I see you'll go and do your work,
Major Hamilton."—Noting my start at the title, he
laughs : "You at least should have Union rank equal
to your Rebel one, I'll try to get it for you. I now beg
your pardon for imprisoning you ; for I see in your
face the fire of patriotism ! "

But he also sees in my face the flame of love !

CHAPTER XXV.

MAJOR BILLY HAMILTON, C. S. A.

"You will report to me before you go ; but the
sooner you make arrangements to start, the better.
Any money or transportation you may want will be
furnished you," remarks the head of the Federal War
Department.

"I shall require two days to make my preparations,"
I say.

"So long ? " he asks impatiently.

"Yes ; to transform myself from a Union to a Confederate officer. For I shall take every precaution, as
no man will go South of the Potomac with a tighter
noose upon his neck than I will, Mr. Secretary."

With this idea in my head, I step out of the War
Office, and make my preparations with corresponding
care and accuracy, but very secretly and very privately.

From my papers I get out the old Confederate commission. Fortunately, time has made its paper slightly yellow. I increase this, and give it the appearance of having been constantly in my pocketbook by fraying its creases, by staining it with water, salt and fresh, by even rubbing it with mud in one corner, indorsing on its back, in military form, my acceptance of it, dating this 1862, and exposing it to long but moderate heat to give my writing the appearance of time.

On the Rebel uniform made for me by my sisters, I impress the appearance of having suffered the hardships of war.

My preparations, which have to be made gradually, especially those in regard to my uniform and my Confederate commission, take me all of two days. It is during this time that cruel military disaster overtakes Mr. Finnaker, of the United States Quartermaster-General's office.

On my first release from the Old Capitol prison, the little patriot had fought shy of me. But learning in some way that I am to receive additional rank in the Union army, he begins to be chummy once more, coming into my room and smoking my cigars and prattling vivaciously of "what we are going to do with the Rebs."

On one of these occasions he is holding forth with great patriotic ardor. "By Bunker Hill, sir, we've got Grant with us now—that Western hero—and he'll go at 'em hammer and tongs! *He* doesn't care for a few lives ; he puts his men in and fights to a finish, he does ; just as I would if I were in command. If ten thousand men are slaughtered, what does it matter, when the country is at stake ? If ten thousand men more are butchered—we've got lots—who counts the cost, so long as we save the Union ? I *must* go down to the front with Grant ; I haven't fought since Gettysburg. If you don't believe me, ask Cushing, who died in my arms as he fired his last gun into the faces of Pickett's Rebs. But then—God help us all—my brother-in-arms, poor Cushing, is dead."

"Well," I reply, "here's something that may interest you. It is apparently on military matters, and comes from Illinois. The servant-girl gave it me in the hall for you. Something from your company, eh, Finnaker ?"

"Oh—ah, yes ! of course—about my company ! " he stammers, apparently astounded that he should receive a written communication from his command of one—which is himself, in Washington.

Then as Finnaker opens an official envelope, stamped with the arms of Illinois, and inspects an official paper bearing the State seal, something horrible seems to happen to the patriot; his face grows ashen pale ; the paper falls from his grasp ; with a low gasping "Good Lord ! I'm drafted ! " he sinks half paralyzed upon a sofa.

Picking it up, I read a short notice stating that he not being present, the name of Napoleon Leonidas Finnaker had been drawn by the United States Marshal at the last draft ; that he is ordered to report himself immediately for active service, he having been assigned to fill up the ranks of the Twenty-Seventh Illinois, now serving in McPherson's Army of the Tennessee.

"My God ! You see I—I'm drafted—*drafted* to fill the place of a dead man ! By the God of War, Hamilton, DRAFTED ! And the slaughter is so awful that substitutes are only for millionaires. DRAFTED ! O Shadow of Death, to be *drafted* is to be KILLED ! "

"Well, you'll have a chance to teach the art of war to McPherson. You'll *have* to go to the front ! " I suggest grimly.

"To the front? We'll see if I have. Not by the tears of my widowed mother L Drafted into '*Fighting* McPherson's ' corps, who leads his men against the Rebel guns as if they were so many rats in a trap. DRAFTED ! Call an ambulance ! I—I don't feel quite well."

And really he is awfully sick, and we have to get an ambulance and send him to the military hospital, done well nigh unto death by a paper pellet, before his first engagement.

But I haven't time to stay in Washington to see the outcome of Mr. Finnaker's sufferings for his country, and report myself at the War Office, where I state to Mr. Stanton my plans.

"Understand me, Major," says the secretary, " I can get all the rubbishy, inaccurate information I want. What I wish from you is a military report of the defences of Richmond, about what you estimate its garrison will probably be when Lee masses his whole army to oppose Grant, and what the chances of a rapid *coup de main* will be against that place and Belle Isle prison by a quick-moving cavalry force."

"I understand you, perfectly, Mr. Secretary," I reply.

"Very well, then, you'd better see Baker about the details."

I do so, and obtain orders for transportation, a supply of Confederate money and a general letter instructing every officer of Federal troops to further my mission in any way in his power.

Armed with this, I take boat from Washington to Norfolk, judging it best to journey towards the Confederate capital as if coming from North Carolina, as less questions will be asked me, travelling from that direction, than if I approach Richmond from the line of the Potomac.

I have carefully thought over my chances in the matter. The risk of detection by Confederates who have known me as Captain Billy Hamilton of the United States Service has been almost swept away by the awful slaughter of the last year. Wat Bowie has died in Maryland. George Thornton, who had spent the two days with me at Frederick, has fallen gallantly in the great cavalry-fight at Brandy Station ; and half of my old classmates at West Point, who had entered the Confederate army, are either dead or disabled. So I, early on Wednesday morning, the 3d of February, 1864, cross from Norfolk to the Navy Yard at Portsmouth, and take the road, escorted by a sergeant and squad of cavalry, towards Suffolk, where the Union lines end and the Confederacy begins.

Arriving at this place, and passing the very last Federal outpost, in fact journeying some quarter of a mile beyond it, the sergeant, having his strict orders, salutes me and turns about his squad.

"Understand me," I remark to him. "An hour from now you come here, enter that grove, and take away what you find left there."

"Certainly, Major ; those are my instructions," replies the non-commissioned officer, and trots away with his troop, along a road whose mud is changing into dust, for the weather is mild and little rain has fallen lately.

The squad of cavalry have no sooner got out of sight than I leap my horse over a broken-down rail fence and ride into the little grove of trees and swamp undergrowth. In the seclusion of an alder thicket, I make a quick and effective toilet, leaving every vestige of Unionism behind me, and half an hour afterwards, where the Yankee major had ridden in, a Confederate major rides forth and takes his way by country roads through the lowland counties of Virginia, arriving that evening, by way of the miserable hamlet called Washed Holes, at a more important town named Jerusalem.

My journey has been uneventful, for the whole country bears the traces of having been foraged over by both sides. A few negroes are in the roads, and I pass one or two farmers ; but they only return the compliments of the season.

I also pass without difficulty a Rebel vidette of cavalry, my uniform apparently answering for me, the lieutenant in command after a few questions saluting, and asking pleasantly : "Where are you bound for, Major ?"

To this I answer : "Richmond !" stating I've been down towards Gatesville, looking up both cattle and timber for army uses.

The country tavern in Jerusalem also indicates I am in a land of war. I pay thirty dollars in Confederate currency for a bed (the title to which I have to dispute with numerous live stock), and two miserable meals.

Fortunately, I get plenty of fodder and corn for my horse, whose comfort I look after personally ; for Roderick must be kept in good condition ; upon his strength and fleetness may depend my life.

The next morning, getting up betimes, I jog along the same kind of country roads to Hicksford, a little town on the Petersburg & Weldon Railroad.

As I have journeyed on, greater evidences of being in a nation in its death-struggle have reached me. There are even fewer cattle ; nothing but negroes are seen in the fields, and the appearance of the railroad at this point indicates that it is on its last legs also ;

that is, if dilapidated rolling-stock and a most execrable roadbed with worn-out rails indicate railroad ineffectiveness.

An hour after my arrival a train comes in with a regiment of Confederate troops bound north. Though the men are mostly bareheaded and some barefooted, and a few of them even say they are hungry, they go off as anxious to meet the Yankees as ever.

While this train is in Hicksford, the problem is forced upon me : "Shall I ride Roderick into Richmond, or journey there by railroad ; for the conductor tells me he can get me a place on one of the cars.

After a moment's consideration, though it would be perhaps safer for me to journey by rail, especially over the bridges that cross the James River I conclude to endure a two days' delay and ride my horse into the Rebel capital—because I may wish to ride him out again in a hurry.

Therefore, after spending a rather sleepless night at Hicksford, I press on by country roads and succeed in reaching Petersburg late on Friday afternoon.

I put up at Jarratt's tavern, I think they called it, and getting Roderick a good feed, about eight o'clock the next morning I say to myself, a quiver in my voice : "This afternoon, Richmond !" and my heart gives a big jump—as what man's wouldn't ?

I have experienced no trouble thus far, my military appearance making the country people friendly and preventing awkward questions. In fact, for a young man not to wear a uniform would excite comment ; nearly every one seems now to be connected with the Confederate service, and the nearer I get to Richmond the more general this becomes. No better disguise could I have on its face than that of a major in the Confederate army, especially with a major's commission *en regle* in my pocket to back up my assertions, if these were necessary.

So I ride on ; with every stride of my steed, thinking: not "Nearer to the Rebel capital," but "Nearer to— my wife !" I am forgetting I'm a Union spy ; I am becoming simply a man journeying to the embraces of his loved one and the delights of home and spouse.

Filled with these feelings, quite early in the after-

noon, I reach the little town of Manchester, and looking across the James River that is pouring over its rocks
and round its pretty islands, gaze at Richmond, on its
hills that slope down to the broad stream.

Here I devote an hour or two to finding out what I
can of the fortifications south of the river and Belle Isle,
the prison camp of captured Union troops. This is on
an island about a mile above the bridges and near the
Manchester shore. I note that this is guarded only by
a low earth embankment and wooden stockade and that
there are, as well as I can discover, only two batteries
of importance immediately south of Richmond. These
observations, I make as complete as I dare, and take
my way across Mayo's bridge.

A considerable number of people, mostly military,
though a few of them are civilians, are going in with
me to the Confederate capital. I have prepared a
forged leave of absence from General Hardee in
Tennessee, but it is scarcely glanced at. The guards
at the bridge, noting my uniform, simply salute me;
though I perceive they examine much more closely
those in the dress of the farmer, the artisan or the
merchant.

I have never been in Richmond, therefore in Washington I have obtained an accurate map of the city from
the United States Secret Service, together with a description of its various hotels, restaurants and principal
thoroughfares. From this I have memorized the main
details of the place, so that I can go about without
asking too many questions. Having mentally pho-
tographed Richmond, I have then destroyed the
map.

In addition to this information, I have also received
instructions from the United States Secret Service to
communicate if necessary, with one, Lemuel Isaacs,
who keeps a small store in a broken-down suburb of
the city, called "The Rockets."

"You whisper in Mr. Isaac's ear 'Cotton is twenty
pence a pound in Manchester, England,'" Baker had
said to me, "and he will reply to you 'So help me
gracious, it is only five cents a pound in Wilmington,
North Carolina.' After that introduction, trust in
Isaacs as you would in me."

Fortified with this information and instruction, I put

up at the old Monumental Hotel, opposite Capital Square and on the corner of Grace and Ninth streets, not caring to register at the more fashionable and better known Spottswood, where too many Confederate officers may be lounging about and too many of the reporters of the Richmond *Bee, Examiner,* or *Despatch* may be dropping in for news items ; but still wishing to select a place at which a Confederate major might creditably live, for all this journey I have kept strictly to my rank in that service.

Therefore, simply stating that I have been on staff and recruiting duties in Georgia, I walk up to the office of that hostelry and register : Major W. F. Hamilton, C. S. A., Atlanta, and find myself living, not luxuriously, but at the rate of nearly fifty dollars a day, Confederate money.

My pen trembles slightly as I write my title. For I, with every move, am putting the halter tighter and tighter around my neck. Once suspected, every man and every woman's hand in all this city will be against me—save my wife's. She, I hope, will be true to one who has shielded her in similar extremity.

But how shall I find her ? How shall I tell her I am here ?

Though Eve is foremost in my mind, I first address myself to the commission on which I have been sent by Mr. Stanton, and after some consideration conclude that to do this effectively it is best for me to see the gentleman at "The Rockets."

Taking my way along Main Street, the sidewalks of which are quite filled by an afternoon crowd, which I inspect with hungry eyes, always looking for one face, one form, my wife's, I am soon tramping through the unkempt streets of what is probably the lowest quarter of Richmond.

For "The Rockets" of that day was the home of the criminal classes, contrabandists of all degrees made it their lurking-place, Federal spies and escapes from military conscription found temporary safety in its dark and dirty shanties ; though these were leavened by a good many workmen from big tobacco warehouses and flour mills in the neighborhood and on the river.

It is not a very large suburb of Richmond. I soon find the sign of

LEM ISAACS,

NOTIONS, PROVISIONS AND CLOTHING.

Isaacs's is apparently a Cheap John store; though in peaceful days, it would hardly seem to be a bargain counter; for I see placarded up in large letters: "Good boots, made of *real* leather, Dirt Cheap, $175." "Genuine Woollen Stockings, just by blockade, $14. These we guarantee not to be Yankee shoddy." "Corn per bushel $10. Good family hams, $225."

As I enter confronts me: "Buy *quick*! This overcoat has just been marked UP from $225 to $300. Things is RISING!"

In the dark interior of the dimly lighted store I inquire for Mr. Lemuel Isaacs; though that seems unnecessary, as there are no customers, and only one person is in the establishment. He is of big black eyes and large hooked nose, and comes to me rubbing his oily hands and saying: "Vat can I do for you? Does you vant a fust-class army overcoat I've just had dyed." He shows me one of a grizzled black. "Three hundred and fifty dollars. It was damned Yankee blue once; now it is patriotic gray."

"No," I reply. "I only want to see Mr. Lemuel Isaacs."

"Dat's my name, mein friend."

"Very well, Mr. Isaacs," I whisper to him. "I "just dropped in to inform you that cotton is twenty pence a pound in Manchester, England."

At this the Hebrew's eyes grow big and gleam affrighted; his nose, which is large, becomes larger and dilated; his florid complexion grows as white as the only sack of flour in his store, which is marked "Cheap at $1 a pound." He looks me all over from head to foot; then his voice trembles as he whispers in return: "So help me gracious, cotton is only five cents in Vilmington, North Carolina;" next, his eyes growing watery with agitation, mutters: "Vat else does you want of me?"

And he trembles as an aspen leaf, as I whisper to him, my voice low and trembling also; "I must know

the number of troops here that are *permanent* in garrison ; not those that are passing through. Home-
guards, Boys' Company, Battalion of Department Employees, etc. You understand."

" Holy Moses, I onderstands. You likes to play vid
a man's life ! " he returns. " But I vill find out for
you by to-morrow ; and you can bet yer life on what
I tells you, Major."

" You can't give it to me sooner ? "

" Impossible—to be dead right. And I s'pose you
vant it straight as a trial balance."

" Yes ; otherwise you'd better never let a *mutual*
friend of ours get his hand upon you."

" Yes, I understand. If de Rebs don't put me
through, de Yanks vill make it hot for me. Vell, I
know which side is going to win. To-morrow is
Sunday ; dis store is closed ; it vouldn't do for you to
come here. Meet me on the road by the bank of the
James River Canal below Butcherstown. At three
P. M. I am dere, vid what you vant—not on paper, but by
passing visper. Look out for yourself ; dat Winder'll
be hell on you if you's cotched ! "

I know this. I have heard of the Confederate Provost Marshal's mercy to spies before. " All right," I
answer. " Three P. M., canal bank," and purchase
from him some clean linen at Shylock's prices, as I
have brought nothing into Richmond with me, and, in
addition, think it wise to carry from his store some
package to give reason for my entering it. Then I go
away, determined to attempt to obtain by my own
observation the knowledge of which I am in search.

It is now quite late in the day. I pick up what information I can, in the bar-room of the Monumental,
as to Home Guards, the Employees' Battalion, the Boys'
Company, etc., for the Confederacy apparently is robbing not only the grave, but the cradle, for food for
powder. So by the time I get to bed I have obtained
a pretty general idea of the permanent Richmond garrison ; so much so that I think I have something
to tell Mr. Stanton that will please that potentate greatly.

But to encourage gossip I have to gossip myself,
and am compelled in chatting with my associates of
the Monumental bar-room, over our whiskey, two dollars per drink, to give greater detail to my proceedings

in Georgia than under the circumstances I would wish. I have also learned that beautiful Mrs. Hamilton is one of the belles of Richmond.

"A namesake of yours, Major?" remarks an old, white-headed department clerk who with senile curiosity has read my name in the register. "A relative?"

"Well, yes," I answer. "By marriage, of course."

Still all the time I feel, even as I take drinks with the few lounging Confederate officers and one or two clerks of the Rebel War Department who have dropped into this tavern, which is cheaper than the Spottswood, that I am placing a tighter noose about my neck than ever man selected and lived."

But to-morrow will be Sunday. I know enough of Eve's religious devotion to be sure one of the Episcopal churches will have her lovely form among its worshippers. To-morrow I shall see my wife !

This thought makes the Union spy's heart beat high and puts a flush of joy and rapture on his face, even in the dangers of the Rebel capital.

CHAPTER XXVI.

BY DAY IN RICHMOND.

That night I hardly sleep, and the next morning am up betimes. I mount Roderick, and riding about the city, take cursory views of its defences, photographing them in my mind as I move along, for I dare not pause to make any close inspection. As I entered Richmond the day before I had noted that there were only two forts of importance south of the city on the other side of the James, one at Magruder's Hill and the other, Battery 18. In all other directions the capital, I now find both by personal observation and reports I have picked up—the careless conversation of an artillery officer at the tavern at Petersburg having been of aid to me—is much better protected.

On the east, north and northwest sides of the city are sixteen batteries, known by their numbers, some of them of great defensive strength, also Forts Jackson and Johnston. These, properly manned, make Richmond pretty safe from armies moving from the Potomac, the Shenandoah or Fortress Monroe.

"South of the James River is their weak point," I think. "There they depend too much on Petersburg and the batteries down the river, which would be of no avail against a quick cavalry raid coming from the west, but south of the James, if the bridges can be seized *in time.*"

Therefore I turn my attention to the bridges on the river and the batteries commanding them.

My inspection, cursory as it is, takes me till half-past ten o'clock—*church-time !*

I return to the Monumental, quite confident my ride has attracted no unusual notice ; too many other Confederate officers are out on horseback, as the city seems quite full of troops ; though most of these appear to be *en route* for the north, for even this morning three regiments have taken trains on the Richmond & Fredericksburg Railroad.

At the hotel I improve my toilet as well as a clothes-brush will dissipate the dust and mud of Virginia roads, and looking at my well-worn uniform, am quite confident I am about as much of a dandy as the most of the officers in Richmond ; for the Rebel gray has grown gradually shabby since 1861.

Suddenly the church bells begin to ring. Then oh, how my heart begins to beat too ! For they sing to me. "Soon I shall see her !" I am no more the skulking spy, with the hand of military justice over him ; I am only a lover who is going to a sweetheart's kisses—a husband who is nearing his wife's arms.

I have already determined to what church Eve will probably go. It will surely be an Episcopal one. Fortunately for my quest, there are not many of them. Saint Paul's, which I am informed is the fashionable parish, where the Rev. Charles Minnegerod will preach, and Saint John's, the old-fashioned one in the Colonial Cemetery, with its quaint gravestones of the last century, upon Church Hill seem the only likely ones.

The first of these is in the heart of the town, just across Grace Street from my hotel, and will probably be the one in which Eve will worship. If not, I must contrive to leave before the end of the service and try the other.

St. Paul's bells are sounding as I step over to it, but

to me they do not seem as loud as the thumping of my own heart. Still, perchance, no more devout creature ever entered that old-time Episcopal Church and bowed before its altar than Major Billy Hamilton of the Confederate service, for no man, even with the guns of battle sounding in his ears—and there were many of those who worshipped in Richmond in those days—ever felt the Angel of Death was nearer to him.

The church is just beginning to fill, but at my request I am assigned to a seat in one of the rear pews. My eyes immediately scan the backs of the ladies who are already seated ; Eve certainly is not yet here.

So I sit and wait, the organ sounding softly to me as the congregation gradually enter, quite a number of the gentlemen being in civilians' dress, members of the Confederate Congress and officials in the State and Treasury Departments.

"Will she never come ?"

Then an awful doubt seizes me. Perhaps my wife is not in Richmond this day. Perchance she is sick? Perhaps—a hundred things may keep her from the House of God on this Sunday of all Sundays !

So I sit, my heart growing more despondent, for the church is now quite full. The President of the Confederacy and Mrs. Davis have just arrived and gone into their pew, I note by a few whispered words that drift to me.

Perhaps I had better walk out before the service begins, and go to St. John's Church.

I have half risen in my pew, which is at the very rear of the church, to step out !

Through swinging doors, I hear a lady in the vestibule say : "Good-morning, Mrs. Hamilton ; your aunt is not here ? "

Another voice floats to me, and my heart stops beating. I know the silvery tones ; they have whispered to me : "Billy, I love you !" too often for me to forget them. Eve is answering : "Thank you, Mrs. Conway ; my aunt is in Petersburg."

Then she enters !

I dare not turn and look her in the face ; but her garments brush me as she passes, I devour with my eyes the back of her graceful head as she floats up the aisle.

And then, oh, how I grind my teeth, for an infernally

handsome, dashing Confederate lieutenant-colonel is walking beside her.

I know I have no right to be jealous. Have I not looked at pretty girls in these fifteen months? Why should not she have a masculine escort—this morning? "Would you make her in her beauty, a nun, you fool?" I growl to myself. But still—still I'd sooner some elderly major-general or decrepit statesman were crawling by my pretty wife's side, than this youthful, erect, dashing, martial figure, who seems so damnably familiar with her ; for I notice him select the Sunday's service for Eve in her prayer-book and they sit quite close together, but that may be because the pew is crowded and ladies' hoop-skirts take up as much room in Richmond as they do in Washington.

Though I strain my eyes, I cannot see much of my wife ; she being some six pews in front of me, but fortunately not in a direct line.

At last my opportunity arrives. The congregation is about to rise for a hymn. Alert with love, I start up so as to get view of Eve. She also, inspired by devotion, rises quickly.

Whether it is my gaze that goes straight to the back of her head, through curls and waterfall, I know not ; but the girl turns slowly. My eager glance catches her side-face ; it seems to draw her beloved countenance fully round to me.

I note the same nut-brown, wavy hair, the same delicate play of features. The same girl I loved and won and lost on the Potomac, is here standing before me, on the banks of the James. The same beautiful blue eyes that I have dreamed of so often in my cell in the Old Capitol prison are looking into mine.

My glance catches her's. Eye to eye, we gaze upon and know each other. I am sure of that, for over those radiant features for one instant has come the pallid hue of death. The next, they are lighted by the sunny rays of love.

Then probably some quick idea of my military danger seems to strike my wife. I note the convulsive quiver—a little hand laid on her heart. She turns from me, slowly as if fighting to conceal her emotion, half staggers, and convulsively clasping its rail, droops over the pew in front of her. Those near her doubtless think it is devotion, for her attitude is willowy as a saint's; but I am sure it is because she knows there is a husband worshipping with her before the same altar, and over his head hang danger and death.

After this I hardly note my surroundings. A great many of the ladies are in black. This I had expected; too many gallant fellows are falling for women not to mourn. The minister's sermon comes to me dreamily, though it is impressive, and delivered by a gentleman of Grecian features and soft German accent.

The music from the organ seems to thrill me in a general kind of way, but I scarcely hear it, being occupied in trying to see the loved figure in front of me. Once—yes twice—I notice Eve half turns, as if to look on me again; then, apparently by a mighty effort, forces herself to the contemplation of her ritual.

And all the time I am praying, harder than any one else in this church—praying to God that he may bless our love—that I may have her in my arms—a wife—this day in Richmond.

The service and sermon are over. The organ is playing the voluntary, and I step out of the church, taking care not to be among the very first, but still decidedly in advance of my wife. I do not wish to put any greater strain or self-repression upon her than possible. My nerves have been braced for this—to her it must have come suddenly as the crack of doom.

I pass into the vestibule, which is crowded with friends meeting friends, and boys waiting for girls, just as if gentle peace were upon the land, and the soft strains of "The Bonnie Blue Flag" were not floating up the hill from an infantry band on Main Street where a Texas regiment is tramping through the city to take train for the battle fields on the Rapidan.

I have already, while in my pew, scribbled my address on a leaf of my pocketbook. This folded up I hold ready to pass to Eve if possible,—as a single unfortunate word may bring about my undoing. For I know each of these devout-looking general officers, and every one of these dashing young military men, would think he had done a very good Sunday's work in driving his sword through the heart of Mr. Stanton's agent in the Virginia capital.

Beautiful girls are passing by me, but to my eyes there is only one, the young lady who is coming behind them. Her half-parted lips giving out quick breaths of repressed joy and fear—her virgin heart fluttering—her eyes blazing like stars with quick intelligence and seeking mine.

Our glances meet; a moment later in the crush for one instant our hands clasp, and with a squeeze of love I leave in my wife's trembling fingers the scrap of paper bearing my present title and address.

In my ear as she passes by I catch a lingering sigh, "Billy."

Suddenly the girl's left hand is held up to her face—for some reason it is bereft of glove. On a dainty finger I see gleam the diamond of our troth, above the golden circlet that has made Eve mine by right of man and God—and I am happy.

But joys are fleeting. A moment later the fixed look leaves her exquisite features. Eve seems as brightly coquettish to attendant cavalier as she did in Washington. "At least," I cogitate, with a curse in my heart, "that handsome young fellow stepping so debonairly beside her imagines she is—*to him.*"

"God of heaven! is she flirting with him? He looks so cursedly pleased with himself, she *must be!*"

After greeting a few friends, my wife moves up Ninth and turns along Broad Street with her gallant in close proximity. Once she turns as if to look back, but apparently restrains herself. I follow at some little distance, noting her step is as light, her carriage as graceful and her figure as rounded as when she first enchanted me—that a year has rather added to her charms than taken from them, and fondly think: "All these beauties this day shall belong to me, her husband!"

Suddenly a spasm of rage flies through me. Eve is crossing Eighth Street. Her facile hand has slightly lifted her skirts to save them from a puddle of red Virginia mud, revealing two as pretty little feet as ever tripped Richmond's streets. A passing zephyr plays pranks with her crinoline, giving me a fleeting glimpse of a limb as graceful in its contour, as lovely in its superb outlines as Venus's very own.

"Great Taylor! Did you see *that?*" is heard behind me. "Didn't I tell you Eve Hamilton had the prettiest ankles in town?"

A side-glance shows me this comes from some boy department clerk. A young infantry lieutenant, scarcely older, is with him. He laughs: "Yes, I saw. She's almighty beautiful. It's an infernal shame she has a husband. Where is *old* Hamilton, anyway?"

"Darn me if I know!" says the other. "Though he'd *better* be about. That cavalry buck there is with her everywhere. I saw him take her into the dance at Mrs. Anderson's last week."

"Do you know his name?"

"No; he's some swell cavalry fellow. He runs with the Reeveses, and the Mayos, and that crowd."

"Which Jakie Suggs doesn't run with," laughs the infantry lieutenant; and he is doubtless right, as his companion has mentioned the names of some of the most aristocratic Richmond families.

But these remarks are not comforting to me. Ye gods, how "*old* Hamilton" wants to chastise these young insolents, but dares not! Ah, it requires a cool head to win in this game of love, with the sword above the lover's head.

So I march on in the crowd, a considerable distance behind her; no one particularly noticing me, uniforms being the rule, civilian dress the exception, though I hear one officer remark to a young lady: "I imagine he must be from some of the new troops from the Southwest."

"Why?" she says, half laughing.

"Well, that major seems *over-fed*," chuckles the gentleman grimly. "He hasn't the gaunt, racing look of our boys at the front."

As the crowd drifts apart, some going off at Eighth Street, others disappearing at Seventh, and gradually becoming less and less, my following my wife and her escort—her gallant, I think now—becomes more difficult.

But, letting them get ahead of me about a block, I note they turn down Fourth Street. Then I quicken my steps, and, passing the corner of Broad and Fourth, look hurriedly down towards Grace Street, and find—to my dismay—they have disappeared.

Eve must live in some one of the houses in the

block of pretty, old-fashioned Virginia residences, but which one? That I cannot immediately determine, as I do not like to inquire. She has my address—I'll hear from her at my hotel.

I hurry back to the Monumental and wait. No letter! To my hints, inquiries, and side-remarks, the few people whom I succeed in engaging in conversation, give me no satisfactory information. Nearly all have heard of the beautiful Mrs. Hamilton; but none know exactly where she lives—they are not in her class in society. If I dared walk up to the Andersons, the Mayos, or some other of the swells, I could find out in a minute. I go in to dinner at the hotel; I can't stomach its eternal pork and stringy beef and bean coffee, though I know I should eat to keep up my strength for the desperate work ahead of me.

Suddenly, looking at my watch, I see it is three o'clock. At half-past I must meet the Jew on the banks of the canal below Butchertown.

Cursing the appointment, I depart for this rendezvous. It is not very difficult to find. Walking along Main Street in exactly the opposite direction to the one I had followed in going to "The Rockets," in the course of a little time I arrive at about the place where I think Mr. Isaacs should be.

The canal is busy, even on Sunday. Boats are bringing corn, fodder, and a few cattle into the capital from the interior of Virginia. Though these last, I should imagine are growing scarce, judging by the tough beefsteaks with which I am furnished at un-heard-of prices at my hotel.

Along the road near the canal, among quite a little gathering of people, who, taking advantage of the fine day, are strolling up the river, I soon run against Mr. Isaacs. That gentleman is talking to some chum of his, but drops him at my approach and regards me with an anxious eye. As I get close to him I notice his lips are trembling, and once or twice he nearly gasps for breath.

I remark to him: "Is the price of cotton in Wil-mington to-day the same as it was yesterday?"

"Ah, so help me, it is always the same, when it is— What price is it in Manchester?"

"Twenty pence a pound."

"Yes sir, I t'inks youse all right.   Here is the information," he whispers to me : "Armory Battalion six hundred.   Department clerks enrolled, six hundred and fifty effective.   Boy company—boys under age for military service—one hundred and fifty.   Two regiments of heavy artillery in de forts ; they may be drawn on, and there may be a brigade left here, but de rest vil all go to the front.   Perhaps there'll be a couple of regiments of cavalry somewhere around, scouting on the outside of the city.   That's as vell as I can find out.   Don't come near me no more."

This about accords with what information I had obtained by my own efforts.

As I turn to go away, consternation comes upon me.

The man who had been walking with Isaacs, and who had moved away from him as I approached, suddenly returns to us.

Our eyes meet.   God of heaven ! it is Shook, the United States Secret Service officer—the one who had cursed me for having caused him to lose his ten thousand dollars reward—the one who had sworn to "do" me to death.

"By the Eternal!" he mutters, then suddenly guffaws : "Oh, Gee Whizz !" as he glances at my Confederate uniform.   With this a sudden devilish lurid glint comes into his gray, unforgiving eyes, and I know that, though Joe Shook will not compromise *himself*, in some cunning way he means to betray *me* to Confederate Military justice,—that Major Billy Hamilton of the C. S. A. is a dead man if he doesn't save himself, and do it very promptly.

In a dazed kind of funk, I have moved a few steps away ; the Secret Service man is chuckling to himself in a low and horrid tone.

A squad of Confederate cavalry, part of the provost-guard, headed by a young lieutenant, is cantering along the road.   The officer greets my uniform with a salute.

With this salute comes sudden inspiration.   I have the power of my uniform and rank.   "Halt your detachment, Lieutenant ! " I cry.   "I have work for you."

The young officer pulls up his horse like a flash, touches his hat and says : "Your orders, Major."

"Arrest that man!" I direct, pointing to my enemy. "Arrest that damned Yankee spy!"

As I speak, the lieutenant's revolver covers the astounded Shook. Three or four of his troopers bring their carbines to a "ready." Two or three more spring off their horses, among them a big, slashing sergeant, who produces a pair of handcuffs.

"By whose order?" asks the lieutenant hurriedly.

"By mine!" I cry. "Major Hamilton, unattached and on staff duty. I know that fellow to be one of Baker's cursed Secret Service." .

"Seize him at once!" At their officer's command, the sergeant and two troopers pounce upon and manacle Joe Shook, whose chuckle has changed into a horrid chatter, and whose face has grown as pallid as the dust of the road on which he is tramping.

"You damned Maryland Union traitor!" he shrieks making a spring at me. "I had you in the Old Capitol Prison for fourteen months!"

"Oh, you did?" jeers the Confederate lieutenant. "God help the good Southerner who gets in that Yankee Bastille." Then he orders sternly : "Gag that scoundrel if he makes any more row."

For Shook is gasping : "He's not a Confederate officer! he's a Union officer—a Union spy!"

"Pooh!" I laugh, to the lieutenant who has turned inquiring eyes upon me. "My commission—my authority." And I produce my paper signed by Jeff Davis and his War Secretary.

Inspecting these and noting the signatures and the seal of the Confederate War Department, the officer salutes again and remarks : "The Old Capitol Prison only contains true Southerners. That Yankee dog had you there for fourteen months, Major ; it won't take us fourteen *days* to finish him. You make your formal charges against him to-morrow morning, to-day being Sunday."

"Certainly," I reply. "At the Provost-Marshal's. At present I am—" I light a cigar ; it is almost the last of the *Bouquets Espéciales* I have brought with me, but still I offer the lieutenant one, which he accepts as if it were a gift from the gods, and continue : "I have been away from Richmond on staff duty in Georgia. This day I shall devote to my wife, as I have been from her for a long time. But keep that cursed Yankee *very* safe."

"You damned treacherous turn-coat!" shrieks my victim, who has apparently forgotten in his despair and rage that he was ordered to be quiet. "Why, God help me—as I am a dying man, he was Provost-Marshal of—"

But he gets no further, for with a crack upon his jaws that makes them quiver, the sergeant growls: "Shut up, you lying dough-face!" and gags the Secret Service man with a clothespin he takes from his saddle-pouch, in a manner that shows he is an expert in the art.

"Oh, we know how to take care of his breed, Major," the non-commissioned officer laughs, then saluting, turns from me, and at a nod from the lieutenant I see Mr. Shook, with his face white as death, run along by the Confederate detachment and disappear, to be shoved into one of the cells of the Provost-Marshal's jail.

I look around; Mr. Isaacs has disappeared. I have shifted the noose that was closing round my neck on to that of Joe Shook, my enemy—where it is like to stay.

But at what a cost! I give a horrid, half-despairing chuckle, for I know I have purchased present safety by absolute destruction if I remain in Richmond until to-morrow.

To the young lieutenant my commission, my uniform, have seemed correct and undoubted; on investigation by the Confederate War Department they will be found absolutely false—my commission issued three years before and apparently not accepted. A scrutiny of the rolls of prisoners will also disclose that Captain William Fairfax Hamilton of the First Kentucky *Union* Cavalry had been captured in Maryland in 1862, and then exchanged.

So far, my commission has been my great safety; but a single doubt of its authenticity once aroused, it will be my worst enemy.

I half moan to myself: "I shall have to leave here now—this very day—before darkness adds the usual increased military precautions of night as regards egress and ingress to any city under martial law. Then in a kind of agonized despair I mutter: "Not before I speak to her! Not till I clasp her in my arms! For my one view of Eve in her grace and her beauty as she has walked up Broad Street, has made me long even more than I did before for the love and kisses of my wife.

Despite all risk I must find and speak to her *at once !*

I hurry back to the Monumental and pay my bill, stating that I will probably spend the evening at the Westmoreland Club.

As I am turning away from the hotel office I suddenly ask, " No letter for me yet ? "

"Why, yes, a darky brought it an hour ago."

It is in her dear handwriting. I tear it open. It reads—joy and rapture !—it reads :

" MY DARLING HUSBAND :—

" Come to me at once. Ask for the residence of Mrs. Sanders, my aunt, on Fourth Street, about the middle of the block between Grace and Broad; left-hand side going up from Grace.

" Oh, what effort it was to keep from showing. I recognized you in church! But I felt that your safety might depend upon my self-control, and I know you came for love of

" Your devoted wife,

" EVE."

Come to *her?* Of course I will !

CHAPTER XXVII.

BY NIGHT IN RICHMOND.

RODERICK is saddled outside. I mount him, dash along Grace Street and up Fourth, and selecting the house make a mistake in it. But I soon find the right one.

An old-fashioned colonial residence, bowered in a little shrubbery, is in front of me, as well as I can discover in the dusk. Lights are flickering through the green Venetian blinds of its front parlor. In that room she is waiting for me.

I nervously open the garden gate. My heavy cavalry boots crunch the gravel of the walk. I have sprung up the steps, and with beating heart have rapped upon the entrance to my own hearthstone.

Even as the knocker reaches the door it is thrown open to me, and I, gazing in, see, standing in front of me, with eager eyes and panting heart and words of love—my wife. Before I am inside the door her kisses are on my lips, her sweet voice is sobbing to me : " Billy ! Billy ! At last, my Billy ! " and I know upon my breast a wife's heart is resting.

Then suddenly Eve archly whispers : " Not another kiss till you come into the parlor. Quick, before the servants see how I adore you."

For I have not been backward with my caresses, and if ever girl got well and thoroughly kissed in short half minute, Eve Hamilton is that one.

A second later we are in the parlor. Suddenly she mutters : "Parted fifteen months!" and is in my arms again.

"Now sit down ; make yourself at home, Billy," she says archly ; then murmurs, looking delightfully bashful : " You have a right to ; it is a wife who welcomes you." With her word she blushes like a rose, and her Garden-of-Eden namesake coming up in her, eagerly asks : " How do you think I look ? "

"Like an angel ! " I cry ; then correct it to "like a *bride.*" and holding her before me, as the quick waves of color fly over her vivacious features, I jokingly query : " This is thy toilet for welcoming coming husband, eh ? "

To this she, hiding her head, half sighs, half laughs : " It is, Billy ! "

Gazing upon her beauty, I know Miss Diffidence means it ; for Eve has made a bride's toilet in my honor. In the soft curls that crown her lovely head nestle a few bright flowers. She wears, simple in make and material, as the sad fortunes of these times of siege and war compel, a gown of soft, light muslin, of so sheer a texture that it gives entrancing view of shoulders that gleam with ivory brilliancy, and arms that seem like driven snow, and sometimes the quick beating of her heart allows delicious glimpses of an exquisite maiden bosom rounded like Aphrodite's. Girded at the waist by some sash of old, by-gone-days brocade, the dress floats down to little feet in garb I recognize. Turning lover's glance on these, I remark: "Hello! Our best ball slippers and silken stockings we smuggled out of Washington."

"Oh, Billy, what eyes you have!" she cries; then laughs: "Yes, of course!" adding rather sadly: "Our finery must last long here. Once gone, it comes not again."

A moment later she whispers bashfully: "Stop kissing me and let me look at *you!*" and gazing on the lines imprisonment has set upon my face, murmurs tenderly: "For *me*, Billy!" Suddenly her eyes light up; she cries: "In Confederate uniform! You've come to join us! I have thought that all this day. O Heaven and Earth, how happy you make me, my husband!"

But even in my extremity I cannot lie to her. I answer: "For your sake alone, I came. I'm still true to my flag."

"But the Yankees imprisoned you."

"Still true to my flag!"

"I—I cannot understand," stammers the girl, passing her delicate hand over her fair brow. Then of a sudden her face grows deathly white. She gasps: "My heaven! then you are outside the laws of war! You've come here to Richmond, with death upon you if discovered."

"But come for you!" I have her in my arms again, and she is weeping now. "For you, Eve! I swore the Confederate flag should not stand between us."

"But you—you cannot *remain!*"

"Only till to-morrow!" I answer brokenly, but determinedly, for I have made up my mind to take this risk, desperate as it is. To-morrow morning I fly; to-night it is my triumph and my love. In this desperate game, some stake I will pull from it: losing my existence, I will have gained my wife.

"You will go away to—to-morrow?" Eve murmurs slowly, broken-heartedly. How her arms clutch me!

"Yes, early to-morrow morning, taking you with me, if I can," I answer.

"Desert my kindred in their extremity?" she shudders; then says reproachfully: "Billy, you've seen now how we suffer?" Here, resolution making her eyes beam, she springs from me and cries indignantly and determinedly : *"Never!"*

"Ah, you do not love me as a wife!" I falter, despair in my voice; then ask sternly, seizing her by her white shoulders and making her look me in the face, though her eyes droop under my glance : "What was the import of your letter to me in Washington? What were the meaning of your kisses to me now?" With this, my arm goes round her waist, for she is sighing and wringing her hands, and tears that make her eyes seem dewy tell me I am winning.

"I—I love you!" she falters; then a sudden determination coming into her eye and voice, whispers : "You shall not reproach me with that *again!*"

"*Then prove it!*"

"I——"

"Prove you are wife to me who have dared so much to prove my love for you!"

"Billy, I *will!*" she cries. Wave after wave of blushes fly over her, each stronger than the other, till face and neck and ivory shoulders gleam like red coral. She is faltering, in so low a voice I scarce can hear : "When you go away to-morrow, you shall not say I do not adore you as well as wife ever loved husband." Her face is hidden upon my breast, and I can feel her virgin bosom throb as if it would burst from the dress that veils its beauty, while I kiss and caress her and thank her for her dear words.

But here she springs from me; a startled, affrighted look flies into her face. She gasps : "What will they think of me? The servants in the house—my aunt, if she learns? Your coming here this *night* and going away to-morrow *morning.*"

"They'll think a husband risked his life for love of you," I answer, my eyes blazing.

"Yes, true heart!" cries the girl, love, passion and devotion in her eyes. "What wife would not dare *anything* for a husband who dares *so much* for her?"

"God bless you! God forever bless you, my bride," I whisper in the shell-like ear that is nestling so near to me, and, gathering her in my arms, draw on to my knee a mass of beauty, faltering with modesty, made very rosy by excited love, and bright with sparkling tears. These last I soothe by caresses.

Then I grow bolder and kiss the dimples on her alluring neck; but she suddenly springs up and laughs: "Have you had any supper, Billy?"

"Lots!" I reply.

"Ah, but you must join me in one meal at home," she says, archly. "Besides, it will look better. I shall tell the servants you are my husband. Then, who shall dare to censure me with being your true and dutiful and loving wife?"

So, after three or four sweet kisses, Eve who has grown strangely bashful and diffident to me, perchance because she notes something in my glance which says: "I am your consort!" runs away from me.

Soon I can hear her ordering supper, telling the servants her husband, Major Hamilton, has just arrived. But once or twice she flits in to me, as if she couldn't bear to have me out of her eyes. On one of these trips she takes my hand, and rather astounds me by kissing it; then runs bashfully away.

A moment after I play a trick on her, for, hearing her coming step I open one of the windows, then hide behind the door.

And she, entering, casts frightened eyes about, and seeing the casement, her face grows ashen, as she sinks down on a chair, gasping: "Bereft!"

But my kisses bring color to her cheeks, till she whispers: "Billy, behave! What will the servants think?"

"Only," I whisper grimly, "that hubby has been a long time away, and knows a good thing when he's got it."

The last time Eve comes in, she whispers: "A moment or two more, my darling, and you shall sit on your own hearthstone with the wife of your bosom by your side;" and so goes from me with a very red face, for I have kissed her pretty dimpled shoulders.

So sitting there quite confidently, I, look upon my modest home, and despite the hand of death which is so near to me, emit a laugh of triumph.

Just about this time there are some steps at the front door. I glance out. As well as I can see, it is the damned Confederate lieutenant-colonel who had escorted Eve from church.

"A little surprise for you, my buck. It'll rather as-

tonish you to know '*old* Hamilton' has come home,"
I chuckle. With this, not waiting for the servant,
with a Don Cesar de Bazan air, I open the door, and
find my suspicions are correct. "Please walk in, sir,"
I remark in blandest voice. "Mrs. Hamilton will be
with you in a minute."

My easy father-of-the-family air apparently astounds
the gentleman. With a surprised and questioning, yet
haughty look, he follows me to the parlor. Then
turning to me he suggests : "You will pardon me, sir,
but I have not had the pleasure of meeting you before."

"No ; I have been away in Georgia and Tennessee
with Hardee and Johnston," I reply. "But permit me
to introduce myself. Major Hamilton, the husband of
the lady whom you honor with your attentions. Eve
will be here in a minute, and I am always pleased to
entertain *her* friends."

"Egad !" I say to myself. "This military cock-a-
doodle will see how my wife loves me, and take his
departure with his sword, if not his tail, between his
cavalry boots."

For at my words, the gentleman, who has been
gazing at me in a somewhat supercilious way, suddenly seems dazed and confused, and I hear him murmur : "Good God !"

"By Yankee-Doodle ! he knows he's got into the
wrong house *now*," I chuckle to myself ; and cry out :
"Eve, come here ; a friend of yours has called upon
us, *dear !*"

And she flying in, gives a muffled shriek and falters :
"I should have told you ! O Heavens ! I should
have *warned* you before ! "

"Warned *me ?*" I say. "It is *he* you should have
warned." And the fire of jealousy lights up my husband eyes.

But she screams out : "No, no ! It is Charley St.
George ! Billy, don't you remember my half-brother ?"

At her words, joy comes to me, and I laugh. And
St. George laughs also, and we three get tittering together ; for Eve has ejaculated : "He was jealous of
you before, Charley—at Frederick. You remember :
your kiss made Billy *so* miserable."

But tragedy crushes comedy.

Upon our merriment the young Confederate's voice

breaks sternly in : "You come under a flag of truce, Captain Hamilton of the United States Army?"

Looking at him, I give a shudder; for I suddenly think : "This is the one man in all Richmond who will know my story of the Confederate Major is and must be a *lie*."

Gazing at me, he suddenly gasps : "Good Heaven! In Confederate uniform—*you?*"

To us both now comes a low, stifled scream. Eve shudders : "My God—Billy!" and commences to wring her hands and mutter : "Sacrificed for love of me!"

Then suddenly my wife is before the young officer, entreating, begging, sobbing, murmuring : "Charley, *Charley*, CHARLEY! You know my husband came for only one thing—love of me. It is my fault. I kept him from my kisses and my arms. That he is here now to demand a husband's rights, is my *crime!* He saved me when he knew I was a spy ; I beg you spare him who comes honorably, not as an enemy, not as a spy, but simply as a lover whom I adore and a husband whom I worship."

To this the Confederate simply mutters in a heart-broken way : "Eve! You forget my *duty!*"

But she bursts out at him : "Charley, you've been kind to me. Though only my half-brother, you've been a brother to me, and as such you're *his* brother —my husband's *brother*. Would you doom him to death? You know that's what it will be. Would you break my heart?"

"Heaven help me!" says the young fellow, who has a noble face and martial bearing. "Eve, I can only do my duty. Think of me—don't put me in a false position ; it is not just to me. I have not courted it; the blame is on Captain Hamilton, who, knowing the laws of the war, came here despite them." Then he breaks out half-despairingly : "For God's sake, Billy Hamilton, why didn't you wait until you knew who I was—that I was the one man in Richmond who would know your story was certainly a lie?"

"He couldn't wait, Charley, he couldn't wait! He was jealous ; he was terribly jealous. God bless him for it, he was jealous!" And the girl is round my neck, with tender kisses, murmuring : "My husband's jealousy proves his love."

And I seem happy, too. Even the fear of death, which is very near, doesn't seem to abate my exaltation. For Eve's kisses are coming to me as strong with love as ever woman's came to man.

"I—I am very sorry," says the Confederate officer, "but I must report this to the Provost-Marshal."

"No, no! Mercy! Charley, for me, your sister— for him, your *brother!*"

"Then if Captain Hamilton will swear to me," "that he has come for no other purpose, disguised, into the Confederate lines, than to claim the love of his wife, for twenty-four hours I will forget my honor and my duty," reluctantly whispers poor St. George, who seems more unhappy than I am. "I will for twenty-four hours forget my oath to my government. Besides this, your husband, Eve, must give his word to communicate nothing he has seen or heard within our lines to the cursed Yankee Government at Washington." This last is added sternly and decisively.

"God bless you!" My wife is round my rival's neck now, but I am no more jealous. I know as true a spouse as ever this world has seen is mine.

"Answer!" says St. George to me. "Then I will go away. On your honor as a man, Captain Billy Hamilton, did you come into the Confederate lines with no other object than to see the wife who loves you?"

Looking into the cavalryman's face which meets mine anxiously, entreatingly, I do not answer him.

"Speak, my husband," pleads the girl—her eyes fixed on mine as if they would burn their way into my soul. "Tell him you're no spy upon your wife's kindred."

Still I do not speak.

And the Confederate mutters: "Good Heavens, I am sorry!" His hand is being stretched for his hat, he is turning to go: my wife, white as a statue now, has uttered a little gasping moan: "O God, a spy!" Then suddenly Eve is again entreating St. George and is holding his arms with her little hands and begging with pallid lips that tremble as they plead: "For God's sake, think!— Don't widow me before I'm a wife! Think—*think*—THINK! Charley, THINK—when I was a little girl you used to be kind to me—when I——

"You sue for a military outcast!" says the young Confederate sternly. "Eve, I'm ashamed of you!" and would stride towards the door.

But I bar his way ; my cocked revolver looks into his face. "Remember, you're unarmed," I whisper ; for, in the safety of his capital and to escort a young lady to church, Colonel St. George has left even his sword behind him. "For your sister's sake, don't make me shoot you!" I plead, for he is still advancing : then cry sharply : "Keep back !"

"Not for a damned Yankee *spy!*" he answers, and springs upon me.

I can't pull trigger upon the brave young fellow ; for Eve is shuddering : "Spare him !"

So he, dashing my pistol from me, we grapple and struggle and fight with nature's weapons : he to imprison me—I to conquer him. Twice I get the best of him, from tricks of wrestle learned in West Point gymnasium ; but he will *not* be fought down ! His muscles have been toughened in a long campaign, while mine have grown inert in a prison cell. God of despair, he has forced me down upon a sofa, he is whispering : "Spy, I have you !" his hands are about my throat to throttle me into insensibility.

But here, a white figure that has cowered in a corner watching us, with moans of despair and faint cries of misery, suddenly becomes a being of action. She flies to where my sabre, thrown from its scabbard, lies on the floor, and raising this on high with both her hands Eve, with all her strength, with the flat of the blade strikes twice upon my conqueror's head.

With a muttered "Jezebel !" at the first stroke ; at the second, Charley St. George staggers and stumbles, and falls senseless upon the floor.

Dropping the weapon, the girl moans shudderingly : "Heaven forgive me ! I have killed my brother !"

But I, inspecting his wounds, say : " With the flat of the sabre ? Nonsense ! Charley's only stunned ; in half an hour he'll be himself again. Bless you, darling, for saving my life !" and would put arm about her.

But she fights from me and cries savagely : "God forgive you ! you have made me raise arms against my country ;" then mutters, contempt in her bright eyes : "Oh, Heaven ! a spy come for the destruction of my city and my race !" Next suddenly starts and whispers tremblingly : "Fly in time ! There is a noise in the next house ; they've heard us. *Fly !*"

"Yes—taking you with me !"

"Impossible !   It would be my death ! They'll never forgive me Fredericksburg !" She laughs in a ghastly way.

"For the information I risk my life to gain, my government has promised free pardon to my wife !

"Ah !"

"If you take the oath of allegiance."

"I take the oath of allegiance to that hated flag? *Never !* " cries the girl, her eyes flaming and in- spired—then a tender light coming in her face, she mutters suddenly : "FLY !"

"I will not," I return, doggedly, "I cannot leave the Confederate capital without a pass at night."

"You must, Billy, you must ! But how—*how*— HOW?" She wrings her hands, then suddenly whis- pers : "I know—one chance !" and runs to the back of the house, where the negro servants, who have heard the struggle, are standing aghast and astounded.

A minute later she is beside me.   Behind her comes a black.

"Quashie," she speaks low and swift, "you must save my husband. You must get him out of Rich- mond to-night."

"'Tain't possible ! "

"You must ! You can do it ; I know you niggers run the blockade whenever you want. Take him by the nigger-way ; get him out !"

"Save a Yank who's killed Massa St. George ? Neber ! "

"He hasn't killed him ; I struck him down with my own hands ; but he's not dead," and she kisses the face of the young Confederate, then begs : "Quashie, save my husband ! Save him as you love me ! "

"Den I saves him ! " mutters the black solemnly. "Dough I neber t'ought you'd ask dis for a Yank."

"God bless you, Quashie ! " cries the girl, and whis- pers to me : "*Go !*"

"Not until you say you love me—you forgive me !"

"Go—you haven't time."

"Not until you say——"

"Oh, is it not proof enough, that I love you, when I would strike my brother down, when I would raise my arms against the flag I love, for *you*, Billy!" she sobs.

"I want your *kisses!*"

"You risked your life, part to gain my pardon, part to—?" in all her anxiety she's blushing like a rose.

"To make you *my own!*" I cry inspired. Her arms are round me; her sweet lips cling to mine. Her soft voice sighs in awful dread, "Go! if you love me!—if you would not have me die in your arms, *go!* You have made me a traitor to my friends, my kindred and my cause—but save your life, my husband BE-CAUSE I ADORE YOU!"

CHAPTER XXVIII.

THE DROOPING COLORS.

"QUICK!" cries Quashie, "or yo'se a gone coon!" He is standing in the hall with a half-filled sack in his hand.

From the house below us women's voices come in excited tones.

Following him hurriedly from the house, I spring upon Roderick, and the negro, throwing the sack over the pommel of my saddle and running beside me with a surprising speed, guides me through Richmond's faintly lighted streets.

A moment after we are up the hill, on Broad Street. The black is leading me towards the North, for I note we cross the tracks of the Fredericksburg & Richmond Railway.

"Won't come to no guards and pickets yet a while," says Quashie to me; then remarks: "Ef dey gits me dey'll raise de deble wid me. An' just to t'ink fo' help-ing a damn Yankee out of de hole! But—" he looks at me as he trots beside Roderick—" yo'se safe, sah. When my missey said if dey kill yo' dey kill har, yo'se safe, if I can make yo'. An' what Quashie ain't up to 'bout dis country ain't no account, no way," he adds confidently.

This proves to be the fact. How I get out of Richmond I don't know ! Were it not for the black, I am satisfied I would have fallen half a dozen times into the hands of the numerous and alert Rebel patrols, which he dodges with darky subtlty. Round piles of lumber, by deserted railroad tracks and unused freight cars—through a dirty creek in which he wades to his waist he leads me. Then the houses growing less frequent, he takes to rough places, and trails probably unknown to any but the negroes, and once or twice conducts me across lots, nosing his way in the darkness through the thickets and underbrush in a manner that astounds me.

So we keep on for hours—all traces of the town have been left behind us long ago. About daylight in the morning Quashie says : " We's got to stop soon, sah. Darsn't travel by daylight ; get gobbled up shuah."

"Where am I ? " I ask, looking at my watch. " We have been travelling nearly eight hours."

"Yo'se on Stonewall Jackson's old battle-groun', Cold Harbor. Yo' Yanks should 'member dat, dat's where yo' got fury," he chuckles savagely. "An I hopes yo' get de deble agin."

But soon after this, getting into what Quashie calls "a nice swamp," he remarks : "We stays heah all day, sah."

"Well—but something to eat."

"I'se looked out for dat. Trust a niggah in the woods. Whaugh ! Whaugh !   What's in dat sack in front of you'se ?"

As he chuckles, the black produces from the bag some bread made of middlings, a few slices of boiled bacon and a piece of beef that for lean, gaunt, stringiness could discount the worst army ration I ever encountered.

"Besides, I'se got some beans to make coffee with." remarks Quashie philosophically, as he builds, with the art of a negro who has been a coon-hunter, a fire that produces little smoke, and producing a tin pan from the sack fills it with water from a creek running by us and proceeds to make his bean coffee. Over this, with the philosophy of an old campaigner, I join him, and if we do not make a luxurious meal, we at least finish nearly everything in sight, for our all-night's travel has made us ravenous.

Then looking at my horse, I say : "We must do something for him. Quashie, you must get Roderick some provender."

"Very well, sah, but I don't want no money," for I have produced a roll of Confederate currency. "Dere's only one safe way to git it, and dat's to steal it. I'll bring you'se some fodder and stuff for yo' nag."

Leaving me in this place, which is secluded enough, though very damp, the darky disappears.

Heavens and earth ! How helpless I feel, knowing practically nothing of the country. For I had intended to go down by a more direct route to the Peninsula, by the Charles city road, on the South of the Chicka-hominy, which would probably—I judge from what Quashie had told me on our night-march—have been my destruction. So, smoking a corn-cob pipe, for I have exhausted my cigars, I wait for the negro.

Presently I hear the sound of horses' hoofs. Crawl-ing to the edge of undergrowth and peering out, I see the gleam of arms going round a turn of the road. A Confederate vidette must have passed me scarce a minute before.

Then I cogitate : "If Quashie deserts me, what route shall I take ? What shall I do ?" and have just about cursed the negro for a traitor, when he returns, bring-ing with him a sack of corn and fodder for Roderick.

After feeding the horse, the negro and I go to sleep, leaving my nag contentedly munching.

That evening, under Quashie's guidance, we again set forth. By swamp-paths and side-tracks, and every round-about way to avoid the main roads of the country, that are picketed with Confederate cavalry, we travel down the Peninsula. About ten o'clock in the evening we pass Tunstal's Station, giving that a wide berth, for the negro remarks : "One side or t'other am always dere, and it's generally us uns."

So, gradually getting nearer Williamsburg and the Union lines we journey on until just after daybreak ; When Quashie whispers : "Stop ! Dar's rangers ahead of us."

But my answer to this is a cry of joy. A patrol of cavalry whose flag floats to the breeze shows me I am in front of United States troops.

"Guess I won't go no further. Dose cursed Yanks

might t'ink I was one of der darned contrabands,"
chuckles the darky.

"All right," I answer. "But don't go until I've
rewarded you."

"No, sah! I saved yo' because I lobe my missey.
But, so help me Gawd, Cap'n, if yo' come here agin,
spyin' out on our people, I'll give yo' away myself.
I'se done a powerful bad t'ing."

"What?" I say. "Don't you want to be *free ?* "

"Not free from *har !* Does yo' want to be free from
har ? "

"No, Quashie, we're both slaves to the same girl,"
I say.

"Yes; dat am de only redeeming point 'bout yo',
sah," chuckles the darky contentedly.

"But you must take a message for her."

"Ob course."

"And this money."

"I doesn't want yer cash."

"It is not for you ; it is for her—my wife. You see
how poor they are in Richmond." And I hurriedly
force on the black all the money of any kind I have
with me, except a twenty-dollar bill.

"Well, sah, I s'pose as Miss Ebe says she's yo' wife,
it wouldn't be quite right if yo' didn't do a little for har ;
specially after she's smashed up my poor massa Charlie
for yo'. Dere's no telling what these gals'll do, sah,
when they git upish."

"Quite right, Quashie," I laugh, for I cannot be
angry with him ; he has done too much for me.

"Here, take this to my wife," I mutter huskily,
for on a leaf in my pocket-book I have hastily written :
"Eve, my darling, the next time I come to Richmond
it will not be as a spy, but as a conqueror." And
jotting down words of love and endearment, I sign it
"Forever your husband."

But I have not much time to lose ; the Confederate
pickets are on the alert. Some half mile away towards
the west a gray squadron appears in the road, and I
spur my horse eastward along the pike to meet my advancing friends, who seem to be in force, for the Rebels
retire without firing a shot.

"Three minutes after, waving a white handkerchief,
I ride into the Union lines and drawing a long breath,

for the first time in a week, feel that I am safe from a dastard's death.

Making my report to the officer in command, but being unable to show anything that indicates I am not a Rebel, for I have dared to carry no Union papers nor insignia with me, I am placed under guard and taken to Fortress Monroe. Here everything is soon made very pleasant for me. My valise that I left in Suffolk, has arrived there; the General commanding, having instructions about me.

That afternoon I take boat for Washington, and early on Thursday present myself at the War Department. Gazing at me, the Secretary smiles grimly, and remarks : "You look as if you had come out of the jaws of death."

For, notwithstanding two days of comparative rest, I am still fearfully haggard and gaunt, from the tremendous strain of my journey to the Rebel capital.

"I have come from Richmond, sir; that is about the same," I answer.

"Well, I never expected to see you again!" he chuckles; then suddenly and eagerly asks for my report.

This I present to him, giving him an account of the various Home Guards' Armory Battalion, Boys' Company, etc., likewise a description and sketches from memory of the fortifications about Richmond.

Concluding I say : "The city is susceptible of attack by a quick raiding party, if the bridges across the James River can be seized *in time*. If the expedition is composed of *two* cavalry commands, the larger assaulting the line of forts north of the capital with sufficient vigor to hold the Confederate troops manning these defences ; a smaller, quick-travelling detachment coming from the West, and on the *South* of, the James River, can probably successfully either raid Richmond, or capture the Rebel prison at Belle Isle and release the Union prisoners there—but cannot do *both*."

"Not raid Richmond and release our prisoners at the same time?" remarks the Secretary testily. "Why not?"

"Because by the time the attacking force has released the prisoners on Belle Isle, the alarm will surely be given in Richmond, and the bridges across the

James River will certainly be so effectively guarded or destroyed, that your raiders will never get into the Confederate capital. You can with good luck either capture Belle Isle or raid Richmond, Mr. Secretary, but to attempt both, will be to fail in both."

"Humph !" he says contemplatively.

Into his meditation I break by asking : "Are you satisfied with my report, sir ?"

"Perfectly."

"Then my reward, Mr. Secretary ?" I demand eagerly.

"I have sent your name in to the Governor of Kentucky for promotion in your old cavalry regiment. You will find your commission downstairs, Major Hamilton."

"But my reward, Mr. Secretary ?" I ask again anxiously.

"To what do you refer, sir ?"

"The guerdon for which I braved a disgraceful death—the pardon for my wife."

"Ah, that shall be made out. I have not forgotten the lady," Mr. Stanton remarks grimly. "I pledge myself the President will sign it. He *likes* to sign pardons. It would have created rather a commotion to have hung the niece of our great Border-State War Senator, eh ?" A very beautiful girl ; I have seen her here in Washington myself. I don't wonder that instead of you catching *her*, she caught *you*. Did you meet her in Richmond ?"

"Yes," I mutter.

"Humph ! A little addition to a short honeymoon, I presume," he chuckles. "Do you think you've persuaded her to take the oath of allegiance."

"I fear not," I answer gloomily.

"Ah, yes ; if we had only the men of the South to fight, we'd have an easier time," remarks the Secretary. "And you, I suppose—you'd like to go to Richmond again ?" he asks.

"Wouldn't I ? But not as a spy !"

"Then I will give you a chance. Your old regiment will march under Sheridan. But this raiding business I shall put in other hands. No man with a wife in Richmond is fitted to burn the Rebel capital. What do you want to do now ?"

" I want to sleep for a week."

So he sends me away, shuddering in my heart as I think, " What may I not have brought upon Eve ? "

Perhaps I should have shuddered more ; for it was on my information that that unfortunate Dahlgren raid was planned, which came to such a horrible ending, and produced so much discussion as to what is civilized in warfare.

The next day I see Birdie, who has taken a handsome furnished house in Washington and lately added to her establishment a prattling goo-goo boy. She is trying to play the Roman matron and not doing it very well.

" You're going to the front. That's where Arthur is —at the front. He's in Torbert's cavalry division. Billy, do what you can to aid my husband when he's in battle," pleads Birdie, who only knows *one* detail of war—that gallant men leave their wives' arms and never come back to them.

" You'll try to save him ? " she whimpers to me ; then suddenly cries : " But I know Arthur isn't coming back. Every time I look at this ring he put upon my finger I see in the diamond my tears ; in the ruby, his drop of blood—oh, if this war were only over ! "

With this plaint in my ear—a cry that bereft women are now raising all over the stricken land, North and South—I leave my sister and ride into Virginia to join my regiment.

Then comes Grant's big campaign—when he fights and flanks, and fights again and flanks again, from the Wilderness to Spottsylvania and North Anna River and Cold Harbor, and here swinging south of the James and assaulting the Rebel capital from the very point I had selected, as weakest, has laid siege to Petersburg.

So the summer goes and autumn comes, and I find myself one of the fifteen thousand sabres that, under Sheridan, Torbert and Custer begin to be known as the *Great* Cavalry Corps.

We have pursued Early into Virginia, and fought up and down the Shenandoah, by the light of blazing barns and dwellings and old colonial manor-houses, till that once blest but now unhappy valley will no more support the struggling armies that tramp over its devastated fields ; Mosby's partisans raiding our communications and destroying commissary and sutlers' trains in our rear, and Bull-dog Early fighting us at the front.

But finally we finish him at Cedar Creek, and as we go into winter quarters in the devastated valley, my regiment, of which I am now Lieutenant-Colonel, both my senior majors having been wounded or disabled, bears on its battle-flag the names of Opequan, Fisher's Hill and Cedar Creek.

For the last battle I find myself brevetted Brigadier General of Volunteers; though Vermilye still commands his horse battery.

During the early winter I once or twice visit Washington on leave. From this point, as opportunity has offered, I have forwarded to my wife money, by the uncertain contraband means of communication between Washington and Richmond. Whether she receives it, I know not, for no letters reach me from her.

In February, 1865, Durant, my Colonel, being invalided, I get orders to prepare for active service, and on the 27th Sheridan begins his celebrated march through Virginia from Winchester to City Point.

The weather is frightful, the rain tremendous. The mud is beyond description ; but we tramp on through it, and report at City Point, Grant's headquarters, on March 26th. An awful ride—a fearful raid ; but Sheridan's cavalry are now ready to help Grant finish Lee.

Up the James River is Richmond, and no man in all the thirteen thousand sabres that moved out with Little Phil to capture the South Side Railway and smash the right of that skeleton line of Confederates which is now guarding Petersburg is more determined than I. My comrades are fighting for the Union, but I am battling not only for that but also for a wife, from whose love the Rebel flag has kept me over two long years.

Then comes Five Forks, and we cut off the last railroad by which provisions reach the Confederate army, and force it either to starve, break out or retreat.

The first it won't do ; the second it can't do ; the third it does, and Petersburg is evacuated on the night of the 2d of April, and Richmond on the same day ; though Ewell, in command of the Confederates, leaves it *blazing*.

Desperately Lee turns up the Appomattox, in search

of safety from our pursuing columns and rations for his starving men—but he gets little of either.

So after six more desperate days, at Appomattox Court House, Lee's wearied and half-starved columns find themselves entirely enveloped. Without provisions, without sleep, they have fought, and marched, and fallen, and died, and dropped out and been captured, to discover Sheridan's cavalry ahead of them and drawn up to dispute the Lynchburg road ; their one avenue to even temporary safety.

It is the morning of the ninth of April. My regiment, after service so hard that we had never seen the like before, are at Appomattox Station, the men half famished, for, if the Rebels starved, we had *no* full stomachs, all this awful ride, when men went to sleep in their saddles ; for what commissariat could keep up to our flying columns when it was hub-deep for wagons in every Virginia road this pouring April weather.

Suddenly every worn-out, dozing and hungry trooper of my regiment becomes as fresh as when he first put foot in stirrup—for the word has been passed " At last we are ahead of Longstreet. Now we've got 'em *sure !* "

But can we hold them—Lee's veterans of four years grimmest war—in their despair—till our infantry arrives ?

Couriers have been sent to the Fifth Corps ; it must be up early this morning, if it has to march all night.

But, as day breaks, our veteran infantry is not in sight.

Nothing for it but to try and stay infantry by cavalry —in these days a military impossibility, and even at that time a desperate thing, the mounted man being already inferior to the foot-soldier for bruising, pitched battle-work.

For we now see them coming, and know by their battle flags we have to do with men who fought and won so many times under Jackson.

" By the god of war ! It will be *hot !* " ejaculates my senior major. " It's the old Stonewall corps— what's left of 'em ! "

By the Lord ! how they come on, in their despair, starving and few of them, but still for one dread hour the old Army of Northern Virginia.

No sign of the Fifth Corps yet! We've *got* to hold them!

On the little hills just behind us our horse artillery unlimber, and their light guns pour shell into them, and as they get near, change to grape and canister, cutting bloody gaps in Lee's ragged columns.

Then we open with our carbines—but stay them not.

The Rebel yell is sounding as fierce as it did at Chancellorsville. The Rebel musketry is as deadly and as incessant as ever flamed from those gray ranks at Second Bull Run, where they smashed Pope to flinders.

Our lines give back or are brushed away. Our losses are enormous; both my senior officers are disabled, and word is brought me that I command the brigade. My regiments, were they not veterans, would be broken, but, still keeping their formation and fighting steadily, are forced from the road, though I contrive to draw them off to our flank and keep my horses within touch of my men.

But our light artillery is still at it. Having mounted cannoniers, as the Rebels come dangerously close, they limber up, and, darting to new eminences, open again—the guns being served with Yankee coolness and deathly accuracy.

So the tide of battle flows against us, for we are gradually driven back some half a mile in that last effort of a starving army.

But every moment that we cling to that Lynchburg road adds to our chances and destroys the Rebel hope; for now blue lines of infantry are coming out of the woods. Chamberlain, by an all-night march, has reached us and is taking position in our rear. Behind him is another brigade. The batteries of the Fifth Corps are getting into place on our flank.

The rebels see it as well as we. Their fire slackens as Gordon is forming them for their last charge. Taking advantage of the lull I order my brigade to mount— so as to be ready to move aside and disclose our infantry

But the Rebels are coming now!

They *must* break through! It is *now* or *never!*

Oh, the wild rush of that ragged, starving column!

They're upon us so quickly, so desperately, that one battery of ours, its horses shot down, is surely lost.

Just to the left of me and my troopers it commands the Lynchburg pike. If it is held all is won ; if it is lost, the Rebel army may break through before our infantry can deploy and form line of battle.

Its guns are served like lightning ! What's danger of explosion now? Cannister and grape, and even powder cartridges, are piled beneath the muzzles of the flaming pieces ; their gunners working like clockwork —in the face of death.

No time to communicate with the division general. Dare I, in this first moment of command, take desperate military chances?

BANG ! BANG ! BANG !

Then comes the answering musketry, the Southern cry, the Southern charge !

My Heaven ! Through the blue smoke about it I see the battery's guidon, and know Birdie to-night will be a *widow.*

"Not if I can prevent that diamond tear, that ruby drop of blood !" I send orders to my brigade to charge with the sabre. To my own regiment I cry : "Follow me !"

As the Rebel line, with its ferocious yell, dashes up the low hillside, our squadrons jump the fence that separates us from them. Wild riders, these Sheridan cavalry lads !

Then Stonewall's ragged veterans surge around the doomed battery, whose guns are fired in their very faces ; but, as they close over it, my brigade, charging with weight of horse and man, strikes them in flank ! Fifteen hundred unexpected sabres flash down upon them.

Ah ! How Jackson's old soldiers fight in their despair, seeming to want to die ! But, worn out from long marching, faint from long fasting, my horse sweep over them and brush them, struggling and deadly to the last, from off that hillside—those that are left of them.

They will *not* have it ! They are forming once more !

Bang ! Bang ! Bang ! go Vermilye's guns again, but that does not phase them ; neither does my carbine fire.

When suddenly, *Crash !* BOOM ! *Crash !* BOOM ! BOOM !

The batteries of the Fifth and Twenty-fourth Corps are opening a cross-fire from both flanks, some thirty guns scourge them with such an artillery fire they have not felt since Malvern Hill and Gettysburg. They pause! they falter!

In five minutes, everything of that thin gray line is swept away.

No! one man I see; the last *fighting* Rebel of the Army of Virginia, still charging and still firing and all *alone!* when, of a sudden, a shell bursts beside him and throws his body into the crotch of a near-by tree, from which it hangs, the entrails dangling out.

A moment later, I am beside Vermilye, who, leaning against one of his brass Napoleons, has a smoking revolver in one hand, a smoking cigar in the other. A pile of dead Rebels mixed with his slain gunners, and some wounded battery horses, who are moaning out their plaint, are his nearest neighbors.

"Thank you, old man," says the artillery captain. "You just connected; I've only a slight bayonet scratch," and he attends to the reloading of his guns. Suddenly he asks: "Did you hear that awful shriek the Johnnies gave as they surged over us?"

"Certainly. Why?"

"That was the *last* Rebel yell you'll ever hear. See!" he points.

Right and left behind us dark and blue columns of the old fifth and twenty-fourth corps are in sight. The leading brigades are already in position.

"Lee's last hope is gone," I mutter; then cry: "By Heaven! there's the white flag!"

"The sign of coming peace," remarks Vermilye, "and I think I hear him sigh: "Birdie;" next he asks me anxiously: "What's the matter, Bill? Are you wounded?"

For there are tears in my eyes. I can hardly see, and my gaze is not upon the army we have conquered, but towards the North where far away lies the Rebel capital; I am thinking of my dear wife who is in Richmond.

So we wait there, one army holding the other in its death-grip.

Suddenly, through the ranks flies "Lee *surrenders!*" Then who can paint the picture?

Pandemonium breaks forth. Those who had doubted, now are sure. From every fence, from each tree-top, from haystacks, from the roofs of near-by farm-houses, where men have climbed to get as near to heaven as as possible in their ecstatic jubilee, comes the cry : " Hosanna ! the war is over ! " Officers who have faced death without a tremor this very day are sobbing like little children. Veterans who have tasted fire and blood for four long years, are weak as swaddled infants in their overpowering joy.

But—the other army ! From the vanquished host across the silvery streamlets of the Appomattox comes a noise. I cannot describe it. Some think that it is joy also, they are so tired of fighting for a losing cause. To me it seems like the long, sighing groan of dissolution, for I know, over there, many stout hearts that have battled long and gallantly, are breaking now.

I have always thought their general's did, as he saw his colors droop, his battle-flags sink, never to float again over the stern array of war—when his starving men crowded about him, and gave defeated " Pap Lee " the same love, the same reverence they would have, had they placed the victor's crown upon his brow this Palm Sunday evening on which drooped the colors of the dead Confederacy.

———

CHAPTER XXIX.

THE ÆGIS OF THE DEAD PRESIDENT.

THAT evening, sitting in my tent—as army wagons have reached us now—one wounded spirit of the other host comes to me. For the armies are fraternizing ; this evening, we are giving our starving adversaries bread, instead of bullets.

My orderly announces : "A Confederate officer would like to see you, General."

I spring up, and see a haggard face. "Charley St. George ! " I cry, my hand outstretched.

He takes it, but mutters : "You had better have pulled trigger on me that night in Richmond, Hamilton. I would have been happier now."

"Nonsense ! You're only twenty-seven. Life is

before you.   Sit down ; have some supper with me."
And I direct my servant, a bright colored boy, to put
everything I have on the blanket which acts as table
and table-cloth.

"Thank you.   I have already eaten of Uncle Sam's
food," he says gloomily ; "but I will take some
whisky."

"Now what can I do for you ?"

"Nothing.   I have come to ask about Eve."

"About her ? " I cry, my heart in my throat.   "She
is in Richmond."

"No, she left it two months ago to join her mother,
somewhere in the valley of Virginia.   Our people in
Richmond were not kind to her, after they knew she
was the wife of a Union spy.   You owe Eve a great
deal, Colonel, for your visit to her," he says sadly, smit-
ing his hands together.   "She must be very poor.
She may be in want.   I can't even leave here until
paroled."

"I'll find her ! " I cry.   "God bless you, St. George
for telling me this.   I'll do everything for her and your
mother."

At which he give me a grateful look and murmurs,
in his old time Southern manner: "I thank you sir !"
and goes away dejectedly as I hurry to my corps
commander to ask for leave.

This my corps commander declines to grant on his
personal responsibility, though he forwards my ap-
plication to Washington.

Where can my wife be ?

I put an advertisement for her in the Richmond *Whig*,
which is still being published and forward another to
the Washington papers.

From the War Department early in May I receive a
hasty order to report forthwith in that city.

Doing this as hurriedly as possible, I enter the
Federal capital, now tremendously excited over the
trial of the conspirators for the murder of President
Lincoln, whose extended hand, bearing peace for the
suffering South, has been paralyzed by the assassin
Booth.

At the War Department, to my astonishment, I am
ordered to report for duty to General Hancock, whose
headquarters are at Winchester.

On the streets, I find the capital enraged and made more bitter than before against all who had aided the "lost cause," on account of the crime of the Northern assassin who had stricken down the President they had loved. In all the turmoil of passion in that capital I have but one thought—tidings of Eve. I hurry to Lucy Bream's; she may be able to tell me something about her niece; and in her parlor, hear news that gives me a chill of horror.

"I'm awfully glad you've come, Billy," says that matron eagerly, though her face has a very anxious look on it. "You're not a day too soon!"

"Too soon for what?"

"Too soon to save your wife and get her out of the country."

"What—do—you—mean?" I stammer.

"You know how the public mind is excited! You are aware how Baker's detectives are anxious to make a good showing. You know how the assassination of our poor martyred President has made the politicians so bitter against the South. Even my husband is very bloodthirsty now."

"Then why didn't he go to the front? He could have had all the Southern blood he wanted when we were fighting," I remark grimly.

"Hush! Don't talk that way. One would think you were not a Union man. Rufus J. had his patriotic duties in the halls of Congress."

"But what about Eve?" I break in anxiously.

"You know she got into an *awful* scrape when she was here in Washington."

"Nobody knows that better than I."

"Oh, yes; you were imprisoned for fourteen months on account of her, weren't you, and even the Senator's influence couldn't get you out. But Rufus is going to speak for you when your name is sent in for a brigadier generalship of volunteers, so you mustn't say a word against him."

"But Eve?" I ask, impatiently.

"Well, my husband tells me that—that they could hang her for those awful Fredericksburg pontoons," whispers Mrs. Bream nervously.

"Baker's Secret Service people are working her case up," continues the matron. "They hate you,

Rod Gibbon, I believe that's his name, told the Senator that you betrayed one of their men, his chum Joe Shook, to death in Richmond. They know a blow at your wife is a blow at you!"

"Yes; they know I love her," I mutter.

"They've got an order for her arrest, and——"

"They know where she is?" I falter.

"Yes."

"What? Where is she?"

"In Luray, Virginia."

"How did they discover this?"

"Well, Eve wrote me. I only got her letter yesterday morning, it was delayed some days in the post-office, I am sure it has been opened. She's living with her mother there; they're very poor. She sent for the clothes she had left here when you ran away with her."

"Luray?" I interject. "God bless you, Aunt Lucy, for telling me where she is! I'm ordered to Winchester —near her."

"You're going?" says Mrs. Bream; for I have sprung up. "You have not received Eve's letter?"

"What letter?"

"The one she writes she sent you?" Here I break out: "The Secret Service—they have intercepted it! I must go at once!"

And I astonish the plump and pretty matron by giving her a nephew's salute, and rush from the house, a tremendous anxiety in my mind. But outside I get my thoughts together, and suddenly give a cry of joy. I clutch a paper that I have carried on my breast through a year's battle and know I have the murdered President's ægis to protect my love, the pardon for which I had risked my life as spy in Rebel capital! And I thank God that though dead, the mercy of the nation's martyr still survives him to guard my love against Uncle Sam's detective agency.

With Lommox, who is still sergeant in my regiment, and has been detailed to accompany me, I hurry to Winchester. Here I am very pleasantly received both by Hancock, who is in command, and General Torbert, under whom I had served in the Valley Campaign.

"We've orders here to place you, in charge of one of the small reconstruction districts in this State; probably because the Government thought your being a Border State man would enable you to understand the people here better than some more full-fledged Yankee. For we want to make everything deuced pleasant to the Johnnies, now they've laid down their arms and are no more Johnnies," remarks the gallant cavalry commander. "You can have your choice of Upperville, Strasburg, Luray, Harrisburg, Charlottesville."

"Luray!" I cry, so sharply it startles him.

"Ay, you know the place," he says. "You've ridden through that valley a dozen times, either after Fitz Lee or from him. But remember, you don't go there to devastate this time ; instead of burning barns, you're to serve out rations. Some young lady there you've seen as you rode through?" he queries laughingly, "made you choose the place so rapidly?"

"Yes—my wife," I answer, and astound him.

"Oh, then, you'd like to get on your road at once?"

"Certainly."

With my order to take command of the district, five hours more and I am in Luray, a pretty little hamlet in that beautiful valley ; one fortunately that had escaped the torch, though the country about it, even on this lovely spring day as I approach it still shows the hands of war. Burned barns and the standing chimneys and charred beams of homesteads marking where the armies had marched the year before.

At the Federal headquarters of this little town, which is occupied now by the wing of an infantry regiment and a couple of squadrons of cavalry for patrol duty, though their troopers' horses are growing fat, I have to give five minutes to business with my second in command, Major Wilcox, of the Foot Regiment.

"You've no idea, Colonel," remarks the major to me, "of the amount of destitution."

"I can guess at it," I say. "I helped to cause it."

"We're issuing rations to over a hundred families, and some of them people of distinction, education and former wealth."

"They are willing to apply to us?" I ask, knowing Old Dominion pride.

"Some of them don't," he says. "There's a very pretty woman, who lives up the main street, haughty as a Juno ; you know these Virginia beauties, and her mother, an old *grande dame à la* Martha Washington, she hasn't applied, though, I fear, they're nearly starving."

"Can't we do something for them ?"

"I have," remarks the major. "I have just ordered rations to be sent them, and added a few little luxuries from our sutler's stores, on my own account. By the bye, the lady is a namesake of yours."

"Mrs. Hamilton ?"

"Yes. You seem excited ; a relative ?"

"Only my *wife* ! God bless you for your charity to her, Wilcox !" I cry and wring the major's hand.

Suddenly my junior's voice becomes husky. He mutters : "Then—I—I fear I have some unpleasant news for you."

"What ? "

"A Secret Service man—one Rodmond Gibbon—wearing a U. S. Deputy Marshal's badge, was here not fifteen minutes ago. He has an order for your wife's arrest for treason."

"And you permitted him to execute it ?"

"I—I had no other course left open to me."

"But I have !" I say cheerfully. "I have a free pardon for my wife in my pocket."

"I'm delighted to hear it !" says the major, briskly.

"Just order a squad of cavalry for me," I direct hastily. "Where do they live ?"

"Not three hundred yards from here. You can see the Secret Service man's and his two assistants' horses in front of it."

Two minutes after, with Lommox and a cavalry squad clattering behind me, I ride up to the house and dismount.

It is a little two-story cottage, amid some slight shrubbery and unkept flowers. As I inspect it all seems quiet inside, though two or three negroes are grouped about, looking in curiously. One of them is holding the horses of the three government agents, who are apparently in the house.

Throwing Roderick's rein to my orderly, I enter the little garden, stride up the path, and rap with my knuckles upon the door, which is minus a knocker.

Nobody answers my summons. The door is on a latch ; I hurriedly open it and stride into the little hall.

A voice, sweet and liquid, comes to me from an adjoining room. It is saying calmly, courageously: "I will go with you, gentlemen. There is no need of using force; I have no other option."

My heart jumps to the accents—they are my wife's.

Then I hear Rod Gibbon's nasal tones, snarling and savage: "By Gol, you played it on me last time at the tavern in Port Tobacco. The jealous wife, eh?—jealous of yourself. By the bones of poor Joe Shook, we'll make the Colonel's heart shriek through you, my beauty. High treason! They're going to hang one woman in Washington now, and perhaps we'll sling up another. By gum, I think I'll handcuff you."

But he gets no further, for throwing open the door I see Eve stand, as beautiful as a Venus, as haughty as a Juno, her eyes blazing, her nostrils dilated. Fronting her is my brutal enemy. Behind her is a lady of the old régime, her face white as her hair and draped upon the wall of the room an old Confederate flag.

Into this group I stride, and say in savage calmness: "You cur, don't dare to touch her!"

"By gum! The Colonel!" cries Gibbon, starting back; then he chuckles: "I'm glad ye're here, so ye kin squirm as I clap my handcuffs on your wife's wrists;" adding triumphantly: "It does me good to arrest her under yer very eyes."

"Put down your hands!" I command and cover him with my revolver.

As for Eve, she has made one step towards me and sighed: "Billy!" then swayed a little; but stood still, too wise to encumber me with her arms, in case of conflict.

"By whose order?" mutters the detective.

"By mine!—the General commanding this district!" I answer. "I have a pardon for this lady in my pocket."

"Great Gosh! From—from whom?"

"From the dead President—Abraham Lincoln."

"Shucks! That ain't no good *now.*"

"Good as his noble soul; and you know it! Now get out of here!" I have given a signal, and the squad, headed by Lommox, has come trooping in. "Hustle this fellow and his followers out!" I order.

"If they make any trouble, put them in the guard-house, for disturbing the peace of the district."

"Curse you!" cries Gibbon; and would spring at me; but Lommox has him by the throat. "Damn you! You murdered my chum, poor Joe Shook, in Richmond! I'll have ye yit! That pardon aint no good unless she takes the oath of allegiance."

"Take the oath of allegiance? Never!" cries Eve, who from a marble statue now becomes an indignant woman with blazing face.

"Then I as her husband will take it for her!" I proclaim.

At my words, my wife gives a gasp—looks reproach-fully at me and commences to sway and tremble.

"That won't work! She's got to take it *personally*, and you know it," cries the disappointed Secret Service man, as he is hustled out by Lommox and his squad.

"*Then she shall!*" I answer.

And we are alone together—the girl's mother, my wife and I. Standing before them, I fear that I have one of the most difficult contests of my life; for I am perfectly aware my wife must take the oath personally, to make the pardon of avail; and she doesn't look like taking the oath now.

Though she has come to me and kissed me, and put her arms around me and murmured: "My husband!" she has pleaded: "For God's sake, Billy, don't try and make me untrue to my cause—to desert it when its banner is torn down."

And the mother has said haughtily: "This comes of marrying a Yankee spy."

"What your daughter and my wife *was*, Madame—only, on the other side," I answer. Then bowing to Mrs. Ashley, I say: "Mother!" at which she gives a ghastly laugh, "I beg you to let me settle this matter with my wife."

Eve's glance seconds my request.

So the Virginia matron, turning away with a stately air, leaves me with my bride.

To her I whisper, my soul in my voice: "Loved one, are we to be parted again?"

"No, no, Billy!" "Never again. I—I have been unhappy enough."

Sitting down, I draw the blushing girl on my knee. To her I say : "To be with me, you must do this thing ! Not that they'll hang you. I don't fear that !" I mutter with a shudder. "But great trouble will come on you and on me, your husband."

"But, oh, it seems so cowardly !" She wrings her hands, though her eyes blaze.

"Eve, shall my visit as a spy to Richmond, when I braved the fate of a military outcast, to gain one look at your dear face, and to obtain your pardon from the Union Government, be *nothing ?*" I ask sternly.

"Ah, that was the price they paid you !" cries the girl. "My safety for the risk of your life. That was why you took the awful risk for me—for me—my husband !" and her teary eyes look gratefully at me.

"Yes ! Now, is it a *living* husband or a *dead* cause ?" I mutter.

Pressing her to my heart, the throbbing of her bosom tells the struggle in it. For one moment she falters, then says, her voice clear as a bell, with determination : "You—YOU !" and adds, with sweet docility : "Billy, I'll do what you wish ;" but, sinking on her knees, buries her head in my lap, almost as if ashamed.

Then and there, for I believe in taking women in their moods, I administer the formal oath of allegiance to the United States to my wife, she sobbing it out after me. Then rising up slowly, she takes the banner of her dead cause from the wall reverently, and fondles it and cries over it, as I saw Lee's veterans do to their battle-flags after he had surrendered.

I step silently out to let her bury the dead thing she had loved.

On the porch there is a noise of moving *impedimenta*. Lommox, with a squad of men, is bringing in not only army rations and provisions, but every luxury in the way of eatables that my thoughtful second in command has gathered up for my housekeeping ; likewise two trunks, one apparently forwarded from Washington.

"Bedad, I don't know what to do with this !" remarks the sergeant.

"Take the provisions to the kitchen," I order. "I will arrange for the trunks."

I step back, and opening the little parlor door, my wife's arms close round me, and the Confederate flag has disappeared.

"Now, darling, you are the wife of a Union general," I say briskly.　"You can do so much good about here.　You know your people's necessities.　We are their friends now."

"Yes, Billy, I'll show them how we Yanks"—she shivers as she speaks—"love these poor surrendered Johnnies!"

"But here are some trunks," I say.

"For me?"　Eve is out in the hall.　"From Lucy Bream!　My clothes!" she cries, and looking at her plain, home-spun gown, her face grows joyous at the thought of pretty dresses: as what woman's wouldn't who had famished for Paris modes and fashions for two long years.

"Hump!　But there's another trunk here," I mutter, looking at a small one marked W. F. H.

"Yours, Billy?"

"Yes, darling."

She blushes brightly, then laughs: "I—I'll attend to that."

A few moments after I hear my wife command: "Lommox, take the General's trunk upstairs and put it beside mine."

"Faith!" chuckles the Irish sergeant, "that's the place I think he has been wanting to get it the last thrae years."

Some little time after the sergeant salutes me, scratches his head, looks curiously at me, and remarks: "Bless yer lady's swate voice, yer honor, she knows me name is Lommox.　She's a beautiful voice that won't go out of my head, and there is a darky sawing wood in the back-yard who knows my name is Lommox, too.　His head's about the size of the one that took the wind out of my stomach on G Street. Yer lady's going to take the oath of allegiance, I makes bould to hope, Gineral?"

"She has already done it.　But why this rigmarole?" I say severely.

"Bedad, between ourselves, don't yer think it would have been better for us both if her swate voice had taken the oath of allegiance thrae years ago—before—

before that pontoon affair?" suggests the Irishman rue-
fully.

"Half an hour afterwards, a girl dressed in white
muslin, with big ribbon sash and delicate hosiery
and slippers, flutters down to me. She cries: "Wasn't
Lucy Bream a darling? She not only sent my old
clothes, but lots of *new* ones." Then suggests bashfully: "How do I look?"

"Like a bride!" I say; "though I've told you
that on two other occasions. This time, however, it
goes!"

"Oh, Bill!"

"Now come with me. I want to register your oath
of allegiance."

"Must I, publicly, to a Federal officer?"

"Yes, dear."

"Very well! I am going to do everything you
say." Her lovely eyes beam on me. She murmurs:
"You see I am going to be a very good wife, Billy. I
have to—to make up for lost time."

So, going with me, Eve registers her oath unaffect-
edly, yet tearfully, in Uncle Sam's book of repentant
Johnnies.

At the entrance of our home, on our return, I see a
stern-looking darky gazing at me.

"By the Lord Harry, it's Quassie!" I cry.

"Yes, sah, and I don't regret saving yo' life, sah,
seeing yo've sent us the best rations in the ole Valley
of Virginia. Reckon Giner'l Grant won't live no higher
to-night than my Sally and me. Dar's gwine to be
champagne on yo' wife's table, sah, to-night. Something I haven't heard pop for four years. Praise de
Lawd, peace, and plenty hath come upon the land."

But this effusion is interrupted by a stately lady,
who steps out and says: "William, my son, dinner
is ready."

"Mother!" I laugh, and give mamma-in-law a
hearty kiss.

"Billy!" cries Eve, "come upstairs and dress for
supper."

"Which room?" I ask, running after her.

"Why, *ours*, of course."

FINIS.

APPENDIX.

* *General Burnside's Testimony before Committee of Congress:*

On the nights of the 11th and 12th of November, after discovering my plan fully to them (Generals Halleck and Meigs) there (at Warrenton), they sat down and sent telegrams to Washington which, as I supposed, fully covered the case and would secure the starting of the pontoon trains at once. I could have sent officers of my own to Washington to attend to those matters, and perhaps I made a mistake in not doing so, as General Halleck afterward told me that I ought not to have trusted to them in Washington for the details.

In reply, General Woodbury telegraphed back, the pontoon train would start on Sunday morning probably, and certainly on Monday morning, which would have been on the 16th and 17th of November, which would have been in time. They did not however start until the 20th, and on that day it commenced raining, which delayed them so much, the roads became so bad, that when they came to Dumfries they floated the pontoons off the wagons. We then sent to Washington for a steamer, and carried them down to Aquia Creek by water, sending the wagons round by land. The pontoons did not get here until the 22d or 23d of November. * * * *

On the 15th of November I started the column down the road to Fredericksburg, not knowing anything about the delay in the start of the pontoons, because the telegram announcing the delay did not reach Warrenton Junction until I had left to come down here with the troops.

*   *   *   *   *

BY MR. GOOCH: Do I understand you to say that it was your understanding that General Halleck and General Meigs, while at your headquarters in Warrenton, and before you commenced the movement of your army, sent orders to Washington for the pontoons to be immediately forwarded to Falmouth?

Answer: That was my understanding, surely.

Question: In your judgment, could the pontoons have been forwarded to you in time for you to have crossed the Rappahannock when you expected, if all possible efforts had been made by those charged with that duty?

Answer: Yes, sir, if they had received their orders *in time*.

Question: Did the non-arrival of these pontoons at the time you expected prevent your crossing when you expected to cross, and interfere with the success of your plans?

Answer: Yes, sir.

NEW YORK HERALD, DECEMBER 18, 1862.

"Radicals of the War Department practically superseded Burnside as they had effectively superseded McClellan. If the army was delayed before Fredericksburg by the non-arrival of pontoons, the radicals were responsible. . . . It was the duty of the War Department to have had the pontoon trains on the bank of the river so that the army might immediately cross."

From a second editorial of the same paper and same date :

"It is not the peril of another advance of the ragged armies of Jeff Davis on Washington, nor the danger of foreign intervention ; but it is the danger of the total loss of the confidence of our loyal people in the success of the war under President Lincoln's administration. . . . Men commanding the confidence of the country must take the places of the blundering fanatics and scheming politicians who distract the counsels of the cabinet, and the places of the incompetent martinets of the War Office.

In Harper's Weekly of Jany. 3d., 1863, appeared The Celebrated Cartoon of Columbia Demanding from Lincoln, Stanton and Halleck her 15,000 Sons Murdered at Fredericksburg.

Columbia is depicted as standing in indignant denunciation of Lincoln, who is dressed as a Western hoosier, with Stanton and Halleck behind him.

Columbia : "Where are my 15,000 sons, murdered at Fredericksburg ?"

Old Abe : This reminds me of a little joke—"

Columbia : "Go tell that joke at Springfield."

This was followed by the Guillotine cartoon attacking most violently the President and War Office.